"I want *you*."

. . . He tugged on her hand and pulled her into his arms. His hold was loose enough for her to squirm away, but shock held her immobile . . .

"I want your body, yes. But I want your passion too. Your love for life glows from you like a light. If you make love with the same verve that you do everything else . . ." He trailed off, but those silvery eyes spoke volumes. Anticipation. Desire. Confidence.

Was he so certain that he could pleasure her? He was all man, arrogant and cynical . . .

The next moment, he proved it. When his lips covered hers, she didn't debate his character. Arrogance had never tasted so divine, she thought vaguely. Then she didn't think at all . . .

GOLDEN FIRES

COLLEEN SHANNON

JOVE BOOKS, NEW YORK

GOLDEN FIRES

A Jove Book / published by arrangement with
the author

PRINTING HISTORY
Jove edition / November 1993

ISBN: 0-515-11231-3

A JOVE BOOK®
Jove Books are published by The Berkley Publishing Group,
200 Madison Avenue, New York, New York 10016.
JOVE and the "J" design
are trademarks belonging to Jove Publications, Inc.

PRINTED IN THE UNITED STATES OF AMERICA

10 9 8 7 6 5 4 3 2 1

What life is there, what delight, without golden Aphrodite?

—MIMNERMUS 650–590 B.C.

Author's Note

In 1952, the great Mexican archaeologist Alberto Ruz Lhuillier entered the chamber of Pacal, or Shield. The Maya king had been buried for over a thousand undisturbed years in the Temple of the Inscriptions, Palenque.

"None can deny that his reign must have been one of the greatest in all the ancient history of the Americas," Ruz said in *The Mysterious Maya*.

Come with me and see what wonders he found. My heroine shares Ruz's love for the Maya, as did John Lloyd Stephens and Arthur Morelet before them. You will see what Morelet saw in 1846, travel where he went as Lina risks her life in the Yucatán to add to their record. Her methods are advanced for these early days of archaeology, but women as bold and adventurous as my heroine would have to be ahead of their time. I've moved the discovery to the Temple of the Sun because Lina, intrepid as she is, could never steal another man's find.

I've combined two loves in this novel. My degree in archaeology, with an emphasis on the Maya, gives me special regard for this story. In addition, Jeremy Mayhew is the only secondary character I've ever created who demanded his own romance. Those of you who read *The Tender Devil* will remember him as the black-sheep brother of the hero. I hope you'll enjoy his journey to his own happiness as much as I enjoyed giving it to him.

GOLDEN FIRES

Part One

We reason deeply, when we forcibly feel.
  —MARY WOLLSTONECRAFT,
   letter 19 (1796)

Chapter 1

THE FIRST TIME he saw her, she was surrounded by men.

In the future Jeremy Mayhew would remember the moment as a turning point in his life; on that sunny April day of 1879, he merely paused with interest. The frilly architecture of the Hotel de Paris made an ostentatious backdrop for the four men who stood, two on each side of the girl. Their exquisite broadcloth coats and embroidered waistcoats proclaimed the status augmented by their jeweled tiepins and rings.

Jeremy's long, fair eyelashes drooped cynically over moody gray eyes. Once, long ago, he reflected, he'd aspired to this rarefied breed. No longer. Gentlemen lived a life that he neither sought nor envied. Their hypocritical, shallow world was more distasteful to him than the rat-infested ports that were his only claim to a land's end.

That life, at least, was bounded by rules he understood: The strong survived, the weak perished. Treachery abounded, but it came with a club instead of a smile. If you paid your debts, and kept to yourself, you didn't make many enemies. You might not make many friends, either, but Jeremy Mayhew had learned long ago to live without friends.

With a will of their own, his eyes slipped once more to the girl. No, he didn't envy the gentlemen their wealth and the entailing responsibilities . . . but this? This, he envied. She was so different from his usual woman. She was flirtatious, yes, but breeding and, even more appealing, *joie de vivre* glowed from every inch of her small frame.

Even on a step above the four young men, she was shorter. But her lack of height only accented her appeal. She was a pocket princess, a lucky young lady whom life had smiled upon, someone who had obviously never known deprivation or despair. She fit here in Monte Carlo, where the sun usually shone and the climate was as temperate as the morals of the Monegasques themselves.

Her cherry-red gown was a stunning contrast to the lustrous black hair worn atop her head in a series of braids and small curls. The princess-style dress was tight from the high, ruffled neck to her hips, where gores flared to the hem. Each gore was inset with white lace. The same lace cascaded from her shirred sleeves. A small red hat adorned with white lace and swansdown perched on one side of her curls, wobbling as she tilted her head and nibbled a white-gloved fingertip.

Her soft, musical voice drifted to him on the lavender-scented breeze. "Really, gentlemen, you're unkind to present me with such a dilemma. I vow I can't choose between you." She looked up at each man in turn.

Jeremy expected her to bat her lashes, but her gaze was direct. "Shall we all dine together? I have such news to share of my papa's plans—" She broke off with a gasp as a gust of wind caught her hat and snatched it loose from its moorings. Like a small, flirty cartwheel, it rolled down the steps to where Jeremy stood at the bottom. He bent and saved the delicate lace and swansdown from the paved drive.

He held the wide eyes that, he could see as he drew closer, were deep blue, and climbed the steps to three below her. He proffered the bit of fluff with a slight bow. "Your hat, milady. Though why it would want to part from such charming company is beyond me." He gazed into beautiful, curious eyes that were framed by spectacular curling lashes.

Before she could take the hat, one of the men, a tall, super-cilious blond, snatched it out of Jeremy's hand and dusted it off on his sleeve. "You've done your good deed for the day, fellow. Now be off with you." He eyed the hat critically as if checking for Jeremy's dirty prints. With a bow deeper than Jeremy's, he presented it to the girl.

Jeremy stayed put, watching the girl watch him. The gentle-man scowled.

Ignoring the blond's disapproval, she took the hat. "It is, I confess, a favorite of mine, though it doesn't seem to share my affection. Should I reprimand it?" She gave it a chiding glance, then smiled up at Jeremy, showing a deep dimple in one cheek.

"You can try, milady, but don't be too harsh. It's such a pretty little thing." He wasn't looking at the hat. Jeremy waited for her blush. To his disappointment, she took the compliment in stride. It was probably poor praise indeed compared to the encomiums usually heaped upon her. Her smile didn't waver as she set the hat back upon her head and stuck a pearl-headed hatpin through the lace.

Her very composure made him more determined to rattle her. Leaning close, he blew gently. The swansdown fluttered, as did the long black lashes. When the bit of dried leaf floated down, it lit on the shoulder of her dress. Holding her eyes, Jeremy licked his fingertip and daubed up the leaf, his touch lingering long enough to be noticeable but not long enough to be impudent. Even through the layers of clothes he could feel the soft warmth of her flesh, and he let his eyes show his enjoyment of that fact. He was pleased to see her smile waver as he tilted his head and blew the leaf away, his pucker lingering along with his sidelong glance.

Her gaze lifted from the strong lines of his mouth. She hurried into speech, her voice a bit higher. "Thank you, sir, for fetching my hat." She held out her white-gloved hand.

Each of the young gentlemen watched skeptically, as if expecting the oaf to shake it.

A thick lock of pale blond hair flopped over his bronzed forehead as, instead, Jeremy bent and kissed her hand in the Continental manner. "It was an honor, ma'am." He straightened and smiled the lopsided smile famous among the women of Marseilles. "I'm an excellent back-scratcher as well, should you need further assistance."

Small white teeth showed in her gasp. At last she blushed. Angry mutterings came from the young men, but Jeremy didn't even glance their way. To his delight, she recovered quickly, and smiled back.

"My maid performs that task quite well, sir, but I thank you for your, ah, gallantry."

Jeremy eyed her beaus, then looked at her and said dryly, "You've a surfeit of that, it seems to me."

She held out a staying arm, shaking her head when her blond suitor and his friend made a move toward Jeremy. "No woman can have too much gallantry."

Jeremy looked from her, to the men beside her, to the facade behind them. Abruptly he came to his senses. The dalliance had been pleasant, but he was here on business. Besides, the only use he had for any woman was something he'd never get from this girl. They had absolutely nothing in common. And common, he thought wryly to himself, was surely what she thought him. He shrugged mentally.

"In that case, mademoiselle, I bid you good day so you may return to that pastime." With a curt nod, Jeremy moved aside to ascend the steps.

"You there! The servant's entrance is to the back," said the blond. Contemptuously, he appraised Jeremy from his scuffed brown boots to his clean but well-worn beige breeches and plain white shirt, then back again.

Jeremy paused. "I don't recall asking for directions. Perhaps you'd like to personally show me where you think I belong?" His tone was soft, but his steely gray eyes glanced off the blond's face. Though the dandy was taller than Jeremy, he lacked the broad chest and powerful legs of his challenger.

And a challenge it was . . . The other young men watched with interest, the girl nibbling at her full lower lip.

The breeze calmed. The sun beat down with merciless clarity on the sweat gathering on the blond's brow, and the lack of it on Jeremy's. This seemed a piddling confrontation to the stranger. His relaxed stance indicated he seldom lost this type of battle—or cared if he did.

When the blond swallowed, his prominent Adam's apple bobbing with the movement, Jeremy's mouth curled down at the corners. Flicking a hand in the air as if he'd just brushed away a bothersome insect, Jeremy ascended the rest of the steps. By the time he paused in the lobby to look about, he'd dismissed the incident. To a man who'd often fought with whatever weapons were handy, be they knives, fists, broken bottles, or even, on occasion, teeth, the confrontation *was* picayune.

The hotel's tasteful but grandiose architectural scheme was repeated in its interior: marble floors and pillars, plush chairs and sofas, sparkling chandeliers and a festooned, arched ceiling centered by a flower-inlaid glass dome. Jeremy's boots left marks in the red carpet as he approached the desk.

The clerk there looked up from his work, his obsequious smile going crooked. "Yes?"

"You've a room being held for me, I believe, by a Sir Lawrence Collier. The name is Jeremy Mayhew."

The smile stayed pinned on, barely, as the clerk flipped through his reservations. He seemed surprised to find one. He swung the huge registration book around for Jeremy to sign. Jeremy did so, then accepted the key the man offered, and the waiting note.

He'd already turned away when the man asked, "What of your bags, sir? Do you need help?"

"I have none," Jeremy tossed over his shoulder. He smiled to himself at the clerk's muttered, "Hpmph!" He was not insulted. In fact, he felt rather sorry for the fellow. How grim for your livelihood and your self-consequence to hinge upon the wealthy, he thought. Much better to have barely a pot to your name, know that fact and accept it, than to live comfortably under the shadow of others. If the fellow knew how much he'd earned in his peripatetic calling, he'd sing a different tune, but Jeremy didn't care what he, or any man, thought of him. He'd chosen his dangerous way of life out of necessity, but now pursued it by preference—for reasons he'd not justify to anyone.

Even himself.

Jeremy ascended the carpeted steps to the second floor and followed the long hallway to his room. He unlocked the door and went inside, resigned to feeling out of place for the next day or so. No expense had been spared here, either, but the opulence was wasted on Jeremy. The green and gold tapestry bedhangings were set off by a gold velvet sofa and chair. The rococo-style furniture, with its ornate carvings, didn't appeal to him. He threw himself sideways in the dainty chair and plopped his scarred boot heels on the adjacent marquetry table.

Pulling the note from his pocket, he unfolded it. *"Please meet me and my daughter in the dining room at seven for dinner, where I will explain my business proposal. Yours, Sir Lawrence Collier."*

Jeremy wadded up the note and tossed it onto the table. Damn. He hadn't brought a suit with him because he didn't own one that fit. He'd been slimmer in build when he left New York six years ago. His preference was to go as he was, uncaring of the scandalized glares. But embarrassing his host was no way to begin what Jean had claimed could be a lucrative business association. And Jean had steered him to many such in the past. He'd have to buy new clothes.

Levering his legs back around, Jeremy stood. He frowned at the room, wishing this snooty English lord had agreed to meet him in Marseilles, as he'd requested. Jeremy sighed and turned to the door.

One lesson he'd learned above all else from these years: Delaying the unpleasant only made it more so. Jeremy slammed and locked the door, then stomped down the corridor and out of the hotel. This quaint little town was becoming more popular now that the rail was through, so he should find a decent tailor who had a few suits made up.

Evangeline Collier grimaced at her reflection in the glass. Her tight gray silk gown would have been sheath-plain without the silver bugle beads. The clever snowdrop pattern was sparse at the heart-shaped bodice, growing gradually denser toward the hem until shimmering snowflakes seemed to float around her feet as she walked. White lace peeped at hem and bodice and trimmed her puffed sleeves. Her hair, dressed now in a cascade of curls, was decorated in back with a diamond hair comb that matched the jewels shimmering at neck, wrists, and ears.

By all appearances, she was an affluent young woman. Only she, her father, their barrister, and their lengthening list of creditors knew the image was as false as the paste jewel. The lovely gown had been lately reworked by her own clever fingers from the voluminous skirts left in the attic by a wealthier relative. In fact, unless they concluded their business soon, she'd have to start rewearing the gowns her swains had already seen—a dead giveaway to the true state of their fortunes.

Evangeline thumbed her nose at her reflection. "You might as well have a sign that says For Sale pasted to your forehead," she said aloud.

Her father, entering in time to hear her remark, stopped in his tracks and scowled. "That's no way to speak, Lina. I swear I've taught you better than that."

"Indeed you have. Perhaps For Rent would be more appropriate." Lina turned away to collect her fan and reticule. "It may come to that if you can't coax enough men to your side using me as bait."

"Lina! I'll not have any daughter of mine be so . . . so—"

"Honest?" Lina snapped her fan open and simpered over it, "La, sir, if you insist, we can perhaps include you in our little venture. A thousand pounds, you say? It's not much, but it will do—"

"That's enough! They'll get twice what they've invested, as you well know."

"I know no such thing. Morelet and Stephens found no gold in their travels. What makes you think we will?"

"Their investigations weren't funded or mounted as ours will be. We can spend months looking, if we so desire. If we're systematic, as Schliemann was—"

"Schliemann didn't have to contend with a tropical rain forest."

"Nor did Troy leave ruins to mark his path. Where there are temples, there must be burials."

"And what then? If gold there is, will you melt it down like Cortez did, or preserve it for the future, as every serious archaeologist should?"

Her father turned away to comb his thick dark hair before her mirror. "That, miss, is none of your concern. I, too, would prefer to keep the finds intact, but I needn't remind you that our future depends upon the success of this expedition. We'll dispense with the finds in whatever way will net the most for ourselves and our investors. The British Museum should be willing to pay a pretty sum if they're anything like the gold Schliemann found . . ." He put the comb down and turned to face her.

She put a soft, pleading hand on his arm. "Please, Father, there's another way. You can take the position offered you by the museum and let me be your assistant. We can sell the estate and pay off our debts, then live on our salaries."

He shrugged her hand off and snapped, "Don't waste your

breath arguing about this again. I'll have no daughter of mine take employment, nor will I give up your heritage without a fight. If you persist in this stubbornness, I may make you stay with your aunt, after all. It's against my instincts to take you along. If it weren't for your drawing skills, I'd not let your blandishments sway me."

Lina drew herself to her full height, and only the paling of her healthy, glowing color betrayed her hurt. "You may try to 'make me' do as you please, but I'd remind you, sir, that I am three and twenty and responsible for myself. Leave me behind if you will, but I'll follow you to Palenque if I have to swim the Atlantic."

Deep blue eyes glared into deep blue eyes.

Finally Sir Lawrence rubbed his brow. "It's my fault for raising you as I have. Your poor mother must be turning in her grave to see her daughter such a hoyden. I should have made you wed years ago instead of letting you accompany me on all my expeditions."

Lina's eyes kindled. "Indeed you should have."

"Now, Lina, let's not get into that again. Young Chambray was totally unsuitable for you, as you've since agreed. You didn't wear your heart upon your sleeve beyond a twelve-month—"

"What do you know of my heart?" Lina burst out. "Or how I felt when Philippe married Marie?"

"Only your pride was hurt, Lina. Admit it."

"Pride, at least, is something we have in common. And know this, sir: I'll not let you endanger mine again. Stop pushing me toward wealthy suitors and let me make my own choice, or I swear to you that when this expedition is over, we shall go our separate ways. If I didn't want to see Palenque as badly as do you, I'd consider leaving you now."

"Lina!" her father whispered through stiff lips.

Grinding her teeth, she whirled and marched to the window. "Now leave me to compose myself. I realize I must appear at my best if I'm to impress this captain Jean thinks so highly of." She arrowed a glance at him over her shoulder. "Live bait wriggling with vigor hooks the biggest fish, wouldn't you agree?"

Sir Lawrence shook his head and didn't dignify her gibe

with a reply. He stalked to the door, opened it, and snapped it closed.

Lina stared through blurred eyes at the drive below. These draining fights had become more frequent as she grew up—or, more rightly, aged. Here she stood, a woman in her prime and proud of it. And yet . . . Somehow she felt that, grown in stature though she was, she'd shrunk in all the ways that mattered. She'd taken life's lessons to heart, but felt weary at the learning.

What was life without joy, ambition without purpose, or maturity without acceptance? As her horizons had literally broadened on her travels with her father, her perspective of the world had narrowed. She'd been both touted in a way she didn't want and scorned for what she couldn't change too many times to avoid the cynicism that now plagued her. When she'd been sheltered on her English estate, it had been easy to laugh, to enjoy life's great adventure, to savor her femininity. But true adventure had taught her the toughest lesson of all: Being a woman in a man's world was little to revel in. That truth she still grappled with. Still refused to believe. Still determined, fool though she might be, to prove false.

Men were now arguing about the meaning of her infant science, archaeology. Of what value was a mere woman's opinion? She'd best keep to her drawing and leave the important decisions to those with cooler heads and sounder logic. While no one had said the words to her face, all had made them clear by deed and action.

Including her father.

At first, she'd argued. With her father, his workers, and finally with the French scholar she'd loved, Philippe. She'd accomplished nothing but a hardening of her father's attitude, snickering from the workers, and anger, then rejection, from the man who supposedly loved her to distraction.

However, Philippe's betrayal three years ago had, with time, changed from a mortal wound to a salutary lesson. She'd eschewed the full trousers and mannish shirts for her more appropriate dresses. The resentment of her gender had faded as she realized Philippe had hurt her pride more than her heart. Realized, too, that scorning her own womanhood was both counterproductive and foolhardy. She'd been impotent to steer her own destiny, much less her father's, as a woman aping a man. But a woman worthy of the name had powers she'd not begun to measure.

Had she not since used those powers to good effect? She'd coaxed her father into taking her along on his most dangerous expedition. She'd wheedled more investors into their risky venture than they'd dared hope for. Now, if she could only charm this captain, whom Jean said knew the Yucatán better than most, into being their shipper and their guide but charging them little more than operating expenses, her satisfaction would be complete.

So why did she wander to the mirror and look at herself with dislike? Sighing, she drew a silver-spangled, tassled shawl over her shoulders. That was easy to answer. Because she liked this role little better than her old mannish one. Both were deceitful; both required smothering part of herself.

Would she never meet the man who could accept her as she was? Neither a wilting violet nor a thorny cactus, but a hardy wildflower that would thrive and proliferate year after year— if only left alone to grow in her own time, in her own way.

Men seemed reluctant to admit that women could think as clearly and even, when challenged, be as brave, as they were. Until she met a man who could accept both her masculine and feminine side, she'd shrink, cajole, and flirt with the best of them.

Unbidden, a strong face capped with pale hair popped into her head. Silver eyes stared into hers with an expression she'd seen often enough to recognize. Yet those eyes had expressed more than physical desire. The loneliness, the sadness behind the boldness had touched her deeply.

He'd reminded her of a penniless boy looking into a window at the shiny red wagon he had no hope of buying. Then, his expression had changed as he'd looked from her to that boorish Baxter. Cynicism had weakened that magnetic pull. He'd left before she discovered his name.

As she went to the door, she reflected that was just as well. Now, when she was about to embark on the greatest challenge of her life, was no time to be attracted to a man. Further contact with that compelling stranger would be disastrous.

When she descended the stairs, she forced a gay smile. She paused at the bottom to accept the proffered arm of one of her admirers, then swept into the vast, muraled dining room with a grace that made her seem six inches taller. The gas lighting flickered on her beaded gown and paste jewels. The silver dress threw her glowing complexion and lustrous dark hair into sharp relief. Even among the throng of women glittering with real diamonds, she was like a crisp, pine-scented air in a stuffy room.

When she reached the table where her father and other admirers sat, she accepted the chair Baxter had saved for her. Of all her beaus, he appealed to her the least. Unfortunately he was also the wealthiest, and he was the investor who would accompany them and report to the others. She looked around the table, but spied no new faces. Her odd tension relaxed as she threw herself with vigor into her role.

Before the soup had been served, she had every man at the table grinning at her tale of how she'd cajoled a Greek worker into letting her see the Acropolis. "Father had confined me to my room, you see, and was not going to allow me to visit the Acropolis as punishment for some misdeed."

Her airy wave was interrupted by her father's mild, "Your 'misdeed,' as you put it, almost cost me my position. Playing dress-up with ancient jewelry worth a fortune was not the best way to endear your father to his coworkers."

After the laughter had died, Lina continued. "As I was only thirteen at the time, the punishment seemed overly severe. I'd longed to see the Erechtheion since Father first showed me its picture. I tried many ways to make the man, an aging Greek with several grandchildren, understand, but I couldn't overcome the language barrier. We weren't facing the right direction, so no amount of pointing seemed to help . . ." She paused to take a leisurely sip of wine.

Baxter squirmed at the long pause. "I say, then, how did you manage the thing?"

Lina daintily put her crystal glass down in the correct position beside her porcelain plate. "I acted out my request. Can you guess how?" Her mischievous, glinting glance went from one attentive face to another.

Baxter rubbed a hand along his jaw. "Dashed if I can see it. How does one act out a building?"

The answer came from an unexpected quarter. A deep voice said over Lina's shoulder, "It's quite simple. She posed as one of the most famous parts of the Erechtheion. I imagine with a sheet draped over herself, even at thirteen she resembled a karyatid, one of those graceful ladies who so magnificently support the south porch. Is that correct, Miss Collier?"

His words were courteous, Lina told herself as she turned her head to look over her shoulder. So why did she feel them grating over her like gravel? She saw a white-coated waiter receding down the aisle and deduced that the stranger must have been standing there for some time after being escorted to their table. They'd all been too engrossed to notice him. Baxter and her other gallants scowled at the newcomer. Jeremy stepped closer, under the blazing chandelier over their heads.

Gone was the laborer; in his stead was an urbane man of the world. From his cropped blond head to his white dress tie and tight black trousers and tails he was sartorial perfection. Lina had to take a deep breath to find voice to answer him.

"Perfectly correct—Mr. Mayhew." Her brilliant smile hid her dismay. *Oh, why did I even get out of bed this morning? This* was the captain she must charm?

Her father rose at the name and advanced toward Jeremy, his hand extended. "It's a pleasure to meet you, Mr. Mayhew. Won't you join us?"

Lina watched Jeremy walk around the table. He was tall, sleek, and powerful, but curiously, he called up images of locomotives more than jungle cats. For his strength was controlled, available at his command, rather than wild and predatory. How she understood that she couldn't say, but as he sat down across the table and met her eyes, she knew he was analyzing her also. And, from the set look about his mouth, he was no happier to know her identity than she was to learn his.

"You seem to know my daughter, though I'm rather at a loss to understand how." Collier sent a half angry, half inquiring glance at Lina.

"We met earlier on the steps when I retrieved her hat," Jeremy replied.

"I see. May I introduce you to these fine young men? Each is interested in the venture I wish to discuss with you." Collier went about the table, starting at his left, naming each Englishman, with Baxter, who was seated on Collier's right, last.

Baxter's infinitesimal nod was more insult than courtesy, but Mayhew only lifted an eyebrow before looking back at Lina. "I didn't mean to hog your stage, Miss Collier, but since none of your swains seemed to make the proper connection . . ."

Somehow he made the apology insolent. He might as well have likened her to an actress and her suitors to idiots. "To the contrary, Mr. Mayhew. *They* understand all that is proper." She turned to Baxter, who shot a triumphant glance at Jeremy. He lifted Lina's hand to kiss it, but froze with her fingers halfway to his mouth when Jeremy again interrupted, even more smoothly.

"Bravo! Thespis himself would be impressed with your ability. If you played the karyatid with as much sangfroid as you do the dignified lady, no wonder your Greek jailer was swayed."

That was it! Lina snatched her hand out of Baxter's and clenched it and its mate in her lap to avoid reaching across the table and slapping that crooked, oh-so-polite smile off Mayhew's face.

With the hard-won control she'd acquired in the past few years, she said evenly, "Again, you err. Thespis would never have noticed my 'ability' because the Greeks would not have allowed me, a mere woman, to act. Women then were to be seen but not heard." Lina paused and let her eyes drift disparagingly over Jeremy's immaculate person. "An opinion still shared by many in the modern world. Unfortunately." To her fury, the sally that made her admirers smirk didn't elicit a blink from her tormentor.

"I've never been so charmingly likened to a primitive," was the suave reply. "Not that I mind, actually. I've seen more to admire, often, in so-called backward societies than I have in 'civilization.' "

Goaded beyond her patience, Lina snapped open her fan and

batted her long eyelashes at Jeremy. Only her father knew her well enough to realize that when she resorted to her fan, an affectation she detested, she was truly furious. He reached out to grab her arm, but she shifted away and leveled a limpid blue gaze on Jeremy.

"Did I imply primitive? How remiss of me. Perhaps simian would be more apropos—if Mr. Darwin is to be believed. While I've been skeptical of his theory in the past, you, Mr. Mayhew, may make me reconsider."

Jeremy threw back his blond head and roared even as Collier moaned, "Lina! What's the matter with you? Insulting a guest so. What will he think of us?"

Between chuckles, Jeremy gasped out, "That your daughter is that most rare and heady of women: a beauty with wit. Though why she uses that rapier tongue on me *is* rather mystifying." Jeremy unfolded his napkin and tossed it in his lap as the first course of turtle soup was served. He might as well have patted a yawn to signify his lack of concern at her hostility.

But when their eyes clashed across the table like crossing swords, Lina knew something bothered him. What, she didn't know. Nor did she understand precisely why she felt as if every hair on her body were standing on end. One thing was certain: This man, whom she'd been so drawn to on their first meeting, deliberately provoked her.

And she was encouraging him.

She took a deep, calming breath and turned a graceful white shoulder on him to engage Baxter in animated conversation.

Only after the elaborate meal had been taken away did Collier clear his throat and broach the subject foremost in all their minds. "These gentlemen shall be privy to our business because they have each invested tidy sums in our expedition. Captain Mayhew, you come highly recommended to us from a trusted source as being intimately familiar with the interior of Mexico. Specifically, we wish to hire your vessel to take us as far as Campeche, then pay you to lead us through the Yucatán to Chiapas—"

"Palenque," Jeremy inserted quietly.

"Precisely. We can negotiate the form of payment later, but

we'll carry much equipment, so we'll require many canoes and mules. Have you the contacts in Campeche to get us the supplies we'll need?"

"Yes." Mayhew watched the light refracting off the cut-crystal glass rotating in his hand.

Lina couldn't read his thoughts. Whatever his failings, she thought tartly, lack of confidence was not one of them. Though she didn't doubt that he could deliver whatever he promised, that surety only made her angrier. She had to bite her inner lip to avoid drilling Mayhew on his qualifications.

"Our party will not be large; it will consist only of myself, my daughter, and Mr. Baxter, who wishes to report personally to the Royal Geographic Society."

Mayhew glanced up at that, one brief, piercing look at Lina, then back at his glass.

"We'll need to hire workers, of course, but I and Mr. Baxter will supervise the project." Collier's acute blue eyes searched the American's face, but Jeremy still studied his glass. "We wish to leave as soon as possible."

When Jeremy didn't refuse the offer, Collier leaned back in his chair with a satisfied air, as if awaiting only the captain's acceptance.

"That's your decision." All at the table relaxed, but tensed again when Jeremy set his glass down, pushed his chair back, and stood. "But not with me as guide. I've little taste to witness suicide."

"Suicide? Nonsense. We know the dangers and are fully prepared—"

"No one can be fully prepared for the rain forest. Even one who has experienced it many times, such as myself. No, Mr. Collier. The Yucatán is no place for you. Much less your daughter."

So, he'd gotten to her at last. She'd known he would eventually. Lina also stood to face Mayhew across the table. "I've lived much of my life in tents. I'm used to rough conditions. You've no right to judge me ineffectual on so short an acquaintance—"

"Ineffectual, Miss Collier? This time *you* err. I judge you a bit too efficient for your own good. But the Yucatán has a way of showing all of us the weakness of arrogance—"

"Oh yes? Then you've learned little in your many journeys there."

Jeremy propped his fists on the table to lean over it. "I've learned that the rain forest is a great, primitive beast that slumbers best when left alone. Toy with it at your peril."

Her narrow eyes met the quicksilver challenge in his. She ignored the thrill chasing up her spine at the double entendre. "I am well read on the area, Mr. Mayhew. I know the privations Morelet and Stephens endured. Don't be deceived by my appearance. I've survived on less than maize and beans."

"Have you awakened with a venomous serpent crawling over you? The Indians call it *nahuyaca*. It can exceed six feet in length. Its bite induces paralysis, burning thirst, retching. Then come livid spots about the wound that soon turn to gangrene that spreads throughout the body. Oh yes, we have no cure. Of the eight people I've seen bitten, cupping and cauterization saved two. The others died." Jeremy smiled slightly when she couldn't hide a shiver, but she swiped the smile away with her retort.

"That is one of the reasons why hammocks are the most practical mode of sleeping. Really, Mr. Mayhew, do you not know that?"

He bowed in her direction in acknowledgment of her hit, but responded equably, "True. However, hammocks, or even nets, can't entirely protect against mosquitoes. And the jungle variety are larger. Then, of course, there's *el tigre*."

"The tiger is indigenous to Asia, not the Americas," Lina scoffed.

Mayhew cast his eyes toward the plaster ceiling. Patiently he said, "That's the Spanish term for the 'jaguar.' It hunts at night. While we sleep. It attacks from trees. Where we sleep." Mayhew glanced from Lina's paling face to Baxter's wooden expression. But dots of sweat popped out on the Englishman's high forehead.

"And then there's the vampire bat. It, too, attacks at night. And of course there are alligators, iguanas, poisonous insects. These are only the animal variety. Some of the Indians are not friendly—"

Collier slammed his hands down on the table and rose. "Your scare tactics won't work, Mayhew. We're going, with or without your aid. We should be able to acquire a guide on arrival, if not before."

Jeremy sighed and straightened. He sent a regretful glance toward Lina. "A pity."

"Don't measure me for my coffin yet," she snapped back. "One wonders why you overemphasize the dangers. Could it be you have plans of your own for Palenque?"

Leaping to his feet, Baxter inserted, "By Jove, that's it! Fellow's been there before. Stands to reason he must suspect the buried riches, ripe for the picking."

Jeremy went still. After a pregnant pause, he murmured, "I'll ignore that remark only because of where we are. Since you won't heed my warnings, then to the devil with you." He started to turn, then sliced a look at Collier. "And for the record, Sir Lawrence, I'd never have agreed to guide you for an interest in such a risky venture. I operate on a cash basis only. Up front." Jeremy turned on his heel and stalked off, his tails swaying slightly with his arrogant stride.

He didn't miss a trick, did he? Lina was torn between grudging admiration and fury. They'd not stood a chance of hiring him since his price was doubtless exorbitant. Still, he could have refused them in a less obnoxious way.

"Surely you can find someone just as suitable," one of the other young men said heartily, but Collier shrugged and slumped back in his chair. Lina glanced at her father. Before she could speak, Baxter took her arm.

"Miss Collier, I could use a breath of air after the stench that rogue left behind. May I escort you to the terrace?"

Lina longed to refuse and retire for a hot soak, but a pleading look from her father made her bite the words back. Keep Baxter happy at all costs, yes indeedy, she thought bitterly. Since her vaunted charm had failed them so miserably tonight, she owed her father better success with their biggest investor.

"I'd enjoy that, Mr. Baxter," she responded politely, and let herself be led away, out to the terrace, where the Mediterranean uttered its siren call.

The terrace was dimly lit by gas lanterns, but their glow paled beside the full moon beckoning over their heads. Lilacs and lemons scented the air, and the waves lapping at the rocky promontory on which the hotel stood lulled some of her unease away. She strolled at his side as Baxter led her deeper into shadows. It wasn't until they were in a dark corner formed by the terrace wall and the side of the hotel that her senses were alerted. She pulled her hand out of Baxter's tightening grip and casually strolled to the wall, ostensibly to peer down at the sea's dance.

"Amazing to think how effortlessly the Greeks plied these waters and others in their tiny ships."

"Let's not discuss archaeology tonight. May I call you Evangeline?" She nodded, but didn't look at him. "Please call me Hubert. We've many miles to cover together, and formalities will soon be as silly as they are unnecessary."

Lina glanced over her shoulder as she thought she heard a footfall, but the waves muffled the sound, and Baxter turned her chin back in his direction. "Evangeline, you already sense my feelings, I know. I'm so looking forward to our journey. What discoveries we shall make. Together." When she didn't pull away, his voice grew more insinuating. "The wealth of pleasure you give can never be matched by mere gold. Oh, my darling . . ."

Lina forced herself not to struggle when he lowered his chiseled mouth over hers. She accepted his passionate kiss passively, even when he bent her back over his arm and deepened the pressure. She found his lips as dry and nauseating as burned beef, but then she only had Philippe to compare him to. Would he never be finished? she wondered as she was forced to breathe through her nose. She sniffed again. Surely that was cigar smoke. She was so involved in sensing another's presence that she didn't at first notice that Baxter's hand had slipped to the front of her low-cut gown. But when he began to ease it off her shoulder, she pulled out of his arms.

She slipped her sleeve back up and opened her mouth to berate him, but was interrupted by a suave voice. "Please excuse me. I came out to enjoy raw nature—and got rather more than I bargained for."

A red tip glowed a bare six feet away. Lina whirled and met silver eyes shining in the lantern light. Their blatant contempt hit her like a slap in the face. She blushed, but drew herself up to her full height. While she was still grappling with words, Mayhew's footsteps receded down the terrace.

Lina whirled on the man who'd caused this humiliating situation. Blast him! Biggest investor or not, he must learn that his money had bought and paid for her smiles and perhaps a kiss or two—but no more.

"Keep your hands to yourself in future, *Mr. Baxter*, or you may get them bitten off." She turned and marched inside the hotel.

Chapter 2

DAMN JEREMY MAYHEW, damn Hubert Baxter. Damn men in general. Lina threw her slippers against her chamber wall, but the dull thud didn't relieve her fury. She tore off her clothes, washed hastily, then rammed her night rail over her head and burrowed into her sanctum. This bed was the one place where she wasn't goaded by male arrogance. And it would remain so—unless she met different specimens of manhood than she'd hitherto happened upon.

Pale hair curling crisply about a clean-shaven, bronzed face, broad shoulders and long, athletic thighs did not a man make, she sneered to herself. Those outer trappings were as superficial as the curves and pretty face that drew men to her. All would slump and sag with time. But honesty, strength, kindness, self-respect were immutable. They firmed with the years, maturity and wisdom growing as the body aged. She had hoped, in her innermost being, to find a man to share her quest for growth.

Baxter, she believed, pursued only self-aggrandizement. On the other hand, in Mayhew she'd sensed a kindred spirit—at their first meeting. The qualities she admired had seemed important to him.

But tonight. . . . The cynical man of the world who'd come to dinner believed only in filthy lucre. That man, who'd delighted in needling her, was as arrogant as her father. And as needful of a set-down. Lina pounded her pillow and counted to ten, but her spirit and thoughts were too restless for sleep. After thirty minutes, she conceded defeat and rose.

She'd just dressed again and decided to stroll down to the lobby to ask for a journal to while away the wee hours when a knock came at her door. She glanced at the ormolu clock on the marble mantel. Ten. She knew of only one man who would disturb her so late. She sighed. She was too weary for more acrimony with her father, but she owed him an explanation, at least. A neat trick, for she couldn't account for her own rudeness to Mayhew, much less excuse her actions to her father.

One look at his expression made her want to slam the door in his face. Instead, she held it wide and closed it gently behind him. Leaning against it, she looked him straight in the eye. "Dress me down. I admit I deserve it. As for what came over me. . . ." She shrugged. "His sarcasm was just more than I could bear without retaliation." She didn't add that his attitude, so different from the strong attraction he'd made plain on their first meeting, had hurt.

Her father's open mouth snapped closed. The anger in his face changed to resignation. "I admit I, too, found him abrasive. Daring to preach to me, when he's naught but an adventurer. Why, he was even ruder, a bit ago." His mouth tightened, but this time she knew his ire was directed at Mayhew.

"Did you see him again?"

"Yes, I caught him as he came from the terrace and invited him for coffee. The fellow was so churlish that he snarled a refusal and pushed past me."

Lina turned away to hide her blush. "Did he seem . . . angry?"

"Yes, by Jove, he did. Much angrier than he was when he left the table." Acute blue eyes narrowed on her bent head. "Lina, what are you keeping from me?"

"He probably has a poor opinion of us both, now," she said. "He thinks you're too arrogant to understand the dangers of the jungle, and he thinks me, ah . . ."

Sir Lawrence braced himself. "Yes?"

"He came upon me and Baxter on the terrace. Baxter was embracing me a bit too . . . passionately, and I'm afraid Mayhew may have misconstrued his words. He probably thinks me little better than a trollop."

Her father groaned. "Why did you let Baxter kiss you?"

Lina rounded on him. "Keep him happy, you said. Pander to his ego, you said. Since we lost Mayhew this night, I thought it behooved me to keep our primary investor content." When

Sir Lawrence still looked disgruntled, Lina put her hands on his shoulders and demanded, "Did you think I could dangle as bait indefinitely and not get an occasional nibble?"

"I hate it when you talk that way." Sir Lawrence shrugged her off, but at her hurt look, he relented and patted her shoulder. "Forgive me, child. I realize I've put you in a difficult situation, but it pains me for anyone to think you . . . loose. Still, as long as we both know it's not true, then Mayhew's opinion really doesn't matter."

Lina's smile conveyed more cynicism than mirth. "No, not now he serves no purpose for you." But her father had turned away to pace, and she knew he hadn't heard her.

"It's odd that he'd be angry at seeing another man embrace you."

"The thought's occurred to me. Why should he care?"

He paused in front of her, his eyes kindling with excitement. "Unless he's interested in you himself. . . ."

Lina backed away a step. "No, Father. No more. I don't have stomach or stamina for another flirtation." She didn't add that her heart thrummed wildly at the mere thought of enticing Mayhew. He was different from the others, she knew instinctively. He had the manners and speech of a gentleman, but any woman who flirted with him would be expected to deliver as promised.

Her father didn't answer, for he was pacing up and down, muttering, as he always did when cogitating. Lina turned away to the sanctuary of her own thoughts.

Had Mayhew not warned her this very night not to toy with him? And yet. . . . The shiver that ran down her spine shook her to her toes with its heady combination of excitement and fear. Perhaps that was why she was so determined to go along on this expedition. She *enjoyed* the thrill of danger.

Never had life felt so dear, nor breath so sweet, as on those occasions when she'd almost lost them. As her father paced and muttered, she thought back to the two occasions when she'd almost died.

The first time, she'd gone rock-climbing with Philippe in Greece. She'd lost her grip and would have fallen sixty feet had not her trousers caught on a thorny tree. Philippe worked a good thirty minutes to extricate her, yet as soon as she was free, she'd insisted they finish the climb to the top. He'd told her she was mad and descended, fully expecting her to follow. She had not. She finished the climb alone, and when she reached the peak, she felt mistress of the world that was spread at her feet awaiting her dominion. Surely God had great plans for her, she'd thought then, else he'd not have saved her.

A second time fate intervened when she went sailing alone. She'd been warned a storm was brewing, but she'd just heard the news of Philippe's marriage and had sought solace in the great equalizer of the Mediterranean. Her tiny boat capsized under a vicious gust. She'd leaped over the opposite side just in time.

For long, scary moments, she'd barely kept her head above the angry waves, but the storm passed quickly. Soon she spied shore, a hazy line on the horizon, but she knew the mist made it seem farther than it was. She concentrated on her strokes and was not greatly afraid—until she saw the triangular fin circling her. She went still, barely treading water, and looked frantically, uselessly, about for a weapon. Flotsam, anything.

That fin paused, ten yards away, then charged, slicing cleanly through the waves. She screamed and closed her eyes. She felt a gentle bumping as something brushed past her. Water splashed her. She opened her eyes to see a great thrashing barely fifteen feet away, then she made out another fin.

Oh God, she was being fought over. Gallantly she tried to swim away, even knowing she couldn't. A dark, slick creature with a pale belly arced out of the water and came down, butting viciously against a sleek gray body. She treaded water again as she realized what was happening. A porpoise battled the shark. Surely porpoises didn't eat people?

The battle was brief but decisive. The gray fin swam away, much more slowly, and the dark body breached the water again. Lina saw blood streaming from several wounds in the mammal's hide. In that instant, she would have sworn the porpoise grinned at her. He whacked his tail against the water, then his fin receded into the mist. Since that day, she'd loved porpoises and had worried at their sometimes callous treatment by humans.

She'd caught a current that carried her to shore. When she reached the beach, she buried her face in the sand and caught fistfuls of it in her hands. Her thoughts had that crystalline edge endowed by danger. As she gulped in savory, briny air, she'd known she hadn't loved Philippe. Known, even more certainly, that she loved life, and that her future happiness would be governed not by whether she had a man at her side, but by something much more basic: her own choices.

From that day forward, she'd accepted her femininity. She'd ceased whining about her treatment by men and worked to gain their acceptance. As a woman. And as an archaeologist. Unfortunately, her efforts had not been fruitful, in the latter quest. Yet.

Those choices had led her here, to this lush hotel, to this role of pretty plaything to men with too much money and too little sense. Still, she yearned for the end—the expedition—too much to eschew the means, no matter how distasteful. Did she long for it so much that she was willing to toy with a man like Mayhew? Again, that thrill shivered up her spine, and when her father at last turned to her, she honestly didn't know what answer she'd give him.

"Lina," he said, taking her hands, "I haven't told you before how vital it is that Mayhew accompany us because I felt confident he'd accept my offer. But you see, he's the only man who suits all our needs. He speaks both Spanish and the Indian dialect of the area; he has the contacts to provide the supplies we'll need and owns a vessel large enough and swift enough to get us there and back comfortably. In addition, he's as familiar with the interior country as is any white man Jean can put us in touch with, and he's friends with the owner of the only plantation near Palenque. In short, we need his services."

Lina's throat tightened as she looked up into her father's pleading blue eyes. Her primary value to him was ornamental, and, invariably, when he asked her aid it was in this manner. Never once had he asked her opinion on which mound to survey, or which tool to use. Even her careful, exact sketches were often discounted with a bored nod. Would she gain the respect she craved if she could coax Mayhew into guiding them?

Probably not. Even so, Lina nodded. "Very well, Father. I'll speak with him." Do I have to prostitute myself to win your love? her eyes asked, but he was as blind as usual.

"Good! Now, on my way up here I heard him ask directions to the casino. Come along. I'll go with you."

Lina paused long enough to put the finishing touches on her toilette. Then she took her father's arm and walked downstairs, across the lovely arc of the Avenue de Monte Carlo to the casino.

Her father paused to admire the recently renovated building. Lights blazed from every aperture, and a constant bustle of people climbed and descended the entrance steps.

"Charles Garnier, the architect of the Paris opera house, built it, you know. Have you ever seen a lovelier sight?" he asked.

The casino was rectangular, but there ended its resemblance to anything so mundane as geometry. Its two stories were elaborately garnished with frilly window ledges and mythological figures rendered in marble and plaster. With its central dome topped by what surely was meant to be a crown, and abutted by two even more ornate towers, Lina thought the building resembled nothing so much as a fancy wedding cake. One too elaborate for her taste.

Even Lina paused in admiration when they entered the vestibule. Around it stood—she counted—twenty-eight marble Ionic columns supporting a gallery. Lovely paintings decorated each end of the gallery, and two enormous bronze chandeliers illuminated all. After her father bought them admission tickets, they handed their wraps and hats to a polite attendant and entered the left doorway, which led to the public gaming rooms.

"Maybe we'll see Blanc himself," her father whispered in her ear, mentioning the man who had made the casino into a thriving enterprise. He looked about at the tables where immaculate croupiers spun roulette wheels. Mesmerized, well-dressed men and women clustered around.

A few trente-et-quarante tables stood about with players seated before the dealer, intent on the cards. But roulette, with its spinning wheel and rhythmic clatter, seemed to be the game of choice.

Lina was not impressed by the parquet floor, gleaming so brightly that every shimmering gas flame above her head was reflected back, nor the lavish paintings and vaulted ceiling. No matter how prettily situated, this room had seen the ruin of too many lives.

Fortunes had been lost at these tables. Reputations ruined. Lives themselves forfeited. Lina wondered if Mayhew had heard the sordid tales of suicide. She was surprised he'd come here. He seemed a man determined to set his own destiny, rather than to risk the mercy of chance.

Even as she thought it, she spied him at a roulette table. A pretty blond woman stood close to him. As she watched, the blonde leaned forward, her full breasts almost falling from her gown, to finger the pile of chips before her as she avidly eyed the spinning wheel. Lina saw Mayhew peering from the notes he'd made on a score card to the placements of the chips on the table.

With a distinctive *thunk!* the tiny ivory ball at last came to rest. The croupier announced, *"Quatorze, rouge, pair et manque."* Lina watched Mayhew nod to himself and make another notation on his card.

"There he is!" Her father took her arm and pulled her toward the table, stopping several paces behind Mayhew. Sir Lawrence tapped him on the shoulder.

He turned, and Lina watched his surprise change to disdain. He gave them the barest nod, then turned back as the croupier said, *"Faites vos jeux, messieurs."*

"Finale quatre," Jeremy called out and placed his bet on the number-stamped table surface. Lina noticed that he put a five-franc chip on the numbers 4, 14, 24, and 34.

When it seemed all interested patrons had wagered, the ferret-faced little man, with an adroit flick of his wrist, turned the wheel in one direction and spun the ball in the other. After it had spun twice, he said, *"Rien ne va plus,"* which Lina knew meant "no more bets to be made."

During the minutes that the ball was spinning, Mayhew kept his back turned to them. Sir Lawrence tried several times politely to get his attention. Once, he cleared his throat; once he said, "Captain, a word, please." He was ignored.

Lina's discomfort was blasted away by anger. No matter what he thought of them, common courtesy cost little. She whispered to her father, "Get us some *plaques*. Since he's so interested in betting, we'll join him."

"I don't know, Lina, if we should spend our dwindling funds so carelessly," her father muttered back.

"We stand to lose all, anyway, without his help," she pointed out.

"Do you want to coax him to our side or beat him at his own game?"

"Whichever is necessary."

Sighing, her father strode to one of the crowded cash desks.

He was gone for a good thirty minutes, long enough for Lina to see several more coups. Each time, Mayhew won on one number, and he consulted his notes before placing his next bet. The odds this time were high enough for him to recoup, with money to spare, his three losing guesses.

Lina got a score card from an attendant and began to write down the winning numbers. She moved closer and eyed the wheel as it came to a stop. If her memory served, the winning numbers had all been clustered in certain points along the wheel. Odd. It almost seemed Mayhew had an idea where the ball would land.

Was she witnessing one of the systems that aimed to break the bank at Monte Carlo? She sniffed. Really, she'd thought Mayhew had more sense. She'd known several gamblers in her time—all of whom had claimed to have a system, all of whom had lost every sou trying to perfect it.

Yet the next coup, and the next coup after that, Mayhew won bigger and bigger sums. By the time her father returned with the chips, Lina saw a pattern in the numbers. Mayhew always bet at the same points about the wheel. Oddly, the wheel seemed to be stopping with reasonable regularity at these points in succession. If she were correct, this next spin should stop in the vicinity of 34. Mayhew had been single-betting on four numbers each time.

This time he bet on 34 and the three numbers adjacent on the wheel. He was using red chips now, which—Lina looked down at the chips her father had dropped into her hand—were worth twenty francs.

As a new croupier spun the wheel in the opposite direction to the previous spin, Lina took a deep breath and walked up to stand beside Mayhew. Just as the croupier opened his mouth to forbid more bets, she tossed four five-franc chips on the

table and loudly called out the same numbers Mayhew had
bet on.

He turned and looked down at her from his lofty height.
She stared innocently back. "I feel lucky tonight."

"Odd that your bets match mine." He raised one sleek
eyebrow.

"Not at all. I've been watching you, you see."

His other eyebrow rose, and for a moment, he looked dis-
concerted, but then he shrugged and glanced back at the spinning wheel. The voluptuous blonde on his other side peeped up
at him and leaned forward, as if to closer watch the wheel.

Lina saw Jeremy look at the woman's offering. She glanced
from the blonde's enormous bosom to her own rounded but
less generous endowment. Without a doubt, she couldn't compete in that quarter. Glumly she watched the woman preen
before Jeremy's gaze. Really, if his taste ran to such . . .
hussies, she had no desire to compete, anyway.

This way would be better. And safer.

Her heart racing, she watched the little ball at last come to
rest—on black 17, a number next to 34. As her five-franc chips
multiplied, she smiled. It wouldn't be necessary to flirt with
Mayhew now. If his system held, all she had to do was keep
betting with him, and before the night was out, she'd have
enough money to hire him.

The next time, she used twenty-franc chips; the time after
that, blue hundred-franc chips. The pile in front of her grew
steadily, yet it was dwarfed by the tower in front of Mayhew,
who was betting at the 180-franc maximum.

Other players began to notice their winning streak, and a
crowd gathered. First the blonde matched their bets, then
other players began to follow suit, until the numbers Jeremy
was selecting were buried in chips. The *chef de parti*, the man
supervising play from a stool adjacent to the croupier, glanced
worriedly at his pocket watch.

Hoping for midnight, Lina thought, and the termination of
play. The man had been eyeing Jeremy suspiciously for some
time, and now he got down off his stool and strode around the
table to Jeremy's side. "It is almost midnight, monsieur, may
I help you cash in your chips?" The elegantly groomed man
appraised Jeremy closely.

"There's time for a couple of more coups, I believe," Jeremy answered politely. The *chef de parti's* smile stayed on his face as he went back to his seat, but since he could see no evidence of anything illegal, he was helpless to stop the drain on his bank.

Jeremy glanced at the pile of chips in front of Lina, then he placed several hundred-franc chips on an area of the wheel he'd not bet on previously. The other bettors followed his lead, but Lina hesitated.

Odd that he'd lowered his wager, for the first time; he'd bet the maximum on the previous spin. He didn't look at her as the croupier spun the wheel, but, with a quick glance at her notes, Lina followed her instincts. Just before the croupier opened his mouth to forbid more bets, Lina wagered 180 francs each on five numbers in the area that, several coups previously, had won. She saw no reason to desert a winning strategy, regardless of what Mayhew did.

Her father, who had been watching her silently, his original disapproval growing to excitement with every win, looked at her askance. "I say, Lina, shouldn't you match him again?" he whispered into her ear.

She only shook her head and watched the wheel.

Jeremy stiffened. He turned to look down at her; her eyes dragged up to meet his. He might have been a magnet, she steel, so inevitably did he draw her. Briefly, her confused feelings were bare for him to see.

Mayhew's feelings, too, were complex, judging from the look in his silvery eyes. "Instinctual players seldom win at roulette," he drawled.

Lina disguised her irritation with a slight smile. She waved her notes in his face. "So I have heard. Systems are much more effective, wouldn't you agree, Mr. Mayhew?"

At the word "system," both the croupier and the *chef de parti* looked at her sharply. Lina's smile broadened when Jeremy's teeth snapped together. He turned back to the wheel.

Lina stared unseeingly at the whirl of red and black. How had he done it? She'd been trying to figure out his system all night, but, unless he was in league with the croupier, she couldn't see how he could divine where the ball would land. Even a dishonest croupier couldn't control the groupings so perfectly. Lina's eyes narrowed as she watched the effortless spinning of the wheel . . . She sucked in her breath in understanding just as the ball came to a stop—on one of her wagered numbers.

With disappointed sighs for the lost winning streak, the other players scooped up their remaining chips and went to cash them in, leaving only Jeremy, Lina, and Sir Lawrence at the table.

Lina's eyes were as limpid and blue as a spring-fed pond when she said sweetly, "Life is much like a roulette wheel, Mr. Mayhew, wouldn't you agree? With every spin we're buffeted by fate, and never know whither fortune sends us—unless we take a hand in our own destiny."

"Get to the point, Miss Collier. It's evident you have one." Jeremy leaned his hips on the table and looked bored. The croupier glanced avidly from one to the other, his hand hovering, prepatory to the last spin before midnight.

Lina consulted her notes and again bet the maximum on the area of the wheel that was due to turn up. Jeremy shook his head at the croupier's inquiry. The man tossed the ball and spun the wheel.

As she watched it spin, Lina went on dreamily, "I only mean that sometimes, with a little effort, we can, ah, stack the odds in our favor." Though she didn't glance his way, she knew the *chef de parti* was literally on the edge of his seat, listening.

"How so?" Jeremy asked.

The amusement in his voice bothered Lina. He didn't seem worried that she'd unmask him. But then, if her suspicions were correct, he hadn't really cheated. Nevertheless, he probably didn't want his system explained. She went on boldly. "Such tiny details decide our destinies. The smallest cog in a wheel, for example . . ." She let her voice trail off and looked up, way up, into Mayhew's smiling face.

Those silvery eyes had darkened to pewter as they skimmed from her expectant features down to the hem of her gown. Lina held her breath, but when Mayhew met her eyes again, his own expressed more admiration than anger.

"How true. Perhaps you wish to discuss your philosophy further? With more privacy, perhaps?"

Lina clutched her father's arm in exhilaration. She'd won! He'd listen to them now. But she only answered languidly, "Indeed. Shall we stroll about the gardens after we leave?" Mayhew nodded and began gathering up his chips.

When the ball clicked to a stop, Lina barely glanced at the wheel before pulling in her chips, so certain was she of winning. Indeed, the ball had stopped as her notes predicted. She had so many chips she had to get her father's aid in carrying them.

"By Jove, Lina, this was a capital idea," he whispered into her ear as he helped her gather up the colorful pile of counters. "We've surely enough to hire Mayhew now."

He turned toward the cash desk, unaware of the half-glad, half-rueful glance his daughter sent after him. She was surprised he'd let her have her way with so little argument, but even he couldn't quarrel with the results. If only she could so easily gain his respect in professional areas. She sighed.

At the wistful sound, Mayhew looked at her thoughtfully. She turned and hurried after her father.

With a snap of his fingers, the *chef de parti* summoned an attendant to help Mayhew with his chips. While Lina waited in line, Mayhew behind her, the *chef de parti* kept pace with her, exchanging pleasantries with various guests. During a lull, he said politely, "Mademoiselle, I am most interested in your theory on fate. Would you care to elaborate a little?"

Smart man, Lina thought. He *had* picked up every hint she'd dropped. Lina couldn't resist; she fluttered long lashes in Mayhew's direction. He stared over her head as if he were not only blind, but deaf. She knew better, and used her sweetest tone in her reply. "Perhaps later, m'sieu. Should my walk prove too . . . boring." Again, she glanced at Mayhew. Again, he seemed uncaring.

Then it was her turn. The polite young man behind the desk congratulated her on her winnings, and began to count. And count. And count some more. Lina's mouth fell open as he reached 30,000 francs and still had a pile to go.

Sir Lawrence kissed her cheek and gripped her hand tightly. Lina couldn't have said, at that moment, who was more excited. Vaguely she sensed murmuring behind her, and she caught the *chef de parti* out of the corner of her eye, speaking to Jeremy. She didn't think anything of it, and turned her full attention back to the cashier just as he counted the last chip.

"Fifty thousand francs," he said, and began to count out crisp, high-denomination notes into Lina's limp hand.

It was a fortune! And made in a few short hours. Lina was so excited that, had not the casino closed, she would have stayed the night at the roulette table. How foolish she'd been to be prudish. Gambling was a thrilling sport, worth the risk. Like rock climbing. She was still staring at the money when her father led her away.

"It's Mr. Mayhew's turn, dear. We'll await you in the antechamber, sir, for our stroll." Gently he pulled the wad out of her hands and put it in her silver-beaded purse.

Jeremy exited the public room ten minutes later, a noticeable bulge in his faultless jacket. Lina still felt a bit dazed, but she caught his airy wave at the man in the doorway. She looked. The *chef de parti*. Smiling, he waved back, then turned inside his domain again.

Before Lina could decide the significance of that, Mayhew offered his arm. "Miss Collier, I understand the casino gardens are lovely. Shall we see for ourselves?"

She nodded demurely and clasped the crook of his arm. Her hand tingled, as if only now reviving from a cold winter. Ridiculous, she scolded herself. She'd held countless masculine arms and had never been so affected.

Excitement was making her imagine things. But that tingling warmth spread to her side, where she brushed against Mayhew as they descended the steps. Sir Lawrence followed silently, looking from one to the other with sagacious blue eyes.

The casino gardens had recently been laid out to match the new facade. Palm trees hovered like guardian angels over tender saplings and juvenile bushes. Budding flowers of exotic and varied types added their heady aromas to the lemon- and lavender-scented air. And the clean Mediterranean breeze, like Nature's dust rag, swept all impurities away.

Mayhew slowed his stride to match hers as they wandered the lantern-lit paths. "Now, Miss Collier, would you care to elucidate how you think my system works?"

Lina had always admired plain speaking, being a direct person herself, but she was rather sorry Mayhew had spoiled her dreamy mood. She withdrew her hand and stopped to look up at him. "It took me some time to figure out. I would call it less a system than an understanding of how the wheel functions. How am I doing so far?"

"Excellently—for a novice. You'd obviously never played roulette before tonight."

She bristled. "Perhaps not, but I've discovered in myself an affinity for gambling. I'll be back tomorrow."

"Unwise, but we'll discuss that in a moment. Continue with your theory."

Really, he was an arrogant so-and-so. She enunciated each syllable as precisely as an elocutionist. "It's obvious that the wheels are finely balanced. They'd not spin so effortlessly otherwise. There are doubtless any number of cogs and arms that are delicate enough to wear, thus throwing off the entire balance, and favoring certain areas of the wheel, depending upon which way it is spun. By observing the winning numbers, I was able to divine a pattern. With your help, of course." She nodded her head regally.

"Gracious of you. And I salute your intuition." He nodded in return, his fair head glinting under the flickering light. "You're exactly right. I have a friend who works in the factory in Strasbourg where the wheels are made, and he told me how they work. Each wheel rests on a steel cylinder with a hollow upper end. A small metal pin fits the wheel into this socket. When the pin wears, the wheel deviates in certain areas with reasonable regularity."

"Good show, Lina!" her father exclaimed, beaming.

Lina smiled, but her glow dimmed when Mayhew's tone hardened.

"Now, will you tell me why you didn't share your theory with the *chef de parti*?"

Of course he'd want to know that. Lina hesitated, searching his face. What a curious mixture this man was. He spoke French so effortlessly, without her own schoolgirlish accent. Yet Jean had said he was American. And he also spoke Spanish and Indian. What travels had molded such a man? That odd thrill ran down her spine again, but this time her shiver owed more to fear. Constant contact with this man would be dangerous. Was she brave enough to risk it? Did she want to see

Palenque that badly? She stared at him so long that her father nudged her arm.

"Mr. Mayhew asked you a question, Lina."

"I think you know the answer to that, sir," she said quietly. "I wanted you to reconsider your refusal to guide us."

"And you didn't hesitate to use blackmail to gain your desire."

Sir Lawrence glanced sharply at Mayhew, but, before he could speak, Lina rebutted handily, "Those who have naught to fear cannot be threatened by blackmail."

Sir Lawrence snatched Lina's purse out of her hand and opened it. "We'll not accept your insults any longer. You and your kind understand only one thing. Mayhew, name your price."

Mayhew seemed unperturbed at the criticism. He leaned back against a palm and appraised his nails. "Let me see, for such an ill-conceived, unprofitable venture—shall we say three hundred and fifty thousand francs?"

Both Colliers gasped in concert. "Y-you're mad!" Sir Lawrence sputtered. "We could buy a magnificent vessel for that."

"Indeed. And this job could cost me that—and more. Despite what you think of me, I set a high price upon my life."

Lina wondered if that were so. He had the ennui of a man who was weary of the world and the little it had offered him. Even tonight, after winning a vast sum against the odds, he'd not acted greatly excited. Yet, he didn't seem one to take chances lightly. He was a paradox. She'd never known a man like him. And hoped she never would again, blast him.

She took a deep breath, then let it out slowly. "Is there nothing we can say to change your mind?"

Jeremy straightened and met her eyes. That shiver ran up her spine again. She backed away a step before she could stop herself.

"Perhaps. One thing." The soft words wrapped about Lina like a silken cord, immobilizing her. Yet, deep inside, she knew she didn't want to flee. She lifted her chin and stared back at him with a calm only she knew was false.

"Well, man? Go on." Sir Lawrence propped his hands on his hips and glared at Mayhew's clean-cut features.

Jeremy didn't even glance at him. "I'd like to acquaint your daughter with my idea, first."

Again, that silvery gaze slid over her, warm and caressing as a touch. Fear and excitement churned in Lina's stomach, but she didn't feel ill. She felt strong. Equal to the glinting challenge present in those eyes.

"Now, see here—"

"It's all right, Father." Lina thrust her purse at him. "Take this to the hotel desk for safekeeping. It makes me nervous carrying so much money." When he still hesitated, frowning, she kissed his cheek. "I'll be fine, don't worry."

"You have my word I'll not eat your daughter, sir," Jeremy inserted wryly.

"For what that's worth." Sir Lawrence snorted. He strode away, calling over his shoulder, "I'll be back soon, Lina."

His ringing footsteps retreated, leaving only the elemental sounds of sea, wind—and Lina's beating heart. She pulled the shawl closer about her shoulders. "Well, sir? What else can we offer you to make you change your mind?" He was silent for so long that she shifted nervously.

Finally, he bridged the gap between them in one long stride and took her hand. "Are you determined to go to Palenque, come hell or high water?"

"Come . . . Hades or high water."

That lopsided smile flickered about his lips. "You're an odd mixture. You look and act so much the lady, yet . . ."

"Are you implying I'm not?" Lina's shock at how well his thoughts had mirrored hers wore off under the insult. And the obvious fact that he didn't mean the comment as critical only made it more outrageous. Lina tried to pull her hand away, but he wouldn't let her.

Jeremy shrugged his broad shoulders. "A lady will perish all the sooner in the jungle. I have no use for ladies." His voice deepened to a muffled burr as he bent to kiss her hand. "But women who know what they want and set out to get it are another matter. That type of woman, I admire." He kissed each of her fingertips.

"Being so similar in character to yourself?" Lina gibed. Her toes curled in her slippers as he sucked her forefinger into the velvety maw of his mouth.

If she weren't careful, he'd consume the rest of her as well. She couldn't really blame him for his misconception. Her boldness tonight had firmed his conclusion that she was brazen. If he'd only known how her knees had knocked together at every coup, and that her threat of blackmail had been exactly that— a threat. There'd been naught illegal in what he'd done, and what kind of person would she be to humiliate a man whose ingenuity had won her a fortune? Just as Lina opened her mouth to explain, however, Mayhew straightened and pierced her with that silver-arrow gaze.

"It's true. I've always gone after what I wanted—sometimes unwisely." He looked over her head absently, his thoughts obviously on a faraway place and time, but then his gaze snapped back to hers. "And I want you, Evangeline Collier."

Lina's fingers jerked in his warm clasp. "What?" she squeaked.

"You seem determined to risk your life on this foolish venture. Since I can't dissuade you, I might as well go along and do what I can to protect you. I have no other pressing business planned for some months."

Lina's nerves jangled at the word "protect," but she was too happy to be put off by his male arrogance. Her fingers tightened about his. "That's wonderful, Mr. Mayhew!"

"Jeremy, please."

"Jeremy. Now, we intend to leave—"

"Don't you want to hear my price?" The soft words arrested her elation.

In a more subdued tone, she said, "That's true, you didn't tell me what you want."

"Ah, but I did."

A small frown wrinkled Lina's smooth forehead. "You did?"

"Yes. I want *you*." He tugged on her hand and pulled her into his arms. His hold was loose enough for her to squirm away, but shock held her immobile.

Dismay rapidly followed, then came pain, and finally, anger. A lifetime of dealing with men who thought her a "pretty child," then a "lovely woman," had made her adept at hiding her feelings. Her eyes, incandescent as blue flames, fixed on his neat tie. "How flattering. What, exactly, do you want of me?"

"I want what you give to Baxter. And more." When she still wouldn't look at him, he lifted her chin with a bold, rough palm and said in a tone to match, "I want your body, yes. But I want your passion too. Your love for life glows from you like a light. If you make love with the same verve that you do everything else . . ." He trailed off, but those silvery eyes spoke volumes. Anticipation. Desire. Confidence.

Was he so certain that he could pleasure her? "Make love." That euphemism men used for coupling. Lina looked deeply into Mayhew's eyes, searching for some understanding, some regard for her as more than a vessel. She saw none.

And she hated him for it. Hated herself almost as much for letting her own actions sink her to the level where this . . . adventurer thought she'd be receptive to his slimy advances. Even in her anger, she knew pain guided her. For there was nothing snakelike about Mayhew. He was all man, arrogant and cynical, withal.

The next moment, he proved it. When his lips covered hers, she didn't debate his character. Arrogance had never tasted so divine, she thought vaguely. Then she didn't think at all. She enjoyed . . .

For long moments, only the wind and sea witnessed Lina's weakness. His lips were so warm, firm yet soft, demanding yet gentle. In his arms, respect became a chimera worth deserting. She gasped in dismay at her own treason, and he took quick advantage, thrusting his tongue inside her mouth. His breath tasted of mints, and brandy, and man. When he left her lips to trail the tip of his tongue down her neck to her collarbone, her head cleared.

She felt dizzy, as if she'd been on a roundabout too long. And her emotions felt as uncertain. He was so sturdy against her, a warm bulwark against the wind and the night. How good it would feel to rest her head against his broad shoulder. No one would see if she did. Except herself . . . The battle between body and mind finally ended firmly as it always had: on the side of reason.

Tiredly, she pulled away. She shook her head when Mayhew tried to pull her back into his arms. "No. I'm not what you think me, though I admit you have cause. Your price is too high." She turned away, but the anger in his voice froze her in place.

"You don't seem to find it so with Baxter. What does that pompous ass offer you that I don't?"

Lina whirled on him. "Respect, of a fashion."

"I admire you. I've already told you so."

"For reasons that mean naught to me." The mystification in his face made her long to kick him. How foolish she'd been to think him different. Exactly so had every man looked at her when she hinted at her craving for admiration for her mind, her ability and her character. Mayhew, like the others, saw only her face and form.

She stepped up to him and stabbed her finger into his chest. "Tell me why you've changed your mind. You sneered at me on the terrace and did your best to ignore me in the casino. Why, suddenly, am I so desirable to you?" To her confusion, Mayhew went a dull color that she knew, in brighter light, would be red.

"That's none of your affair," he growled. "Since I'm so contemptible to you, we've nothing left to say to one another."

"For once we're in agreement. A jolly good night to you, Mr. Mayhew. And good riddance." Lina stalked off, her skirts rustling with outrage. He should count himself lucky he'd not received the slap he deserved. Her steps slowed when he tossed a last taunt after her.

"And by the by, your ladyship, our little talk owed nothing to your threat. You see, I myself told the *chef de parti*, before I left, my erstwhile 'system.' He was most grateful, and said he'll remove the wheel and check the others. So go back to the casino again at your own risk."

He'd followed her tonight only to humiliate her with this . . . insult, she realized. She was tempted to turn around, thumb her nose at him, and drop several dockside insults she'd learned from her travels. But she didn't. Despite what *he* thought, she *was* a lady. That knowledge was scant comfort as she stalked away. Alone.

Secure in her breeding, mayhap, but no closer to fulfilling her womanhood. So what? she sneered to herself. She'd been weary of male arrogance even before Jeremy Mayhew strutted into her life. So why, deep inside, did she mourn his loss?

Repressing stubborn tears, Lina hurried to meet her father.

Chapter 3

LINA PACED THE chamber, hands to her hot cheeks. She shook her head violently at her father's persistent questions. "No, I'll not tell you the deal he wanted, and that's the end of it! Just believe that you would find it as unacceptable as I."

"You let me be the judge of that. What else can we offer him save money?"

"Naught. We'll have to get another guide. Now please, Father, I'm exhausted. Let's both go to bed. In the morning things won't look so bleak."

Sir Lawrence left, banging the door behind him. Lina stood for a long time staring out into a night that, despite the gay lights of Monte Carlo, seemed bleak indeed. If they couldn't find another guide with good qualifications, the expedition's success could be at risk. Did it really matter? she asked herself wearily. The venture they'd put together with such high hopes was probably as doomed as her own ambitions.

Was she always to be viewed as a pretty woman with one use? Jeremy had seemed so different. Had she vested him with qualities he didn't have only because she longed to at last find them in an attractive male? If so, her awakening had been both rude and propitious.

Lina pressed her forehead against the cool windowpane. With the iron will so counter to her appearance, she pushed the doubts away. After Philippe's betrayal, she'd eschewed entanglements easily enough—until Mayhew. She told herself he was as insensitive and single-minded as other males. She'd not let that last disturbing encounter distract her from her goals.

She loved archaeology, from beginning to end: searching innocent hillocks for telltale signs of remains, to seeing one of the relics she'd wrested from the earth on display at a prestigious museum. Women, she believed, were just as suited to this new science as were men. In some ways, better suited— women heeded their instincts more readily. But convincing others, her own father in particular, would take unwavering commitment and toil.

There, in the hot, lush jungle, Palenque awaited her. No man, no matter how attractive, could rival the mysteries it posed. *Good-bye, Jeremy Mayhew,* she told herself resolutely. However, as she sought her bed, Lina could not quite add *and good riddance.*

Lina rose at dawn, feeling as sullen as the orange sun pushing its way through glowering clouds. She washed and dressed in her favorite cherry-red gown. As she adjusted her swansdown hat, she winced at the recollections the ensemble inspired.

Turning away from the mirror, she marched downstairs. Her combative mood was not calmed by the sight of Mayhew lounging in a lobby chair, smoke wreathing about his head. He gestured with his cheroot, and the three young men gathered about him leaned forward at his words. Lina wondered why their investors seemed so intent.

None of them noticed as Lina strolled closer. When she was within earshot, she heard Mayhew saying gravely, " . . . can't believe they'll find much of anything. The Maya of today seem to know nothing of gold work."

"As today's Egyptians know little of mummification?" Lina inserted sweetly. "But I believe our three friends would agree that mummies abound in Egypt."

Mayhew's head swiveled in her direction. His brows rose. He made a leisurely survey of her figure that would have angered her, had she not already been furious enough to spit nails. How dare he look at her so, after what had passed between them? As if she were a cherry cobbler, and he, hungry for sweets. She turned a cold cheek to him.

The three young Englishmen sprang up like startled kangaroos. They began speaking at once.

"Sorry, Miss Collier, didn't see you—"

"A fellow's got a right to question where his blunt's going—"

"Stands to reason I should talk to an objective party to see if my allowance has been well spent. My father would fry me if I didn't . . ."

Lina nodded politely. "Of course, I understand. But we would have been glad to answer your concerns." Her icy blue eyes tried to freeze Mayhew on the spot, but he calmly blew a smoke ring above his head. He stayed sprawled in his chair, and the insult was not lost on her.

"Beg your pardon, Miss Collier," the eldest young Englishman said, acting as spokesman for the group as he usually did, "but this chap surely knows more of what to expect since he's traveled Mexico so widely. I may have to reconsider my contribution—"

"And I," chimed in the other two lads.

No money had actually changed hands yet, Lina knew. Their investors were supposed to write drafts on their banks once the expedition's departure was booked. Lina gritted her teeth to keep from flinging Mayhew an accusatory look. Instead, she eyed each boy, for that's all they really were, her age or not.

"A gentleman's agreement is just as binding as a contract. You don't need me to remind you of that. Besides, Mr. Mayhew can't know what he's talking about. Until the Mayan ruins are explored more thoroughly, no one can say with certainty what types of remains are present."

"That's true," the spokesman said, "but we didn't realize the expedition was so dangerous either. It's not the thing for you to go along. . . ." The brash comment trailed away as the young man blinked into Lina's flashing eyes.

Her voice was even, but the effort of control left nail marks in her white-gloved palms. "That is not for you to say, sir. Withdraw your support if you must, the three of you. It may take us longer, but we'll still find sufficient funds to finance our expedition. Please be good enough to inform my father of your final decisions." Lina began to turn on her heel, but a soft voice stopped her.

"Perhaps you should approach a new contributor." Mayhew stubbed out his cheroot in the crystal ashtray adjacent to his chair. He rose and took four steps forward, until Lina had to tilt her head back to see his face.

Not that seeing him helped, for his features were unreadable. "On your recommendation, sir? Not likely! If this is evidence of your helpfulness, then spare us any further aid."

"You err, Miss Collier. I didn't accost these fellows and try to sabotage your expedition. I—"

"He's right, Miss Collier," the spokesman interrupted. "We, ah, accosted him as he was asking about the schedule to Marseilles. All he's done is answer our questions."

That gleaming blond head inclined in thanks. "As truthfully as I could, I might add. But just because I doubt you'll find gold, doesn't mean that I think the expedition is pointless. It should be conducted in a calm, thought-out manner, however—by males. The jungle is no place for a sheltered female."

At least he hadn't been vindictive, as she'd at first thought. Lina's resentment lessened marginally. Losing these three young men would set them back weeks, maybe months. But go they would, even if they had to spend the gambling winnings she'd hoped to use on their personal debts.

Lina's stance, spine straight, head flung back, was eloquent of determination. "One day, that will change. One day, gentlemen, women will be as prevalent on digs as men. And by the saints, if I have to beg in the streets, I will be one of the first." Again, Lina tried to turn away, again Mayhew stayed her, this time with a gentle hand on her arm.

"I admire your determination. To show how much, shall we say five thousand pounds?"

Lina's eyes widened, but the gray ones she searched were as opaque and secretive as silvered glass. "Are you offering to invest?"

"Yes. I've always wanted to discover what tales those fantastic pyramids would tell if they could speak. And since you're determined to go, well funded or not, you might as well have the equipment you'll need."

While she was still stunned by the offer, their youngest investor piped up. "I say, if he believes so handsomely, then my one thousand should be safe enough." Shaking their heads, the other two Englishmen turned away, but Lina didn't even watch them go.

Mayhew's offer more than made up for their loss. Before she could accept, however, she had to know—"Why? Why do you invest after haranguing us on how risky our venture is?"

"I told you why. I want to know what secrets Palenque holds." When she still stared at him, sarcasm tinged his voice. "Despite appearances, the sum is not so vast to me."

"And what do you want in return?" she asked guardedly, hoping for a different reply from last night.

Mayhew glanced at the young Englishman, who blushed. "E-excuse me. I-I've not breakfasted yet." He tipped his hat to Lina and walked in the direction of the dining room.

"Shall we stroll in the sunshine and discuss this further?" Mayhew extended his arm. "My train doesn't leave for several hours."

Lina barely brushed his sleeve with her fingertips. They were silent until they reached the sea wall not far from the hotel. They peered down at the antics of the waves. The crisp breeze tore at Lina's hat, and when two of her pins came loose, she pulled out the last one and prudently removed the confection of lace and feathers.

"May I?" Jeremy took the hat and brushed the swansdown with his thumb, an odd smile playing about his lips.

She glanced from his caressing thumb, to his lips, and turned away to lean her elbows on the wall. What did he think of, to put such a . . . wistful look on his face? There again was the man she'd met on the steps, whose vulnerability had drawn her so profoundly. He handed the hat back and leaned next to her.

"Odd how wrong initial impressions can be. The first time I saw you, I thought you a princess, sweet, beguiling, and innocent. You don't look like a virago with an iron will and a sharp tongue to match."

His voice was teasing, so she couldn't take offense. Besides, of the two descriptions, she preferred the latter. "Nor are you the lonely, idealistic man you first seemed to me," she responded lightly.

When she paused, he turned his head to look down at her with arrested gray eyes. "Go on. What do you think I am?"

"A man who's had to kick and claw every step of the way in the life he's made for himself—and who's become hardened in the process." When his head reared back, she knew she'd pegged him accurately.

What might have been pain darkened his eyes, but then he abruptly turned away and tracked the sea wall, beckoning her to follow. He didn't stop until they were sheltered by a large tree, invisible to other strollers.

Lina's heart knocked against her ribs, but she accepted the large hand he held out. He drew her deep into the shade, under his arm. She felt a similar tension in his lithe frame. Was he angry at her estimation of his character?

He didn't sound so when he said huskily, "If you're so wise about human nature, tell me what this means." He turned her into the circle of his arms and kissed her.

So simple a word, so complex in execution, Lina thought while she still could. Jeremy's previous kiss had been full of passion's promise; this one spoke to her heart. His lips were gentle, eloquent of what he dared not say. That losing themselves in the finding of each other would leave them enriched, not impoverished. That the self-knowledge she sought in the vast world was here, within her grasp. That he was the man to share both journeys with her.

The urgency he communicated raised, like Lina's relics, her buried hopes and dreams. She'd been right about him, after all. He was her kindred spirit. They belonged together. When Jeremy finally lifted his head to look down at her, she sagged against his chest.

He brushed her temple with a feathery kiss. "Do you see now what I want from you? Your body, yes." He touched her temple, "But this." He caressed the side of her pounding heart, "And this. The latter two, I suspect, you've given to no man."

That angered her slightly, giving her enough strength to pull away and stand as she preferred—on her own two feet. "And what have you to give in return?" she asked. "You don't strike me as a man who likes entanglements."

After a long pause, he answered steadily, "My protection, my passion, my money, and my expertise. Before your dig is finished, you'll need all, I imagine."

Did he really think those sufficient recompense for her good name? She took a deep breath to calm her rising ire. Her own actions had led him to his erroneous impression. They couldn't progress in a business or a personal relationship until he knew the truth.

Even as she parted her lips, however, he finished roughly, as if goaded, "I didn't seek this attraction, I assure you, nor, I realize, did you. But if we end this now, we'll each spend the rest of our lives wondering—what if? And I don't know about you, but I like all my ends neatly tied up."

So now she was an end to be wrapped up and put away, like a ball of frayed yarn. Lina snapped her mouth shut and walked around him to stare out to sea. The last of the euphoria she'd experienced in his arms settled to a cold, determined lump in her stomach. Just as she'd resigned herself to his loss, he offered not only his guidance, but his own money. Palenque had to take precedence over her own foolish fears.

This man did not threaten her, she tried to tell herself. The promise of his kiss was not matched by his words. Like every male, he wanted in return more than he was willing to give. But her heart, and her esteem, were hers alone to gift or retain as she pleased. She needed him, yes, but only in a business sense.

His passion was a trap. Like Philippe, he thought her a sensual little woman who needed protection. But since she'd not give him the one thing he wanted above all, how could she honorably accept his bargain? Lina gave a disgruntled sigh and turned to rest her elbows behind her on the wall. Her eyes settled upon the casino and narrowed.

Of course! Caution receded under the heady rush of excitement. What better place than Monte Carlo to make such a bargain? And it would give them each incentive to dig as quickly and efficiently as possible. "Very well, Mr. Mayhew. I accept your terms—on one condition."

"Yes?"

"That we treat our bargain like a wager. You bet your money, your expertise, and your . . . protection"—Lina's voice stumbled over the last word before she finished—"against my, ah, person and, ah, passion."

Mayhew's brows shot up so high they were lost under the locks of hair curling on his forehead. "You do love to gamble, don't you? Just for the sake of argument, let's say I agree. You've listed the stakes, but what is the wager?"

"You seem convinced we'll find no gold at Palenque; my father is convinced we shall. I am uncertain, though given the huge sums the conquistadores plundered from various New World tribes, I lean toward my father's opinion. Whoever is right, wins." Lina might have descended from Cortez himself, so bold and reckless did she seem at that moment.

A sardonic smile twisted the beautiful lines of Jeremy's mouth. "What an interesting idea. But the advantage, it seems, is all yours."

"How so?"

"Come, Miss Collier. All my stakes will have to be delivered up front; yours, late in the expedition, if ever. Is this a fair bet?"

"Perhaps 'daring' would be a better word." *For us both, if you only knew,* she thought. His mere presence was a threat to her. Twice now he'd kissed her and turned her world on its head. She could only hope that, once in the jungle, they'd both be too weary for this unwelcome passion.

"Perhaps I might be persuaded . . ." When she gave him a blinding smile, he drawled, "With a little on account."

Her smile faded. She gritted her teeth as that gaze ran over her, warm and soft as a silver-fox muff. "That's my proposal, sir. Take it or leave it."

They stared at one another, each oblivious to the packet that steamed by in the bay, tooting its whistle. Gulls screamed overhead. The breeze stiffened, sending waves crashing into the sea wall. Fine mist settled on Lina and Jeremy, glinting in the sunshine like tomorrow's promise.

"Done, Miss Collier," Jeremy finally answered quietly. "But I have a condition of my own."

"Yes?"

"You're not to give to others what you deny me. Do you take my meaning?"

"To the last nuance, sir." She gave him a curtsy no less graceful for its mockery. "Mr. Baxter would be angry if he knew of your demand." Not to mention astonished, she thought wryly. How could she deny something she'd not granted?

Jeremy's shrug was eloquent of indifference. He smiled at her, as if grateful for her sacrifice. "Good. Now, I'll go on to Marseilles and roust up my crew. If you and your father will give me a list, I'll purchase your supplies, up to five thousand. Marseilles is bound to have a better selection. First . . ." Jeremy pounced on her. "Let's seal our bet in a much more interesting way than a handshake."

Lina turned her head away from his descending mouth. "Your word will do." She squirmed out of his grasp and hurried inside the hotel.

"Come along, Mr. Mayhew. Let's tell my father the news."

"As you wish . . . Lina. But I follow only so long before I get the urge to lead."

The double entendre was subtle, and she pretended to miss it. "You'll be doing that soon enough . . . Jeremy." They smiled at one another.

Their amity lasted through the encounter with Sir Lawrence and Baxter. The moment Lina entered the lobby, she spotted her father pacing, muttering to himself, and she knew he was worried about her. He whirled to stalk the other way and saw her. Baxter, looking glum, leaned against a nearby pillar.

Sir Lawrence growled, "Where the devil have you been so early . . ." His words trailed off when he saw Jeremy. He glanced from his daughter, to Jeremy, and back. A thoughtful look settled on his patrician features.

Before he could speak, Baxter brushed past him and caught Lina's arm. "Did this . . . oaf force you to go with him?"

Lina pulled her arm away just as she felt Jeremy take a long stride forward. She sent him a pleading look. He ground his teeth together, but stopped.

"No. He invited me for a stroll, and I accepted. Do you object, Hubert?" *My activities don't concern you, sir,* her eyes said, though her voice was calm.

"I . . . guess not. I was merely concerned he'd try to take advantage of you."

As you did, Hubert? But Lina was more concerned with averting an argument than causing one, so she merely nodded.

"Have you heard the news, Lina?" Sir Lawrence asked.

"About our two young friends? Yes, I was present when they withdrew their support."

Baxter glared at Jeremy. "I don't doubt your role in that, Mayhew."

"Whatever do you mean?" Sir Lawrence asked.

Before Baxter could respond, Lina inserted, "Why they changed their minds doesn't really matter now. I've wonderful news, Father. Mr. Mayhew not only will lead us, but he's investing in our cause."

The diversion worked beautifully. Sir Lawrence started, then smiled broadly. "By Jove, that's capital! We're delighted to have you, my boy."

The sour look about Baxter's mouth grew surly as Jeremy shook Collier's extended hand.

"Thank you, sir," Jeremy responded. "And before you ask, your most charming daughter changed my mind. I'm convinced that, gold or no, exploring Palenque will pleasure me greatly." Jeremy glanced at Lina, his eyes less bland than his words.

Lina turned away to disguise her hot cheeks. "I'm starved. Shall we breakfast together and finalize our plans?" The three men trailed her to the dining room, Baxter marching in the rear.

If Jeremy felt uneasy at his rival's hostility, he gave no sign.

After they'd ordered, Sir Lawrence said, "I see no reason for delay. When can you be ready to depart, Mr. Mayhew?"

"Within the week, I imagine. I need time to take on cargo in Marseilles, and as I told your daughter, if you'll give me a list, I'll purchase your supplies up to the limit of my investment."

Sir Lawrence cleared his throat. "Which is?"

After a cursory glance at Baxter, Jeremy tossed out, "Five thousand."

"Francs?" Sir Lawrence looked a bit disappointed.

"Pounds."

Lina closed her father's open mouth with her fingertip. She felt Baxter stiffen beside her. "Most generous, isn't he, Father?"

"*Most* generous," her father agreed. "You will, of course, get back double on your investment, if I'm right about the gold."

"*Too* generous," Baxter sneered. "You've made your contempt for our venture plain. What changed your mind, Mayhew?"

Under Baxter's insinuating look, Lina studied her glass as if she'd never seen crystal before. She cursed her fair skin. Maybe they wouldn't see her blush in the dim dining room.

"Several things, not least of which is the same curiosity that drives you, Baxter. Or is an inquiring mind the divine right of the gentry and something we poor plebes cannot aspire to?"

Baxter shoved back his chair and leaped to his feet. "By God, no man makes mock of me, least of all—"

"Sit down, Hubert." Sir Lawrence tugged Baxter back into his chair. He gave Jeremy an equally stern glance. "Let's get one thing clear right now, both of you. Bickering benefits no one. Each of you keep your differences to yourself. We'll have challenge enough in the jungle without being at one another's throats. I am the leader of this expedition, and I'll countenance no more outbursts when our very lives may be the price. Agreed?"

Lina was surprised at her father's plain speaking. She'd not thought he'd do anything to anger Baxter, but on reflection, she realized his concerns were valid. She'd been around acrimonious digs before. Very little of value had been accomplished. Nor did she relish the idea of being isolated in the jungle, the personal trophy between two fierce competitors. She held her breath as she awaited her suitors' responses.

"Agreed." Jeremy sipped carelessly from his water glass.

"Dash it, Lawrence, he insulted me. You can't expect me to take that without retaliation," Baxter growled.

"By my recollection, there's blame enough on both sides." Sir Lawrence softened his tone. "It would pain me to lose your support now. I respect your capabilities. Schliemann himself told me you've got the ideal scientific mind. I want you with us, Hubert, but only if you can work with us *all*—as a team."

"I notice you're not threatening to dismiss Mayhew," Baxter grumbled. At Sir Lawrence's raised brow, he admitted grudgingly, "Not that I blame you. Without him to lead, this would be a very short trip." Baxter took a deep breath. "Oh, very well. Provided Mayhew keeps his tongue bridled, I'll be bland as bread pudding."

"Excellent!" Sir Lawrence leaned back to let the waiter set his breakfast before him. "Could I trouble you for pencil and paper, my good man?" After the man had served them, he came back quickly with a pad and sharp pencil.

Sir Lawrence jotted down items between bites, filling several pages before he was satisfied. The others ate silently, watching him. He muttered to himself, stuck the pencil above his ear, and handed the pad to Baxter. "What do you think? Have I missed anything?"

Baxter studied the list; Jeremy studied Lina. She took a careful bite of ham, trying not to let her hurt show. She'd been on far more digs than Baxter. But she squelched the pain, swallowed the ham, and met Jeremy's probing gaze defiantly. His gentle smile was almost her undoing, but she controlled herself by taking a big sip of juice.

"I can't think of anything else." Baxter handed the list back to Sir Lawrence.

"Good." After the dishes were cleared, Collier ripped off the three top sheets and handed them to Jeremy.

"Your investment should more than cover this. I figure we can purchase mules and more food when we reach Campeche."

Jeremy glanced at the items, then folded the sheets and put them in his pocket. "I hope to be back within a week, two at most. But a word of caution, gentlemen. You've not picked the best time of year to visit Chiapas. It will take us about a month, with good winds, to reach Campeche, and by then, the rainy season will be in full earnest."

Sir Lawrence slapped his forehead. "Didn't even think of that, by Jove." He hesitated, then asked, "When would the dry season be?"

"Late in the year."

"Can't wait that long. I've heard rumors that someone else is mounting an expedition. If we're to be first, we have to go now."

Jeremy shrugged and stood. "That's your decision, but it will cause us considerable hardship." He shook Collier's hand again, then held out his hand to Baxter. After a tiny hesitation, Baxter shook it.

"Godspeed, Mr. Mayhew. We'll be looking forward to your return," Sir Lawrence said. All rose and walked Jeremy to the door.

"Will you come to the station with me, Miss Collier?" Jeremy asked politely.

Baxter's head veered around, but he relaxed when Lina said, "I'd rather not. I wish to retire to my room for a rest." Lina uneasily accepted Jeremy's hand salutation.

"Very well. *Au revoir.* Until next week." Without a backward look, Mayhew strode from the hotel.

With him went the starch in Lina's spine. If the entire expedition was to be pervaded by the same tension, they'd all end up raving lunatics.

"I'll see you both for dinner," Lina murmured, then trudged up the stairs.

However, upon reaching her room, tired as she was, she still couldn't sleep. Her skin felt so prickly she had the urge to scratch. Extreme stress always made her feel itchy. And here she was willingly seeking an environment where the climate, both literal and emotional, would enhance this reaction.

She smiled wryly to herself. She'd better take plenty of salve along.

Rising, she pulled a wrapper over her undergarments and poured herself a glass of water from the carafe beside the bed. She sat on the window seat looking out over the sea, sipped and asked softly, "Who are you, Jeremy Mayhew?"

Immediately, she felt better. Truth was like a hungry tiger: Face it squarely with all the weapons at hand, and it often slunk away; run from it, and it consumed you. The analogy seemed especially fitting as she recalled Jeremy's lithe, dangerous grace.

She quit scratching her arm as she speculated on the circumstances that had made him so cynical about life and women. If he ever discovered her own deception, he was not likely to change his opinion. She'd have to pray that her father was right about the gold.

If he were wrong? She set the glass down and clasped her arms about herself. A shiver rippled down her spine as she saw herself lying naked in Mayhew's arms. In the quiet of her own mind, at least—but God forbid, not her heart—she admitted the thought of losing the bet didn't trouble her as it should.

Put simply, she wanted sex with Mayhew. And he knew it, damn him. That's why he wouldn't leave her be. So what? She'd probably never wed. Virginity could quite possibly be a burden in the world she hoped to carve for herself. She'd go much further in archaeology as a mature, experienced woman than as a maid.

There, the truth was out. Of course, knowing the truth
didn't make her free; quite the contrary. She'd be trapped
with Mayhew for months on end, first on a ship, then isolated
in the jungle. The only defense she'd have against these dark
urges would be her escorts and her own doubtful morality.

Would they be enough? Decisively she rose. Only fate
and God would decide. But whatever happened, she'd see
Palenque. Lina threw off her wrapper and dressed again. She'd
go to the casino. Gambling would help quell this restless-
ness . . .

A week to the day after Mayhew's departure, a porter
knocked on Lina's door. "A Mr. Jeremy Mayhew begs an
audience, Miss Collier."

"Thank you, I'll be right down," Lina called.

The desultory appraisal of her appearance suddenly became
meticulous. This royal-blue taffeta dress was one of her newest.
It swept tightly across her hips to gather in the back in a white
lace cascade that fluttered to her knees. The skirt was tight to
her calves, then flared to the floor, where more lace peeped.
The bodice slashed deeply to her bosom. Only white lace
protected her modesty. Lina carefully cocked the tiny hat at
a jaunty angle and pinned it on.

She nodded at her dashing reflection. "Quite a coincidence,
old girl, that you chose this gown on the day he'd said he
would arrive." She stuck her tongue out at her mirrored image
and turned away.

For a woman who'd lost a good portion of her winnings
in the past week, she felt wonderful. Thank God they'd be
leaving soon. Her daily visit to the casino had become the
high point in her stay. She took a set amount each night
and never played after losing it, but since she'd lost every
day for a week, she'd made a good dent in her earlier winnings.

So what? she asked herself as she swaggered down the
stairs, hips swaying. Her good humor wavered when she spied
Jeremy arguing with Baxter. She eased closer to listen.

"Who the deuce gave you the right to purchase her clothes?"
Baxter snarled, trying to snatch the boxes Jeremy held.

Jeremy raised them high and to the side. "Her father did."

Baxter's mouth dropped open; so did Lina's. Sir Lawrence was fiercely protective of the proprieties, especially where his daughter was concerned.

"I don't believe you," Baxter said flatly.

"I'll lose some sleep over that, I can tell you." When Baxter's eyes narrowed and his fists bunched at his sides, Jeremy said wearily, "Enough! I only meant that, as the hired guide of this expedition, it's my right to see that you're all properly attired. I've purchased clothes for you and Sir Lawrence too."

"Wouldn't it have been easier just to admit that rather than get in an argument?" Lina asked, coming down the last few steps to their side.

Jeremy's eyes swept over her provocatively. The smile that stretched his lips was even more so. "Perhaps. But it wouldn't have been near as much fun." He ignored Baxter's scowl and bowed.

How he moved so gracefully holding three large boxes was a mystery to Lina. Did nothing shake his self-confidence? "These are for me, I assume." She held her arms out, but he shook his head.

"I'll carry them up for you."

"The devil you will," Baxter growled, coming toward Lina. "Send them up with a servant."

Lina shot Baxter an annoyed look. Without his intervention, she might have done exactly that. "Come along, Mr. Mayhew. You can leave them inside the door."

Huffing in frustration, Baxter stomped off.

When they reached her room, Lina hovered near the open door. "Set them on the bed."

He did so, then wandered to the window. "You're lucky to face the sea. The view is lovely from here."

"Yes, lovely. Now, let's go find my father—"

"In a moment. I'd like you to open the boxes first." Jeremy turned, propping his broad shoulders against the wall.

His gleaming eyes should have warned her, but her skin was prickling so that she only wanted him out of her room. A luxurious bedchamber, scented with roses, was not conducive to keeping the distance she needed to maintain between them.

She stalked to the bed and tore into the boxes. The heavy twill split skirts were beige, practical, and ugly. The thin white cotton blouses were a little better. They were trimmed at short sleeves and V-neck with lace. A wide leather belt, heavy boots, and socks were in the second, smaller, box. The last box was smallest of all.

She opened the lid curiously. She gasped when she held up a batiste camisole, low-cut and trimmed in lace. She could see Mayhew through it. The smile playing about his lips looked all the more seductive through the gauze.

"Why bother? Such a garment is hardly worthy of the name." She stuffed the camisole back into the box on top of the others. "And you had no right to buy such things for me."

"You'll be glad soon enough at how thin they are. I hope you have some cotton petticoats." His voice softened. "I bought them purely for your comfort, I assure you."

"Ha! You've probably not had a pure thought since your schooldays."

Jeremy uncoiled his long length and came toward her.

She steeled herself not to back away. Thank God the door was open.

Jeremy glanced into the empty hallway, then clasped her shoulders. "I confess I've not had one pure thought since meeting you." He dipped his head and kissed the warm, scented hollow of her throat. "And I also admit I bought the garments thinking how beautiful you'd look in them."

Lina pulled away as his lips wandered lower. "You'll never know, will you?" Her response was too slurred to sound as tart as she wished. She straightened her hat and moved to the door.

"I suspect I shall. Of course, if you want to put me out of my suspense, I shan't mind."

Stopping, Lina turned her head. His raking stare was more explicit than his words. She was tired of playing the mouse. The role of cat was much more to her taste. She blinked at him impishly. "Why, if you're wondering what I'm wearing now, it's quite similar to your, ah, gift. Except that it's pink, sheer, and embroidered only where it has to be."

At his quick intake of breath, she smiled in satisfaction. She swept regally to the door, feeling his stare burning a trail after her. "Come along, Mr. Mayhew."

He followed, still peering at her. "This round to you, my dear," he said beneath his breath as they descended the stairs in search of Sir Lawrence. "But the match has only begun."

"Now that, sir, we can agree on."

"And I do *so* love physical sports," Jeremy drawled.

"Why are you blushing, Lina?" Sir Lawrence asked a few minutes later when they found him basking on the terrace.

"Ah, we, ah, rushed down the stairs to find you."

"Mayhew!" Sir Lawrence rose and extended his hand. "It's a pleasure to deal with a man of his word. Did you find everything?"

"Down to the last shovel."

"Excellent. When do we leave?"

"My ship is victualed and waiting. We can take the evening train if you can all be ready."

"Lina?" Sir Lawrence looked at his daughter.

"If I get a maid to help, I should be packed in time."

"You should all probably put most of your things in storage. The humidity of Campeche will not be good for silks and laces," Jeremy said.

"Fine, fine." Sir Lawrence strode off the terrace. "We'll sort through our belongings and meet you downstairs at four, then all go to the five-o'clock train together."

Lina turned and descended the terrace steps.

"Where are you going?" Jeremy called after her.

"I've a quick errand to run. I shan't be long." Lina strolled around to the front of the hotel, her reticule swinging jauntily. A whim had taken possession of her, but she'd always believed fortune favored the bold. Besides, as important as this bet was, one thing was even more vital to her: Mayhew would *not* get the best of her. Once he did, she'd have a tiger by its tail and have no way to dismount.

The analogy made her blush, but she staunchly continued on. When she came to the expensive men's salon she'd passed several times, she entered.

"Yes, mademoiselle? May I help you?" The natty salesclerk seemed surprised at seeing her in this male domain, but his courteous smile remained fixed—until she told him what she wanted.

"For my father, you see," she explained hastily.

His open mouth snapped shut. Shrugging, he went behind the counter.

By the time they reached the dock in Marseilles, the sun straddled the horizon. One of Jeremy's men awaited in a dinghy to row them to the clipper. The harbor was crowded with vessels of every size and type, but somehow, as they weaved around the various anchorages, Lina knew none of these squat, ugly steamers or practical packets belonged to Jeremy.

They veered around an enormous steamer, and there, straight ahead, a long, sleek vessel easily rode the swells. Her sails were furled, but even hobbled, she seemed a race horse quivering at the gate. The vessels around them were nags in comparison.

Jeremy's eyes drank her in. Lina watched his face, feeling a slight pang. Somehow she knew he'd never blessed a woman with such pride and approbation. He probably never would. Her head snapped back around. When they passed under her bows, Lina made out the name of the clipper.

As part of her classical education, Lina had studied world mythologies. She sighed and looked at the figurehead. Yes, her hair was long and blond. No, she wasn't beautiful as she stared straight ahead, her eyes fixed firmly on the present. How sad.

"The *Verdandi*. Is that Italian, Mayhew?" asked Baxter.

"No. It's Norse. My mother is Norwegian. I named my vessel in her honor," Jeremy answered somewhat curtly.

Or as a constant reminder to yourself? Lina wondered. Verdandi was one of the three Fates of Norse mythology. Lina knew it was no accident that Jeremy hadn't selected Urd, Fate of the past, or Skuld, Fate of the future. Jeremy Mayhew's course would always be set firmly in the present.

Lina's gloomy thoughts were interrupted by her father's exclamation.

"She's so big! But—isn't her hull made of iron?"

"Steel. The same size skin is lighter than wood, believe it or not, because the plates are so much stronger they don't need to be near as thick. I've had her in many a pounding around the Cape of Good Hope and the Horn, and she's come through like a trooper."

"How is she rigged?" Baxter asked, peering upward at the hull towering above them.

"She's a square-rigged bark, of course. She's called a medium clipper, but since she was built in Maine, most seamen call her type of vessel a down-easter. She's almost twenty-five hundred tons, so she can carry a goodly cargo. I had the topgallants and topsails split to allow for easier handling. Even loaded, I'd match her speed against many a steamer."

As he spoke, Jeremy rose to help steady the dinghy. He indicated the rope ladder that had been thrown over the side for them. "You first, Baxter."

"But surely Miss Collier—"

"Should come last. For obvious reasons." Jeremy looked significantly at Lina's skirt.

"Oh, I see. Very well then." Baxter began to climb. Sir Lawrence followed, then Jeremy attached the rods to the sides of the dinghy so it could be hauled aboard and nodded at his seaman. The man sprang onto the rope and clambered up it, agile as a monkey.

"I'll go first. All you have to do is hold on tightly and move with rhythm. What's in that box you've clutched all the way from Monte Carlo?"

"A present. For you," Lina answered sweetly.

Jeremy's brows shot up. "Now why does that alarm me?" He picked up the box and sniffed. "I don't smell smoke. Hemlock, perhaps?" He casually twiddled with the string, then whisked off the lid before she could protest.

"Not now!" she cried too late.

As his fingers rustled through paper, then lifted out the contents, Lina wanted to dive into the sea. She'd intended to leave the box in his cabin. She'd not wanted to be present when he opened it.

He whistled as he held the sheer men's drawers up to the sunset. "I've had some interesting gifts from women in my time, but this . . ." He bent so he could see Lina's averted face. "Tops them all. Or should I say bottoms them all?" He traced the flush that traveled higher up her face. "Most intuitive of you, my dear. I'll think of you whenever I wear them."

Lina threw back her head. "That's enough. Tit for tat, Mr. Mayhew." Lina could have kicked herself at her word choice when his eyes dropped to her breasts.

"Really?" he drawled. "I shall be delighted to accept those terms for our relationship." He carefully folded the garment and closed the lid. Propping the box under one arm, he stepped on the first ladder rung and began to climb, using his free hand.

When she was two steps up the ladder, he paused and glanced over his shoulder. She had to look up then. Gleaming silver eyes sparkled in the roseate sunlight. Goodness, he had strong legs, and . . . Her blush burned hotter at her thoughts. His next comment did nothing to appease her discomfort.

"But there's one thing you should know, Miss Collier. Your gift is not quite as useful as you probably thought. For you see, in the jungle, I don't wear nether garments. So much more practical without them." He grinned at Lina's mortified sound. "What's that?" he asked when she muttered something.

"Shameful," she repeated, sniffing.

"Quite, ma'am. No doubt, at one time, your gift shall come in handy. Perhaps we can model for one another." His hearty laughter boomed over the water as he resumed his climb.

Lina followed steadily, wondering what had possessed her to make such a scandalous purchase. She peeped up at his flexing thighs and buttocks, going scarlet all over again. The image his words had conjured would not quit her brain, especially with such a view as inspiration.

This expedition hadn't even begun and already she was wondering how she'd survive it dignity—and something even more important—intact. Groaning inwardly, Lina climbed aboard the *Verdandi*, wondering if past or future would hold the most sway over her present.

Chapter 4

THE VERDANDI WAS as pristine on the inside as she was on the outside. Care gleamed in her swabbed decks, her polished brass lanterns and bells, her oiled doors and oak trim. Lina looked around for Jeremy to praise his ship and saw him conversing with the carpenter. She'd barely set foot aboard and already was forgotten. Mentally she shook her head at her own contrariness. The less she saw of him, the better.

A man wearing a blue peacoat and billed cap strode up to where the newcomers stood. He tipped his cap to Lina. "Sure, and 'tis a fittin' sight ye be. A pretty colleen for a pretty lady."

Lina hadn't thought the figurehead especially attractive, but she smiled at the Irishman's compliment. His ruddy skin and broken nose were topped by a wicked mop of black hair. There was the spark of the devil in his blue eyes. He was about Jeremy's age.

"Why, thank you," she replied. "And who might you be?"

"Mack Menefee. First mate. The cap'n asked me to escort his guests to their cabins." With a flourish, he offered his arm.

Baxter stepped into the officer's path and captured Lina's reaching hand. "Lead on, my good man."

The Irishman's bold grin wavered, but he shrugged and guided them amidships, where a broad companionway led below. Cabins stretched on both sides of the corridor. A door near the steps opened as they passed. A young boy, bed linen in his arms, exited. He ducked his head at Lina's glance, his freckles disappearing in a sea of red.

Lina was more interested in the cabin behind him, however. Based on its size and elegance it must be Jeremy's, but she glimpsed only a massive carved four-poster and a brilliant oriental rug before the lad closed the door.

Mack stopped. "This is Cal, our cabin boy. He serves as our steward when we have guests. If you need anything, ring for him." Mack introduced Cal, who bobbed his head, his Adam's apple keeping time.

Lina gave the shy adolescent her warmest smile. "And a braw lad he is. A hearty good day to you, sir."

Pale blue eyes peeped up at her through curly brown locks. "Ma'am. Sirs." Cal scurried off.

Mack opened the second door and waved Sir Lawrence inside. "For you, sir. I'll send a seaman with your bags." The next door Mack opened for Baxter.

The Englishman gave Lina's hand a last proprietary squeeze before disappearing inside his new domain. He missed her grimace, but the Irishman quirked a smile. Lina met his amused gaze coolly.

He tipped his cap, the action saying "Yes'm, I'll mind me own affairs."

Lastly, on the opposite side of the corridor, he ushered Lina through a carved walnut door into a cabin sequestered from the others. Gasping, she stopped past the threshold.

She stood on a blue-green sea cavorting with dolphins, mermaids, and naiads. The plush carpet was complemented by pale oak furniture accented with mother-of-pearl inlay. The bedstead was carved to look like an opening oyster shell. The linens were palest sea-foam green shot through with silver threads. The delicate spindle-legged vanity held an assortment of ivory scrimshaw bottles and pots. A window seat cushioned with aqua silk looked out an ovoid, inviting portal to the sea.

Mack nodded, obviously pleased with her delight. "The cap'n discovered the profit in leasin' his lady to the wealthy and had this cabin and the others done up special."

Lina turned away from the curiosity in his eyes. If Jeremy wanted his mate to know the terms of his most recent agreement, it was up to him to divulge them. "Thank you, Mr.—"

"Mack, 'tis." With a cocky wave that matched his grin, Mack exited the way he'd come—with confidence and verve.

The cabin felt empty but a good deal more peaceful after he'd left. Lina set about unpacking, deciding grimly she'd be wise to enjoy her boredom while she could.

The next evening, her thoughts proved prophetic.

When they exited the Mediterranean, the formidable mass of Gibraltar glowered down at the two men arguing over dinner.

"By Jove, Mayhew, for a supposedly educated man you show a peculiar ignorance of political affairs—"

"Ignorance is bliss in this case, Baxter," Jeremy retorted, rotating his claret glass between his palms. "I've had enough personal intrigue to last me a lifetime."

Lina's fingers paused in twisting her dinner napkin. She looked up. Jeremy glanced at her, then snapped his glass down on the elegant dining table, as if regretting the anger that led to the revealing comment.

"That I couldn't comment on, but surely as the heir to a shipping line, you were taught you had a duty to your name to perpetuate its interests." Baxter shoved back his empty plate and tossed his napkin aside.

"The docks of New York teach rather different values than the halls of Eton and Oxford." Jeremy picked up his glass again and toyed with it, apparently uncaring of Baxter's distaste.

Though Jeremy spoke to Baxter, Lina had the feeling the comment was directed at her.

Touch me not. Was the warning for himself, or for her? Lina had to know. "And what are those values, Mr. Mayhew?"

The claret glass swiveled more slowly as Jeremy murmured, "All of them can be condensed into one simple precept: In his lifetime, a man has only one totally reliable ally . . ."

"Himself," Lina finished quietly.

Jeremy tipped his glass to her. "Or, perhaps, herself?"

Tears stung the backs of Lina's eyes. How could he be so perceptive, yet so cynical, all at once? At least she still hoped, and reached out. Jeremy's dreams, if he'd ever had any, had atrophied.

She stood, snatched a fresh blood-red rose from the vase centerpiece, rounded the table and set his glass down. She curled his fingers around the flower stem, placing them carefully so the thorns wouldn't prick him, picked up his other wrist and crossed his arms on his chest.

Then she stood back and cocked her head. "There. Rest in peace, Mr. Mayhew. If you truly live your life by such philosophy, then you're more dead than alive." Lina picked up her skirts and walked away, leaving a profound silence behind.

Only when she reached her cabin did she allow her tears to fall. They were bleak company as she sat in the lovely window seat and watched the wild, beckoning life of the sea. The gray swells were as turbulent and fathomless as Jeremy's eyes. And, of a sudden, she knew the life they hid was equally cold and dangerous.

Resting her head on her arms, Lina wept. For the loss of girlish dreams, and for the man who might have fulfilled them, had she not met him too late . . .

Too late. He'd met her too late. Jeremy clenched the rail with one hand and held the rose to his nostrils yet again. The aroma was faint on the blustery, salty wind. The story of his life, he thought bitterly. Moments of happiness almost forgotten. Remnants of decency almost lost.

And now, when the uncaring shell he'd built with such care had almost harbored him, *she* came. A rose atop the refuse of humanity. Taunting him with her beauty and pristine scent.

That, too, was a lie. Had he not seen her quiescent in Baxter's passionate embrace, heard the whispered intimacy she did not reject?

She was no pure virgin to make him feel so . . . inadequate. So old and jaded. Yet the memory of her eyes when she gave him the rose, glittering with unshed tears and untold longings, stabbed at him in a region of his body he'd thought long dead. She, too, bore her own secret grief, but she'd not let it sour her. Like Aimee.

Jeremy waited, but the usual searing pain had a dull edge. He tested her name aloud. "Aimee."

Her sweet face framed by blond hair appeared in his mind, but the picture was hazy, overlaid by a different persona. Had his initial attraction to Lina been because of her similarity to Aimee? The two women were of a height, both proud and stubborn, but now he realized Lina was very different from Aimee. Her lovely face had no cupid's-bow mouth or serene brow. The mouth was wide, mobile, the expression vibrant with life. Raven hair flowed like incarnate night down her shoulders.

Their differences went beyond the physical, yet the two women shared a quality that had drawn him to both—a passionate love of life. It glowed in all they did, from their bouncy steps to their ready smiles. Aimee's gentle persistence had won his stepbrother's guarded heart and the couple were ecstatically happy, according to his mother's letters.

Almost, Jeremy could be sorry that he had no heart left to give. If earthly happiness had a name, it was surely Evangeline.

The unbidden thought made him grit his teeth. Never again would he open himself to agony. And he didn't want to be there when Lina, too, lost her illusions, as she inevitably must. Give it time, Jeremy longed to warn her. Your father will never treat you equally, you'll find no gold at Palenque, and you'll never be accepted as an archaeologist. Dismiss your illusions and save yourself the pain.

Jeremy looked down at the rose, drooping now from the damp and wind. Deliberately, he crushed it, barely aware when a thorn pierced his palm. He opened his hand.

The mangled petals still glowed crimson, like the blood staining his palm. The crushed rose had released its dying elixir. The scent filled his head, making it swim with longings he could ill afford.

Slowly, inching his hand over the rail, Jeremy forced himself to let the petals go. He watched them drift away on the breeze, then float down to the water and drown in the wake. He was left with the stem, decimated and forlorn.

Repelled, he tossed it overboard, trying not to equate it with what his life had become. He stalked to his quarters, ignoring that hurting region in his chest.

The denial required more effort than usual.

Midnight still found Lina tossing and turning. Finally, she lit the lantern beside her bed, rose and sought her dressing gown. She'd seen a small bookshelf in the dining room. Maybe losing herself in someone else's tragedy would make her sleep.

Barefoot, she peeked down the empty corridor. It was dimly lit with lanterns. She stole out, not wanting to encounter anyone in her scanty attire, and ducked into the dining room. She pushed the door wide until she could dimly read the titles. She debated *Ivanhoe*, then decided *Clarissa* was more to her taste, with its cold seducer and sad ending.

Holding the red leather volume to her chest, she rose. However, as she turned to the door, it snicked shut. Lina froze, her heart tapping nervously at her ribs.

"Silly. It's just the movement of the ship." Her own voice sounded breathless instead of reassuring. With her free hand, she felt in the darkness for the wall to trace it to the door.

She touched something hard, warm, and smooth. Too late, she gasped and tried to back away. A powerful hand caught her wrist and held her still while a match scraped and flared, allowing her to see Jeremy's face as he lit the lantern.

She swallowed and held the book to her chest like a shield, conscious of her low-cut night rail and robe. Both were cotton, brought for comfort and to be worn in the privacy of her own tent. But the look on Jeremy's face as he turned the lantern down to a luminous glow reminded her of his questionable motives in buying the lingerie. His bare chest was broad, lightly dusted with fine, fair hair, and his back rippled with muscles as he turned to set the lantern down. Lina's veins swelled with rushing blood. Excitement? Or fear?

"Your evening constitutional finds you looking well." Jeremy appraised her from her toes, to her quivering knees, to her hips and on past the swells of ivory flesh to her pale face. "But you came too far, you know. Baxter's cabin is next to your father's."

Fear dissolved in the face of the insult. His voice sounded strange and she scented brandy on his breath. She didn't have to defend her virtue to a sot. She pulled at her wrist, but his grip only tightened.

She divided a scornful look between him and the full brandy decanter he'd set behind him on the table. He'd obviously depleted his personal stash and had come for more. "Thank you for the directions, but I can find my own way. Now let me see, was his the right or the left from this side? We must be sure I don't mistake your cabin for his, mustn't we?"

The lonely yearning there shook her to her toes. How often had she seen it in her mirror? She had not the strength to deny them both. Right or wrong, she had to give the tender shoots of need a chance to flower into trust.

She saw the pain in his eyes as she stepped back. He sat up, bracing his hands on the table. But she didn't leave. Slowly, blushing, she pulled her robe tie loose and shrugged out of the garment. It fluttered to the floor. Jeremy's strangled groan gave her confidence. His hands tightened on the table edge until his knuckles whitened, and she felt his yen to grab her.

Quickly, before she could change her mind, she untied her last sanction of modesty. The abrupt exposure should have made her cool, but warm silver poured over her, molding her into woman. His woman.

He held out his hands, drawing her with the richness of his male ardor. "Come."

She went, her bodice gaping wider with every short step. When she stood in front of him, it slipped to her waist. She caught it, too shy to reveal herself totally.

She started at the first gentle touch of his hands. He molded her in sail-hardened palms, learning her texture and weight. He cupped her rounded flesh, then rotated his palms against her aroused nipples.

"Perfect," he whispered. A silvery flash struck her soul like lightning before he bent his head. His warm breath forecast his intent, but the shock of his mouth still made her quiver. He flicked his tongue at one aching nipple, then bathed it in his mouth.

Her chest heaved with her excitement, abetting his intent. By the time he left one nipple rosy with need to devote his attention to the other, she was limp in his arms. Vaguely she sensed him reaching out. She heard a faint sound, then the scent of crushed roses mingled with the brandy aroma.

Cool velvet soothed her heated skin. Her heavy eyes opened to see him rubbing crushed roses onto her breasts. The pleasant contrast of soft petals and tough hands made her eyes drift shut again. She lolled in his arms, trusting, expectant.

He didn't disappoint her. He blew the petals away, then brushed his cheek along the smooth, flower-scented swath of

flesh. His hair and nascent stubble tickled, making her excru-
ciatingly sensitive to the suckling that followed. He licked and
nibbled every inch of her exposed torso until her very knees
failed her.

Gladly she fell, for the arms that caught her were strong and
able. He swept her up, bending his head insatiably again as he
started to the door. When he turned, her feet caught the brandy
decanter. It shattered on the planked floor. Brandy splattered
them both. A shard of glass stung her bare foot.

The twin shocks made her eyes flick open. She met her own
gaze in the mirror behind the table and blinked. Dear God, was
that her? That wanton with flushed cheeks and swollen lips?
She squirmed, turning away from the sight.

His arms tightened as he moved to step over the glass, but
then he saw her face. He went still. He set her by the door,
away from the glass.

Shamed and cold, she pulled her gown up and fastened it.

"Go. If you come to me it will be willingly, not in the
passion of the moment."

For an instant, her eyes met his. Chilly fog had obliterated
the silver lode, but she knew untold riches awaited her—if she
were brave enough to mine it.

She fled, her hand to her mouth to hold back the sobs,
not even aware that her weight forced the shard of glass
deeper with every step. Or that she left a trail of blood on
the planks.

When the knock came a few minutes later, Lina was still
crying. She wiped her eyes on her gown sleeve and took a
deep breath to steady her voice. "Who is it?"

"Jeremy."

She worried at her lip. Dear God, she was so humiliated.
She wished she could turn the ship around and never face him
again. But when she sat up, her mirror shamed her. Nothing
had happened tonight she had not sought. No wonder he
thought her experienced. What was it about this man so lonely
in his strength that made her ache to comfort him?

"Miss Collier, you've nothing to fear from me. I only want
to see to your foot."

Lina looked down. Blood stained the linens. She'd noticed
a few darts of pain, but had been too upset to care.

Lina's mouth tightened. She deserved a flailing and a hair shirt, but facing Jeremy would equally serve as penitence. She rose and reached out to open the door before she remembered she'd left her dressing gown in the dining room. She turned down the lanterns to a feeble glow, sneering to herself at her laggard modesty.

Jeremy's face was expressionless as he entered and handed over her robe. He turned away and set out a clean towel, a small bottle of medicine, and a long pin, tossing her book on the floor. He turned up the lantern on the small table.

Lina grimaced at his gentlemanly back as she drew on the robe and tied it tightly. Then she limped over to the chair he indicated and sat down.

He folded his powerful legs sailor-fashion, spread the towel on his lap, and turned her foot up on his knee. Lina swallowed, trying not to remember how recently those work-toughened hands had touched her. But now he was impersonal, intent only on removing the sliver of glass.

The twinge as he probed was minor compared to her ache to stroke the hair away from his frowning brow and replace it with a smile. She looked away instead.

"Ah, there it is." She tensed as a dart of pain flashed up her ankle, but then she heard a slight ping as he flicked the glass into the copper pail he pulled away from the wall. He swabbed her cut. She gasped at the sting.

Then he blew on the wound. The cool, pleasant sensation only made the ache in her chest more marked. With a quick dabbing of cream and a plaster bandage, he was done. Not once had he looked at her. Did he despise her as much as she despised herself?

She put her foot down and watched him rise, clean the long pin, and wrap his supplies in the towel. However, as he did so, she saw a rusty red in his own palm. She stood and caught his wrist. When he stiffened, she tried not to show her hurt and turned his right hand up.

A dark thorn impaled the tough skin. Streaks of dried blood indicated its depth. The small wound was already oozing and looked to be some hours old.

"Why did you see to my wound and ignore your own?" The words were out before she thought. Lightning flashed through her for a split second before his long gold lashes shuttered it.

"I'm right-handed. I was going to get Cal to do it in the morning." He tried to pull away.

The explanation was facile, for this must have happened before Cal retired, but she didn't argue. Gently but firmly, she led him over to the same chair she'd recently occupied and pushed him down.

The tense set of his mouth relaxed into a slight smile as he watched her bustle about, cleansing the pin and spreading the towel over his knee. "Miss Nightingale, I presume?" He picked up the lantern and extended it.

She sniffed and plopped it back down. "I'm no saintly lady with a lamp. Now, be still before I'm tempted to whack you with it."

He tossed back his rich blond head and laughed. "I don't think Florence would approve of your bedside manner."

His laughter was so rare and treasured that she was unnerved. "I'm not very good at carrying torches either."

His grin was wiped clean. "Who asked you to?"

So, a toss in a bunk was all he wanted of her? Well, hadn't she known that from the beginning? She twisted his wrist a bit harder than she'd intended as she turned his hand over. "Be still."

He didn't move a muscle as she probed for the deeply embedded thorn. Even when she poured a capful of antiseptic on his palm he didn't stir. But when she blew on his hand, he jumped. His quickened breathing made her own heart beat faster.

Mellow moments later, the words slid over her like a caress. " 'Such dulcet and harmonious breath that the rude sea grew civil at her song.' "

"Do you quote Shakespeare to all your passengers?" She sat back on her heels, releasing him.

"Only the ladies." He added dryly, "For the inimitable Mr. Baxter, however, I reserve something a bit more caustic."

" 'Out, out, damned spot'?" she quipped.

He grinned. "I was thinking more on the lines of 'A lunatic lean-witted fool.' "

"Unfair. Hubert is very intelligent."

"If you say so." He rose and collected his supplies.

Now the tension had eased, she had to ask it. "Why do you pretend to be uneducated and uncultured?"

He stopped tying the towel up, then twisted the knot harder than necessary. "I don't."

"Yes you do." The late hour and the lonely creaks of the ship were not caution enough. She blocked his path to the door. "Like tonight at dinner, and the way you dressed when you came to the hotel. Judging from this ship"—she inclined her head at the ivory bottles—"you can afford to buy Baxter several times over. Yet you pretend otherwise. Why?"

He caught the bundle tightly under his arm. "I despise social climbers and the world they inhabit."

"But why?" If only he would answer, maybe she could begin to understand him.

He flung the bundle down and advanced.

She lifted her chin and stayed put. She would have an answer whether he barreled over her or not.

"Need I remind you, Miss Collier, that this is neither the time nor the place for such a discussion?" Jeremy lifted a hand as if to touch her bare shoulders, but dropped it when she met his gaze squarely.

"This is a discussion I'd rather share here and now than in the jungle."

"Very well, if we're having a true heart-to-heart—why did you choose to read *Clarissa* on this particular night?"

"Perhaps I was in the mood for tragedy."

"Or perhaps tonight you used it as a lexicon, to paint me as the seducer Lovelace, yourself as the innocent?" His gaze raked her luxuriously. "Luckily, we know both images are false."

Attack was always the best defense, she thought wearily. And Jeremy had become a master at both. Was he so adept at fending off the truth? "Very well, keep your armor tight about you; I will do the same. Let our deepest wounds remain untreated."

His swift intake of breath proved his understanding. He curled his fingers about his right palm and strode for the door.

Stiffly, she opened it, armored against him—and herself.

When he paused on the threshold as if to speak, she didn't look at him.

He sighed softly, then strode into the dark.

Where he chose to belong. She told herself to leave him there, for she loved the sunlight. If she couldn't coax him out with her, they had no basis for even a superficial relationship.

Long into the night, she stared at the planking above. Her wounds lay aching where no one could see them, hurting the more at her knowledge of how joyously they could have healed one another.

For some days after, the voyage was uneventful. Lina took to avoiding everyone, even her father and Baxter. Jeremy seemed equally intent on ignoring her, a truth she fiercely told herself to accept. She had better things to do. She'd previously only sailed on passenger packets, so she was curious about the *Verdandi*.

With a little coaxing, Cal made a good tutor. Today Cal shepherded her from one end of the deck to the other, his shyness easing as he explained the various watch duties. "We scrub the deck and prepare for sailing durin' the evenin' hours, then we paint or repair sails durin' the day till the first dogwatch."

At her puzzled frown, he added hastily, "That be the four P.M. to six P.M. watch where we make the ship ready for the night and shorten sail. The second dogwatch is after supper when things is generally easy 'less we have a storm."

In her brief time aboard, Lina had noticed that the crow's nest was never vacant. She peered up at the tiny dark patch on the rounded cheek of the sky. "What about him? Doesn't he ever rest?"

Cal followed her gaze. "S'cuse me, ma'am, I thought everyone knew—we ain't never without a watch or a helmsman. That changes jest 'bout every hour."

"The view from up there must be wonderful."

Cal sighed wistfully. " 'Tis so. Maybe someday they'll let me take a turn."

"Are you still in training?"

"Yes'm."

"I'd love to see the sunset from there."

"Aw, you're jest a girl—" Cal coughed and excused himself, beating a hasty retreat.

Lina still glared after him. Then her face smoothed and she hurried after Cal. "You're quite right, Cal. Your explanations are *so* informative. And you're only fifteen? Amazing." She clasped his arm, aware that Jeremy's fair head turned from where he stood beside the helmsman. She smiled wider at Cal and fluttered her eyelashes.

The lad strutted toward the companionway, tossing a smile at the seamen who watched him enviously. He patted her hand, unaware that he was playing right into it. "Would you like to see the hold now?"

"I'd love to." Though she concentrated her attention on Cal, Lina was more aware of the dark suspicions trailing her into the hold. Good. Let the arrogant beast wonder.

She squelched her momentary guilt at the trouble Cal would incur. If she were quick, no one would be the wiser. She dutifully admired the spacious but orderly hold, then, as they went back up to the living-quarters deck, she asked, "Oh, by the by. Do you have an old pair of breeches I might borrow? The wind's quickening and these skirts are awkward."

Cal scratched his freckled nose. "I got an old pair, but I don't think the cap'n'll want you above. A squall has—"

"Just for a brief peek? You can help protect me." She batted her eyelashes again.

Cal's chest puffed out. "I'll be right back, ma'am."

"Please call me Lina."

He bobbed his head and disappeared down the crew's companionway. A few seconds later, Lina heard steps and saw shiny black boots descending from above. She looked desperately about, unwilling for Jeremy to question her now. She ducked into the closest cabin and eased the door shut. When the steps passed, she sagged in relief. Her hand was on the knob before the bright pattern of the oriental rug caught the corner of her eye.

She released the knob and turned around. A sign would have been superfluous—everything in this cabin proclaimed "captain." From the log sitting open on the black lacquered oriental desk, to the chronometer balanced on a special gimballed stand, to the exotic knickknacks hailing from every corner of the globe.

Lina wandered to the glass-fronted bookcase. Books on sailing sat comfortably next to Flaubert—in French—and Chaucer. A few modern novels were sprinkled among the others like spice. Lina tilted her head to read the titles. She smiled. Of course. What self-respecting sea captain wouldn't want copies of *Moby Dick* and *Voyage to the Bottom of the Sea*?

The copies of *Pride and Prejudice* and *Jane Eyre* were surprising, but supremely satisfying. Perhaps Jeremy truly was a closet romantic, after all.

Feeling as if she were peeling away Jeremy's masks, Lina opened a case and took out an innocuous-looking book at random. She flicked through the pages—and almost dropped the book. Did people really *do* such things? Her ears burned as she glanced around, expecting her father to pop out of the bed curtain. Gingerly, she turned to the title page and read aloud, *"The Kama Sutra."*

The name meant nothing, but the pictures were most elucidating. She paged through the volume, growing curious as her embarrassment eased. She was so intent that she didn't hear the door open.

"Find anything interesting?" Jeremy closed his door and strolled forward.

Lina jumped and hid the book in her skirts. "Ah, no, not really." She made to replace the tome, but Jeremy snatched it out of her hand.

His eyebrows rose. "You've peculiar taste for a lady."

Why did circumstances always incriminate her unjustly? Her hurt made her lash back: "And you've peculiar manners for a gentleman."

Jeremy thumbed open the book and held it out to her, his eyes never leaving hers. "Ah, but I never said I was a gentleman."

She steeled herself not to blush and glanced at the page, where two naked bodies copulated in a position that should have violated Newton's laws of gravity *and* motion. "I'll have to try that sometime." Lina swept her skirts to the side, adding, "And I, sir, never said I was a lady."

"That's what I like about you." Jeremy closed the book and set it back in its place. He caught her arm as she tried to pass him. "Remind me to pack it in my kit before we leave. Trees and rivers should offer intriguing possibilities, wouldn't you say?" He stroked her forearm through her dress.

Lina pretended numbness even as fire flicked up her arm. "I would say, sir, that from what I know of you, you need no book for inspiration."

He leaned closer until his breath fanned her warm face. "True, my lady—I have you. And the memory of you."

The peculiar mixture of reluctant tenderness and sheer male hunger he emitted had her scurrying for safety.

"By the way, Cal is looking for you."

She froze two steps from the door. "What did he want?"

"He didn't say. In fact, he was unusually surly when I questioned him. Must be the power of your charm."

Relieved, she opened the door.

Escape was nigh when he added, "Use it sparingly, all right? He's only fifteen."

The words accompanied her down the corridor where she found Cal knocking at her door. Guilt made her voice warm as she accepted the breeches he'd bundled into a canvas sack. "I'm sorry you had to look for me. Thank you so much, Cal. You're a credit to your ship." She kissed his cheek and watched his freckles disappear.

Whistling, he strode off.

She wasted no time, more determined than ever to climb to the crow's nest. Maybe the breeze would blow the cobwebs from her brain. The dungarees were snug through the hips and belled at the bottom. She ignored the temptation to approach the mirror and tucked her plainest cotton blouse into the waist.

The best time to go would be during supper. Most of the men would be at mess, and sunset should follow shortly after. She sat down at the window seat to wait, crunching an apple. When the uncomfortable memory came of Eve's fate after she ate the apple, Lina dismissed it. The only toil and travail would be Jeremy's, as he gnashed his teeth and roared at her to come down. Lina smiled and took another big bite.

As soon as the supper bell sounded, she snuck down the

corridor. She paused behind the half-closed dining room door
and listened.

"—don't know why she's late. I'll check." A chair scraped
back and her father's familiar steps approached the door.

Lina bolted for the deck, glad of the old canvas shoes Cal
had lent her. She flattened against the steps as the door opened,
but her father had already turned in the other direction. She
didn't wait to see him read the note she'd tacked on her door
which said she was tired and would not be at dinner. She scaled
the last steps.

Above deck, she appraised the activity. A couple of sailors
sat mending canvas, and more were in the yards trimming sail
for the evening. No one even glanced her way as she pulled
the cap down over her ears and tried to mimic the easy sailor
gait as she strode to the mainmast, where the crow's nest was
located.

She cricked her neck back and looked up—way up. Her
heart skipped a beat as the bottom of the platform seemed no
more than a dot on the horizon. She reminded herself that she
was an experienced climber and reached for the shrouds.

Two swaying steps up, she divined the vast difference
between climbing a stable mountain and supporting herself
on swaying rope as the ship bucked beneath her. She glanced
down at the suddenly appealing deck, but, stubbornly, she
reached higher.

No, dammit, she'd not retreat. She'd resolved two years
ago to live life to the fullest, the proprieties be damned. If
she were to establish herself in a man's field, she couldn't
afford feminine frailty. This was something she wanted to do;
nothing would stop her.

Least of all her own fears.

She climbed twenty more feet before a gust of wind made
her slip. For an instant she felt nothing beneath her but air
before the movement of the ship down into a trough slammed
her back into the shrouds. She braced her feet, rested her cheek
on the back of her hand and panted. She waited until her heart
quieted, then forced herself to wait longer, learning the swell
and retreat of the waves.

She climbed more ably then, beginning to enjoy the caress
of the breeze. She kept her gaze on her hands, not looking up
or down.

Had she looked down, she would have seen the seaman frowning up at her. He cupped his hands and shouted, but the wind was louder. Then he hurried off.

Lina was too intent to notice the rising swells. She'd become accustomed to the rocking and learned when to time her steps. She hazarded a glance up. The platform was only ten feet away now. Thank God, for her palms had chafed at the unaccustomed activity.

The peculiar color of the sky alerted one part of her brain, but determination remained preeminent until she'd boosted herself over the flimsy basket inside the close confines of the platform. The young seaman there turned to her in surprise.

"What'd you come spell me for? I's jest gettin' ready to go down and help batten down for the storm . . ."

Lina barely heard him as she jerked off the cap and tossed her head, letting the breeze comb her hair. She turned slowly in a circle, appreciating the panoramic view of white-capped seas and . . . green horizon? Shouldn't the sky be painted with the glory of sunset?

The seaman's missing front tooth would have made his gape comical if she hadn't read such horror in his expression. His words finally sank in.

The storm!

She clasped the flimsy plank edge of the crow's nest and looked around, critically this time. The seas were no longer poetically white-capped; they bristled and bared angry white fangs. Why hadn't she felt the humidity in the air? Sweat trickled down her back despite the wind.

Now that she was still, she realized she was not as immune to seasickness as she'd hoped. And that putrid horizon accentuated her queasiness. She took a deep breath. "Well, I'm between wind and water now."

The young able seaman smiled weakly at her quoting of the sea truism and added glumly, "As will I be when the cap'n gets wind o' this."

Lina swallowed her rising nausea and forced herself to look down. Dizzy, she sank back, but her spine soon stiffened again. She'd make it. All she had to do was concentrate on her steps and pretend the deck wasn't sixty feet below. "I got myself into this, so I'll get myself out. Will you guide me down?"

The sailor hesitated, then hefted himself over the edge, braced his feet, and extended his hand. "Ready when you are, miss."

Chapter 5

"READY." LINA FORCED a smile past the acid in her throat and clasped his hand. At that moment, the *Verdandi* rode the back side of a strong wave. The young sailor was forced to release her and grapple for his own safety.

She felt the lurch clear through her stomach to her spine. She pulled her extended leg back into the basket. "I'm . . . not sure I can. I feel so . . . awful." Her eyes widened. She leaned over the side of the basket away from the seaman and retched. The undigested apple tasted terrible, but she felt slightly better when she was done.

The young sailor watched her with mixed worry and frustration. "Here, let me light the lantern for you." Bracing himself against the rigging, he did so, then lashed the lantern to the platform. "I'll go down and fetch some rope. Maybe we can lower you down. Aye?"

Shakily, Lina saluted. "Aye, aye." The yellow glow was feeble company, but, as night swallowed the last sickly rays, she was glad for the fitful light.

As if rebuking her for her arrogance, the heavens opened and added to her misery. The lantern hissed, but was shielded so well that it didn't extinguish. She was stuck here now. As sick as she felt, she'd never get down safely in this gale. She leaned her head back and let the icy rain beat her in the face.

Sheer pride had brought her here; she only hoped it would sustain her.

A few moments later, she lifted her head. Voices? He couldn't have returned so soon. She felt the platform shake, then a familiar scowl glowered at her above the basket.

"You silly little twit. Do you have a death wish?" Jeremy vaulted over the side, his movements lithe and easy despite the churning seas. He dropped a thick coil of rope at his feet and removed his heavy slicker to spread it over the top of the basket.

He bumped her hip with his as he folded his long length into the cramped space. "Move over."

She tied herself into a tighter knot, but still his legs had to rest atop hers and his torso rubbed her from hip to shoulder. "Ar—aren't we going back down?" She tried to steady her chattering teeth.

"When the storm eases, I'll lower you down. Now it's too dangerous. The pitch of the ship would slam you from mast to mast like a puppet." He took a silver flask from his pocket and offered it.

She swigged the brandy, glad of the warmth that watered her eyes and rinsed the sour taste from her mouth. Strengthened, she offered, "Maybe I c-can climb."

In the intimate glow beneath the slicker, his eyes flashed. "You're still shaking. Come here." Efficiently he returned the flask to his pocket and pulled her under his arm, rubbing her chilled legs with his own thigh, her arm with his hand.

The hard, warm contact stopped her shaking and eased her nausea. However, her mental stress grew. She was acutely aware of the thin, soaked cotton shirt and even thinner batiste that were her only protection. The other night had proved that they were forbidden fruit to one another, all the more tempting when they were alone.

However, Jeremy's impersonal touch was reflected in his voice. "The squall shouldn't last long."

"Are we safe up here?" The groaning masts had frightened her at first, but even the precipitous pitching seemed less frightening—now he was here. She was too thankful for the craven thought to shame her, as it would have in other circumstances.

"We should be, provided the mast doesn't break." His calm slipped as he growled, "But this post was not designed to be manned in a storm."

"I'm sorry, Jeremy. Truly I forgot about the storm."

"What in the devil were you thinking of?"

Peace. Self-determination. Pride. How could she explain such motivations to a male who allowed females only one purpose in his life? Still, she had to try. The urgency held all else in abeyance, even danger. "Do you think only men have pride?"

She heard the perplexity in his voice. "What does such a foolish stunt have to do with pride?"

"Haven't you ever done something just to prove to yourself you could do it?"

"Well yes, but I'm a man—"

"Precisely why I did it. I get enough pats on the head from my father. I'll tolerate them from no one else, do you hear?"

"I could hardly fail to."

She snapped her mouth closed and tried to pull away. He wouldn't let her. "This time you can't slam your door and lock me out."

"I? Lock you out? You've the reverse of it, Jeremy." She cupped one small hand over his heart. "It's you who have locked yourself away."

Lina's own heart beat loudly in her ears at Jeremy's sudden stillness. Why must she always be so blasted honest?

"Astute of you, angel."

So soft the words, so strong their impact. She felt the change in him as he pulled her close again and kissed the top of her head.

"So small, but so determined. Like . . ."

"Like whom?"

"It doesn't matter. Someone I used to know."

Someone he'd cared for deeply. The hope soaring in her breast slowed to a flutter. "Tell me. Please."

The wind howled, the sea roared, but Lina heard only Jeremy's soft, "Her name is Aimee. She's my brother's wife."

She caught her breath. Oh God, this explained so much. Here was the insight she'd sought—and she wanted to close her eyes and ears.

"It's not what you're thinking." He pulled his arm away and rested a forearm on his upraised knee. "We were never . . . intimate."

"Except in your heart." She, too, pulled away.

Was it a lull in the storm, or did the very air seem to hold its breath? "How do you understand so much? You barely know me."

"Sex is an appetite to you, Jeremy. It's your feelings you hoard. If this . . . Aimee touched your heart, you must have loved her passionately."

For the first time, she was seeing the real Jeremy, the raw human being motivated by raw human emotion. Yet, if some unobtainable female had sent him over the seven seas, then the depth of his love might as well consign him to Davy Jones's locker. Never, ever could she reach him. In her misery, his next comment took a moment to penetrate.

"You remind me of her, you know."

She frowned, torn between insult and hope.

"Your zest for life gleams from you, as it did from her, even though she was as fair as you are dark. You also have a basic curiosity and optimism that allows you to find the best of human nature in the most unlikely of places. It's a rare quality, but one I admire."

"You have it too, Jeremy, though you try to hide it."

She felt his body shake and turned to comfort him—until she realized he was laughing. Never had she heard mirth so bitter.

"And that, angel," he finally gasped, "is proof of your optimism." Suddenly, his hands were on her shoulders and his weight pressed her against the basket. "Don't seek goodness in me. It's long gone."

And he proceeded to show her exactly how sweet evil could be. Lips, tongue, and hands bade her enjoy her fall from grace. At first she resisted, but their wet clothes were gossamer guards for her wavering chastity.

Why hadn't her father ever told her to beware? This skin-to-skin contact was pleasurable beyond description. No wonder, she thought dimly, no wonder so many children were born out of wedlock. Her hands curled of their own accord, then turned traitor and wrapped about his neck. She lay in his arms, poised between heaven and hell, lightning blazing, thunder booming, yet the storm in her mind made the power of the elements mundane.

Lips so warm and giving could never be evil. The more she

sipped, the more he filled her. His tongue dipped in concert with hers, evocative, arousing. When his mouth escaped her seeking, she tried to pull him back, only to gasp a deeper need when he spread her over his lap and cupped the vee defined by her tight pants. She bowed in his arms, the surging seas calling to her blood until her head whirled from the twin tempests.

And then thought was denied her utterly, for his mouth, its warmth and softness bliss upon her chilled flesh, explored her breasts through the fine cotton. He made husky little noises as he claimed each peak, then leisurely forayed the valley between.

"Angel, angel, fall with me," he purred against her flesh. "Forget the storm. Think of me." He picked up her hand and pulled it to the front of his pants.

For one compulsive moment she traced the wonder of him, so full of life and mystery. Why not? Where better to find the answers she sought than here, blessed by Nature? Just as she reached for the top button of his pants, however, a violent gust ripped the slicker loose. Rain beat down upon her like icy tears. She blinked, removed her hand, and forced herself to sit up.

His arms tightened, as if he'd not let her go, but when she pulled harder, he allowed her the width of the tiny platform. She stared at him. He stared back, his eyes as bright and charged as the lightning clashing over their heads. His wet golden hair molded the fine shape of his skull. The bouncing lantern cast odd, moving shadows over his face, starkly outlining its purity.

Never had she been so aware of his male beauty—or of his male power. Was that lightning she smelled? Or sulphur? Surely only a devil could tempt her beyond thought.

He crooned, "Come, angel, let me shelter you." He held his arms wide.

The wind made his shirt billow about him like a cloak; she fancied steam rose from his flaring nostrils. "No." She inched farther away.

He inched closer, his crooked smile enough to tempt a nun. "You know you want to."

"I don't always want what's good for me."

Pain flashed across his face. His arms dropped. "As I myself warned you, did I not?"

"Oh Jeremy, that's not what I meant, and you know it. You're good at heart—"

"It's my goodness that causes this?" He brushed a thumb over her distended nipple.

She caught his hand and kissed it. "No, it's your goodness that made you let me go. I'm not frightened any longer. You distracted me magnificently."

He groaned, then hauled her back into his arms. "Damn you, you twist my guts in half. Hush now. Be still. We'll just wait it out. Together."

There, in the protective circle of his arms, she remained, listening to his strong heartbeat. For once, she let her womanly instincts have sway and believe that the man was as steadfast as his heart.

When the storm quieted as suddenly as it had arisen, Lina pulled back shyly. "Thank you."

"For what?" He cleared his gruff voice.

"For not pushing me. For . . . staying with me through the storm. I feel much better now."

"Wish I could say the same," he muttered, glaring down at the front of his pants.

Since she knew she wasn't supposed to hear the complaint, she pretended not to, but she hid her smile by looking over the platform. The deck, dimly lit by the emerging moon and by lanterns, seemed even farther away than it had in daylight.

Lina took a deep breath. "I'm ready when you are."

Jeremy picked up the rope and began tying a rudimentary harness.

"No." She covered his busy hands. "I want to climb down under my own power."

He tossed her hands off and kept working, but his jaw had tensed.

"I mean it, Jeremy. That thing would terrify me, for I'd be helpless. At least I control my feet. I would have come down already if I hadn't felt sick, but I'm better now."

"So much for your trust in me." His eyes sliced up to hers.

"I'm sure you'd be very careful, but even a man of your talent can't control the waves. Please, Jeremy. This is important to me."

She knew from his frown that he didn't understand. His hands tightened. Then, sighing, he loosened the knots and coiled the rope neatly, hanging it on the side of the platform. "I go first."

He eased over the basket. "Put your feet exactly where I tell you. Understand?"

She saluted saucily. "Aye, Cap'n!"

The climb would have been difficult in the best of circumstances, but the rigging was wet, and the moon still struggled in and out of clouds. Jeremy went slowly, watching her feet and hands.

"Now. Third rope down and to your right," he said. "Not there!"

She slipped. One foot struggled for purchase in thin air as a wave bore her weight away from the rigging. Jeremy freed a hand and pulled her back—at the price of his own safety. She was no sooner stable than his extended reach pulled him off balance.

He fell backward, his arm flailing as he tried to fight the pitch of the ship and pull himself into the rigging.

Lina braced her feet and grabbed. She caught only his shirt, tearing the stressed fabric. She had to let go or fall herself. Helplessly she watched him struggle for the eternal journey up the wave. Then, as the *Verdandi* rode down the swell, gravity became his ally, throwing him back into the rigging. He latched onto the wet, slippery rope.

They both rested, panting.

When she could breathe again, Lina said mildly, "I'm an experienced climber, Jeremy. Kindly watch out for yourself, else you'll have *me* falling trying to catch *you*."

Jeremy's grin was roguish. "I'll be careful, angel. When I fall with you, it will not be into the sea."

Lina climbed quickly after that. Jeremy glanced at her now and again, letting her set her own rate. They were only ten feet above deck when Lina heard someone call her.

"Shut up, Baxter! Don't distract her now."

Lina looked down at her father. Even in the dim lanterns, his frown was thunderous. She stifled a craven urge to scurry back up to the crow's nest and suffer Nature's less imposing tantrum. Instead, she climbed down, jumping the last few feet to the deck that was swarming with concerned onlookers. Seamen clustered around.

Baxter hurried over. "Are you all right?" He appraised her from head to toe, lingering on her wet shirt. Lina glanced uneasily at the staring seamen and crossed her arms. Only then did she notice the rip in her sleeve.

Jeremy quirked an eyebrow when Baxter glowered at him, then turned slightly sideways until the wind displayed the tear in his own shirt.

"What the deuce has been going on up there?" Baxter growled, reaching to pull Lina under a shielding arm.

When Jeremy jerked his head, the sailors scattered.

"Nothing." Lina pulled away from Baxter and braced herself to meet her father's eyes.

"You were up there a long time," Sir Lawrence said calmly.

From long experience, Lina knew his true feelings were anything but calm. She couldn't control it; she blushed. "We had to wait for the storm to die before we could come down. You know that."

"Hmph. Well, you can tell me all about it. Below with you and get out of those wet clothes before you catch your death." He hustled her to the companionway, then paused to address Jeremy. "Thank you, Captain. She'll not be so foolish again. I'll see to it."

Straight-faced, Jeremy replied, "Good luck, sir."

When they reached her cabin, Sir Lawrence caught Lina's upper arms. "Dammit, Evangeline, can't you ever think of anyone but yourself?"

Lina jerked away. "No! Like father like daughter, wouldn't you say?"

Sir Lawrence's fair skin reddened. "How dare you speak so to me! Just look at you. Displaying yourself so . . . so . . . "

"At least this time I was on display for myself rather than for men I don't give a farthing for."

"Baxter was furious, I tell you. If we weren't in the middle of the Atlantic, I believe he'd consign us both to the devil."

Lina smiled bitterly. "Indeed. I'm only a toy to Hubert Baxter, but he doesn't share well—"

Sir Lawrence sank down on the window seat. "Oh Lina,

credit me with some sense. I've noticed his particular atten-
tions to you. Why do you think I've been so determined not
to lose him? He'll make a good match. He's a bit arrogant,
perhaps, but you need a strong man. Before this trip is out, I
believe he'll come up to the mark."

Lina ran her hands through her wet hair so hard that her
roots smarted. "Why can you not comprehend that I *don't want
a husband*?" Certainly not a man of Baxter's ilk. Lina glared
at her father and squelched the other image that appeared in
her mind.

"What else is there? Angel, I only want what's best for you.
You're too lovely to wither away in a moldy museum. You
should have the brood of children your mother and I were
denied because of her health."

Lina cupped her elbows, her throat tightening at the childhood nickname he so seldom used anymore. How had Jeremy
known the one endearment to turn her to mush? "Father,
please. Listen, for once. If I ever wed, and I probably shall
not, it will not be to a snob like Baxter. I want someone as
comfortable with peasants as with princes, who will not set me
on a pedestal but stand beside me, both feet firmly planted on
the ground." She hadn't admitted her deepest feelings to him
in years. Maybe this time, just a bit, he'd understand?

"Where did you get such queer notions?" Sir Lawrence rose
to his full, imposing height. "It's Mayhew you want, isn't it?
What has he done to encourage you?"

Lina turned away to hide her watering eyes. Why did she
still try to reach her father? They shared the same name and
the same blood, but little else.

"Or perhaps I should say—what have *you* done to encourage
him? Answer me, Lina!"

Goaded, she dashed her tears away and whirled. "As much
as I dare. And I've enjoyed every moment of it!"

Sir Lawrence groped for the window seat and sagged down
as if his knees would not support him. "Are you saying what
I think you're saying?"

"Not that. Not yet. But, if we find no gold at Palenque, then
I will keep my side of the bargain." The horror on his face only
made her more reckless. At least he was feeling something.
"Didn't you wonder why he so abruptly offered his aid? It

wasn't the power of your persuasion, my dear pater. It was the power of my pulchritude."

There, it was out. Wise or not, she was glad. It was high time her father understood the depth of her own determination. What would he do? Forbid her to see Jeremy? In other circumstances, she would have giggled. He could hardly do that. She watched her father closely, hoping for a strong reaction. Even if he slapped her, he'd have to acknowledge her at last as a person, not just his daughter, and admit only her boldness had saved the expedition.

He struggled with words for several moments, then groaned, "Oh God, this is what comes of letting you have your own way so much. I knew I shouldn't have let you wheedle yourself into this expedition."

Lina blinked. Pain swamped her until she wondered she could stand. As usual, he saw her only as his baby daughter, an ineffectual female instead of a woman becoming worthy of the name. Somehow she managed a cold, "There wouldn't *be* an expedition without me." She strode to the door and flung it open. "Now please leave and think about that."

Sir Lawrence wearily stood. When he came even with her, however, he stopped. "Lina, you are my daughter, and I'll do all in my power to protect you from this . . . this scoundrel who foisted an infamous bargain on an innocent."

Cleopatra would have envied Lina's brash smile. "Again, dear pater, you err. It was I who suggested the bet." She shoved him out the door and bolted it.

The smile faded; her knees wilted. Lina slid down the door to the floor, buried her face in her knees, and tried to forget that last look on her father's face.

It was best this way, she tried to tell herself. She'd put herself beyond the pale. When this expedition was over, they'd go their separate ways.

No more trying to please him, taking him tea in the morning or gin and tonic at night. No more beaming when he complimented her sketches. No more hiding her pain when he patted her on the head and told her to run along so he could work. Lina told herself fiercely she was glad.

The moisture that ran down her cheeks, however, told her otherwise . . .

* * *

Jeremy stood at the helm, guiding the *Verdandi* with steady hands. He needed the familiar feel of her. She was the only woman who had never hurt him. She'd borne him away from New York and helped him heal. She'd taken him around both capes through storms that had sunk untold steamers. She'd guided him through many an adventure and saved his life more times than he could count. She'd made him rich.

One thing she could not do, however: She could not protect him from his own feelings. Especially when the source of his confusion sailed with him.

No, Jeremy. It's your goodness that made you let me go.

How many years had it been since someone believed in him?

His grip tightened on the great wheel. The *Verdandi* quivered. He took a deep breath and forced his hands to relax, guiding her back to her course before the wind. As he stared at the luminous foam evanescing beneath the moon, he admitted that for too many years he'd run from, no, worse than that, *denied* his own feelings.

Lina, like Aimee, drew the best and worst of his nature. Simultaneously he wanted to protect her and grab her. She appealed to him as no other woman had—even, he was growing to realize, Aimee. Here he was, about the business of his ship, forty lives dependent on him, and all he could think of was a bit of a girl with more courage than sense.

Lina looked nothing like the figurehead on the prow of his ship, but still, she reminded him of the *Verdandi*. Both were game, steady, and able.

He grinned. And both had a cut to their jib that set his heart to pounding.

"Wipe that grin off your face, you cur, else I'll do it for you." Sir Lawrence stood at his side, his hands clenched.

Jeremy turned his head and met that rage with an honesty he owed Lina. "Astute of you, sir. I *was* thinking of your daughter."

"You have no right to think such lustful thoughts. She's an innocent. And shall remain so. Do you hear?"

Jeremy's heart lurched in alarm before he realized that the father was, naturally, the last to know. "Does it occur to you,

Sir Lawrence, that my expression owes as much to admiration as it does to, ah, lust?"

"Well, of course, she's a lovely girl. Looks just like her mother."

While Jeremy suspected Lina had inherited her iron will from her father, he was tactful enough not to say so. "I don't mean that sort of admiration. It's her spirit, grit, and intelligence that draw me, even more than her looks."

What had possessed him to admit that? He'd learned the hard way not to interfere in familial strife, but he hated the hurt in Lina's face at her father's inability to see her talent. Something drove him to add, "She's more your daughter than her mother's, I suspect. If you can accept that, you'll go a long way toward solving your disputes with her."

Sir Lawrence took two great strides forward and thrust his face into Jeremy's. "I don't need a ruthless adventurer telling me how to manage my daughter. Keep your opinions— and your hands—to yourself or suffer the consequences." Sir Lawrence stalked away.

So much, Jeremy thought ruefully, for good intentions.

Breakfast the next morning was strained. Lina ate her oatmeal daintily, outwardly composed. After one look, she ignored the reproach in her father's eyes and the suspicion in Baxter's. To the devil with them both. Almost, she could hope she *did* lose the bet.

Her vague smile of pleasure faded when her father said, "Lina, I demand that you move into my cabin. There's room for a bunk."

Lina sighed. "Father, I'm not up to this now. Can we not at least have a peaceful breakfast?"

"Certainly. After I have your agreement."

Lina shoved her half-eaten oatmeal away. "You're not going to get it in such a fashion. You should know that by now."

Sir Lawrence swallowed the last bite of his buttered bread and tossed his napkin on his empty plate. "Lina, I declare you'd cut off your own nose just to spite me—"

"Better yet, your own, if it doesn't quit poking into my affairs!" Lina stood.

Jeremy opened the door, took one look at the scene and made to back out again.

Lina tossed him a glare. "Coward. This whole mess is partly your fault."

Jeremy pointed a forefinger at his chest and mimed innocence.

Lina's firm mouth quivered, but she stifled it. "Yes, you."

Jeremy closed the door and entered to take his seat. "I'm at your command, madam."

Lina sniffed. "Certainly. Just like every other man in this room." She sat down again. "Captain Mayhew, my father wishes me to share his cabin. What do you think of the idea?"

Jeremy raised an eyebrow. "Why, I think you'll both be rather uncomfortable, but I'll have a bed set up if you wish it."

Lina challenged her father. "Hardly the attitude of a man who has nefarious plans for me."

Sir Lawrence glanced at Baxter uneasily.

Baxter's spoon clattered into his empty bowl. "Dash it, I didn't want to believe it, but. . . ."

"But what, Mr. Baxter?" Lina asked softly, ignoring her father's warning look.

"But, well, my faith in your intelligence is misplaced, it seems." He traded a disparaging glance between her and Jeremy. "You're as weak-minded as the rest of your sex, if you find this . . . sailor appealing."

Aware that Jeremy had stiffened beside her, Lina rested her chin on her hand and contemplated Baxter's red face. "Weak-minded? Perhaps. But weak-willed?" Lina stood, flattened both palms on the table and leaned forward. "Most assuredly not. I won't be gammoned, bullied, or cajoled out of either opinions I hold dear or relationships I choose to pursue. And that, Mr. Baxter, is what you find deplorable in me, regardless of your opinion of my morals."

"Lina! Why must you be so—"

Lina straightened. "You brought this up, Father. You might remember I asked for some peace and quiet. But I'll have no one sit in silent judgment on me—or my friends"— Lina glanced at Jeremy—"without defense."

Baxter gripped the table edge, and, apparently, his temper. "Miss Collier, it's not your character I question, but those who would lead you astray—"

Jeremy continued buttering his bread as he interjected mildly, "I'd remind you, sir, you eat at my table and sail on my ship. Two things I will readily remedy if you say the word." The eyes that glanced up flashed like the knife he held.

"You'd like putting me ashore, wouldn't you?" Baxter leaned back in his chair. "Oh no, Captain. I'm part of this expedition and shall remain so."

Jeremy swallowed a bite of bread. "Who said anything about putting you ashore?"

Baxter looked confused, but a smothered laugh escaped Lina. She sat back down. "Any second now you're going to hoist a skull and crossbones, aye, mate?"

Jeremy gave her a cheeky grin. "Aye, and a magnificent pirate's wench you'd make."

"And what if I'd rather be captain?"

"Why, I'll cross swords with you anytime, me lovely." Jeremy bit into his bread with strong white teeth, but his eyes never left Lina. She blushed.

Sir Lawrence glanced between the two, apparently aware of the improper undertone to the repartee, but not quite sure how to stop it.

Baxter had paled as the implication struck home. "Why, you—"

Sir Lawrence burst out, "Aren't you finished yet, Lina?"

Lina didn't like the look on Baxter's face. She took a sip of her tepid coffee, wishing she'd never invited Jeremy to stay. "No."

Jeremy sighed and put his bread down. "I cry quarter, Baxter. Forgive my little joke. If she were my woman, I'd be protective too."

Baxter relaxed marginally.

Jeremy added, "Your property is safe—for the moment."

The words might have appeased Baxter, but they had the opposite affect on Lina. " 'Property'? Would you care to elucidate?"

Jeremy wiped his mouth with his napkin. "I was trying to spare your modesty, but if you insist—do you prefer 'inamorata'?"

"I prefer 'lady,' but since I'll obviously not receive that courtesy from you, 'woman' will do." Lina snapped her head around in Baxter's direction. "And take that smug look off your face. We both know the truth of our relationship, even if this poltroon doesn't."

Jeremy burst out laughing. "I've been called many things, but never a poltroon. The, ah, lady has a way with words." The laughter faded from his face. "Why don't you save us both some time and tell me the truth of your relationship?"

Lina stared at him. So, he was getting suspicious. Why not tell him? *Then he'll leave you be.*

While she struggled with herself, Baxter rounded the table and put a hand on her shoulder. "I'll be happy to, Mayhew. It's not official yet, but sometime in the near future Lina will make me most happy."

Jeremy stared at that caressing male hand. "Angel? Is this true?"

Sir Lawrence gasped at the familiarity. "How dare you, sir?"

Lina was aware only of the plea in Jeremy's eyes. Here was an even better defense, for she knew this man well enough now: He lived by his own code of honor, even if it was a bit different from the world's. If he thought her betrothed to another, he'd leave her be.

Silence would preserve her modesty and possibly her sanity, but still the words were torn from Lina. "No, it's not true."

Sir Lawrence groaned; Baxter's hand tightened.

Surging to her feet, Lina flung off that encroaching touch. "Nor shall it ever be."

Jeremy's shoulders heaved with his relief, but Lina had already turned to the door. There, she paused. "But that does not give you leave to consider me fair game. I came on this trip to further my *intellectual* experience—and that is all."

Jeremy fingered the gold inlay in the sugar bowl. "Understood, Miss Collier. I honor your decision. Honor is important to us both, is it not?"

That cursed bet. What had possessed her to make it? Lina felt her own skin tingle at the way Jeremy caressed the curve of the sugar bowl. With a frustrated groan, she flung open the door and fled for her cabin.

* * *

Jeremy watched her ankles flash beneath her skirts as she rounded the door before he looked back at Sir Lawrence. "What did you say, sir?"

"I said, you haven't taken my warning seriously, it seems. For the last time—leave my daughter alone." Sir Lawrence joined Baxter.

Jeremy lifted a cynical eyebrow. How many times in his life had men such as these looked down their patrician noses at him? "What a united front. But it's your daughter you need to convince."

Baxter was already rolling up his sleeves. "Since an appeal to your chivalry is obviously useless, shall we barter in terms you better understand? Shall we say—whichever of us is still standing has the right to press his suit? The other will desist."

Jeremy grinned and sprang to his feet with savage energy. A fight was just what he needed to clear his head. And if, in the process, he could make Baxter's face a little less appealing to women, well, so much the better. "Done! But let's retire abovedeck, where we'll have some room." Politely, he held the door. They swept outside to the deck.

The crew paused in their myriad tasks to stare. When Jeremy tossed his jacket over a capstan, the activity both above and on the deck came to a virtual standstill.

"Fight," the whisper began with Mack.

It grew to a shout as it went from sailor to sailor. "The cap'n's fightin' the fancy bloke!" A crowd gathered. Coins and small items of clothing were tendered, but the pickings were slim. Only the two new crew members bet against the captain.

The others had seen him fight.

Grinning hugely, Mack held up a ten-pound note to match Sir Lawrence. "Easy money."

Jeremy didn't chide his crew because the wind was steady and no storms or vessels had been sighted. Besides, when he was setting such an example, he could hardly enforce discipline.

"Shall we say, the open space is the ring?" Jeremy walked off the distance between the wheel, the poop, and the starboard and port rails. "No blows allowed below the belt. No kicking, biting, or scratching."

Baxter flexed his fingers, then formed them into admirable fists. "Agreed. I should tell you, Mayhew—I've been coached by some of England's best prize fighters."

Jeremy bowed slightly. "And I should tell you, Baxter, that I've fought on many of the world's toughest docks." He assumed the classic fighting stance. "But I confess I prefer the manly art of pugilism myself. I shan't use any of my dirty tricks—unless you make it necessary."

For the first five minutes, the two men circled one another, exchanging experimental, brushing blows. Then, egged on perhaps by the eager men, Baxter landed a crushing right on Jeremy's jaw.

Jeremy's head popped to the side, but he recovered and countered with a punch square to Baxter's arrogant chin. Baxter's head jerked backward, and he stumbled.

An overeager crewman caught him and flung him back into the makeshift ring. "Right-o, gov," he mocked in a broad Manchester accent, "prove what an Englishman's made of."

As Baxter complied, rushing forward on the balls of his feet, Jeremy sidestepped and whirled, boxing Baxter's jaw when he turned. Baxter was expecting it, however, and he drew back, lessening the force of the blow.

Jeremy was caught off balance, and his nose took the full brunt of his clumsiness. He grunted and stumbled backward, a hand to his stinging nose. It came away red. He swiped it on his sleeve.

Baxter grinned. "Had enough?"

In reply, Jeremy held up his fists, blood still dribbling down his face. This time, he was ready and ducked the punishing right, returning a meaty blow to Baxter's flat belly.

"Ooof. . . ." Baxter bent double, holding his stomach and gasping for breath.

"Had enough?" Jeremy taunted.

His head still down, Baxter rushed, catching Jeremy about the waist and forcing him back against the rail. He rained blows on every body part he could reach, ribs, thorax, even vulnerable throat.

Jeremy did likewise, but they were too close for much leverage.

Mack pulled them apart and led them to the middle of the deck again. "Round two." He stood back.

Baxter's feet weren't quite as agile, but his arm didn't seem in the least tired to Jeremy. As his head jerked back after a blow to his jaw, Jeremy wondered if the girl were worth it. His returning blow had more force than he realized for Baxter fell to his knees, his hands cupping his own nose. Jeremy would have grinned at his own unwitting reply if his face hadn't been so sore.

Red and clear fluid oozed between Baxter's fingers and dribbled down to the deck.

Mack began the count. "One, two, three. . . ."

Baxter stood, wavering on his feet. The sailors cheered, their enthusiasm bouncing from stem to stern—and below.

No one noticed as a new, lighter step sounded on deck.

Jeremy circled warily. Baxter's face was a bloody mess, and he suspected he didn't look much better. The Englishman's blows were clumsy now, but still had considerable force, as Jeremy learned when he ducked too slow. Jeremy groaned over his bitten tongue, but he subdued the searing pain and retaliated with a punch to Baxter's stomach that he hoped would end it.

Baxter went greenish but kept his feet. Like a man caught in syrup, he slid forward, slipping in his own blood, but still coming.

Jeremy sighed and flexed his fists for the final blow.

It was pitiably easy. Jeremy drew back his right fist, aiming for the point of Baxter's chin.

"Stop! Are you trying to kill him?" Lina pushed through the men who all towered above her and caught Baxter in her arms. When he fell, she went with him, cradling his head on her lap. She glared up at Jeremy. "If this juvenile display is over me. . . ."

At her tone, the seamen melted away. The new crewmen were several pounds poorer. And Sir Lawrence's ten-pound note resided in Mack's pocket.

However, Jeremy only noticed the steely glint in Lina's eyes that matched her voice. Here, he feared, was a far more formidable opponent than Baxter. What, exactly, had he won? He rubbed his aching knuckles, reflecting ruefully that Lina would more than likely tell him what he'd lost.

Chapter 6

"BAXTER WARNED ME you were coarse and uncivilized. Here is graphic proof." Lina looked down at the blood on her dress and hands, her anger heightened by guilt. She hadn't thrown the first blow, but she'd started the fight—the minute she made her preference for Jeremy clear.

Why hadn't she put the project first? What had possessed her? Here, his rakish air accented by bruises, stood her unrepentant answer.

"My own wounds were not self-inflicted, madam."

"Your Viking forebears would have been proud of you, no doubt, but I'm disappointed, sir." Lina brushed Baxter's silky hair away from his neck to feel his pulse. It didn't seem sluggish. In fact, it leaped to her touch.

Jeremy fingered his swollen mouth. "My opponent, I'd remind you, was a man whose ancestors painted themselves blue and worshiped stone while mine were writing down their history in runes."

"You twist history for your own ends as you do everything else." Lina searched her pocket for a kerchief, but found none. She glared up at Jeremy. "The least you can do is fetch bandages and water."

Jeremy opened his mouth, then snapped it closed when a weak voice interrupted, "That won't be necessary, m'dear. Your sweet hands are restorative enough. Your concern pleases me." Baxter cupped her cheek.

Jeremy stiffened, but Lina had already pulled Baxter to a sitting position. She looked from his puffy face to Jeremy's bruised one. How long had Hubert pretended unconsciousness?

Even more important—"Which of you issued the challenge?"

Baxter swiped at the blood on his lips; Jeremy stared at the masts.

Lina gritted her teeth and removed her supporting arm from Baxter's shoulders. "Just as I thought. Your self-consequence never ceases to amaze me, Hubert. Did it not occur to you that I have no need—or desire—for your protection?"

Baxter swayed, then caught himself with his hands. "But . . . how did you . . . ?"

Lina stood and tried to wipe off her hands, but the blood had dried. "You'd not hesitate to blacken Jeremy if you could, but you're too honest to lie."

Baxter groaned as he levered himself up. He teetered on the balls of his feet before he spread his legs, bracing himself against the ship's roll. "I apprehend you don't believe the same of him, since he remained silent. Decent of you not to, ah, blacken me before the lady, old chap. Or, perhaps, 'clever' would be a better word? You knew she'd figure it out."

Lina stared at Jeremy. His face remained unreadable at Baxter's taunting. He stood impervious to the ship's movements as if he were wood and canvas instead of man. She looked at his boots, fully expecting them to be rooted to the planking. In truth, sometimes he seemed not only wedded to his ship, but glued to it. No mere woman could ever compete with the stern Viking damsel that led him forward, always forward.

Lina swallowed her pain and said lightly, "For once I'm in agreement with you, Hubert. Decency did not keep the captain silent." Lina gathered her skirts to leave.

Jeremy spanned the space between them in one stride. "What in hell does that mean?"

"It means, Captain, that you remained silent not out of courtesy, or even regret, but because you don't give a damn what anyone thinks of you. Least of all a woman." Regally, Lina walked away, unaware of the way Jeremy's face changed.

Baxter noticed, however. His blue eyes narrowed.

At the companionway, Lina whirled. "In the interests of amity, perhaps it would be best if we avoid one another for the remainder of the voyage." And her last words floated softly to the two listening men. "I begin to anticipate the snakes, the jaguars, and the natives. . . ." She disappeared down the steps.

Silence pervaded in her wake. The *Verdandi* herself barely moved as the wind died down, leaving her an elephant instead of a bird. Jeremy's face had resolved itself into its usual calm expression—but his hands were fists at his sides.

Baxter cleared his throat. "Well, we've naught to show for our little bout save aches and bruises, what, old man?"

"Did you expect her to admire you?" Jeremy asked remotely.

Baxter shrugged, then winced and rubbed his stomach. "I confess I was not thinking very well at all. Sheer anger drove me, but it seems I might have mistaken the matter. She's none too partial to you either."

"Good. That's just the way I like it. See the cook. He has bandages and astringent." Jeremy strode off, either unaware or uncaring of Baxter's skeptically arched brow.

Then, muttering "Ow," Baxter rubbed his forehead and stumbled below.

Lina was true to her word. She seldom left her cabin, except to stretch her legs on deck. She ate sparse meals in her room and turned away if either Baxter or Jeremy approached.

Under other circumstances, Jeremy would have persisted, but he sensed his fight with Baxter had hurt her for some incomprehensible reason. Perhaps, if left alone as she'd requested, she'd calm down and tell him why she was angry. So he bided his time, refusing to admit his own hurt, even to himself.

A day out, the brooding shipboard ambience had spread to elemental dimensions. Jeremy awoke to a pregnant sky hanging huge and heavy over the *Verdandi*. He cursed the luck of another storm now, when the coast was almost in sight. He hoped the wind pushed them in the right direction. He hurried from one end of the ship to the other, personally overseeing the furled sails and battened-down hatches. He tested the pumps and reoiled them as a precaution, snapping orders to his men all the while. They scurried to obey him.

Eyeing the reddish horizon, he tested the wind in the ancient way—with a wet fingertip—then he sought out his slicker. No squall this time.

Such was the fate of mariners who sailed to Mexico in the rainy season. Madness. Lashing down his cap, Jeremy hurried back above deck. "Help man the pumps," he snapped to the helmsman. "I'll take over." The man hurried below.

Jeremy had barely touched the huge wheel before the deluge broke. The rain didn't bother him; the wind did.

For an Atlantic storm, this one was a bitch. It reminded him more of the violence around the cape than the usually genial northern latitudes. Slickered sailors rushed about the deck, lashing down everything from stem to stern. The most experienced able seamen toiled aloft, furling most of the acres of canvas.

Then, tasks complete, the tars braced themselves against wind and wave as they had upon the seven seas, trusting their lives to their captain and their ship. Even hobbled, the *Verdandi* bucked at her restraints. She quivered, eager to bound up every wave, then lope down the other side, like a racehorse with more heart than sense.

Blinded by wind-lashed rain, Jeremy could barely steer her safely before the wind. If these gales caught her beam side, they were doomed. His arms ached within an hour; within two hours, they were numb. Still, the wind didn't relent. Spray chapped his face; salt stung his eyes. But he was used to both.

The roaring sea didn't frighten Jeremy, nor did the hungry whitecaps that licked over the *Verdandi* every few seconds. But the course of the wind—what if she drove them toward shore and didn't let up? They could go aground.

The eternal battle between man and sea was one he'd always relished, but Lina must be scared witless. Should he reassure her? But he dared not leave his post, even to Mack.

When a hot cup touched his mouth, he groaned his thanks. Avidly, Jeremy drank the hot buttered rum Mack held to his lips, welcoming the sizzle down his throat. When it hit his belly, his sore throat cleared enough for him to shout, "Have you checked on the passengers?"

"Groanin' in their beds, the lot o' them," Mack responded with a chuckle Jeremy saw, but didn't hear. "Can I spell ye, mate?"

Jeremy shoved his cap back to try to see the sky, but he got an eyeful of icy rain. He shook his head to clear the moisture and shouted in Mack's ear, "I'm good a little longer. See if you can help the passengers."

Mack returned a few minutes later. "Both the gents be passed out, but the lass is green as pea soup."

Jeremy's shoulders were fiery now. He'd suffered other, longer storms and remained at the helm, even if a few times he'd had to lash himself upright. Jeremy looked from the menacing whitecaps, to the black hole that led below.

He held his breath as the next wave hit. The icy submersion retreated quickly, taking his indecision with it. Lina was sick and terrified. She needed him. "Take the wheel, Mack. I'll be back when I see to her."

Mack's cup froze halfway to his mouth. As hot rum splashed on his feet, his open mouth closed abruptly in a curse. He tossed aside his cup and took the helm. "Aye, Cap'n."

Jeremy hurried below. Most of the lanterns had guttered out in the wind and rain that seeped below, but the *Verdandi* was his home. He felt his way to the last door off the corridor and shoved it open.

Weak lantern light showed him tumbled covers, tousled black hair, and a white face with a greenish tinge. Jeremy admired the sleek white calves twisting restlessly in the folds of her nightdress. Gently, he pulled the sheet up to her waist.

"Lina, how long is it since you've eaten?" He brushed the black silk cloud away from her clammy face.

Her eyes fluttered open. "Go away. Let me die in . . ." She inhaled and began to gag. She pulled herself to the side of the bed and hung her head over the bowl on the floor, coughing up nothing but phlegm.

Jeremy could only squat and support her head until the spasms passed. He picked up the cloth from the nightstand, ignoring its pungency, and turned it to a clean spot to wipe her lips. When she lay back weakly, he carried the bowl to the chamber pot and emptied it, then washed it and his hands. Replacing the bowl, he said, "I'll be back in a moment."

He hurried to the galley, heated water, then put several items on a tray and hastened back. She hadn't moved.

Poor baby. He set the tray beside the bed and touched her flushed cheek. "Angel, your lips are cracked. You must drink something or you could get seriously ill."

Her eyes didn't even open. "Go 'way."

Jeremy had never suffered seasickness, but he'd seen it often enough to empathize. "I know food is the last thing you want right now, but it's the best way to settle your stomach." Cupping the back of her head in his palm, he lifted her and held the cup of mint tea to her mouth.

She tried to turn away, but was too weak. Some of the tea dribbled through her lips. She swallowed and looked as if she might gag, but he set the cup down and rubbed her stomach in soothing, circular motions. When she was limp and relaxed, he held a morsel of sea biscuit to her lips. She accepted it listlessly, drinking more tea to get it down her parched throat.

For an hour he ministered to her, feeding her tiny sips and bites, then waiting ten minutes to be sure she held them down. He was so intent on seeing color return to her face that he little heeded the tossing of his ship, and when he did, he realized Mack had as steady a hand as any. The one time the thought occurred to him to check, Lina coughed on a bit of biscuit and held a hand to her mouth. Hastily he rubbed her stomach, sighing when she subsided back against the covers and took his hand.

"Thank you, Jeremy. You're an angel of mercy. I believe I'll actually survive."

The smile was weak, but her dimple peeped at him. All thoughts of Mack, the storm, even the *Verdandi*, that most devoted of mistresses, flew from his head. Reality became the intimate circle of light, Lina's trusting clasp, the serenity in her indigo eyes. In a dim corner of his mind, he knew this moment would be a turning point in their relationship.

But the old barriers did not topple easily.

Under the guise of wiping her brow with the clean towel he'd brought, he pulled away. "I'm not sure I like being called an angel—angel."

Her dimple deepened. "At the moment, you look the part, even if a devil is more to your taste." She ran her hand from one side of his head to the other.

His frown disappeared as he realized that he must be outlined by the light behind him. He chuckled. "I assure you it's a trick of the light. I wear no halo."

Her hand came to the side of his face. She traced each crease in his cheek, then ran her fingertip under his eyes. "No?" she asked huskily. "Then what made you fly to my aid during a storm, when all your thoughts should be for your ship?"

He swallowed and thought vaguely, *I must relieve Mack.* In a moment. The trust and admiration in her eyes soothed the inner wounds he'd seldom acknowledged and never touched. How had she known they were there? "Mack's a capable seaman, but I really should go above." Even as he spoke, Jeremy realized the wind was beginning to die. Still, he tried to rise, but she pulled him back down.

"Why do you always do this? Every time I get close, you pull back. The *Verdandi* has survived the last hour. She'll survive a bit longer." Looking determined, she propped two pillows behind her back and sat up. "Jeremy, tell me about your past. Your life before the *Verdandi.*"

So simple the question; so difficult the answer. Had she been a stranger, he'd have found it easier to open his lips and his feelings. But she was not a stranger. It felt so blasted right to be here with her, isolated in this intimate circle of light from the world, the storm, his ugly past. Here, embodied in this girl of small stature and mighty character, lay all he'd spent years denying himself, hoping that, one day, denial would equal indifference.

Hope. Shared laughter. Shared tears. Sex with meaning. In short, a future to be enjoyed instead of endured. Yet, if he reached for that future, he risked a hurt that would surpass all the many hurts of his past.

Lina, too, traveled only in the "best" society. How could she build a future with a wharf rat?

While he battled with himself, Lina picked up his hand and ran her finger over its calluses. "Your poor hands. You don't ask your crew to do anything you won't, do you?"

Shamed, he snatched his hand away and rose. "Unlike Baxter and his ilk, I've had to work for every dime I own. So sorry if you find that repulsive, my lady."

Before he could slip away, she caught his hand close again. "You misunderstand, as usual." And she pressed her lips to each of his calluses, one after the other. "These scars are to be admired, not reviled, Jeremy." Her voice, muffled against his hand, hit him like a bolt from the blue.

He teetered where he stood, the tenderness in her velvet lips rocking him to his moorings. A great urge to snatch her close almost overwhelmed him, but a knock at the door restored his sanity. Sighing, she released him. He stuck his hand in his pocket and called, "Come."

Mack poked his head around the door. "All's right and tight, lad. We rode the storm like troopers. Sent us right to shore. The coast is in sight. What are your orders? Do ye want to have the usual damage inspection?" Mack sent a knowing look at Lina.

Jeremy made the mistake of looking at Lina to offer his excuses. Those solemn blue eyes stole the words from his lips.

"Please. Stay. The *Verdandi* doesn't need you now." Her voice softened to a whisper. "But I do."

Jeremy saw a hand gesturing Mack away, heard a voice say, "The inspection will wait. I'll be along soon."

Blinking, Mack closed the door and retreated, leaving a profound silence in the lovely cabin.

Jeremy was poised between door and bed—duty and delight—but couldn't seem to move toward either.

Flipping back her covers, Lina rose, swayed, then padded toward him. Apparently she was unaware of the light silhouetting her figure. Jeremy was very aware of it. Somehow he kept his hands at his sides even when the heat of her body touched him, so close did she come.

Dear Lord, how he longed to warm himself. And her.

"Jeremy, come. Sit with me. You've helped me. Now let me help you." Taking his big, rough hand, she led him to the window seat. "Tell me why you left New York." She pulled him down beside her.

Jeremy wished he could be as unconcerned at her scanty attire as she seemed to be. How many women would sit with him alone, so dressed, and encourage his confidence? So many times she'd trusted him, believed in him. Would it hurt him to give her a few of the answers she sought? Maybe then she could understand why they had no future.

"I left because I couldn't bear to stay. My father was dead, the dynasty he hoped to establish through me buried under a mound of debt. Only by selling every ship, the house, every stick of furniture, could I settle the bills and buy the *Verdandi*. Even then, I was four seasons paying her off."

Those blue eyes never wavered, even when he paused. Her sweet compassion drew him on, but the painful memories were shared in a low tone, as if the softer he spoke, the less he hurt. "My father began to drink too much shortly after my mother left us when I was just a child. You see, my mother believed that he killed her brother, who came from Norway and joined with my father in a shipping enterprise. She wanted me to go with her, but I refused."

Lina gasped.

His smile exuded no mirth. "The sordid tale gets no better, I fear. Are you sure you want to hear it?"

"Yes," she whispered, tightening her clasp of his hand.

"My father died under a cloud of suspicion, even though he was innocent. I know now that anguish at my mother's desertion led him to behave as he did, but it still wasn't right for him to . . . to . . ."

"He poisoned you against her, didn't he?"

"Yes. But it wasn't until years later, after his death, that I saw that. By then, she was married to a powerful New York shipper by the name of Garrison. He was a widower with two children. I guess my mother threw all her instincts into raising them as her own, since I refused to see her. Her adopted son, Luke Garrison, and his father hated me for the pain I'd caused my mother and they did all they could to blacken me in the New York shipping community."

"And did they succeed?"

"Almost. Without the intervention of Aimee . . ."

Lina's hand clasp loosened.

He didn't want to talk about Aimee. She'd obsessed him for too many years, so he hurried on, "The end result was that she helped me prove my father's innocence. Our warehouse manager killed my mother's brother when he caught the scoundrel stealing part of a shipment. The manager then planted evidence against my father, knowing the two had been arguing over the division of the company."

He couldn't see Lina's eyes, for she was watching their clasped hands. "And then?" She cleared her hoarse voice.

"Once we proved my father innocent, even posthumously, much of my bitterness ended. Events made the Garrisons reappraise my, ah, status in the family. I was somewhat reconciled with my mother after I was, ah, wounded when the manager shot at Luke, my stepbrother."

"Aimee's husband?"

He hesitated, then admitted, "Yes."

"You jumped in front of Luke, didn't you? To save him for Aimee?"

His hand tightened in shock around hers. When she winced, he released her. "How did you know?"

"Because when you love, Jeremy, you do so deeply. I've known that about you almost from the beginning." Now it was Lina who rose and turned away, cupping her palms about her elbows.

"Lina, what's wrong?" Jeremy rose and circled her until he could see her face.

She lifted her chin and said bravely, despite the tears brimming in her eyes, "No one will ever replace Aimee in your heart, will they?"

Jeremy stared. He tried to form a clear picture of Aimee, but it wouldn't come. He hadn't seen her in years. But Lina, she would ever after be indelibly imprinted on this cabin—and on him.

The surety was too much too quickly. "Well, I've bored you long enough. I really must see to the inspection now."

Jeremy paused at the door, twiddling with the handle. "Ah, if you need anything, my cabin boy is at your service. I'm . . . glad you're feeling better. You'll need all of your strength to face the jungle."

Lina stared at the closing door and somehow willed the tears away. Her head still ached, and her diaphragm was sore from her spasms, but otherwise she felt normal. Physically, at least. Thanks to Jeremy.

Emotionally, she felt knotted into a thousand tangled strings. Thanks to Jeremy.

How could he be so kind, even tender, one moment, then so distant and cold the next? Her heart had ached at the physical toil that left such calluses. And she ached more now she knew the emotional toil Jeremy had suffered at a very young age.

Poor lad, to be caught between his mother and father. No wonder he didn't trust women easily.

Should she be heartened that he'd at last shared some of his feelings, or depressed at the confirmation that he'd been in love with his stepbrother's wife?

The unpleasant answer stared her in the face. As usual, she faced it squarely.

This attraction was doomed. She could never compete with a ghost. Nor did she want to try. That was just as well, Lina tried to tell herself. If the coast had been sighted, they'd be docking at Campeche soon. Distractions of any sort were now unwelcome; nothing would deter her from her purpose.

"Palenque," she whispered. Her eyes closed, she visualized the majestic carvings, the long buildings, the steps to the pyramids. Soon, very soon, she'd follow in Stephens's footsteps to the top of the Temple of the Sun. Her lips curved as she felt the warmth of the sun upon her face, smelled the rich scents of the jungle. Feeling a bit more at peace, she sought her bed.

However, when she fell asleep, it was not of Palenque that she dreamed.

Eden surrounded the two lovers. Not even fig leaves protected their modesty. Lina couldn't see the girl's face, but she recognized the strong neck capped by waving golden hair. The man was kissing the girl, his hands moving over her bare skin. A misty waterfall enwebbed the two figures in glistening angel-hair streams. Wild orchids of every hue clustered on the banks, and softest moss made a bed that put feathers to shame.

Lina was pushing aside the undergrowth to move closer when *he* strode out of her dreams. How could he still smell of the sea, and brandy, and damp wool? When his tough palm cupped the side of her face, she turned into it and kissed it. The hand jerked back, then returned to trace the living hollows of her throat. Even in her half-awake state, Lina felt the conflict that touch conveyed. Jeremy.

Sweet reality. And sweeter forgetfulness.

Still warm from the lovely dream, Lina was bolder than was her wont. She tilted her head to trap his hand in the warm curve of her neck. "You're warmest to me when you think I'm unaware. Has it not occurred to you that the same tenderness when I'm full awake might aid your cause?"

He squeezed her shoulder lightly. "Minx. What cause is that?"

Lina's eyes opened. Her lips stretched into a smile more sensual than she knew. "You were not so obtuse in my dream."

The caressing hand went still. Gray eyes flashed with a desire that no longer frightened Lina. Then the strong arms of her dream hauled her into an embrace that seemed but the culmination of her interrupted bliss. She sighed in relief and met his kiss.

Here, she belonged. Sometimes dreams were more true than reality, she thought. She felt closer to Jeremy at this moment than she'd ever felt to anyone. Right and wrong were but limitations imposed by a society that would inhibit a woman's natural right to pleasure.

The defiant thought was her last for long, leisurely minutes. He ministered to her in a different way now, patiently feeding her passion with drugging kisses and caresses that softened her bones—and her head.

When his hands wandered beneath her gown to trace her legs, she stiffened. Jeremy gave a shuddering groan against her lips, but slowly, painfully, he raised his head.

"Lina, is this what you want?"

She stared up at him. The lamp beside the bed bathed the hairs on his arms, in the vee of his chest, and his luxurious mane until he glistened with the luxury that had sent them on this quest. Outside, and, she was coming to believe, within, Jeremy Mayhew was pure gold. He offered untold spiritual wealth to any girl bold enough to meet his challenge.

The golden wager. Since that reckless night in Monte Carlo, she'd put the wager out of her mind. But now, as she stared up at the man who tonight embodied that substance, with all its inherent danger and allure, she knew the impulse that had led her here had been the wisest choice of her life.

If she shared all with him, perhaps the feelings he hoarded would enrich them both. Aimee could not hold him in her arms and make him forget; she could. Again, she would gamble.

Lina closed her eyes in assent and lifted her arms to his neck. "Don't be angry with me. Afterward."

His voice shook with tender laughter as he swept her close again. "Angry with you? Angel mine, you're the closest thing to heaven this wanderer has ever known."

Lina's eyes popped open. For three eternal seconds, the real Jeremy was bare in those gray eyes. She saw again the man who'd so drawn her outside the Hotel de Paris. Lonely, vulnerable, yearning, but gentle with the true strength only the powerful possess. Those eyes came closer, closer, both sapping her will and infusing her with the serenity of a woman loved. Then his lips covered hers, conveying all the emotions his eyes had finally admitted.

The quiet knock didn't impinge on their communion. Nor did the opening of the door, or the shocked gasp, or even the hasty footsteps that approached the bed.

"Lina!" A hand hauled on the back of Jeremy's shirt.

Jeremy muttered a protest and swatted at the intrusion. Lina's eyes fluttered open when the drugging pressure of his mouth lifted.

They rounded, matching her gaping mouth. "Father?"

Jeremy shoved a shaking hand through his hair and sat up, pulling Lina's gown chastely down past her knees again. The slap rocked his head on his shoulders and brought his fists up in the protective stance that was second nature to him.

Sir Lawrence didn't back off, even though his skin was pale and his hair mussed from his bout of seasickness. "Come on, then. For violating my daughter, you pay. I don't care if you beat me senseless, at least I'll land a few blows on that falsely handsome face."

Ruefully, Jeremy dropped his fists and slowly rose. "Baxter has taken care of that for you, but if you wish to add to his handiwork, I'll not stop you."

"So! You admit you deserve punishment."

Jeremy looked from that aristocratic, fuming face to Lina, who sat quietly, her skin still glowing from his touch, her mouth ripe with the womanhood he'd so nearly brought to fruition. "Punishment? Aye, sir, the flames of hell should scorch me for forgetting my sacred vow. Punch away at your leisure." And Jeremy offered his chin to Sir Lawrence.

Obviously confused, Sir Lawrence turned away from Jeremy's closed expression to appeal to his daughter. "Well, girl, what have you to say? If that isn't just like you, to be quiet when, for once, you should be talking. What happened here?"

Lina didn't even glance at him. She stared at Jeremy until tears misted her vision. Here again was the man too jaded to believe in anything, least of all an emotion he couldn't touch. She should be thankful, she reflected vaguely, that her father interrupted. If it hadn't been for the dream, and his trusting confidences, she'd never have let things go so far.

"Lina! Dammit, answer me!"

Under the guise of brushing back her hair, she dried her eyes with the sleeves of her gown. "Nothing happened, Father, but a kiss that was as false as the man who gave it."

Jeremy's head jerked back. But Lina felt little pleasure at her invisible blow, for Jeremy countered quickly.

"Inspired by a society bitch as false as her paste jewels." Swiveling, Jeremy stomped out of the cabin, ignoring Sir Lawrence's angry protest.

"Now see here, you shan't speak to my daughter like that!"

The door banged shut. Sir Lawrence turned on his daughter, but went still when he saw the two shimmering streams down her cheeks.

Sir Lawrence sat beside her and took her hand. "Child, don't carry on so. He's not worth it."

Lina sniffed and wiped her eyes on her sleeve. A white square wavered before her eyes. She accepted it gratefully. Pristine and smelling vaguely of his cologne, the kerchief both comforted the adult Lina and revived memories of the child he'd so often bandaged, hugged, and read to. Their problems had begun in her adolescence, when she no longer followed him about like an adoring puppy.

The tears came faster then, and she grieved for the loss of that happy past even as she wondered what the future held.

"Oh Father, why are things so muddled?"

He drew her to his bosom and said into her hair, "My dear, I wish I could tell you life is fair and that happiness is yours for the reaching, but you know I'm not one to give false comfort. We can only strive with the gifts God gave us and accept that without tragedy there is no happiness."

Lina tilted her head back against his shoulder. "You think I should let him go."

Sir Lawrence brushed her chin with his fist. "You're a fighter, my girl, and you're not one to shrink from unpleasant truths. That, you received from me. I finally understand that you care for this . . . man, but he'll give you only unhappiness. If you couldn't build a relationship with Philippe, who had so much in common with us, how can you build one with this homeless adventurer?"

Lina closed her eyes in pain. He echoed her own thoughts, but aloud, the words battered her like stones. "You're right, of course. But you don't really know him. If you could see him as I do, when his guard is down—"

"I know nothing of his past, but it must have been a difficult one. He's a handsome man, but I suspect his emotional scars are hideous. Such men do not make good husbands, even if that is his intent, which, frankly, I don't believe."

Neither did Lina. And she agreed about Jeremy's hidden pain, but oh, how she longed to kiss him and make him better. Inside and outside.

She didn't want to spoil this rare accord with her father, however, so she only said, "You haven't been so understanding in years."

"You've been like a prickly pear of late, child. But I can't bear to see you hurting so, over such a man. It's my duty to comfort you and guide you."

That stung, but her smile didn't waver. "Thank you, Father. I'll think on all you've said. However, the jungle will probably make this discussion moot. The only feelings that will be troubling me shortly are exhaustion and eagerness."

Sir Lawrence frowned. "Eagerness?"

"To see Palenque, of course." *I'm an archaeologist, too, Father. Before this trip is out, you'll recognize that.* The silent vow gave Lina strength enough to accept his condescension without protest.

He patted her cheek. "Of course. Are you better now? I came to check on you as soon as I could leave my own bed."

She cocked her head critically. "I'm fine now." *Thanks to Jeremy.* "You don't look as though you feel bad any longer."

He shuddered. "I've never been so sick I've wanted to die, but now the seas are calmer, I'm much better. I can't wait to land. Mack tells me we'll round the coast of Yucatán by noon tomorrow and dock at Campeche."

"Thank God."

"Sleep tight, my dear."

"I shall, Father. And . . . thank you for caring. I'm sorry I've been so irritable of late. I just want you to see that this expedition is important to me, too. Not as your daughter, but as an—"

"Yes, yes, well, I'm weary. We'll talk more later. Good night, Lina."

Shielding her hurt, Lina said, "Good night."

Lina subsided against her pillows, but she suspected she'd have a very bad night indeed. Her brain revolved uselessly, like a top gone amok. Images of Jeremy haunted her: kissing her, calling her false, touching her, jerking away. And they say women are fickle, she thought tartly.

Her father was right. Jeremy was their hired guide who stood to gain from this expedition if they found gold.

And even if they didn't.

She shoved the thought away. Her attraction to him was so strong only because she was past the age when most of her peers were married and either expecting or shielding a toddler in their skirts. In a man's best fashion, she wanted Jeremy only for one thing.

She'd not allow him into her heart even if, one day, she allowed him into her body. Lina punched her pillow until a few feathers flew, but the resolve did not ease her mind. Dawn was exciting the sky into a rosy glow when she finally, fitfully, slept.

The streets of Campeche were quagmires from the recent rains. Lina blessed the forethought that had made her change into her heavy boots, for she sank almost to the ankle with every step. The mud squelched as she lifted her foot, as if burping after it had gorged itself. She wrinkled her nose in time to catch Jeremy's grin. She glared and returned to the onerous task of putting one foot in front of the other. They'd not exchanged a word yet today.

Her father had handled their disembarcation with the skill born of years of traveling. Here, they would exchange their trunks for boxes that could be carried by mules, which they would obtain once they reached the interior. First they'd sail up the coast, berth the *Verdandi* in a safe Gulf of Mexico harbor, then begin their journey in earnest: by canoe, navigating the waterways as close to Palenque as possible. Only on the last leg of their journey would they obtain mules and workers.

Since this was the last large city they would visit, they must first take on the supplies they'd been unable to obtain in France. Lina recalled the altercation between Jeremy and her father only this morning over that very subject.

"Hammocks? Mosquito netting? I brought perfectly good ones from my time in Turkey."

"The mosquitoes here are more numerous," Jeremy had said curtly, "and require a different defense, but suit yourself." Jeremy continued appraising the supplies in the hold, ticking them off on the list he carried. "Are you sure your clothes are adequately cool and comfortable? You'll probably need more than the few items I supplied."

"Quite sure. I'm no tyro to extreme conditions." Sir Lawrence slammed his trunk closed and locked it.

Jeremy sucked the side of his mouth, and Lina knew he was squelching his temper and his tongue, but he only continued his inventory. "How much quinine did you bring?"

"All I could obtain. Lina, Hubert, and I are already taking it."

"Are you sure you won't change your mind and take the Mayan remedy instead? I take it, and I've never contracted malaria in all my travels here."

"Heathen superstition." Sir Lawrence sniffed. "You've just been lucky."

Kindling gray eyes stared at Lina. "That remains to be seen, but I've always been a gambling man."

Lina turned away to hide her blush, glad that her father was sorting through his pots and pans.

Jeremy propped his shoulder against the bulkhead. "One pot, one skillet. Leave the rest."

Sir Lawrence dropped a metal teapot into the box with a clang. "No silverware, or plates? Ridiculous. Besides, we can't all survive on such meals as can be prepared in two pots."

"Sir Lawrence, 'survive' is the definitive word here. Once our perishables are gone, we'll probably live as the Indians do, on what food we can wrest from the jungle. But even more important, if we're attacked by natives, the less our mules have to carry, the better chance we'll have to get away."

Sir Lawrence opened his mouth to argue, but closed it abruptly when Jeremy added casually, "Of course, if you prefer, you can leave some of the screens, shovels, and trowels behind instead."

Despite her anger at Jeremy, Lina smiled. One really had to admire his grasp of human nature. What a pity he couldn't turn that incisive eye upon himself.

Sir Lawrence had reluctantly removed the largest pot and skillet, then slammed the trunk lid closed.

Now, as Lina made her way through the ancient Puerta del Mar entranceway that linked the dock area to the city proper, she hoped all their disputes could be settled so easily. Even if it required bowing to Jeremy's authority. Lina paused to look around while the men bartered at a ramshackle grass-topped hut for sturdy baskets and wooden crates.

Three blocks north she could see the imposing but weathered Fort Soledad. Its stone buttresses were crumbling, but in its day it must have made a formidable barricade against the pirates who razed the area.

Lina had made it her business to read about the city when she realized they'd be stopping there. She found it as charming as described, an interesting mix of the New World and the Old. She saw a majestic Spanish *señora,* complete with rosary and mantilla, entering an ancient church. Two young women dressed in colorful skirts and thin blouses, their skin dark and shiny with health, tripped up the steps behind her, jabbering in a tongue unfamiliar to Lina.

Further on, a lodging displayed its menu on a blackboard: grilled fish, black beans, and sweet potatoes. Diners sat at a charming array of tables and chairs shielded beneath a woven awning. A half block down the street, Indian vendors sold fruits and vegetables that were wholly unrecognizable to Lina except for the corn. Even some of the corn, however, was an odd color, speckled as it was with dark and red kernels.

She craned her neck, but couldn't glimpse the other fortresses the city held. Fort San Carlos interested her in particular, for it had underground passageways linking homes to the fortress. Women and children had used the tunnels to hide during pirate raids. She hoped she'd have an opportunity to explore them.

Though Lina was enchanted with the sights and sounds, everything looked so . . . exotic. She'd been to Spain many times, but there she'd never had this same sense of being an outsider.

Was it the strange smells, or the heavy humidity in the air, or the mix of humanity that made her feel alien? For a moment, she was chilled despite the sunlight that had finally made itself decent and paraded overhead. How would she feel, she wondered, when she was on a canoe destined for the interior? She started when Jeremy spoke in her ear.

"Having second thoughts?"

Her skin tingled as she pretended indifference by watching her father and Hubert haggle over the price for the mound of boxes and baskets. "No. Just wishing I could see more of the city. You mistake my frustration for fear."

Jeremy scratched his chin. "That's easily enough remedied. We can sail from here on the evening tide, so we'll have several hours to wander about. What do you want to see first?"

"Fort San Carlos."

"Shall we go?" Jeremy caught her arm.

Lina planted her feet. "But what about Father and Hubert?"

Jeremy followed her gaze and grinned. "I offered to bargain with the old coot, but your, ah, friend insisted he and Sir Lawrence must become accustomed to dealing with these people."

Hubert offered first one note, then two, but the stooped old man who manned the hut kept shaking his head and screeching something in a strange tongue. Neither of the parties seemed troubled by the lack of verbal communication, for that universal language—the Yankee greenback—was interpreter enough. They'd exchanged most of their remaining funds when they reached Marseilles.

"And then they intend to visit the marketplace to purchase dried foods and coffee. The tea that's available here is not, I fear, what you're all accustomed to. You'll soon find that your own supply will not last long in the humidity."

Lina hesitated, glancing between her father and the intriguing narrow, tumbled streets. She didn't want to be alone with Jeremy right now. It was too soon to test her new resolve. Yet, the fort certainly sounded more appealing.

"Come along, angel. We don't have much time." Jeremy's mouth tilted in that crooked, challenging smile.

Damn him, he knew she didn't want to be alone with him. He also knew this was their last chance to converse privately, probably for a very long time. Maybe, just maybe, he wanted to apologize.

Not likely, she scoffed to herself. But she stared for a long moment into those quicksilver eyes and knew that, once again, she couldn't resist his dare. Without giving herself time to change her mind, she walked up to her father and tapped him on the shoulder.

"Father, Jeremy is going to show me about Campeche. We'll be back in a couple of hours. Shall we meet at this restaurant for an early dinner?"

Sir Lawrence patted her hand. "Certainly, child. Have a nice time." And Sir Lawrence watched intently as the old man hefted a box and turned it this way and that to show off its sturdy construction.

Smiling wryly, Lina went back to Jeremy. "I'm ready."

Jeremy inclined his head at Sir Lawrence. "Are you sure he heard you? He didn't seem to protest."

Lina didn't share Jeremy's surprise. "He's like that when he's concentrating. Once his bargain's done, he'll recall every word."

Conspiratorially, Jeremy offered his arm. "To adventure, my lady."

Lina took his arm, and they strolled off, disappearing in the motley, milling crowd.

Neither of them realized then how very prophetic his words were to be . . .

Part Two

History is the witness that testifies to the passing of time; it illumines reality, vitalizes memory, provides guidance in daily life, and brings us tidings of antiquity.

—MARCUS TULLIUS CICERO,
"De Oratore," II, 36

Chapter 7

THE VERY AIR teemed with incongruity. They passed a pile of donkey manure, its pungency overcome four steps later by the pleasing aroma of crushed cacao beans. Lina paused to watch the old Indian woman work over her wide stone *metate*. The woman's face seemed as wide and comforting as her hips. Her sun-darkened skin wrinkled even more as she gave a friendly, gap-toothed grin. She appraised the pretty foreigner, then said something in a guttural tongue. Jeremy answered and offered a couple of coins.

"I'm going to have a chocolate. Would you like one? I warn you it's different from what you're accustomed to."

"Why not? I want to try the authentic foods of the area." Lina watched in fascination, unaware that Jeremy looked doubtful. He shrugged and turned to watch the old woman.

She scooped the crushed beans into two earthenware cups and used a rag to lift a bubbling kettle from her small fire. The pleasant scent intensified as water gurgled over the paste. The old woman split a handful of crushed sugar cane between the two cups, sprinkled something from a small vial, then stirred both to a froth. She offered the first cup to Lina with a gnarled hand, watching anxiously.

Lina sniffed. It smelled alluring, but what were those dark specks? Blowing on the liquid, Lina took a tiny sip. "Mmmm." The taste of chocolate bathed her taste buds, far richer than the European style she was used to. She'd taken a deeper sip before she realized what the dark specks were.

She coughed and gasped for air, her eyes watering. "Pepper! Why didn't you warn me?"

"I did. You said you wanted to try the authentic taste. You've just sipped the brew Montezuma offered Cortez, minus the sugar of course. That was a Spanish addition." Jeremy drank and swirled the fluid in his mouth, apparently unconcerned with the fiery aftershock. "Truly an elixir fit for kings."

Lina sipped more cautiously but found the taste addictive despite its bite. How odd. She'd never have thought pepper could so well complement the mellow taste of the chocolate. She peered at Jeremy. "How is it you know so much of archaeology?"

The cup in Jeremy's hand paused, then lowered. "Do you, too, scorn those who are self-educated?"

That "too" was illuminating, but Lina kept her eyes lowered as she swirled the liquid in her cup. "Not at all. I saw your personal library on the ship. It was most impressive. But the interest seems an odd one for a sea captain."

Jeremy's stiff shoulders relaxed. "You may be surprised to find we have more in common than you suppose. My interest derives from the day I saw my first Mayan ruin. What tales could those artful stones tell, I wondered? These people had their own language and writing and obviously their own religion, yet what motivated them? Why did they desert the proud cities they built with such toil? In short, my dear, I did not exaggerate when I told you that I, too, yearn to visit Palenque and delve further into the mystery of this great people."

The cup forgotten in her hand, Lina listened. No one, not even Philippe, had echoed her own feelings so exactly. Again that strange bond she'd often felt with Jeremy tugged at her. He stared over her head, his magnificent gray eyes trained on the misty reaches of time he seemed to feel but not see. Then he looked at her.

Lina heard a splashing sound, but she didn't even know the cup had tilted in her grip until Jeremy gently removed it. "Would you like some more?"

Unable to speak, she shook her head. Jeremy gulped the last of his chocolate, then plunked both cups down before the old woman, nodding his thanks. Taking Lina's arm, he led her away. "To the fort. If you still want to go?"

An invisible current traveled up her arm where he touched it, strengthening the link Lina felt, if only in her mind. Still, her sensible half urged her to return to her father, but the words burst from her lips of their own accord. "I can hardly wait."

As they strolled the picturesque streets, Jeremy talked, his voice blending curiosity and warmth for his subject. "Actually, I probably know almost as much about the Maya as you do. Do you know what the primary currency of the peoples of the area was, and still is, to a lesser degree, today?"

Lina frowned thoughtfully. "It's believed they used shells, jade, and cacao beans. But surely Spanish currency is used today?"

"In the cities, perhaps. But in the outlying areas, to this day, the bride-price often includes cacao." Jeremy stopped and subjected her to a leisurely appraisal. "I wonder what you'd fetch?"

"More than you're willing to pay, no doubt." Lina tried to pull away.

He tucked her arm securely in his again. "It's certain your price would break the back of the poor mule who had to carry it."

"Or of the poor man who had to pay it?" Lina shot him a sideways glance, then wished she hadn't, for the one he returned singed the hair at her temples.

"Perhaps the price would be cheap, considering the other, ah, interesting compensations you'd offer."

For mesmerizing minutes he held her only by the strength of his light touch and the power of his gaze. Inwardly Lina battled herself, for he always managed to insert sexual banter into their conversation, even an intellectual one. And why, damn him, was she so susceptible to it, when similar advances from Baxter made her skin crawl? Pride reared its head, but Lina was finding that her baser impulses were equally powerful.

And that, my girl, is why you shouldn't have come on this little jaunt. The jungle would offer threat enough without endangering her self-esteem as well. She'd resolved to keep him at the same distance he held her. He toyed with her, as he had proved by scorning her after her father discovered them together.

This time, she'd not be swayed by the silver in his tongue or in his eyes. She'd come with him only because she longed to see the fort—the sooner the better. Pulling away, she forged ahead, hoping he wouldn't see the torment in her eyes at the choice he'd forced upon her.

He hurried after her. "Lina? What have I said?"

She bit her lip and managed, "Nothing of any import. Which way now?" She hated that cynical twist to his beautiful mouth and felt a pang at the knowledge that, this time, she had put it there.

However, as he stalked off in the opposite direction, she ruthlessly quelled her regret and followed him. The scent of salt grew stronger, carried on a stiff breeze, and she knew they must be approaching the Gulf again.

The fort was all she'd hoped for. Its battlements still stood tall, all the more impressive for the dents put there, Lina supposed, by ancient cannon balls. Its massive wooden gate was open on huge rusty hinges. The occasional sightseer, like herself, entered and exited on the stone walkway trod smooth by countless feet.

"Would you like to go up on the roof? The view of the sea is wonderful from there."

Lina answered equally politely. "Yes, please." Jeremy led her up the walkway lined with luxurious foliage Lina couldn't recognize, much less name. The winding staircase that led to the battlements was also worn smooth. Their steps echoed down the well with a martial sound. Lina wondered how many times this charming fort had seen battle. Even now, when Mexico was not at war, guards thronged the enclosure.

When they at last obtained the roof, Lina drew in her breath. From here, the Gulf stretched like a crystalline carpet, clear blue and sparkling. In the distance, Lina saw several ships, looking like toy sailboats. Closer in, she glimpsed several swimmers, their athletic strokes taking them cleanly through the water. In a different direction, an ornate church tower poked authoritatively over the trees, as if sternly watching its flock.

Jeremy rested his elbows beside her on the sturdy wall and nodded at the cannon still bristling in their ports. "I've often thought that Mexico could be a world power if it were not so torn by political strife."

"Porfirio Díaz certainly seems more interested in lining his own pockets than in instituting true reform."

Jeremy glanced around uneasily at the guards lounging against the battlements. "I wouldn't espouse such opinions."

As if to verify his fears, an officer climbed to the roof and growled at the lolling guards. Immediately they snapped to attention.

Intent on her rebuttal, Lina didn't see him. "Díaz can't have spies lurking everywhere."

The officer stared in their direction when he heard his commander's name. He came several steps closer, catching Lina's attention. His insolent appraisal made her move closer to Jeremy.

She lowered her voice. "Surely, dictator or no, he allows foreigners some freedom of speech."

Jeremy pulled her under his arm. "It is exactly that attitude, milady, that infuriates other countries. The world is not like your little insular British isle."

"More's the pity." Even as they glared at each other, Lina knew the source of their antipathy was not political.

When the officer snapped something else in Spanish to his men, spun on his heel and descended the steps, Jeremy relaxed and released Lina. "Indeed. Pity is certainly due any nation so arrogant as to believe that all the world should follow its ways."

"Why in heaven's name did you invite me here if you only wanted to fight? We could have done that at the dock."

Jeremy sighed and ran his hand through his hair. "I wanted to apologize for my . . . behavior the other night. But you diverted me. I swear you're enough to anger a stone."

Lina had to smile. "I've been thinking exactly the same about you." But she backed up a pace when Jeremy reached out to trace her cheek. "Shall we just say, I was not blameless either? Please accept my own apology. Then let's put the incident behind us as the inconsequential matter it was."

The warmth in his eyes had cooled by degrees, making them Arctic-gray. "As you wish. We'd best return before your father worries." Jeremy swung about and led the way down the stairs and out the gate.

They were halfway down the street before Lina remembered he hadn't showed her the tunnels. She trotted along, head down, unaware of the officer who exited the fort gate and followed. Jeremy, too, concentrated only on his angry strides.

Lina was busy telling herself she'd finally put Jeremy in his place. He'd leave her be now, and she could concentrate her energies on her work.

Why, then, was she so miserable?

Lina stared at the ground so she wouldn't have to watch that indomitable back, or that distinctive, swinging stride. She was so intent on not watching Jeremy, in fact, that it was some moments before she realized she'd wandered onto a side street. She stopped and glanced around. Her heart leaped in fear, but she inhaled and turned slowly in a circle, seeking familiar landmarks. She saw none—until bells pealed and she glimpsed the church. Two blocks down, it fronted on this street.

The heavy doors swept open and people spilled down the steps. Mass must have just ended. Lina cocked her head and tried to calculate. Based on where the steeple had been situated from the fort, she needed to turn left to find her way back to the docks.

Slowly, as if she hadn't a care in the world, Lina strolled up the street, ignoring the curious glances sent her by male and female alike. She knew her dress and hairstyle set her apart, but she hoped she didn't look as vulnerable as she felt.

By the time she reached the church, the steps were empty except for one young man. Her attention was caught by the stealthy way he looked up and down the street. He saw her, hesitated, then exited. He carried a long bag wrapped about his shoulders. He wore the tight pants and full shirt in the Spanish style, but his strong features—high cheekbones, blade of a nose, and almond-shaped dark eyes—had looked out at Lina from many a Mayan engraving.

Lina was so busy watching him that she didn't see the man blocking her path and careened into him. "Excuse me," she said automatically, stepping around.

He said something and caught her arm.

She froze. He was the officer who'd overheard her at the fort. Had he followed to question her? But no. He caressed her arm through her dress, and the look in his eyes needed no translation. He was young and not unhandsome, but his familiar touch revolted Lina.

Keeping her smile steady with an effort, she tried to pull away. He didn't release her. Her Spanish was very limited, but she knew what *bonita* meant and *bar* was apparently the same in Spanish.

She shook her head emphatically and pointed toward the dock. *"Mi padre."* This time when she tried to pull away, he jerked her along after him. Lina had opened her mouth to scream when the officer fell backward. Lina was dragged with him for an instant, then, blessedly, she was free. She gathered her skirts to run, but a grunt made her peek over her shoulder.

His hands cradling his gut, the officer slid down the side of the building to the ground. The Indian man who'd exited the church last said something cutting in Spanish, then he approached Lina.

Lina was still poised to run, but he stopped three steps away. "It's not wise for you to be in the streets alone." His English was perfect, if oddly accented.

Lina released her skirts and peeked around his broad shoulder. The officer still sat stunned on the ground. "I know. Thank you so much for your help. I got lost. Can you direct me to the docks?"

"Allow me to escort you." Politely, he shouldered his loose bag and thrust his hand toward the street on the left.

Lina was curious about the contents of his long sack, for it had an odd, bulky look, at once soft and round, as if it were padded. However, she walked in silence, dreading the choice words Jeremy would peal over her head. He was not likely to let her forget that her first action after she set foot on Mexican soil was to get lost.

"Why are you in Campeche?"

Lina started. "I'm here on a scientific expedition into the interior."

"Another archaeologist."

He gave the word an odd resonance, as if he either despised her kind or admired it. Whatever his feelings, he was obviously not indifferent. Lina glanced at his profile and was struck once again at how his sloping forehead and beaked nose resembled his ancestors'. For a moment, she was chilled, wondering if he really led her to the docks as promised.

Then he grinned, flashing those dark eyes at her in an admiring, nonthreatening way, and she relaxed. "I've never seen such a pretty archaeologist before."

She flushed. "Thank you. I'm part of a larger party, of course." It wouldn't hurt to add that, even though he'd saved her from a possibly unpleasant experience.

"And where will you excavate?"

Lina had the feeling he was intent on her answer, even though he casually scuffed at a stone as they walked.

"Palenque."

He nodded as if he were not surprised. He opened his mouth, but Lina held up her hand. There it was again. Her name being called.

"Over here, Jeremy!" she yelled in reply. "Thank you, but my friend is looking for me. I'll be fine now."

The Maya subjected her to a last intense appraisal, as if he searched not her body, but her character. Then he nodded and melted into the crowd thronging the streets.

Thus Jeremy found her—standing still, staring after the strange man, a perplexed expression on her face.

He caught her arm and shook it. "Have you lost your mind? What do you mean wandering off alone? I've been looking for you for ages."

"Hmmm?" She focused on Jeremy. "What did you expect me to do? Sprout wings? I couldn't keep up with those great strides of yours."

He dragged her after him. "You're an accident waiting to happen. I must be out of my mind, leading you into the jungle."

"You were out of your mind long before you met me," Lina muttered.

"What did you say?"

"Never mind. You can release me now."

"Not bloody likely." He pulled her closer to his side.

If she hadn't been so angry, she would have been touched by his obvious concern. All thoughts of the Maya flew out of her head. "We're here."

"What?" Jeremy glanced around and saw Sir Lawrence waving at them from the outdoor restaurant. "Oh." He walked a few steps more, slowed, then said rapidly, "I'm sorry. I was lost in my thoughts and didn't realize you weren't behind me until it was too late. I'll not make the same mistake again."

"You were angry, you mean."

Jeremy didn't lose a step. "That too. As you were."

"Yes." Uncaring of what her father and Baxter might think, Lina tugged on his arm until Jeremy stopped. There would never be a safer time than now. "I may not get another chance, so . . . Jeremy, you're a very attractive man and I'm drawn to you, but I came here for one purpose, and nothing will deter me from it. You obviously don't want entanglements any more than I, so shall we base our relationship strictly on business from now on?"

Jeremy had gone very still. "And what of the bet?"

Lina smiled and waved at her father to indicate nothing was amiss even as she said through her teeth, "I always meet my obligations, but I still don't believe it will be necessary."

She started to move forward again, but Jeremy interrupted grimly. "Wait a minute. You've had your say. Now it's my turn." He waited until she looked at him, then he ticked off on his fingers, "One. Now that we've reached the Yucatán, you are to obey my orders without question. Your life may depend upon it. Two. You're right. I don't want 'entanglements' either. But you're not to give to Baxter the favors you disallow me."

Never had she hated that arrogant male grin more than now. "Finished?"

"Not quite yet." A strong brown hand caught her chin and lifted it. "Lie to yourself, angel, but I know better. You want me almost as badly as I want you. But I'll bide my time. Soon enough you'll be leaping into my arms voluntarily. For now— this is three."

In full view of her father, Baxter, and any number of total strangers, Jeremy kissed Lina squarely on her surprised mouth. He took his time about it, too, until her stiffness relaxed in his arms. Only when her mouth opened did he let her go. He whistled, long and low. "I'd love to progress to four, but will, regretfully, await a private moment."

Lina pulled away and mustered her scattered wits. She searched for words, but the "how dare you" she longed to fling at him was a relic of too many bad melodramas. No indeed. He needed more forceful retribution. She contented herself with a quiet, "You'll regret that."

Her back as erect as a Mayan stele, she stalked inside the lacy iron gate to her father's patio table. She tensed for the expected tirade, but for once, she was glad to see, his anger was directed at Jeremy.

"How dare you make my daughter a public spectacle?"

Lina smiled wryly. What a pity Jeremy didn't sport a waxed moustache. He should twirl one, warning women of the roué lurking behind that fallen angel's face. "Please, Father, not now. We've made scene enough already. No harm done."

Across the table, Baxter made a rough sound, but for once, he held his tongue. His eyes switched rapidly back and forth between the speakers.

Jeremy slouched back in his chair. "Perhaps you found the encounter inconsequential, my dear, but it was the best appetizer I've ever tasted."

Her father's arm tensed under her hand. He half rose, but she jerked him back down into his chair. "He's merely trying to provoke you. And I think I know why."

Lina folded her hands in her lap, hoping she looked more composed than she felt. "I don't know why you suddenly want to cry off, but it shan't work, Jeremy. You made a commitment, and we hold you to it."

Jeremy's arm, which had been swinging casually over the back of his chair, went still. "Your perception never ceases to amaze me, Lina. What a pity you can't see yourself so clearly."

"Nor can you."

Swinging his arm again, Jeremy said, "See how well suited we are, m'dear?"

Lina inhaled deeply. "Why do you want to quit?"

"That's my business." Jeremy lifted a hand for the waiter. "Shall we eat now and discuss this on the voyage home?"

"You bounder," Baxter burst out as soon as the waiter departed with their orders. "Should have known a gentleman's agreement means nothing to you—"

"Never mind that now," Lina interrupted. "I don't understand. You've been into the jungle many times and left without a scratch."

Sighing, Jeremy faced forward in his chair and clasped the table edge, his posture as direct as his words. "I've never had more than my own neck and my cargo to worry about before. You've made it eminently clear today that you have no more idea how to take care of yourself than a babe. I'd be so busy worrying about you that I could make careless mistakes that would endanger us all."

Sir Lawrence glanced at his daughter. "What's he rattling on about, Lina?"

Lina bit her lip, but forced the admission out. "I strayed a couple of streets over when we were heading back to the docks. But I came to no harm. You're making a to-do over nothing, Jeremy."

"This time—in a populous city. The jungle, however, does not give second chances." As if cued, the heavens opened in a deluge. Rain hit the ground with such force that it spattered them even under the awning. Jeremy spread his hands. "Can't you all see that this expedition is doomed from the start?"

"I see, sir, that a promise means naught to you," Sir Lawrence retorted. "I can't make you guide us, but by God don't expect us to cry coward along with you."

Baxter growled, "To the devil with you, then. No doubt we can find another guide now that we're here, Sir Lawrence."

As the two men conferred quietly, Lina's heart sank to her sturdy boots. He couldn't desert them now, when they needed him most. And the bet? So much for her pretensions. This man had learned years ago to put himself first; apparently his safety meant more to him than his desire.

When the food came, Jeremy applied himself to it quietly, ignoring the surrounding debate.

Lina stared at her own plate, then forced down a bite of shark. At another time, she might have been surprised at its tender, moist flesh, but at the moment she barely tasted it. This, then, was the way it ended. She'd never see Jeremy again. She tried to tell herself it was for the best, but her eyes unaccountably misted. No doubt the vegetable sauce was spicy.

Next to her, Jeremy shoved back his half-full plate and murmured for her ears alone, "Can't I say something to dissuade you?"

Equally softly, she answered, "No. Even if we have to use a map to get there and can't obtain a guide, we'll go. Aside from the fact that our personal fortune is at stake, so are our professional reputations. After we've raised such high hopes about the size of our expedition, do you think we can go back to our peers and say, 'So sorry. We lost our guide'?"

"No, I guess not." Jeremy stared into the gathering darkness. The rain had stopped as abruptly as it came. "But surely you value your life more than your reputation."

"No, Jeremy, I don't." Lina lowered her voice still further until she whispered, "And this difference will forever make a relationship between us impossible. God didn't put us here to age. He put us here to *grow*. Without challenge and self-respect, life is meaningless anyway."

Lina rose and sent her father and Baxter a brilliant smile. "I'm going back to the ship to pack."

Her father waved her on. "We'll follow shortly, after we make some inquiries at the dock." Sir Lawrence sniffed disdainfully. "Mayhew, be so good as to unload our supplies. And don't fear about your investment. You'll get double on it, if the finds are as rich as I expect. Unlike some, I always keep my word."

Then Lina's hurrying steps took her out of hearing range. Only the redolent darkness witnessed her tears.

As the sailor rowed her out to the *Verdandi*, the restless seas rolled even more before Lina's blurring eyes. Abruptly she realized she cried not for herself, or even for the adult Jeremy. She cried for the little boy who sometimes looked out from the man's eyes. The little boy who had been hurt so badly that he could never trust again . . .

Standing on the dock, Jeremy watched Lina disappear into the night. His hands clenched on the fear still churning in his stomach. Good God, if he'd come to care so strongly for the mite that losing her for fifteen minutes in a crowded city could unman him, what would it do to him to watch her die of snake bite, or to be eaten by alligators, or ripped to shreds by wild boars, or speared by Indians, or . . .

Jeremy forced the horrendous visions away. He'd kissed her before the others only partly to warn Baxter off. He'd had to reassure himself of her safety. Thank God she'd not realized the stew she had him in. As usual, she thought the worst.

But his last desperate gamble hadn't worked. With, or without him, they'd go. He hadn't lied. They'd all be in grave peril if he had to watch Lina every second. Yet how could he let them go with anyone else, or, God forbid, alone?

He shuddered. Dammit, he should have followed his instincts and hightailed it out of Monte Carlo back to Marseilles that first morning after he'd met her. Now, like it or not, he was committed. Cursing fluently in Norwegian, French, Spanish, and English, Jeremy swiveled and sought out Sir Lawrence to say what he must.

"Jolly good." Sir Lawrence clapped him on the shoulder. "Knew you'd come 'round."

"Did you?" Jeremy asked dryly, but Sir Lawrence had already turned toward the docks.

Baxter, however, fell into step with Jeremy. "Why do I have the feeling that a certain dark-haired lady had more to do with your change of heart than conscience?"

"So? Didn't she have a great deal to do with your participation on this expedition?"

"Too true, old boy."

"Being the *gentleman* you are, Baxter, no doubt you don't need reminding, but I won our little bout. You leave me a clear field with the lady."

Baxter rubbed the fading bruise on his cheek. "I could hardly forget. However, if the lady changes the rules, I can't be churlish, can I?"

"What the hell does that mean?"

"It means, old boy, that if Evangeline Collier decides she finds me attractive, I shan't reject her."

Jeremy's strides lengthened to match his brisk tone. "Two days into our journey, you'll be making yourself as unattractive as possible, I assure you."

It was Baxter's turn to frown. "What?"

"To the true rulers of the jungle—the animals. Out there, you're not God's loftiest creation. To everything from mosquitoes to alligators, you're just another meal."

"Nice try, Mayhew. But I don't scare so easily." Baxter leaped into the shore boat and settled himself comfortably next to Sir Lawrence.

Jeremy followed. "You will, Baxter. You will."

Lina almost had her bags packed when she felt the movement of the ship beneath her. She slammed her trunk closed and ran outside, careening into Jeremy, who had his hand raised to knock on her door.

She stared up at him, unaware of her pleading expression.

He closed his eyes briefly. "Don't look at me like that. I changed my mind."

Lina sighed until her shoulders lifted. "Thank God."

"Why so glad, angel?" Jeremy caressed her cheek with a fingertip.

"I'll feel safer, knowing you're there."

"That's all?"

"Yes." Honesty forced her to add, "I'm glad you're keeping your word as well. I knew my judgment wasn't that bad."

That lonely hunger flickered in his eyes, but was as quickly gone before she could reach out to it.

Stepping back, he said obliquely, "I hope God grants you the opportunity to say the same several months from now. Be in the dining room at eight in the morning. We'll dock soon after, and I want you all ready." His shoulders erect, he stalked off.

Lina closed the door, wondering what that obscure comment had meant. Then her frown brightened into a slow smile. He really was concerned for her safety. But she was looking forward to those months he obviously dreaded.

She could take care of herself. And anything she couldn't handle, she could leave in his capable hands. Serenely she prepared for bed. She was asleep within minutes.

Above, Jeremy paced the deck, pausing occasionally at the side to stare into the gloom. He really should seek out his bed, for it would be long indeed before he felt a feather mattress again. But he knew he'd only toss and turn.

The rain forest was both the most beautiful—and the most dangerous—place he'd ever visited. Yet he saw to it that business brought him here often. Tonight, with only the serene seas to stare him down, he asked himself why.

Could Lina be right? Had he become so cynical that he was indifferent to his own survival?

No. He couldn't accept that. Yet . . . before Lina dropped her hat at his feet, he couldn't remember the last time he'd truly enjoyed himself. Since then, he'd had many pleasurable memories—and only some of them had involved physical contact. Merely watching her eagerness for life pleased him and somehow made his own life more interesting. However, it was that verve, that curiosity he so admired that would endanger her in the jungle.

Jeremy wiped his sweaty palms on his pants, then stared at his hands. Even in the capricious moonlight, he could see them shaking. Disgusted, he stuck them in his pockets, but he could not deny the sick dread in his stomach for the morrow.

Sir Lawrence and Baxter didn't concern him so much, for they were basically egotists. Nothing would occupy them as much as their own safety. But Lina . . . she'd be as likely to chase a butterfly and trip over a snake.

He kept a lonely vigil through the night, watching the stars cede to dawn. Only when Venus gave a last peek, then disappeared to rest did he realize he'd wandered from starboard to the prow. Resting a possessive hand on the bowsprit, Jeremy stared as the orange sun vaulted over the waves, growing brighter at its exertion.

When he shaded his eyes, Jeremy realized that, for the first time in a long time, he was looking toward the future. A future that, God help him, hinged on the next months—and the fates he'd long ago learned he couldn't control . . .

Chapter 8

THEY HAD ALL eaten by the time Jeremy arrived. His clean hair smelled deliciously of sandalwood. He'd changed into a thin cotton shirt with ties at the top and khaki pants tucked into knee-high boots. His slim waist was accented by a sturdy belt from which depended a long knife, two pouches, and a pistol holstered around one thigh. Another, slimmer knife was sheathed to his calf.

Baxter snorted a laugh. "Good God, Mayhew, you look as though you're going into warfare."

Sir Lawrence chuckled. "I hope you don't expect us to carry that arsenal on our persons."

Jeremy folded his arms and waited until their laughter died.

Lina silently ruminated on yet another feature of the man who was as multifaceted as a fine diamond.

And as hard. How could he make her mouth water and her heart pound with foreboding all at once?

That grim stare turned on her. "Why aren't you wearing your boots?"

"I . . . didn't think it necessary since the first part of our journey is by canoe."

"You will wear your boots from now on—waking *and* sleeping. Canoes turn over; hammocks flip; we may have to rise suddenly in the night."

"Now see here, Mayhew, there's no need to be so autocratic," Sir Lawrence protested.

"No?" Jeremy unfolded his arms and leaned his palms on the table, hovering over them like a portent.

A gilded lock of drying hair flipped forward over his face,

making Lina yearn to brush it back. But she didn't dare. No trace existed of the lonely boy now; this man was as tough and dangerous as the land he loved.

"Each of you listen very carefully. I've neither time nor stomach for the niceties. Civility is not only wasted in the jungle, it's dangerous. If I say something to any one or all of you, whether it's couched as an order or a request, you are to obey without question or hesitation. If I don't have your agreement on this point, our voyage ends right here."

Steely gray eyes sliced around the table. Everyone nodded, but apparently that wasn't sufficient. "Baxter? Do you agree?"

"Guess so."

"What?"

"Yes, blast it."

"Sir Lawrence?"

"Still don't think you have to be so rough, but yes, I see the sense of what you're saying. I'll obey you to the letter."

That acute gaze sharpened on Lina. "Well?"

Lina fought the urge to bob her head and curtsy. "Yes, of course."

Jeremy straightened and sought the chair at the head of the table. "Good. Now, the rules are as follows. You don't touch anything without asking, you don't drink from the water without asking, you don't eat berries without asking, and most of all—*you don't wander off without asking*. I want everyone within my sight at all times."

"But surely it's all right to touch the flowers and plants," Lina protested.

"Some of the plants and flowers here are not only poisonous, their sap burns the skin." Jeremy's even tone hardened when she still looked doubtful. "This rule, as are the others is for your own safety. Disobey it, and you'll pay the consequences— if the jungle doesn't get you first."

"Dammit, Mayhew—" protested Baxter.

"Now wait a minute—" began Sir Lawrence.

Jeremy's fist slammed down on the table, rattling the cutlery and dishes. "That goes for you two as well. A second's hesitation can be the difference between life and death."

"And what, pray, do these 'consequences' entail, you . . . despot?" demanded Sir Lawrence.

Jeremy looked amused. "Why, I'm a benevolent despot, Sir Lawrence—but if you insist, I'll let you make your own mistakes. The consequences I'll leave to your fertile imagination." Jeremy stood. "You have an hour before we dock. I suggest you use it bathing. You'll not get a chance at another bath for some time. Now, if you'll excuse me, I have a ship to tend to."

Bemused, Lina watched the door close behind him. She wasn't sure whether to be offended or amused by Jeremy's lord-of-the-jungle attitude. Here, she had a feeling, was the real Jeremy, stripped of masks and subterfuge. As for her own reaction to him—she felt like a cat being stroked the wrong way, waiting for a mere change of direction to begin purring.

Obviously Baxter felt no such ambivalence. "Arrogant bounder! He's not indispensable to us yet."

"Unfortunately for us, Hubert, at this point he is," Sir Lawrence inserted, "as he, apparently, well knows."

Lina smiled wryly. Ever practical, her father.

"Where the devil are you going, Lawrence?" Hubert asked.

On his way to the door, Sir Lawrence replied over his shoulder, "Why, to bathe, of course."

An hour later, fresh and cool in her crisp cotton, feeling clumsy in the heavy boots, Lina stood at the railing, peering at the approaching verdure. Here, her real journey began. The island of Carmen lay flat and narrow like a salamander, sunning itself between the Gulf and the Laguna de Terminos. They sailed through the passage between the island and the mainland, allowing Lina her first glimpse of the city where, Jeremy had told them early on, they'd obtain mules for the brief trip to the Palizada River, the first leg of their journey.

Luxuriant foliage bordered the sandy beach, but a wide swath of jungle had been cleared for pretty frame houses. Lina glimpsed an open space fronting the houses and deduced the town had piazzas. Red, white, and purple flowers clustered along the square under the majestic foliage of banana trees Lina recognized from her botany studies.

The city of Carmen sustained itself mainly through log

commerce, where the various abundant woods the rain forest boasted were floated in, stripped of their bark, and warehoused to await export. Lina recalled Jeremy's geography lesson as she watched a new load of logs, lashed together like a crude raft, floating through the Laguna de Terminos's murky waters, vying for steerage with various craft ranging from flat-bottomed barges to canoes and sailing ships.

"Why are the waters dull?" she asked when Jeremy strode to her side to watch the anchor cable drop. "The Gulf is so blue."

"The Laguna de Terminos got its name because it's the delta for hundreds of jungle rivers. As for its color, these rivers bring untold miles of river sediment with them." Jeremy eyed her critically, from her loose white shirt, down past her split skirt, to her booted feet. "Much better."

Lina smiled wryly as he turned away to where her father oversaw the loading of his precious equipment. Jeremy had not been complimenting her person, nor would he for a very long time, if ever. She'd wanted things on a business footing, hadn't she? Lina turned back to the rail, inhaling deeply.

Beneath the sea scents, she detected a new aroma. At first she couldn't isolate it, then she realized the very air smelled . . . green. Alive with plants of every description. In the distance Lina could make out the hazy coastal state of Campeche. Via the Palizada River, they'd pass its border and feed on their liquid roadway into one of the mightiest Mexican rivers: the Usumacinta. There, they'd wind with the river a tortuous path through the jungle, finally obtaining the interior state of Chiapas.

"Palenque." Behind her closed eyes, Lina visualized the place she'd dreamed of visiting since her father first read to her from John Lloyd Stephens's copious accounts, and showed her Frederick Catherwood's meticulous drawings. The intrepid adventurers had laid the cornerstones for current Maya archaeologists. Stephens's *Incidents of Travel in Central America, Chiapas, and Yucatán* and *Incidents of Travel in Yucatán* colorfully detailed his travels to over forty sites. The tomes were treasured friends to Lina, as warm, intellectual, and informative as their author.

At last, she had her chance to add to his records. Was it arrogant of her to want to improve upon them? Doubtless

Stephens would have thought so, as her father did today. Wistfully Lina wondered why men apparently couldn't comprehend that women, too, were drawn by the lure of the unknown. That curiosity had drawn her halfway around the globe, to delve for herself into the wonders Stephens had described as "All was mystery, dark, impenetrable mystery, and every circumstance increased it."

She glanced over her shoulder, itching to disembark. For the past thirty minutes, sailors had sweated to bring all their endless boxes, crates, and trunks from the hold, each checked off on Sir Lawrence's master list.

To that gentleman's obvious irritation, Jeremy peered over his shoulder. Occasionally he ordered a box set aside over Sir Lawrence's protests. When the last box was loaded, Jeremy strode to the final shore boat to leave.

"I'll go procure our mules and arrange for our canoes once we reach the Palizada. I suggest you make a last tour of your quarters to be sure you haven't left anything. I'll see you ashore."

Straddling the rail with a long leg, Jeremy looked at his first mate. "Four months, to the day. It's a week or so to get to the plantation, but we'll allow a month traveling time, to be certain. That will give us about three months at the site. That should give you plenty of time to deliver the goods to New Orleans and return. If we're not here, wait. If we don't come within a week, you know how to reach Don Roberto. I'll send word to him if we're delayed."

"What if we can't finish in three months?" Baxter asked, coming to the side.

"Then you'll have to mount another expedition. Three months is the time we agreed upon." Jeremy began swivelling at the waist to hoist himself over into the shore boat, but Sir Lawrence held up a staying hand.

"What if the finds are richer than we expect and take longer to extract?"

"Three years wouldn't be sufficient to wrest Palenque's secrets from the ground, Sir Lawrence, if the site is anywhere near as complicated as Copán or Tikal."

When her father looked as if he might argue, Lina touched his forearm. "A bargain's a bargain, Father."

Jeremy's eyes kindled. "Indeed, Miss Collier."

Then he'd vaulted over the side and was gone, thankfully unaware of her blush. Sir Lawrence and Baxter, however, stared at her.

"Ah, I'm going to check my quarters." Lina fled.

By noon, they'd finally sailed to the landward side of the Laguna de Terminos and, after several trips, sailors had ferried their equipment ashore to the waiting mules. From the railing, Lina could see Jeremy striding about, himself ensuring that each crate and trunk was securely lashed. The three Indians who had leased them the animals watched the restless foreigner. They tilted back their broad-brimmed, flat-crowned hats and shrugged in their colorfully embroidered shirts.

They reminded Lina of snails watching ants; they increased her own impatience. She drummed her fingers on the railing. "At this rate, we'll not make it ashore until dark."

Next to her, Mack laughed. "Jeremy's got the patience 'o Job when he needs it. Ye'll be glad o' that, lassie, 'fore we meet again."

An hour later, remembering the comment, Lina tried to reconcile yet another aspect of Jeremy into a cohesive whole, even as she knew she'd never understand him. The man she'd known heretofore had certainly not seemed patient. However, no other term defined his tolerance as he simultaneously dealt with twelve obstreperous mules, three loitering muleteers, and three impatient Britons.

For the third time, Jeremy once more held Baxter's mule, but the skittish female might have defined the truism "stubborn as a mule." Every time Baxter's boot touched the stirrup, she shied sideways.

Securely atop her own mule, Lina shoved her hat forward on her head to hide her smile. Discriminating animal. Apparently Baxter's charms didn't appeal to the four-legged variety either.

"Fiend seize it, Mayhew, hold the bag of bones still!" Once more, Baxter warily lifted his foot, but the mule turned its head.

Though the mule couldn't understand Baxter's words, it apparently took exception to his tone. On the many digs she'd attended, Lina had ridden burros, oxen, camels, and even, once, an elephant. Now she read intent in the muddy brown eyes.

"Uh-oh," Lina breathed. Then, as she realized everyone else watched Baxter instead of the mule, Lina shouted, "Hubert, watch o—"

Too late. That stocky neck lunged. Big yellow teeth clamped down on Baxter's raised thigh.

"Owww!" Baxter danced on the ball of his other foot as he batted, unavailingly, at the mule's head.

Jeremy pulled his pistol and brought the butt down between the mule's eyes. Blinking long lashes, it let go. Still wailing, clutching his thigh, Baxter slid to the ground.

One of the muleteers kneed his own mount closer, protesting, but Jeremy slapped his pistol back in its holster and snapped a reply. The man sullenly returned to his place at the head of the line.

Lina dismounted and knelt beside Baxter, who was gingerly feeling his leg. "Take your pants off and let me see the bite."

Baxter opened his eyes widely at that. "I was wondering if I'd ever hear you say that, Lina . . ."—Baxter looked above Lina's head—"again."

Lina didn't need to turn her head to know why Baxter had tacked on his addendum. On the ground before her, she saw Jeremy's shadow go very still, then move away.

"You bastard," she hissed, surging to her feet.

Baxter stood, wincing. "It's for your own good, my dear. He's not for you." He rubbed his thigh, but Lina saw no blood dotting the heavy canvas.

"And neither are you!" She gave him her back, half regretful the mule apparently had only bruised him.

Jeremy made soothing sounds as he tried to calm the skittish mule, but she snorted and bared her teeth every time he reached for her halter. Lina peered at the head of the line, but found no help there.

The three Mexicans had hunched their shoulders and gave every appearance of napping. Lina's mouth turned down. Her Spanish was limited, but she'd read enough Latin literature to know the word *macho*. Their male pride had apparently been offended at Jeremy's remark, so now they refused to help.

Muttering under her breath, Lina went to the packs holding their food supplies, opening and closing several until she found what she wanted. Then she strolled toward the mule, murmuring, "There, old girl, I don't blame you. I wouldn't want to carry two hundred pounds in this heat either. But you see, we need you . . ."

Jeremy glared at her over his shoulder. "Get back, Lina. She'll break your bones like sticks if she decides to kick."

"Shut up, Jeremy," Lina said in the same even, unthreatening tone. "Leave the poor thing alone. You males, that's all you understand—dominance."

Lina skirted Jeremy and went to the mule's head. Those dark brown eyes followed her warily, but when Lina held out her hand, the mule's nostrils flared. Lina inched closer, talking all the while, a pile of dried apples extended in the middle of her palm.

His hand hovering over his pistol butt, Jeremy watched Lina's ungloved hand angle within range of those angry teeth. The mule sniffed one last time, then dipped its head and daintily lipped the apples out of Lina's palm.

Lina stroked the middle of its forehead, hoping mules liked that touch as much as horses. Apparently so, for the mule gave her one last assessing look, then, chewing, it remained still as Lina's hand brushed its neck. "There, you see?" she said to Jeremy. "She just needed a little understanding."

Under a tree, still favoring his sore leg, Baxter snorted. "Or could be she recognized a kindred spirit."

Lina's stroking hand didn't pause. "Or it could be she's choosy about who mounts her."

Jeremy burst out laughing; Baxter's pale skin reddened.

Sir Lawrence, luckily, was already making notes on the flora and fauna.

Embarrassed that anger had made her so frank, Lina jerked the reins from Jeremy's hand and mounted the now quiet animal. "Can we go yet?"

Jeremy held Lina's former mount for Baxter, still chuckling. His voice shook a bit when he answered, "I was just thinking of the mule's name."

Seated, Baxter looked down at him. "And what's so bloody amusing about that?"

"Her name is Angelina."

Baxter grinned at the two females. One swished its tail in disgust; the other would have, if she'd had one.

"See," he crowed. "Two of a kind. I told you!"

Masculine chuckles accompanied Lina down the trail.

Her disgust didn't last the afternoon, however, for as they departed the coastal plain, the vegetation thickened. Even Jeremy's rearguard presence couldn't distract her from the new sights and smells bombarding her thirsty senses. Nor could the daily rain, which had begun its usual start-stop dance, dampen her enthusiasm.

She was glad that her oil-covered wide-brimmed hat shielded her from the patter seeping through the trees, for her eyes had much to do. Some of the trees she recognized. The willows had the typical trailing branches, but she'd never seen one so large in England. She had to tilt her head back to see the top. She also knew what a bamboo looked like, but what was that tree with the enormous leaves?

A bright yellow frog jumped down a leaf as she watched, darting out its tongue. Eight legs fluttered for a split second from its mouth, then were gone. The frog gulped.

Lina gulped too. She tried to remind herself that enchanted as her surroundings seemed, the harshest rule of life reigned supreme in the jungle: eat or be eaten.

Yet, as her mule swayed from side to side with each sure step, Jeremy's warnings were lulled, along with her body. This was life at its finest; what could she do but enjoy it?

With its usual fickleness, the rain stopped. A small clearing allowed Lina her first sight of the vastness lurking beyond the little path worn by civilization.

The suffused lighting offered by the misty day lent an enigmatic glow to the forest. Vine-garbed trees, some thin, some thick, some whitish, some dark, towered supreme. Like sleepy giants they nodded over the fairy flowers flaunting rainbow hues that cavorted at their feet. Bushes bloomed with more revelers, their red and purple blossoms preening, aglow from the recent rain.

Lina started as a brilliant flash of red exploded above her head. Her heart slowed as she recognized the ibis, its curved beak and long neck graceful against a bit of sky. Then, with an effortless flapping of its great wings, it disappeared above the treetops. Lina deduced they must be approaching the river, for she also recognized the distinctive ringed neck and tufted crest of the kingfisher, though of a larger variety than its northern cousin. Now Lina watched the trees instead of the ground, wondering if she'd spy more aquatic birds.

The thought had hardly left her when her mule stumbled on a rotten log, then bleated and danced sideways. The loose stirrups left Lina's heels. Her hands had become lax on the reins, so her grab was abortive. The mule reared. Lina was already off balance, and the movement unseated her.

She gave a little squawk more of self-anger than pain as she landed half on, half off the path. The bushes looked lush and inviting as a green mattress, but in reality prickled her legs like the devil. Her teeth bit her lip as her head connected with the hard path.

Meanwhile, the mule proved yet again that Angelina was a misnomer, for she ignored her erstwhile friend, leaped over Lina and the rotten log, and bolted up the trail. Lina was preparing to sit up when Jeremy's voice came softly above her.

"Lina, be still. There's a snake two feet to your right, but your head is in my way. I'll have to make my way around before I can get a clear shot."

Only then did she hear the hissing. Ever so slightly, Lina turned her head. Her blood ran cold. She couldn't have moved then even if she'd wanted to.

A snake was uncoiling itself from the split log. She was so close she could clearly see the dark brown and gray trapezoids decorating its muscular, writhing back. The triangular head raised, displaying a yellow throat. Its tongue flicked repeatedly at the air, and she knew it sensed her heat, but she would have sworn those flat dark eyes stared straight into hers.

She sensed the snake was bunching to strike.

Not heaven or hell could have stopped her then, for she read her death in those cold eyes.

She tensed all her muscles for a powerful lunge just as the snake hissed loudly, baring its fangs, and struck.

A shot drowned out Lina's scream. A foot away, the reptile's head erupted backward, severed cleanly from its body.

Momentum carried the rest of the snake, however. Part of the corpse, pulsing blood, landed on Lina's arm.

She jerked away, swallowing another scream, and scrambled to her feet. She was shaking so much she could hardly stand. Vaguely she sensed movement, then Jeremy was there. He caught her in his arms before she could topple.

"You dimwit, keep your goddamn eyes on the path, or so help me I'll tie you to your mount."

For once, his harshness didn't bother Lina, for she could feel his heart pounding as hard as her own. "Yes, Jeremy."

He pushed her slightly away, holding her shoulders, and eyed her with concern. "Did it bite you?" He lifted her arm, then stiffened when he saw the blood. "Oh my G—"

"No, no, I'm fine. It's the snake's blood." She shivered and burrowed her face into his chest. "Thank you."

Mules pounded up the path. For the first time, Lina realized the others had not known anything was amiss and had gone on ahead. Lina pulled away and teased shakily, "Did you think only snake bite would make me obey one of your autocratic commands?"

He didn't smile. "The commands are for your own good. And I meant what I said. Watch the path, or be tied to your mule. I was afraid something like this would happen. But I can't always watch your back."

He stalked off to examine the snake's remains.

Sir Lawrence leaped off his mule and ran to his daughter. When he saw Jeremy bending over the seven foot corpse, he froze. "Lina?"

"No, Father. Jeremy shot it before it struck."

Sir Lawrence closed his eyes. "You have my undying gratitude, Mayhew."

"The best thanks you can give me is to help me keep an eye on your daughter." Jeremy looked up at the two muleteers who had accompanied Sir Lawrence and said something.

They nodded, then one dismounted, wrapped the long body in a coil and stuck it in a hide bag, which he tied to his saddle.

"What's he doing with the carcass?" Sir Lawrence asked.

Jeremy grinned. "Fresh meat."

Lina gagged and covered her mouth.

Sir Lawrence blinked. "You're joking."

"Fresh meat is not so easy to come by here as you might think. Snake tastes pretty good, actually. Rather like chicken."

Pale-faced, Lina stared at the bag. "What was it called?"

"That particular variety carries various names here in the Yucatán, but I think the name they're now calling it in Brazil is most appropriate." Jeremy collected Angelina, who seemed calm now as she wandered back their way, nibbling at the ground cover beside the path. The animal snorted when Jeremy pulled its head up, but trotted over to Lina obediently.

"Which is?" Lina put her foot in the stirrup.

"Fer-de-lance."

Lina mounted. "French for lance head." She shivered, fumbling for her reins. "Appropriate. Are they . . . numerous?"

Jeremy collected his own mule, then swung lithely aboard. "Oh yes. But the bushmaster is even more venomous. I've seen one twelve feet long. They're not as aggressive, however, nor as prevalent."

Sir Lawrence also mounted. "Which is the one you told us about in Monte Carlo?"

"The *fer-de-lance*. The Indians call it *nahuyaca*." Jeremy smiled at the two grim Britons. "Actually, this escapade may be for the best. I suspect you'll each watch very carefully where you're going from now on. Shall we? The mules get lazy when they stand."

The two Indians had already started back up the path.

"Wait." Sir Lawrence turned his mule sideways.

"Yes?"

"Mayhew . . . do you have an extra pistol?"

Lina sent her father a sharp look. He hated weapons, and had never understood the English gentry's obsession with hunting.

Jeremy shook his head. "But Don Roberto will probably sell you a weapon when we reach his estate."

"Very well. I guess it will have to wait. Lina, I'm going to ride in front of you. Watch where you're going." Sir Lawrence turned his mule up the path.

Lina didn't need the second admonition. For the brief hour it took them to get to the river, she never released her reins, and only peeked at her beautiful surroundings.

Behind her, Jeremy relaxed in his saddle and even started whistling.

The boatmen were waiting, paid and alerted by the Indian Jeremy had hired at Carmen. Their broad dark faces were impassive as they studied the foreigners. They wore thin cotton trousers and nothing else, though their wiry torsos gleamed oddly in the restrained light. As Lina dismounted from Angelina and approached, her nose wrinkled. Every exposed part of their bodies seemed to be coated with some foul-smelling distillate. Lina wondered why.

She watched as Jeremy spoke to them. Their expressions didn't change, even when he put a hefty number of coins in their outstretched palms. A deposit, Lina presumed. She unlashed her personal knapsack from Angelina and tossed it to the ground, then approached a pack mule.

"Leave that, Lina. The boatmen have to balance their loads carefully, anyway," Jeremy explained, coming up behind her. Lina watched doubtfully as every man bent to the task of unlashing crates, then stacking them on the bank, where two of the boatmen took over. Experimentally they hefted each crate, set it with care in a long, narrow canoe, then replicated the process.

Lina glanced uneasily at the west as Jeremy and the others toiled.

"Please, let me help," she said yet again.

Jeremy wiped his brow on his sleeve and followed her gaze. "No need. We're almost finished. We don't plan to travel far tonight anyway." Jeremy returned to his loading.

Some minutes later, Baxter pressed his knuckles to the small of his back and arched his spine. "Thank God that's over." He smiled at Lina and offered his hand. "Will you ride in my canoe?"

She was still smarting from his false insinuation to Jeremy, but before she could say no, Jeremy did so for her.

"She's riding with me, Baxter. For the whole of the trip."

"I can make my own—" Lina began.

"Fiend seize it, Mayhew, you're not invincible either."

"I'm better able to protect her than you are."

"Not if you'll give me your gun."

"Not likely."

Lina tried again to interrupt. "Please, I'm quite capable of—"

"You're our fearless leader, Mayhew. So you should take the lead canoe. Lina will be safer in the middle."

"Precisely. With me at her side." Jeremy's smile showed too many teeth. "Like the *gentleman* you are, you can go before her."

Lina closed her eyes and leaned against a tree, reflecting that she'd never heard "gentleman" made to sound like an epithet. But then she'd never met a man like Jeremy Mayhew.

Scratching at her arm, Lina shoved away from the tree, trying to think of a way to put a stop to their bickering. Already it was starting, and the sun hadn't even set on their first day.

Her mood wasn't brightened by the way the boatmen watched the row. Stained teeth only a shade lighter than their skin stretched the tough brown faces. They glanced knowingly from the two men to Lina, their comprehension unhindered by the language barrier. Lina scratched at her skin again. Her rash of frustration seemed worse than usual.

Sir Lawrence had already climbed into one canoe, standing uneasily as the fragile craft rocked under his weight. When he was secure, he glared at the two younger men.

"Devil take you, Baxter, you promised to cooperate. Lina should ride with Mayhew. He's the only one who knows the country, after all." Sir Lawrence jerked his head toward the middle canoe. "Lina, get in."

For once glad of her father's arrogance, Lina hurried forward. Now her arm was burning, and she scratched at it harder. Jeremy turned to offer her a hand, stepping in front of Baxter as he did so.

He surged forward and reached for her blouse.

Lina backed away, putting up her hands to protect her buttons. "Are you crazy?"

He didn't mince words. The next thing Lina knew, the buttons had popped under his tug and she was stripped to her thin chemise. Jeremy tossed her blouse aside, shaking his fingers as he did so.

Only then did Lina see the tiny black bodies scurrying up his wrist. She looked down. Her arm was covered in tiny welts, and now she felt the prickly sensation of the ants crawling toward her neck. Swallowing a scream, she brushed at her burning skin, but Jeremy returned from the river, shoved her hands away, and dumped a hide bucketful of water over her shoulders.

Lina sighed as the burning sensation eased. She looked up. "Thank you, Je—"

His stare was riveted on her chest. She froze, her eyes slicing sideways, to see every man present looking in the same direction, with varying degrees of interest. Her father, of course, was appalled.

Automatically Lina looked down. The dark tips of her breasts showed through the wet batiste. She crossed her arms over her bosom and turned her back to the men, desperately searching for her knapsack. Damn Jeremy and his paper-thin chemises.

A brown hand wavered in her vision, holding the canvas strap. Somewhat hoarsely Jeremy said, "Are you looking for this?"

Lina snatched it. "Yes." Lina tore the buttons loose and fumbled inside, then she hesitated, holding the dry shirt up to her chest.

Jeremy turned his broad back. "I think I'll make an adequate screen."

Keeping Jeremy between her and the river, Lina stripped out of her wet chemise, put on a dry one, then buttoned a clean shirt, tucking it into her skirt. "I'm ready." Calmly she folded her chemise and fetched her trampled shirt, but her cheeks told a different story.

"Well, come along, then," Baxter snapped.

Neither Lina nor Jeremy glanced at him.

Jeremy's forefinger traced her cheekbone. "Sorry, angel. In this case I thought your personal comfort more important than modesty." He turned her shirt back to look at her arm.

Lina frowned over the dots of pus already forming under the bites. Her skin didn't burn any longer, but it was itching like the very devil. "What kind of ants were they?"

"A more virulent type than you're used to. They have been known to sting animals to death. Even . . ."—Jeremy hesitated, then apparently decided she needed to hear the truth—"small children."

Lina scratched harder after that, then walked to the middle canoe. She didn't like the way the boatman stared at her, but she smiled at him hesitantly anyway. Jeremy assisted her in the tricky maneuver of entering the canoe without tipping it over, then eased in beside her. As soon as he was seated on the rear seat, he poured some of the powder from one of the pouches at his belt into his palm, then added water and mixed it to a paste. Pulling her arm across his legs, he spread the yellowish paste over the bites.

Immediately the itching eased. "What is this stuff?" Lina sniffed her arm and coughed.

"Never mind. Plants you've never heard of. I learned my first visit here that the natives of this land know far more efficacious remedies for its perils than modern medicine." Jeremy's strokes moved higher, then switched to the side of her neck.

Lina leaned into his hand, her eyes drifting closed. The gentle gurgling of the swift river was as hypnotic as Jeremy's touch. The river breeze played softly on Lina's heated skin, seeming cooler than before. Birds of every variety thrummed their throaty harmonies above the banks, some forte, some pianissimo. Even when the rain began again, Lina's pleasure wasn't spoiled. The drops felt like heaven's dew upon her skin, a pleasant contrast to the warmth of Jeremy's hand.

Then his touch was gone. Lina's eyes opened to see Jeremy rinsing his hand in the river. Her father was glaring back at them from his position in the second canoe.

Lina smiled secretively as she admired Jeremy's superb profile and spied the red spot high on his cheekbone. He'd not wanted to stop touching her any more than she'd wanted him to stop. Where was the harm in that? she asked her puritan side.

Plenty, it snapped back. One touch leads to another. Lina trailed her fingers in the water. The silky slide half veiled her hand, making it both sleeker and more attractive in its milky whiteness. All her life, she had been sensual, in the literal sense of the word. She'd accounted herself lucky that she was more sensitive to life's pleasures than, say, her father or most of her friends, but now she wondered.

Taste, sight, scent, hearing, and feeling. Lina loved to eat, to see new sights, she planted mostly fragrant flowers in her English garden, she adored classical music, and as for feeling . . . Lina frowned at the image of Jeremy's bare torso that leaped into her mind.

No wonder she was so susceptible to him—he delighted every one of her senses. She looked up at him.

The sky was growing roseate. His profile was stark, unabashedly masculine against the feminine color. She saw him evaluating the closest bank. Did he never rest?

As if he felt her gaze, he turned his head. His eyes seemed to catch the setting sun, then that fire was doused by a frown. "Get your hand out of the water."

"But you did—"

He leaned over, caught her wrist and pulled her hand out of the river. "I'd think your experiences today would have taught you something. You disappoint me, Lina."

She sat up straight, her sensuality a burden now instead of a boon. "So sorry. I keep forgetting you're perfect."

He chuckled harshly. "Not even to my mother." When she stared at him curiously, he dropped her hand. "Now listen. This is the first day of our journey, and you've already narrowly escaped snake bite and you've been bitten by ants, both through sheer carelessness—"

"Now wait just a minute! I didn't know my mule had broken open a snake's den—"

"She never would have unseated you if you'd been holding on properly. And it's not a good idea to lean against the trees here."

Lina was too honest to deny the twin truths. The words seemed stuck in her throat, but somehow she forced them out. "You're right. You've come to my aid twice today, and I'd be churlish to deny the fault was mostly mine. I promise to be more careful."

Jeremy's smile was perfunctory. "Good." And he returned to his vigilance.

Hurt, Lina likewise stared at the banks. That invisible wall between them towered as high as ever. Only when she was

hurt or in danger did a gateway open. Lina told herself she
didn't care, but it was several long moments before her white-
knuckled grip on the sides of the canoe eased.

The lead boatman called something back to them. The next
took up the call, and Jeremy answered, then turned his head,
cupped his mouth, and extended the verbal chain. The last
three replied, then the first canoe began veering toward the
bank. The others followed.

Lina sighed. "Thank heaven. I was beginning to think we'd
spend the night on the river."

"Too dangerous," Jeremy replied. "The jaguar hunts at night,
often from trees, and we can't see to navigate. No, we'll go in,
set up camp with a fire, and post a guard."

The unloading was easier than the loading, for they took off
only provisions, pots, and hammocks. Feeling as if she had to
carry her weight, Lina volunteered to cook supper. One of the
Indians soon had a fire going and watched curiously as she
used their fresh provisions to make a stew.

Meanwhile, Jeremy surveyed the perimeters of the clearing.
Baxter washed his socks, then both men drew out the hammocks and fine mosquito nets.

Sir Lawrence set up a mat covered with an elaborate net
tent he'd purchased in England, then stood back and briskly
brushed off his hands. "Good. Much more civilized than those
dashed things."

"Civilized, maybe. But practical?" Jeremy shrugged. "But
I won't try to dissuade you. The mosquitoes will do that."

"They can't be that much worse than the ones in the
Mediterranean."

"Whatever you say, Sir Lawrence." Jeremy scooped up a
bite of the lamb, carrot, and potato stew Lina had made.
"Hmm, very good."

The Indians were more cautious, using their fingers to nibble
a piece of lamb. Looking surprised, they pulled long flat pieces
of bread from their own supplies and used them to scoop up
every bite, juices included.

When one saw Lina's curious glance, he offered her a piece.
She turned it cautiously, sniffed it, then scooped up a bite of
stew. Hmm, not bad. She scooped up another bite with the
savory utensil.

Jeremy smiled. "Do you like Central America's staple?"

Lina nodded, her mouth full. When she'd swallowed, she asked, "What is the bread called?"

"A tortilla. Before our four months are out, you'll be sick of the sight of them, I predict. When our fresh food runs out, we'll be limited to beans and tortillas if we can't find game."

Doubtfully Lina turned the flat, hard piece of bread. "But who will make them?"

"We can buy them from the Indians, but if I have to, I can do a fair job myself. I've subsisted on them before." Jeremy leaned back on his elbow and sopped up the last of his juice with another tortilla.

With some relish, Jeremy assigned Baxter to clean-up detail after dinner. Baxter grumbled but rinsed the dishes in the river. The sun's last rays danced on the water, wavering on the ebb and flow before the throaty darkness swallowed them. Lina slapped at her wrist.

As soon as he'd finished eating, Jeremy had accepted some of the paste offered by the Indians, and was busily rubbing it on his skin. "Lina, this stuff doesn't smell good, but mosquitoes find it equally unpleasant. I suggest you try it."

Lina took one whiff of the little clay pot, then shook her head. "No thank you. Surely the smoke from the campfire will keep them away." She slapped at the side of her neck.

Jeremy grinned and kept rubbing.

As the velvet night shrouded them, the bites came more frequently. The three Britons tried moving closer to the fire, but that only allowed them to see the living fog whirring about their heads.

Lina couldn't slap fast enough. She tried turning her collar up; she tried wrapping her skirt about her knees and pulling a serape Jeremy had purchased for her over her shoulders. The mosquitoes always found an opening.

Finally, with an exasperated groan, Sir Lawrence stood. He snatched up a lantern and his notebook. "I'm going to bed, early or not. Good night."

Baxter hunched his neck down in an obvious attempt to lessen his exposed area and sent an exasperated look at the Indians, who had wrapped themselves in coarse serapes. Two were already snoring, their home remedies either very effective or they were accustomed to the bites. One sat on a fallen log, his old musket propped in the crook of his arm. His profile, lit by the flickering fire, was as strong and mysterious as the land that had birthed him.

As she squirmed and slapped, Lina wondered what he thought about as he stared into the jungle. She turned, but couldn't see a blasted thing beyond the circle of light. The droning in her ears was driving her as mad as the voracious bites. The fact that only occasionally did Jeremy slap at his skin somehow made her discomfort worse.

She surged to her feet. "I cry quarter. These pests have vanquished me. Will you how me how to set up my hammock?"

Jeremy stood. "I'll do it for you." He took a lantern and examined the trees circling the little clearing, casting the light up, down, and around before he was satisfied the trees were vacant of dangerous occupants. "Here, hold this. Take it with you if you need to, ah . . ."

Lina nodded, ducked behind a leafy, low-lying bush, then emerged, one urgent need subdued only making her itching more acute. "Hurry, Jeremy."

Efficiently Jeremy had unrolled a hammock on the ground. Now, as Lina watched, he pulled the strings at each end through a fine netting before he tied the strings around the branches of two adjacent trees. Carefully he flipped the netting down to cover the hammock entrance, pulled the netting ends taut to seal them, then stood back and waved his hand.

"Your couch awaits."

"I wish," Lina muttered. She'd slept in a hammock once, and found the way it conformed to her body restful, but she still preferred her creature comforts.

She glanced at her father. The lantern inside his makeshift tent outlined his own struggle. He slapped constantly, twisting and turning. Finally, he blew out the lamp and pulled his blankets over his head.

Great. This would be a long trip. Lina cocked her head and contemplated her own refuge.

"The trick is to be fast," Jeremy warned. "Otherwise you'll get the critters in there with you."

Nearby, Baxter was attaching his own bed, having watched Jeremy closely.

Jeremy took the lantern. "Ready?"

Lina slapped for the dozenth time at her neck. "Let me take off my boots—"

"Dammit, I told you, no! If we have to take back to the river in the night, you'll have no time to search for your shoes."

"It's hard enough getting in a hammock barefoot, now you want me to do it in clumsy boots."

Jeremy stood as unyielding as the towering trees.

"Oh, very well." Lina caught the netting in both hands, timed herself, then flipped it up, swiveled at the hips and plopped herself down, all in one movement. She was congratulating herself when she pulled the net down and pushed with her feet to allow momentum to help her adjust her weight.

The hammock swayed as, in her haste, she pushed too far. She fell sideways, her feet caught in the netting, and bumped out on the ground, her posterior taking the brunt of the fall.

Jeremy made a choked sound, set the lantern down and offered his hand.

She glared at him. "See? I feel like an ox in a china shop."

"Here, let me help." He disentangled her feet and lifted her under the shoulders. "I'll hold the netting for you as you get in."

Lina brushed his hand away, her pride more bruised than her anatomy. What had happened to her on this day? She was not usually accident-prone. "I'll not have you babying me for four months. I need to learn."

Propping her hands on her hips, Lina walked around the contraption. It looked simple enough, lying limp and quiescent, as if awaiting her to take shape. Must be the netting that made it tricky.

Scratching her cheek, Lina braced herself, then rushed it. A flip, a swivel, a duck, and she was there, the netting shielding her from the bites.

Again, she was fine until she brought her feet up. Then the hammock jerked violently from side to side as she tried unavailingly to balance herself. She fell harder this time, her feet once more caught.

She leaned back for a moment, her gaze tracking the strong thighs, slim waist, and broad chest to Jeremy's blank expression. "Don't bother. I see that crooked slant to your mouth."

He laughed. "I'm sorry, but you do make a picture. If you won't let me help you . . ."

Lina snatched her feet loose and scrambled up. "Go do whatever great white hunters do and let me figure this out for myself." His quirked brow allied with that devastating smile only made Lina more determined.

She waved him away. "Go."

He went to fetch his own hammock and spread it near hers.

This time, Lina approached her enemy cautiously, swinging it to see how it settled, propping a knee inside and swaying to test its high and low points. Finally, she took a deep breath and did her little dance, each movement carefully synchronized. This time, Lina waited for her weight to settle before she cautiously pulled her feet up. Almost there, almost there.

A hoarse scream sounded, echoing through the jungle. Lina started violently, her feet automatically reaching for terra firma. The hammock swayed. She slid out in an ignominious heap. A blur of motion caught the corner of her eye.

Jeremy had run to one of the long crates. As she watched, he drew out a rifle, its barrel gleaming in the firelight, dumped out a box of cartridges, and began loading them into the breach.

Lina went very still. Whatever had made the sound was apparently too big for the pistol. Lina scrambled to her feet.

The Indians started awake and inched as close to the fire as they could. The one on guard held his musket at the ready and turned in a slow circle.

"Dash it, I knew he had another gun!" Baxter stomped over to Jeremy. Jeremy held a finger to his lips, pulled his pistol, and offered it, butt first, to Baxter.

Her father flipped back his own net and ventured outside. "What was that?" he asked her.

"I don't know, but—"

The scream was closer this time. The hoarse cry had a raspy, hungry quality that made Lina swallow and reach for her father's hand.

Jeremy chambered a round and beckoned. "Get over here to the fire, both of you."

"Why?" The two Lawrences spoke together.

The fury in Jeremy's eyes acted on them like buckshot. They moved.

As she hurried, Lina wondered why Jeremy was staring at the trees. The thought had barely left her when she heard a rustling above her head.

She looked up—straight into two spots of jungle fire that burned an eerie green.

Chapter 9

MESMERIZED, LINA STARED into eyes that engulfed her like the jungle: wild, unfathomable, dangerous. As her vision adjusted to the darkness beyond man's feeble fireglow, she made out the laid-back ears, the proud head covered in spots. The rest of the powerful body was hidden by the huge leaves.

El tigre.

Lina knew the jaguar was second only to the lion and tiger in strength. It stalked its prey, then pounced.

Often from trees.

"Lina, Sir Lawrence, back away. *Very* slowly," Jeremy ordered softly.

They needed no second command. Somehow, Lina knew to keep the eye contact as she moved. She had the eeriest feeling the big cat was reluctant to attack. Perhaps it sensed the guns trained on it; perhaps it had recently fed; or perhaps it merely feared the scent of man.

"Shoot, Mayhew!" hissed Baxter when Lina and Sir Lawrence were ten feet away.

"Sometimes if you confront them, they back off."

Lina glanced at the others out of the corner of her eye, but she didn't stop until she was even with them. Jeremy stood ready to fire, one foot braced before him, the rifle snug against his shoulder. Baxter aimed the pistol like a man experienced with firearms.

The Indian with the musket stood farther back, his weapon clasped to his side. Easily accessible, but unthreatening. He muttered something to one of his friends. Soft-footed, the man inched over to Jeremy, one eye on the jaguar, and spoke.

159

Jeremy shook his head and replied, his gaze never leaving the cat. Now that Lina and Sir Lawrence had moved off, its ears had perked up again. It still seemed wary, watching for any movement, but its powerful neck had relaxed slightly.

The Indian didn't look happy, but he said nothing else. Lina noted that he sidled two steps until he hovered at Baxter's elbow. She wondered what he'd said to Jeremy.

Baxter apparently didn't notice the man. "Dammit, are we going to let some overgrown cat keep us out of our beds? Let me shoot it, Mayhew."

"Not yet. Can't you see it's hovering, uncertain? It knows there are too many of us for it to attack stealthily."

Baxter took a half-step forward. "Well, I—"

Jeremy grabbed his shoulder. "Stop right there!"

The cat stiffened again at Baxter's movement. Simultaneously the Indian beside him snatched at the pistol. It misfired. The blast echoed through the jungle, eliciting a flurry of squawks and grunts from hidden wildlife. Cursing, Baxter struggled with the Indian over the weapon.

Next a sound reverberated through the jungle such as Lina had never heard. The jaguar bared its fangs in a deep-chested, harsh roar, proclaiming its dominion—and their intrusion.

Its tail extended like a rudder, it jumped.

Instinctively, Lina screamed. Even as she backed away, part of her marveled over the animal's beauty and agility. Sleek muscles bunched beneath the gleaming, mottled coat as it bounded gracefully into the firelight.

Jeremy fired a warning shot at its feet. The big cat froze as a patch of jungle peppered its paws. Then, tail switching, *el tigre* tensed its haunches for another lunge.

Luminous eyes transfixed Baxter and the Indian. The pair had frozen in an embrace that would have been comical if their position had not been so perilous.

Jeremy waited until the last possible moment, but when the cat sprang, he fired. Six feet of tensile strength were shattered by a bit of steel. The jaguar collapsed midair, its vitality obscenely denuded into a hide that would adorn some rich woman a world away.

Blood pulsing from the chest wound, the jaguar gave one last coughing, defiant cry, rested its head on its paws, and died. The green eyes remained open, sentient for an instant, before they went flat. Lina bit her lip and looked away.

Guilt and fury almost choked her. Here, they were the invaders. The jaguar had only protected its territory.

Jeremy roughly propped his rifle against a tree. "Satisfied, Baxter? Look at her teats. She was suckling a cub."

Horrified, Lina swerved back around. Indeed, with the belly half exposed, Lina could see the telltale matted rings around the female's nipples.

The Indians clustered around the body, conversing in low tones that grew progressively angrier as they gestured from the jaguar to Baxter, and back again.

Jeremy snatched the pistol from Baxter's limp grip and snapped it in his holster. "For your own protection."

"What are they yammering about?"

"I imagine you'll soon see," came Jeremy's grim response.

Sir Lawrence approached the body to measure it. He made several notations in his notebook.

No one noticed as Lina hurried to their food, snatched something, picked up a lantern, and circled the tree where the jaguar had crouched. She glanced from the clearing, safe and open, to the thick brush. She held the lantern high with a steady hand. The circle of light flickered, then disappeared in the jungle.

Baxter and Jeremy still glared at one another.

Jeremy tilted his hat back. "Baxter, how in the name of God can you come here, expect to work with these people and even, if you can get away with it, steal their heritage, and still care so little about their culture?"

"I don't need a rootless adventurer to lecture me on Mayan customs." But, with a guilty glance at the lifeless form on the ground, Baxter moderated his tone. "What with the frequent depiction of jaguars in their art, one can only conclude that the jaguar was a god to the ancients. But surely the Indians of today are not so primitive. Why, one of our boatmen even wears a cross."

"The jaguar is still sacred to them. Even the Christians among them are devoted to their land, as you are, doubtless, to English soil. And the jaguar is lord of the earth for good reason." Jeremy's eyes darkened as he looked at the lifeless form on the ground. "If you want to live, I suggest you remember one thing: In this jungle, *we* are the invaders. The animals will treat us as such, and we must adapt ourselves accordingly."

"You mean retreat." Baxter sniffed.

"When prudent." Jeremy turned his head, then whirled in a circle. "Where's Lina?" he asked sharply.

Sir Lawrence's busy pencil faltered. When he saw no trace of his daughter, he surged to his feet. "Dash it, she's gone to look for the cub!"

Jeremy had already loped out of the clearing, grabbing a lantern as he went. Sir Lawrence and Baxter followed on his heels.

"Lina, where are you?" Baxter called.

"Daughter, this is no time—" Sir Lawrence broke off when he barreled into Jeremy.

Turning his head, Jeremy put a finger to his lips. Sir Lawrence peeked around one of his shoulders, Baxter the other.

On the ground before a large hollow tree, Lina knelt next to a playful bundle of fur. Supine, the cub batted at the palm frond she used to tickle its belly. It growled and bared pearly white fangs, its claws extended as it reached for the frond.

Sir Lawrence gasped. "Get it away. It may hurt her."

But Lina seemed unafraid. "You darling. I'm so sorry we killed your mama. You'll have to come with us—"

"That's not a good idea, Lina."

The shining white oval of her face beamed a happy smile up at them. When she saw Jeremy's expression, however, the glow dimmed.

"Why not?"

"You can't lead a jaguar, cub or not, through the jungle like a house cat."

As if to verify his words, the little cat stared up at the huge shadows who'd brought the strange starfire with them, blinking in the light. It rolled warily to its feet and backed into its hollow log. The alert green eyes glimmered with refracted light.

Lina rose and faced them. "Why? It will die if we don't take it."

"It will probably die if we do. How do you propose to feed it?"

Lina's face lit up again. She bent and picked up a can, turning it so they could read the label.

Jeremy scoffed, "A wild jaguar won't drink canned milk—"

"Oh no? Then how do you explain that, my intrepid jungle guide?" Lina pointed.

The men looked down, noticing for the first time the huge concave leaf Lina had filled with milk. Most of it was gone.

Baxter snapped his fingers. "So that's how you did it. Wondered why the little beast wasn't afraid."

"This cub has probably never even smelled man before," Lina pointed out. "Why should it fear me?"

"The cub's about the right age to be weaned," Jeremy reflected aloud. "The mother had probably not let it drink its fill for some time. Even canned milk probably tasted good to it."

"See? By the time we run out of milk, it will be eating."

Jeremy crossed his arms and planted his feet. "Indeed. Are you going to hunt for its raw meat?"

Lina mimicked his authoritative stance. "If I have to."

"Dammit, woman—"

"There's another alternative, you know," Sir Lawrence pointed out.

Blue eyes glared at him. "Stay out of this, Father."

Gray eyes widened with interest. "What's that?"

Sir Lawrence jerked a thumb over his shoulder. "Let them take him."

Jeremy swiveled and peered at the approaching lantern. One Indian nudged the other, nodding toward the hollow log. Both bent down to get a better look and apparently saw the luminous green eyes. They rose abruptly.

Baxter backed up a step. "Why are they looking at me like that?"

"How would you feel if someone had, shall we say, defaced the Trafalgar Square lions?"

Baxter scowled.

"I see you take my point. I suggest you stay close to me for the duration of the trip." Jeremy waited until the Indians had disappeared as silently as they'd come before turning back to Sir Lawrence.

"Interesting option, sir, but not workable. I've never heard of an Indian raising a jaguar as a pet. I believe they'd be appalled by the very idea."

"There's no choice, then," Lina said, turning toward the hollow tree.

Jeremy grabbed her arm. "Agreed. The poor little bugger will have to take his chances."

Lina's shoulders sagged. When his touch gentled, she twisted free of him. "Listen to me! We're responsible for the death of this animal's mother. If we leave the cub to die, we'll be living examples of all these Indians despise. Please, Jeremy. I'll take care of him by myself. I promise."

Jeremy sent an appealing look at Sir Lawrence, who approached his daughter.

"Lina, you haven't thought this out. I'm sure the cat would be a great deal of trouble. Getting into things, hungry all the time—"

"There's a reason for the saying 'Curiosity killed the cat,' Lina," Baxter inserted.

Jeremy sent him a surprised but approving look before he hammered at Lina again, "And in this case it may kill the girl who follows it."

Lina shook her head. "My mind's made up."

When three male jaws jutted out, she dragged the milk residue to the front of the log, and gently picked up the cub when it emerged. "Don't you see? This isn't some whim of mine. In a way, this cub represents both the reasons we've come here and the reasons the Indians are distrustful."

The cub had stiffened under the unaccustomed touch, but when she set it in her lap and stroked it under its neck, it relaxed. "If we leave it to die, we're invaders no better than Cortez, or Pizarro, despoiling these people's heritage and leaving destruction in our wake."

Sir Lawrence frowned at this repetition of an old argument; Baxter scratched his chin.

Jeremy, however, had gone very still, intent upon Lina's upturned, determined face.

"And we *are* different from them," Lina insisted, trying not to look at her father. "We came here in an attempt to understand the wonder and mystery of this land. How many people get the chance to so closely observe a jaguar cub in its native habitat?"

The cub had grown restless. When she held it gently in her lap, it turned its head and latched onto her restraining hand. She gasped.

Jeremy swooped down on it and lifted it by the scruff of its neck, then used his free hand to help Lina up.

Two deep fang marks on the side of her hand welled with blood, but she merely pulled a kerchief from her pocket and wrapped it about the wound. Jeremy handed the cub to a surprised Baxter. He held it, kicking and clawing, at arm's length. The grasp at its scruff pulled the little face into a grimace that offered a hint of the formidable temper to come.

"You win, Lina," Jeremy said gently, brushing her hair away from her face. "But let this,"—he lifted her hand—"be a lesson to you of what can happen here to the best of intentions, if they're misguided. Perhaps you should realize now that this land doesn't want to be discovered, or even admired by the rest of the 'civilized' world. Just like that cub"—Jeremy jerked his head toward the struggling cat—"it wants to be left in peace."

Lina shook her head. "I don't accept that. Surely these people want to know more of their own rich past."

Sir Lawrence swatted at his neck. "This is no time for a philosophical discussion. Dawn comes early. I suggest we retire." He picked up the lantern and gestured them ahead of him.

Lina went obediently, aware finally of the mosquitoes feasting on her. Still, Jeremy's words ran through her head with all the clarity of Mr. Edison's amazing phonograph, which she'd heard once at an exhibition. " . . . this land doesn't want to be discovered, or even admired . . . it wants to be left in peace."

The words seemed more dirge than lullaby as the hammock accepted her weight. She rocked from side to side, secure in the knowledge that the cub was tied to a tree, as safe in their circle of light as they. Yet her mind could not rest, despite her self-assurances.

She couldn't accept his appraisal. Why, her entire field of science was predicated on the benefits of the pursuit of knowledge. They weren't just treasure hunters, as he seemed to think. Archaeology was important not only to mankind's past, but equally to his future. Only in understanding history could they avoid its mistakes.

Guiltily Lina thought of the stack of bills on her desk at home. But surely they weren't wrong to want to share the glories of a lost era with the Western world—were they? Of what benefit were the artifacts to anyone, even the Maya of today, buried under the growth of centuries?

None. Lina tried to turn on her side before she remembered she couldn't. The droning of the frustrated mosquitoes pleased her. Finally, the soothing night wind, the crackling fire, and the rustling trees drowned out Jeremy's warning. She slept peacefully until near dawn.

The nightmare came.

How could she fly? That buzzing sound surely didn't come from her? Next, she stood at a distance and watched the giant mosquitoes sucking the blood from a Mayan king. He withered rapidly into a husk and blew away, his former grandeur now dust on the wind. The mosquitoes buzzed angrily and turned toward her, looking for fresh prey.

Dear God, their faces. Human caricatures of herself, her father, and Baxter.

Screaming, she tried to sit, and only ended up tangled in her netting. Soft footsteps approached, then firm hands freed her and pulled her out of the hammock against a strong chest.

"Hush, Lina. It was only a dream." Jeremy stroked her hair. "Listen. Hear the birds? It's almost dawn anyway. Come, finish out my watch with me."

Her heartbeat slowing, Lina sat beside Jeremy and watched dawn tinge the sky with a delicate glow. Birds heralded the new day just as they did at home, but the cries of every pitch and decibel sounded different. Both clearer and more melodious . . . freer, somehow.

For long, peaceful moments, Lina sat with Jeremy on the riverbank. She couldn't see more than ten feet away, for on both sides the river was surrounded by trees of every size and composition. However, she could hear. Beneath the birdcalls she caught an occasional grunt and rustle; she knew unseen wildlife abounded around them. With Jeremy so close, she wasn't frightened, but she felt, once again, that she was a stranger in a land harsh even to natives.

Finally, among the strange rhythm of life, she caught a familiar tap-tap-tapping. Straightening, she smiled her delight. "A woodpecker!"

Jeremy pulled her back in the shelter of his arm. "Of course. Everything here doesn't have claws and fangs—"

"Just prickles," Lina teased, running her fingers down Jeremy's muscled forearm. To her delight, goose bumps marked her passing. When she would have teased his other arm, Jeremy caught her hand.

"If you're implying I'm prickly, madam, you're right." Jeremy kissed her bandaged hand. "You've only to touch me to make me prickly—especially in one key spot."

Now it was Lina who tried to pull away, Jeremy who held her close to revel in her blush. "I suggest you remember that the next time you make free with my person I may want the same privilege." When her eyes darted away from his, he relented and released her to continue his lecture. "Some of the wildlife you'll recognize as similar to your own."

An enormous butterfly fluttered by as if to verify his claim. It was bright blue, with black markings, its wings so delicate the rising sun limned their structure as it flitted from flower to flower on the riverbank.

When it had flown away, Jeremy asked gently, "What did you dream, Lina?"

She shuddered. "I . . . can't talk about it yet." She glanced over her shoulder. The cub sat on its haunches, wearing the feline equivalent of a pout. Its rope was badly frayed in the parts it could reach. "I was going to ask how he did, but I can see."

"He wasn't happy at being tied up and took his frustration out in typical fashion. Jaguars are nocturnal, so he wanted to roam. I imagine he'll sleep soon."

Indeed, the proud little head drooped, then snapped upright again. Poor baby. Lina rose. "I'll feed it before we leave. Maybe he'll sleep then."

The cub stiffened when she approached, bared its fangs and hissed a hoarse cough that Lina knew was a warning. She stopped, poured milk into the clay bowl, added sugar and stirred, then shoved it within the cub's range. It took a swipe at her hand, and only her quick reactions saved her from a bad scratch.

She sat down a foot out of reach and crossed her ankles, propping her elbow on her knee, her chin on her hand. "You might as well get used to me. I'm the closest you'll get to a mama now."

The cub hissed at her again, sniffed the milk, then lapped hungrily, giving her an occasional wary look. When the bowl was dry, a pink tongue came out and licked the milk rim away from its mouth.

Lina laughed her delight. "You darling. You're nothing but a baby trying to be an adult."

At the pleasing sound, Jeremy turned from packing their hammocks into a crate. He watched Lina talk softly to the cub, an odd expression on his face. Then he caught Baxter's eye and returned busily to his task.

Baxter gave the Indians a wide berth, which was easy for him to do since they ignored him as beneath their notice. One of them went to the tree where they'd hung the jaguar skin to dry overnight and untied it, rolling it up with some difficulty since the skin had stiffened overnight.

Rounding the pile of waiting crates, the Indian passed the cub. The jaguar blinked in obvious confusion, its whiskers flickering as it sniffed. Then, in a lightning movement, it bounded to its feet and leaped to the end of its tether, tripping the Indian.

When the man fell, the pelt went flying. Happily at first the cub gamboled over to the fur, but when the familiar spots didn't move, it stopped. The green eyes widened as it lowered its head and sniffed, investigating the dead smell underlying the familiar scent it had waited for all night.

The Indian scrambled up and approached the cub to reclaim the pelt, but the little jaguar spat at him, ears laid back, eyes green slits.

The Indian glared and tensed, but Lina caught his arm. "Please, let him say good-bye."

The Indian obviously didn't understand her words, but he couldn't mistake the tears in her eyes as she stared at the vibrant, spotted bundle atop the lifeless one.

Jeremy slammed the last crate closed and approached, saying something. The Indian nodded and walked over to his canoe to dip it free of the rainwater that had seeped in overnight.

Her arms crossed about herself, Lina watched the cub paw at the pelt gently, then harder. He circled the shining skin, shoving with his nose, even nipping, but the pelt didn't move. Finally, the cub flopped down and rested its cheek against the soft fur, making short little grunting noises that sounded, to Lina, like sobs.

She turned aside, unable to watch any longer. Jeremy drew her close, patting her back, until she swallowed and pulled away. She wiped her eyes on the heel of her hand and straightened resolutely. "Is there anything I can do to help?"

Jeremy stared down at her, his features shadowed under his hat. His forefinger wavered in midair, then skimmed under her eyes so lightly she barely felt it. "You already have. Just by being you."

She inhaled sharply, but before she could speak, he whirled and retreated to his tasks.

For the remainder of that day, he seldom met her wondering eyes, rowing and poling as necessary along with the boatman. For the hundredth time, Lina wondered about Jeremy's childhood. Underneath his tough veneer lurked a tenderness he was careful to hide. What had hurt him so?

That night on the ship, passion or loneliness had loosened his tongue, but beyond the bare bones of the tragedy of his father, she knew little of the meat and substance of his past. He claimed to love his mother now, but said he'd not been back to New York in years. Somehow she knew he had no close feminine relationships at all. How, she wondered despairingly, could a man give love who'd never received it?

Clenching her jaw, Lina stared at the riverbank instead of at that enticing profile. She was a fool. Love bore no relation to the feelings this man stirred in her. Even if she wanted it to—which she didn't—she couldn't let that sappy emotion sway her. Her "love" for Philippe had devastated her once. Those tears now seemed a foolish indulgence.

And yet her heart chided her subterfuge. She'd never been good at lying to herself. She longed to share everything with this difficult, lonely man who needed love more than anyone she'd ever known. Her body, her thoughts, her dreams, her ambitions. But her lips were locked as surely as her heart unless Jeremy provided the key.

He would not. Perhaps, indeed, he could not. Those twin truths were among the hardest she'd ever had to accept, but accept them she must.

Depressed, Lina spoke little that day. Aside from the meals of cold beans, tortillas, and native figs, Lina's only activity was trying to build a relationship with the surly little cub. It slept in the canoe with them atop its mother's pelt. They'd tried to take the skin, but it had spat and clawed so that they finally rolled it up in the pelt and loaded it thus into the canoe. As soon as they were under way, Lina unrolled it, carefully tethering the little cat to a crate.

Like Lina, it seemed depressed, dozing fitfully through the day. The rains came intermittently, sometimes hammering at them, sometimes tapping. The jaguar simply curled into a tighter ball; the boatmen poled on, apparently impervious. Lina supposed that, eventually, she'd become accustomed to being soaked to the skin. At least the heat made it unlikely she'd catch a chill. She pulled the sopping poncho away from her skin, but it only seemed to cling the tighter when she let it go.

Even the scenery appealed less. She couldn't see much when it rained, and when it didn't, the haze of heat and humidity hung like a gauze curtain over the land. She'd long since given up trying to name the trees. Some had leaves as broad as a giant's hand; others seemed bedecked with fairy lace. Still others sprouted with flowers and odd-shaped fruits. The trunks varied in hue and texture from smooth white to rough black-brown. Many were valuable, for several times they passed piles of dyewoods lining the banks, apparently awaiting transportation to the Laguna de Terminos.

"What are you thinking?"

Lina hesitated then turned to Jeremy. "I'm wondering if these woods are as limitless as they seem, or if one day they'll be overforested, like those in Europe. They seem so vast . . ."

"I imagine the Pilgrims thought the same when they came to the New World. Yet American loggers are pushing farther and farther west to feed our population expansion." Jeremy stared at the passing banks, a brooding expression on his face. "And America is a much richer nation than Mexico. If you had a choice of feeding your family or saving your land, what would you do?" He took up his oar again and rowed, as if he knew her answer.

Indeed, there was only one. Lina knew she'd make the same choice humanity had, through the ages. She leaned back against the side of the canoe, sad at the futility of choices life sometimes offered.

The entire party seemed subdued that night, even the cub. Lina awoke once from a restless slumber to stumble into the bushes. The jaguar sat like a small idol with unwinking emerald eyes staring into the brush. When dawn came, she swore he'd not changed position.

As the morning progressed, the river narrowed, rushing rapidly along its banks. Some of Lina's apathy lifted, for the brisk breeze made the avid mosquitoes seek easier sustenance. Even the sun paid hesitant calls from time to time. It illuminated the slime-covered logs dotting the riverbanks. That one looked odd, Lina thought, staring at the barrel shape that narrowed oddly to . . . She gasped as it moved. The narrow end opened and she saw a deep, pink throat, the roof of the mouth lined with rows of sharp teeth.

"An alligator!"

Jeremy glanced at the bank. "We've only passed dozens just this morning."

Surreptitiously Lina tapped the sides of the canoe.

Jeremy laughed. "We're quite safe. They seldom attack canoes."

Lina shivered as two more "logs" snapped at each other, hissing, before they subsided back into the mud. Now that she looked closely, she spied the ugly snouts poking above the ooze.

At first the third day seemed as boring as the second. At Sir Lawrence's request, they rowed on right through lunch, relieving the boatmen so they could wolf down the *totoposte,* a type of dried tortilla, plantains, and cold black beans.

They all joined in the cold repast. Each of the travelers, for differing reasons, felt a like urgency to reach their destination. Perhaps that urgency accounted for Jeremy's relaxing vigilance.

He didn't notice when the dragonfly, its four wings living rainbows in the sunlight, buzzed their canoe, apparently attracted by the light flashing from Lina's ring. She turned her hand this way and that, growing still with delight when the creature lit on her hand, its wings fluttering slowly now so she could see their delicate musculature.

Then she tried to bring it closer to study it more thoroughly, for it was much bigger and brighter than the ones she was used to. It buzzed off, only to zoom in and out, frustrating her. Kneeling, she leaned farther and farther over the edge of the canoe, turning her hand, trying to coax it back.

She couldn't see the drifting, rotten tree floating before the lead canoe. The boatman's warning cry as he veered to miss it barely impinged on her concentration.

The next boatman passed down the warning. Jeremy said, "Hold on, L—"

He turned his head a second too late.

The canoe jackknifed sideways as the boatman shoved his pole against the shallow side of the river. Lina had time only for a startled cry as she toppled, headfirst, into the middle of the river. The swift current took her quickly downstream. She swam strongly against it.

The boatman behind made a grab for her, but missed, as did the one after, for they'd already maneuvered too far to the side of the river to avoid the tree.

Jeremy threw his paddle down so hastily it fell atop the cub, who did immediate battle with it. Even when the oar fell sideways, the cub still clawed and bit at its enemy, growling ferociously.

Jeremy barked something to the boatman. The man tried to turn the canoe, but their boat jolted as the boatman behind them was unable to turn aside in time to avoid hitting them.

Meanwhile, the current carried Lina ever farther downstream, though she swam gallantly against it. Her head bobbed under water, making Jeremy inhale sharply, then quickly reappeared and he realized she'd only thrown off the heavy poncho. Jeremy glanced around him, but the welter of boats would take some time to untangle and turn.

Lina would be exhausted by the time she made it to them. He'd have to help her. He was bending to remove his boots when he saw it.

A dark shape whipsawing up the river behind her.

Jeremy straightened abruptly, his heart shooting to his mouth. No time to remove his boots. Precious seconds were wasted as Jeremy withdrew his knife and stuck it between his teeth. Jeremy tossed his pistol to the boatman, hoping the man could shoot, then shoved hard with his feet against the seat of the canoe and dived into the murky water.

It tasted foul, but he hardly noticed. He was far upstream from her, but the current aided his agile strokes and powerful kicks. He closed the gap rapidly. Now he was in the water, he couldn't see the alligator.

But he knew it was there. Would he make it in time?

He couldn't even risk withdrawing the knife to warn her, for he might drop it. Vaguely he sensed shouts from the lead boatman and hoped Baxter was a good shot with a rifle—and that he'd get a chance to use it.

Then Lina was upon him, swimming strongly, still unaware of the powerful tail slicing cleanly through the water after her.

Coming closer. Ten feet. Eight . . .

Jeremy had time enough to register the expression on her face as she drew even, but his anger would have to wait. Carefully he drew the knife from his mouth and grasped the hide-bound hilt firmly. The tree should be almost even with them. "Try to catch the tree and put it between you and us!"

Her happy smile faltered when she saw the knife, heard the "us." She looked over her shoulder. That pink throat was much more imposing up close, gaping to display the razor-sharp teeth reaching for her kicking legs.

She didn't waste time in screaming, or freezing. Using her arms more strongly, she pulled herself forward, kicking sideways with her legs. The tree was so close it blocked the sunshine from her face. She took a deep breath and dived under it, then grabbed at the far side. It was slippery under her grasp, but desperation gave her strength. Her second grab held. She rested her cheek against the slimy bark, then lifted her head and peered from one end of the log to the other. Why hadn't Jeremy grabbed it with her? Had he . . .

Then she heard the splashing.

Remembered the knife between his teeth.

She closed her eyes, but imagination couldn't be worse than reality. Hugging the log with both arms, she kicked with her legs and pulled her weight upward. The one glimpse showed her little but a white miasma of boiling water, long legs wrapped about a leathery green body that whirled frantically to dislodge the weight on its back.

The tree slipped from Lina's numb hands. She made an abortive grab at a branch. The dead wood broke, and she was left with a sturdy club in her hands. Using her legs, partly floating, Lina swam backward to avoid being caught in the struggle.

She saw the flash of the knife before Jeremy sank it into the head, but he had to hold on with one arm, and the movement was awkward. She knew he must be aiming for the eye because he couldn't tilt the head far enough back to reach the throat. He only slashed the reptile's cheek—obviously angering it in the process.

It gave a hissing roar that terrified Lina and struggled so furiously to dislodge Jeremy that he had to tuck the knife in his teeth and hold on with both hands. The alligator spun again, dipping Jeremy in and out of the water.

Lina held the branch to her chest with icy hands, aware Jeremy wouldn't be able to hold on much longer. But was she brave enough to help him?

Then she saw the blood on Jeremy's leg.

Her nails dug into the stave. Not stopping to think, she grasped the stave in both hands, stopped kicking and let the current carry her straight to Jeremy and the alligator.

Unable to get the leverage to wield it like a bat, she did the only thing she could. When that white throat was exposed on the turn, she turned the pointed end of the branch skyward and drove it upward with all her might. The hole that appeared to ooze blood was pitiably small.

Then Lina was caught in those stubby front legs, her throat stinging under the scratches, the leathery skin abrading her arms and face.

The animal hissed and stopped spinning, its beady eyes staring straight into Lina's. She was too close to use the stave again. She kicked, trying frantically to get away. The branch slipped from her fingers, leaving her defenseless as that ugly snout turned toward her.

Lina closed her eyes, not wanting to see as well as feel, so she didn't see Jeremy take immediate advantage of the distraction she'd provided.

He slipped sideways and drove his knife deeply into the alligator's throat next to Lina's little scratch. Lina smelled a hideous, acrid scent and opened her eyes in time to see Jeremy stab again. Blood muddied the water around them, and farther down, near the reptile's hips, the water was stained yellow.

Then the great beast went limp. Lina was able to shove it away. Jeremy tucked the knife between his teeth again and helped her make for the bank. They pulled out of the river, mottled with reptile blood and their own, collapsing on the bank. They stared downstream.

The alligator rolled listlessly a couple of times, and sank. Its blood rapidly dissipated until nothing remained of its death throes but a faint stench. Soon that, too, was gone.

Birds called about them and insects buzzed. Lina knew the rhythm of jungle life would have continued the same whether it had been them or the alligator who perished. She dropped her head against the bank. Mud had never felt so good.

Then her pretty patch of blue sky was blocked by gray eyes looming over her like a thunderhead. Jeremy stabbed the knife into the ground next to her head. Lina flinched.

"What in hell do you think you were doing? I told you to hold on to that tree, not use part of it to attack the gator." Jeremy rested his palms on each side of her head, half lying atop her.

His strength and heat struck some visceral chord within her, but his arrogance also infuriated her. "I was only trying to help! The thing was trying to drown you and it was my fault you were in the water at all—"

"That's the first sensible thing you've said since we started on this blasted comedy of errors."

Lina pushed at him. He didn't budge. "Get off me, you oaf." Lina felt something growing against her leg. Her breath caught.

His eyes had grown even darker. This emotion, she knew, was far more of a menace to her pride than mere anger. Her heart tried to climb out of her chest, and she knew from his smile that he felt it. "Not until you say you're sorry for disobeying me. Prettily."

Lina gritted her teeth. "Go to hell."

A little groan escaped him as she struggled. "I've been there these three days past."

"What does that mean?" Lina went still and glared up at him. "Why, it's been an exciting trip so far—"

Jeremy reared back to look at her, the sensual haze lifting from his eyes. "Exciting for whom? My God, woman, in three days' time, you've been thrown from a mule, almost been bitten by a snake and eaten by an alligator, plus you've decided to take a wild jaguar as a pet. And the Usumascinta gets more dangerous the farther we go in."

Lina arched an eyebrow at him. "Surely your life would be simpler if I just disappeared? I can see I'm a vast trial to you."

Jeremy's fingers tightened on her shoulders, then he pushed away from her and swiveled until she saw only his flexing jaw.

Lina shoved her wet hair back and sat up. "I'm sorry, Jeremy. I haven't deliberately gotten into trouble. This is just such a lovely place, I can't help being curious about it. I am a scientist, after all. But I promise to be more careful."

"I've heard that before. Not very long before you fell into the river."

Lina rested a hand on his tense forearm. "Thank you for saving my life. Is there anything I can do to make it up to you?"

That touseled blond head turned. Even with his hair wet, his clothes torn and bloodstained, he still exuded a potent masculinity that made her toes curl in her wet boots.

"Yes," he said softly. "I'll let you make it up to me. You've shown me hell for three days. I think I deserve a little glimpse of heaven for saving your life."

Lina swallowed. "And what's that?"

Jeremy cocked his head, listening, then he smiled that bold adventurer's smile. "Come on. I'll show you."

Lina accepted his hand and squished out of the mud with him. "But . . . the others—"

"They got caught upstream in some roots. It will take them a bit to work their way back to us. They'll see where we climbed out of the water. But just in case . . ."

While she blinked in shock, he unbuttoned his sodden, ripped and bloody shirt and threw it on the riverbank. Then he held out his hand again. "Come."

Such a little word, but loud with the challenge shimmering in those silvery eyes. Lina hesitated, looking over her shoulder at the river. It carved a serpentine path through the jungle, and she knew it would be some time before her father caught up to them.

She looked back at Jeremy. His broad chest glistened with moisture, the gold hairs glowing in the sunlight, limning the purity of his muscles. His strength had just saved her from an ugly death. He favored one leg, and she saw that one of his boots was ripped, but his bleeding had stopped, and she didn't think the injury was serious.

It could have been. She owed her life to this man.

But did she trust him?

Even more germane—did she trust herself?

The answers were beyond her control. With a life of its own, her hand caught his strong one and clung as he led her deeper into the jungle.

Chapter 10

THE POOL BROKE suddenly from the brush, like an oasis succoring the desert. Lina stopped in delight and spun in a slow circle. A small waterfall gurgled down a cliff, its exuberant spray marrying with the serenity of the pool, begetting a veritable bower of flowers.

Lilies as huge as dinner plates floated on the quiet end of the little pond. Flowers of every hue from deepest violet to dazzling white grew around the water, some bedecking bushes, some twining about trees, others nodding atop delicate stalks.

Lacy butterflies and corpulent bees flitted from banquet to banquet, grizzled with pollen that would spread the bounty of life. Energetic fish flashed in the pond as they grazed near the surface. One bold fellow leaped out of the water, his scales rainbow-hued in the sunlight, swallowed an unwary fly, and plopped back home. The pond rippled. Myriad, disturbing reflections caught Lina's attention.

She finger-combed her filthy, tangled hair and tried to brush the worst of the mud off her shirt, but it was hopeless. She hesitated, then said in a rush, "I know why you brought me here, and it's very improper, but I'm so filthy and the water is so inviting . . . Will you turn your back until I'm undressed? I'm going to keep my chemise and drawers on."

Jeremy's strong mouth trembled, then he politely turned his back. "Most proper. I can assure you the only dastardly designs I have on you at the moment are as a back scrubber."

Lina chuckled. "I remember a time, oh so long ago it seems now, when you offered me that service." She bent and wrestled off her boots.

"And such a lovely shade of pink you wore to go with your cherry-red gown. Perfect as you were, I think I prefer you the way you are now."

Lina paused in the act of rinsing her shirt by the water's edge. "What do you mean? I'm the same." She stepped out of her split slip and skirt, rinsed them and spread them out.

"No. The real Lina isn't a pocket princess, content to sit upon her pedestal, as I confess I first thought." When water splashed, Jeremy inched back around.

Lina tossed her head back under the water, unaware of the picture she made. White throat arched, eyes closed in enjoyment, she displayed the blatant vee of her bosom. The more salient parts of her anatomy were hinted at beneath the bluish gauze. She straightened, glistening, emitting a joy that led Jeremy straight to her side as surely as Polaris guided the lonely traveler.

As he came, he said, "The real Lina is an adventurer who embraces life as fiercely as she shares it." Holding her eyes, he tugged off his boots and socks, throwing them willy-nilly where they landed.

"Like you, Jeremy?" she whispered. "With one important difference."

His fingers froze on his belt. "What do you mean?"

She didn't want to spoil the bliss of the moment, but she felt so close to this man. They were alone, their barriers lowered by the danger they had just shared. Were they low enough?

"Sit. Let me see to your leg." She waded to the edge of the pond, afraid to look down at the clinging chemise. The water was around her waist now.

Jeremy's gaze drifted downward, then, his abrupt movements testifying to his feelings, he sat on the bank and let her roll his pants leg up. She turned his strong ankle this way and that to examine the long gouges. They were superficial, thank God. A smile played about Lina's lips. "The gator must not have liked the taste of your boot."

"No, he didn't like the bite of my knife. I've seen gator wrestling done a number of times. I never thought I'd try it myself." Gallantly Jeremy watched her face, but as if he couldn't help himself, he traced the rim where batiste met skin.

"But I never knew I'd have so much at stake. We're both lucky to be alive, you know."

Lina pulled his leg into the water and used her palms to soothe away the mud and dried blood. "I know that. But I know that every day of my life, Jeremy." Her lashes lowered, but he must have caught the hint of sadness in her eyes.

"And you think I don't."

She tugged his leg fiercely to her bosom. "Please, Jeremy. Be honest with me, and yourself. Why do you continually put yourself in danger by coming to places like this?"

Cupping her face in his palms, Jeremy leaned so close that his breath brushed her cheeks. "I'll answer your question if you'll answer mine first. Why are you so reckless, Lina? I saw the look on your face as you swam against a swift jungle river current. Fear? No. Distaste? No. You *enjoyed* yourself. What is it in *you,* Lina, that brought you here?"

Lina tried to pull away, but he held her face steadfast. Nothing could shield her from the power of those gray eyes—least of all her own honesty. "It's not something I think about, but I guess I'm determined to live life on my own terms and not impose the limitations on myself my father attempts. If I were his son, I'd not have to fight to go on every dig, or be forced to ride in the middle canoe. I am a capable person first, not just the female my father sees." The passionate tenor of her voice softened. "Besides, something even more basic drives my, ah, recklessness. And truly, I don't deliberately get myself into trouble."

"I know that. I think I also know what your more 'basic' drive is."

Lina held her breath. The liquid tenderness in Jeremy's eyes seeped through her pores more deeply than the water.

"You love life, Lina. It shines in everything you do. You fell off the mule because you were so enchanted by your surroundings. You fell out of the canoe chasing a blasted dragonfly. Why do you think I was so reluctant to lead you here?"

His understanding of her character gratified Lina. No other male had ever seen past the pretty casing God had cursed her with. Could he be so honest with himself? "It's your turn, Jeremy. Tell me why *you* come to the jungle so often."

Jeremy tried to drop his hands but she caught his wrists and cradled her cheek into one of his palms.

A long sigh escaped him. "Like you, I've never given it any thought. I just knew that something drew me here, but . . . you may be right. I enjoy danger for the exact opposite reason you do. I . . ."—he swallowed—"I haven't much cared if I lived or died for too long now. Until . . ."

"Until?" Lina whispered. She turned her head and kissed his palm.

"Until I met you. I see this jungle anew through your eyes, Lina. And it is a lovely place. You fit here, you know. Beautiful. But dangerous."

Giddily Lina hugged him, her breasts tingling to the hard warmth of his bare chest. There was hope for them after all. But they'd had enough seriousness for the nonce.

It was time to play.

When he would have kissed her, she pushed with her feet and backstroked to the middle of the pond. "Join me. I dare you."

That crooked smile was devastating. "I've never been one to turn down a challenge. Especially when the reward is so sweet." Molten silver ran down Lina's face, to her arms, lingering on her breasts. She reveled in the warmth.

Slowly Jeremy removed his belt, then his fingers went to the buttons of his breeches. Lina's paddling legs went still. She floated, waiting, torn between yearning and fear. Now that he was opening his guarded heart to her, inch by inch, she knew the moment would come when she would not be able to resist the allure first exchanged on the steps of the Hotel de Paris.

Jeremy glanced over his shoulder at the turn to the river, then back at her wide eyes. Looking disgruntled, he joined her in the water, pants and all.

"Thank you, Jeremy." Lina tried to imagine her father's expression if he found them emulating Adam and Eve. The picture refused to come.

He waded closer to her. "As I told you, drawers are superfluous in the jungle. Your modesty needs protecting." An uncomfortable look flashed over Jeremy's face. His hands went under the water. He wriggled a bit, his hands in the area of his hips, then sighed in relief and added grimly, "As does my own."

Lina had a fair idea of what he meant, but splashed water under her arms to hide her smile. "I wish we had some soap."

Jeremy leaned over to a thick-leaved plant and snapped off a couple of stems. Squeezing juice into his palm, he then rubbed his hands together and held them wide, displaying a thick lather. "See? The jungle provides. Come here, and I'll wash your hair."

Lina caught his wrist and sniffed. "Not exactly attar of roses, but it's better than alligator pee."

Chuckling, Jeremy ran his hands through her hair. "That's another thing I like about you—your honesty."

Guiltily Lina closed her eyes, wondering what he'd say if he knew his presence here had been perpetrated on a lie. No time to think about that now. She groaned as he rubbed her scalp from forehead to nape and back, his strong fingers gentle yet firm. "Blasted honest, my father always said. I fear I've been a sore trial to him."

Jeremy muttered something that might have been agreement or denial, pulling her long hair out in a thick rope, winding it about his hands to suds it. He snaked it over her shoulder and used the rope as a sponge to wash her arms and collarbones. Goose bumps pimpled Lina's skin. "That feels so good."

Jeremy didn't reply, but his breathing quickened.

The feathery glide of her own hair stroked lower, circling the edge of the chemise that was virtually transparent in the water. Lina didn't know what she revealed to him as he sank back in the water, drew her head upon his chest, and cupped water in his palm to rinse her hair.

Lina knew nothing but sheer sensual delight. The bites, the dangers, the heat and discomfort of the past three days washed away with the grime. A little bit of heaven Jeremy had promised her. Where better to find it than here, in this little bit of Eden?

He cradled her against his shoulder now, floating with her half atop him. He'd broken another leaf against her neck and now rubbed in soothing, circular motions. The pattern widened gradually, so when his gentle palm enclosed her breast, it felt right. The heat of him sank through cotton, to flesh, through muscle and bone, warming Lina clear to her soul.

Her eyes drifted open. Propping her cheek on his shoulder, she looked up at him. His eyes had darkened to that elemental gray that portended storms, lightning, and doom to her virginity. She owed this man her life. If, in giving herself to him, she could teach him to revel alike with her in God's greatest gift, then the price was small. She was too shy to voice her feelings, however, so she lay in his arms and let him feel and look his fill.

"It's only a matter of time for us, you know," he whispered, his mouth full even before it took hers. "There's too much between us now to allow for losers. We truly made a golden wager, Lina. We'll both win."

He tipped her head back and kissed her, his lips as languorous and silken as the water. Soothing, however, they were not. The storm in his eyes somehow lodged in her breast. She knew naught but the thunder of the strong heart pounding beneath her, and the answering lightning in her own.

His hands kneaded her breasts, then rubbed back and forth over the nipples that stood proud for him. His lips opened, slanting across hers. His tongue slipped into her mouth, then invited her own to dance. Awkwardly, but gladly, she dipped and swayed with him, trusting his lead. Groaning against her lips, he clasped his legs about hers, stroking his hips against the rich curve of her buttocks.

They heard nothing until the voice came closer, outrage echoing over the pond. "Evangeline! Have you lost your mind?"

Jeremy's legs slid down. Lina sank into the water, the loss acute—until she surfaced to the full blast of her father's fury. His hands flexed at his sides as he stared at them from the shade of the surrounding trees. His face was indistinct, but his voice was reprimand enough.

Lina brushed her hair back, confused at the abrupt transition from ecstasy to humiliation. She looked from the snickering boatmen to Baxter's stony expression and sank into the water until only her face was visible. Jeremy pushed her behind him.

"We were both filthy, Collier. We exchanged only an innocent little kiss. You have my word."

Innocent? Lina felt the slick warmth between her legs and was glad of Jeremy's shielding back. Blast her fair skin.

Apparently Baxter wasn't fooled either. "Fat lot that's worth."

Lina felt Jeremy grow still, then he said mildly, "I didn't see you jumping into the river after her."

"Oh, so you were exacting payment, is that it?" Baxter fumbled for his pocket and withdrew a bulging wallet. "Men of your kind always expect payment. You'd do well to remember that, Lina."

The Indians' eyes left the guilty pair and settled on something more interesting.

Sir Lawrence knocked Baxter's hand down. "Take these savages back to the canoes. Lina, come here."

Jeremy waded out, throwing his arms wide to display his breeches. "See?"

Sir Lawrence glared at the bulging front of Jeremy's trousers. "Indeed. We were just in time."

With a last scathing look over his shoulder, Baxter wheeled and used the side of his hand to chop at the brush, obviously wishing it were Jeremy's neck. The Indians followed.

Jeremy handed Lina her rinsed shirt and skirt, turned, and planted himself in front of her.

Sir Lawrence bristled. "She's my daughter. I have far more care for her good name than some . . . roisterer whose idea of a cultural evening is a taproom brawl."

Lina dressed as quickly as she could with her shaking hands, for she felt Jeremy's tension.

"Do you, Sir Lawrence? Or is it your own good name you have a care for?"

"Why, you—"

"If you truly put your daughter first, you'd not push her toward an egotist like Baxter."

"I know what's best for my daughter."

"No you don't, Father." Lina circled Jeremy. "You never have."

"Lina, what do you see in this man? Some stupid wager could never account for—" Sir Lawrence glanced at the pool.

Lina's anger softened. In this, at least, he was like other fathers. He couldn't visualize the daughter he'd swaddled as a sexual being.

Couldn't she make him understand? Just once? "I see a man who saved my life. A strong, private man who will, when he learns to love, make some lucky woman sublimely happy." Lina heard Jeremy's swift inhalation, but she didn't turn her head.

"Men of his stamp don't wed, Lina. And even if he did, is gallivanting around the globe any way to raise children?"

"You should know."

Her father paled. "That's not fair. When your mother died, I had no choice but to take you with me or let servants raise you."

"I know, Father. And I'm not repining. My point is that 'gallivanting,' as you put it, didn't harm me."

Sir Lawrence rubbed his forehead and flicked a glance at the pool again. "Didn't it?"

Lina's mouth trembled, but she managed, "It was only a bath and a kiss."

"This time. You'll ride in my canoe from now on."

"No." Jeremy spoke for the first time since Lina had begun arguing with her father. "She's safer with me."

"Oh, indeed. She fell out of the canoe under your vigilant eye."

"My God, Father, look at his leg. He risked his life for me. Could you see Baxter diving into the river after me? Or"— Lina swallowed—"would you?"

"The question is moot because if you'd been with me, I'd never have let you fall out." Sir Lawrence took two steps forward. "Come. We've lost enough time. Ride with me so I can protect you as is my right."

It always came down to this, Lina thought sadly. His "rights," his "name." She was a walking Collier, not a vibrant woman with her own talents and flaws.

"Lina," Sir Lawrence said again, offering his hand. "Come. We need to discuss where we want to dig first anyway."

Her eyes widened. Would he consult her at last? Sir Lawrence smiled slightly, apparently confident of her choice. Jeremy only looked at her with those opaque gray eyes.

Sir Lawrence had insulted him when thanks were in order, yet Jeremy stood indomitable, inviolate. Nothing could hurt him, it seemed—for the simple reason that he let no one close enough. Their communion in the pool had vanished with the ripples.

He'd never coax, or even ask. He'd let her make her own choices.

And a choice it was. Scylla loomed on one side, Charybdis, the other. Lina clenched her fists, threatened equally by the engulfing whirlpool of need Jeremy represented and the monstrous, ancient yearning for her father's approval. Jeremy needed her, and she him, but if she chose to ride with him, the rest of the trip would be unbearable.

In a way, the choice was even more difficult, for Palenque itself was at stake. She'd come too far and worked too hard to have the dig ruined because of friction between her and her father.

Yet as quiet gray shadows enveloped her, she knew she couldn't be like the selfish society women who had obviously driven Jeremy to roam. Not even for her father, not even for her own determination to prove herself, could she reject this man.

"I . . . I . . ." She felt Jeremy stiffen. Lina moistened her lips and took a deep breath.

Inspiration struck. She exhaled slowly. "I think I should ride with Baxter."

Her father nodded. "Sense at last."

Jeremy scowled. "I won't allow it."

Turning her back on her father, Lina rested a hand on Jeremy's tense arm. "Please, Jeremy. It's a good compromise. We're only three days from the plantation. I'll be careful. I promise. Besides, Baxter is a good shot."

Jeremy shrugged her hand off. "Do as you wish. But I've seen your idea of careful. Just don't expect me to jump into the river after you a second time." Despite his limp, he managed to stomp away. He shoved a limb aside so hard that it swung back and smacked him in the forehead, but he didn't even pause.

The angry rustling of his passage faded, then died, leaving her lonely and tired. The flowers seemed drab now, the pool filled with sediment. The fragile understanding they'd

built here was spoiled just as surely. What did he expect her
to do?

Lina gritted her teeth over her rising tears. Dammit, she
would not be a fickle female. She was an archaeologist first,
a woman second. A tear oozed out, but she angrily swiped
it away.

Sighing, Sir Lawrence sheltered her under his arm. "Come,
child. You'll forget him once you're among civilized people
again. Remember why we came here."

Exhausted, Lina let him lead her away. She didn't contradict
him, but she knew Jeremy's image would be engraved on her
heart until she was very, very old.

For the next three days, for once she followed her father's
advice. Ignoring Jeremy's glares and Baxter's overtures, she
read and reread every journal they'd brought that even men-
tioned Palenque. When her eyes crossed from too much reading and her pages got wet in the frequent rain, she occupied
herself with the cub.

Slowly he was coming to rely on her. She fed him, watered
him, and played with him when he allowed it. The milk was
almost gone when, one evening as she sat by their fire, an
Indian brought her a fish he'd caught, jerking his head at the
cub. Lina wrinkled her nose, but fetched a knife and labori-
ously began boning the large, flat-bodied fish that resembled
a flounder.

Deep male mirth distracted her. Lina looked up, scales on
her fingers, to see Jeremy laughing. The Indians goggled at
her, then they, too, began to laugh, pointing and elbowing one
another in the ribs.

Lina threw the knife down. "What's so funny?"

Jeremy's voice shook. "The sight of you boning a fish for
a jaguar who'd as soon eat it whole, and your hand with it, is
rather humorous, you must admit."

"He's just a baby. He might choke." Lina gathered up the
meat she'd trimmed, piled it on a large leaf and carried it to
the cub.

He watched her with unblinking green eyes until she set the
leaf down near his feet. He bent his head, sniffed. A rough
pink tongue came out and licked. His head swooped down.

The small mound of meat disappeared, then the speckled head came back up. The cub swallowed twice and looked for more. Lina had sat near to watch him eat, and when he sniffed her hand, she was delighted, thinking he was growing to accept her. Then those fangs bared, and she barely scrambled away in time.

The Indians laughed so hard they had to sit down. Lina glared at a stifled sound from Jeremy. "If you say I told you so . . ."

"Me?" He spread his hands.

Lina marched over to the fish, picked it up by its fin, then tossed it to the cub. Rumbling with contentment, he made short work of the fish—bones and all. Still, Lina hovered over him protectively, and when he gagged, she supported his head and patted his back. He regurgitated, then more carefully lapped up the residue. Then he flopped down and suffered her stroking hand without batting at her as he usually did.

"Charming," Baxter said from his seat by the fire. "I've seen hogs eat more delicately."

Lina didn't even glance at him. She continued smoothing the soft fur until the little jaguar rested its head on its paws. Only then did she see the way Jeremy watched her.

No amusement was evident now. As she rose, he swept her with an encompassing stare. The words seemed torn from him. "You'll make a good mother someday."

"Will I, Jeremy?" She took two steps toward him, the firelight flickering in her eyes. "And what kind of father will you make?"

Their gazes held until Sir Lawrence cleared his throat. "Time for bed, everyone."

Whirling, Jeremy went to set up the hammocks.

The Usumacinta had grown wilder with every league. Finally, the party wound through the jungle to a point their boatman found significant. He pointed at one side and said, "Tabasco," Then he pointed at the other and grunted, "Chiapas."

Chiapas! Palenque! Lina threw off her lethargy and sat up. The river was wider, coursing them slowly beneath an avenue of giant trees, but she saw no mountains. Disappointed, she sat back and picked up her book again.

"Aoooo!"

Lina dropped her book. "What was that?"

Baxter, too, had stiffened. "I don't know."

Lina tapped the boatman on the shoulder, struggling for the Spanish, but he merely jerked his head at the trees without losing a stroke of his oar.

Lina frowned. Then two more screams joined the first. Turning her head, she called to Jeremy, "Someone's screaming! Shouldn't we stop?"

Jeremy yelled back, "It's only the *aluates*. Monkeys."

That first howl had elicited a chorus of otherworldly sounds. She had to cover her ears. "Dreadful. They sound like lost souls."

But the constant screaming, day and night, soon deadened her sensibilities. In fact, emulating Jeremy, she learned to be wary when the noise stopped.

The forest grew more imposing as they neared Palenque. Twice they diverged from the Usumacinta to the smaller tributary Jeremy called the Río Chico, then poled slowly along the even narrower, muddier Chiquito.

Here immense trees reached for the sky. Some had skeletal branches stripped of growth; others formed a veritable cornucopia of plant and animal life. Lying back in the canoe, soporific in the sweltering noon heat, Lina saw orioles darting in and out of their woven nests, yellow dots against a sea of blue. A giant vulture, its black and white plumage topped with a virulent red crest, lofted above them on the breeze the trees smothered at river level.

Seldom did man pass here. No one had to explain that to Lina, for the animals themselves made it plain by the way they exhibited little alarm. Giant lizards slithered down trees into the mud as they passed, their skins varying in shade from brown to purple. Leathery heads turned in mild curiosity, then dipped again to feed.

Tapirs lifted ugly snouts out of the water and trotted into the gloom. The sun itself had to struggle for preeminence against the choking growth. The unending verdure grew wearing, so imposing and primeval that Lina felt insignificant. Occasionally a tree Jeremy called a *jolocin* would relieve the ubiquitous green sea with giant pink blossoms, but even their beauty couldn't interest Lina. She was so eager to reach civilization again—even one built by people long dead—that the landing, finally, in Chiapas, was anticlimactic.

Her boatman, with an exuberant heave of his oar, pulled them into a wide lagoon and paddled to the side. Lina stared at yet another bank of lush grass and sighed, thinking they were stopping for lunch. She hopped out and stretched her cramped muscles.

Jeremy helped wrest his canoe to the bank, then joined her. "What do you think?"

"Of what?"

Turning her with a hand on her elbow, he pointed. "There. The mountain of Palenque."

Lina gasped. A four-sided mountain that rather resembled a trapezium, as Morelet had said, towered against the hazy blue horizon. She squinted, but couldn't see anything resembling buildings no matter how she turned her head.

"How long?"

"We can walk to Don Roberto's from here. He's only twenty miles away from Palenque. In the morning, we can lease horses from him and cover the last distance in a couple of hours."

"In the morning?"

Jeremy grinned at the disappointment in her voice. "I could use a bath and a real bed. They'll be our last for some time. Besides, I could never reject Don Roberto's hospitality. You've waited twenty-odd years. Surely you can wait one more night."

"I guess so." Lina went to help unload.

When their supplies stood on the bank, Jeremy paid the boatmen. He held his arm out, palm up, toward the path worn to the lagoon. "Just follow that. It will lead to the rancho. I want to thank them."

Lina went to each boatman and said, "*Gracias*," then bestowed on each a shy smile and a ten-peso tip. They nodded gravely. One looked at Jeremy and said something.

Dull red highlighted his defined cheekbones, but he just waved her away when she cocked an inquiring brow. "I'll follow shortly. Don Roberto is expecting us, and the entire household speaks English."

Lina followed her father and Baxter, who'd not even bothered with good-byes. They rounded two curves in the path, then stopped in shock. On one side, dense jungle stood. On the other, civilization ruled.

A corral filled with horses stretched in the distance. Close in, Lina smelled pigs and saw sheep and goats grazing on the edge of the jungle. A dazzling white plaster building rambled over the man-made clearing, fenced all around with long reeds obviously wrested from the jungle. Crude log storehouses and barns abutted three sides. A Spanish mansion this was not, but when they swung open the gate, they saw that the front door, at least, would have befitted any Castilian grandee.

Eight feet tall and five feet wide, the fine mahogany had been carved with a complicated coat of arms involving a lamb resting between a lion's paws. The handle was of wrought iron, shaped like a lion's paw.

Sir Lawrence was already pulling the tarnished brass bell beside the door. A pretty woman, wearing only a thin chemise and bright skirt, answered the door.

"*Señores! Señorita! Bienvenido.* Where is Jeremy?"

Jeremy, huh? Lina's eyes narrowed on the woman's lissome shape.

"He's paying our boatmen," Sir Lawrence replied. "We appreciate your—"

"Don't keep them standing, Carmen," a booming voice said.

The heavy door was flung wide to display a gleaming hardwood floor. The narrow foyer was lined with dark family paintings and sparsely filled, elaborate armoires.

Lina was more interested in the man who held the door in a work-roughened paw than in his home. His crest was appropriate, for his graying mane was as thick and bushy as any lion's. His thick brows topped piercing dark eyes that encompassed their travel-stained weariness in one experienced sweep.

"Come in, come in," he roared. "Carmen, get them some juice."

Carmen was still peeping anxiously around the edge of the door, but she answered, "*Sí, papa.*" She disappeared into an adjacent corridor.

Doors opened along it. Women exited, obviously drawn by the commotion. Don Roberto preened as his pride of females encircled him.

He introduced the six girls, all younger than Carmen, but Lina was lost in the sea of Spanish names. Sir Lawrence performed the same service for their party. By the time Carmen returned with a tray bearing a pitcher and three glasses, Lina was wilting. The plethora of exuberant humanity was too much after the isolation of the last week.

Again, Lina was swept by that piercing gaze. A big hand caught her arm and pulled her to the ladder-back chair next to the door. "Sit, señorita. Before you fall."

Lina obeyed. She gratefully sipped the yellowish, tangy juice he offered. Even tepid, it was delicious. "What is it?"

"Mango juice." Out of the corner of his mouth, he rapped something in Spanish. When she finished, he helped Lina up and himself escorted her to the last room off the long hallway.

One of his daughters had already turned back the cool cotton sheets for her. She bobbed her head shyly at Lina's thanks, then took Lina's boots when she removed them.

"Rest, señorita. Tonight, you must dance. We always have a fandango when Jeremy comes." With the air of a man who knew women—inside and out—he kissed her hand and watched her sit down on the bed, his arm about his daughter.

"But I'm so filthy—"

"I'll have a tub made ready in an hour. You can bathe before the fandango. The sheets will wash."

Quietly he closed yet another carved mahogany door. Lina's lids already felt heavy. The veranda door was open, but a latticed screen kept out the ever-hungry insects. It was still hot. It was still humid.

But the clean crackling straw mattress felt like a cloud. For the first time in days, she was alone, no snoring Indians on one side or grumbling Baxter on the other. No buzzing mosquitoes, or incessant rain, or glowing eyes staring at her from the wilderness.

She slept.

Darkness enveloped the room when she awoke. She stretched, feeling rested for the first time in weeks. The knocking came again, and she realized the sound must have awakened her.

"Yes?"

"Your bath is ready, señorita," Carmen said, opening the door.

Even in the dim chamber illuminated only by the hall lanterns, Carmen seemed a living flame in her red lace dress. Lina's heart sank. All she had were skirts and blouses.

She was not so churlish as to make her discomfort known. "Thank you, Carmen."

Carmen nodded carelessly, turned up a lantern and picked up the brush on the heavily carved dressing table.

Lina leaped off the bed. "I'm sorry, is this your room?"

Carmen nodded, then set the brush down and offered a brief but kind smile. "No matter. Tonight I sleep with my sister. Come with me. I show you the bath house."

An hour later, Lina felt clean, truly clean, and refreshed. She was making her way toward the patio behind the house when another sister caught her arm, offered something, then scurried after Carmen.

Lina found herself with an armful of soft cotton. The white dress had a low, ruffled neckline embroidered with silver thread. The wide sash was silver; the same silver thread wove through the voluminous hem. Lina hurried to her borrowed room and gladly threw off her clothes, feeling like a woman again.

She turned to leave, but the wavery mirror on the wall broadcast a reflection that displayed too much excitement for her liking. She borrowed some of Carmen's pins and piled her hair atop her head, but she could do nothing about her hectic flush. Or about the eagerness in her eyes for the sight of one man. Hopefully, he'd not find her face as transparent as she did.

Taking a fortifying breath, Lina went in search of the music, her toes already tapping to the music that rippled on the air like Spanish magic.

On the patio, Indians sat under the overhang, playing odd reedlike instruments. One thrummed a lute and another played a guitar. The music was a lilting Spanish country tune Don Roberto obviously remembered fondly, for his foot tapped as he listened. *"Muy bien, muy bien,"* he called to his men.

They grinned and redoubled their efforts. Jeremy sat next to Don Roberto, conversing in easy Spanish. "And how will the cacao crop be this year?"

Don Roberto frowned, opened his mouth, then shrugged.

Jeremy noticed the hesitation and wondered what he'd been about to say.

"Good, good, as always. I am a fortunate man, Jeremy. Once I get Cesar settled, I can retire to my rocking chair and watch my grandchildren play on the lands they will one day inherit." A shadow crossed his face. "If only *madrecita* were here to see it with me."

Jeremy shifted uncomfortably. "I was sorry to hear of your loss. I wasn't sure if this was a good time, but your agent assured me we'd be welcome—"

Don Roberto nodded vigorously. "*Sí, sí,* always. She loved you like the second son she always regretted not giving me." Don Roberto grinned as Baxter stumbled over an intricate step Carmen tried to show him. "Perhaps you should relieve your friend. Carmen will not be happy if he spoils her new slippers."

"He's no friend of mine," Jeremy muttered before he could stop himself. He hoped the sisters would continue to keep Baxter busy once . . . Jeremy caught his breath.

Don Roberto leaned toward him, but when he saw Jeremy's attention elsewhere, he shifted his imposing bulk in his massive carved rocker to broaden his view. "Ahh, I see." He gave his eldest daughter a sympathetic glance, then he smiled and leaned back to watch.

Shyly she stood on the edge of the light, her hair as velvety and shiny as the star-studded night. Seeing it so contained instead of in its usual braid merely whetted Jeremy's appetite to tumble it about her shoulders—and his own. The thin cotton lovingly molded her curves as the wind built for yet another rainy night. Silver trim glittered in the bouncing lantern light, accenting the value of her physical and spiritual beauty.

She paused and looked around, and instinctively Jeremy knew she searched for him. Her beautiful sapphire eyes sparkled, and her skin had never been a purer ivory.

The music faded from his consciousness; he didn't feel Don Roberto's probing stare. His world had narrowed to one girl and the world he could have with her. He'd risen, but he stayed rooted, shaken to his very bones, wondering why he had taken so long to see it.

She was precious to him.

She was perfect for him.

He wanted her body—and her heart.

He clenched his hands on the need to hoard her, protect her from Baxter and any other man who dared approach. Yet Lina would be angry at his impulse for the simple reason that it was not necessary. The second revelation struck him with equal force: He trusted her. He, who had distrusted women all his life, believed in this valiant sprite.

The man who won her need never fear she would stray. She was incapable of lying, or subterfuge. She was as sure and steadfast as the ship that had brought them together.

The man who wins her love will be fortunate indeed. By a simple substitution of pronoun, he echoed her own description of him earlier that week. Jeremy searched his feelings, but his gut didn't shrink in fear of that simple little word, as it had for so long. Too long.

Happiness was not gifted to humanity along with life. It had to be earned, with toil, tears, and tenacity.

God knew he'd toiled enough. Tenacity was all that had kept him going sometimes. But tears . . . for the first time in years, he felt them welling in his eyes as he watched her. And he knew, with a certainty Lina had forced upon him, that denying his feelings had almost lost him the ability to feel.

Joy carried him forward. He was unaware of Don Roberto's understanding appraisal, or of Baxter's glance at Lina above Carmen's head.

Lina spied him. Her mouth trembled into a smile as her eyes met his. The dancers, the bouncing lights, the scents of the banquet all faded from Jeremy's senses. He heard nothing but his beating heart, saw nothing but a small girl with generosity enough to persist in the face of his rejection. What matter that she'd known another man? In his arms, she'd forget all but him.

No more would he turn away from her for fear she would hurt him. Whether he won or lost their golden wager, the rest of his life would be dross without her. He moved toward her to take what was his.

A handsome young man stepped in her path and clicked his heels together. "Señorita, I am Cesar, son of Don Roberto. I regret I have just returned from business in Campeche. May I have the honor of this dance?"

Jeremy stopped, blinking, as Cesar kissed the hand that belonged to him.

Lina looked around Cesar, then at the expectant sisters. She let Cesar put her hand on his shoulder and moved with him to the gay country tune. He said something that made her laugh.

Jeremy's jaw tightened. A big hand fell on his shoulder. "He will leave her alone once I explain to him."

Jeremy turned and smiled wryly at Don Roberto's wise face. "Am I as transparent as that?"

"Only to one who knows you well." He watched as Lina matched Cesar's complicated steps. "I approve your choice, Jeremy. I've never heard of a female archaeologist. Is she as intelligent as she is lovely?"

"Yes."

"*Muy bien.* I wish you joy of her." As Baxter bowed his thanks to Carmen and hovered on the edge of the patio, obviously wondering how to break into Lina's dance, Don Roberto added, "And I wish you luck. That one wants her too. And he does not always play fair."

But it was not Baxter who concerned Jeremy. Lina's attraction to Baxter had obviously died. Cesar, however, was a bold, handsome duplicate of Don Roberto in his youth. And Jeremy had often thought that Don Roberto could give charm lessons to Don Juan. As the music segued to a stop, he hurried forward.

However, at a signal from Cesar, the musicians fired up again. This tune had a rapid, bold staccato that was the natural inspiration for clapping hands and stomping feet.

Jeremy stopped. Dammit, he didn't know how to dance the flamenco.

But Lina apparently did. Yet another skill learned in her travels, probably. Glumly Jeremy watched as Lina circled Cesar, her elbows high in the air as she clapped her hands and turned her head, staring at her partner all the while. Her stamping feet made the full skirt billow about her legs. The wind displayed a pleasing glimpse of ankle and even, on occasion, a scandalous length of calf.

Cesar's handsome face came within kissing distance of Lina's as, their necks arched in opposition, they circled, hips thrust forward, feet stamping. They reminded Jeremy of trumpeter swans—who mated for life. Before he stopped to think, Jeremy surged forward.

The expression in those Latin eyes was one he knew. He tapped Cesar on the shoulder.

Cesar's feet slowed, but didn't stop. He frowned. "Jeremy, my friend. But not now—"

"It's good to see you, Cesar. But I've yet to dance with the lady. And I saw her first."

The rose in Lina's cheeks climbed to her forehead. "But your leg—"

"Is fine."

Cesar glared, but then Don Roberto rumbled at his side, "Come, son, tell me if your journey was fruitful." He caught his son's arm and pulled him to the side of the patio, whispering in his ear.

Jeremy waited long enough to see Cesar's face fall with disappointment, then he bowed to Lina. "Madam, I request the honor of this dance."

"Request? That's your idea of a request? Where's your club and bearskin?" But Lina's irritation dissipated on a sigh as Don Roberto nodded to the musicians. They struck up the flamenco music again.

"Come, angel. Dance with me." Did his own yearning arouse hers? Jeremy wasn't sure, but when his foot tapped, hers did likewise. He'd observed the flamenco many times, and this night had watched the movements closely. He'd always had a good sense of rhythm. He was also attuned to her, and sensed when she would turn, or quicken her steps.

Those on the sidelines clapped, urging the musicians on. They complied, playing faster. The space between the two dancers narrowed as the steps grew more intricate.

Dance in, circle. Retreat, approach, circle. Trousered legs brushed full skirts. Skirts fluttered as woman backed away.

Man advanced, his very feet stomping his desire.

The tempo quickened.

Gray eyes flashed like the silver on Lina's gown, warming the feminine curves that were so close, yet untouchable. Blue eyes beckoned, basking in the flames, only to retreat behind long, teasing eyelashes. Lina tossed her head and laughed. Her hair tumbled free, bouncing with all her gaiety and life, flicking him in the chest as he turned, her eyes never leaving his.

Mesmerized, Jeremy duplicated her every movement. Had she danced to a precipice and beyond, he would have followed. The passionate music thrummed in his blood.

Touch her. Hold her. Keep her. The words ran through his fevered brain, far more invigorating than a pale one-two-three. His feet pounded with the rhythm of his heart, but no matter how perfectly he matched her, she was ever just a touch away.

The clapping from the sidelines slowed, then faltered. Silently, the others watched. The flamenco was always passionate. But this . . . this was a mating dance.

Jeremy's virility, all tensing muscles and untempered power, was a perfect complement to Lina's wild beauty. Her lips were parted, as red as her cheeks. Her hair seemed to have a life of its own, curling about Jeremy's shoulders and neck like clinging arms.

Now they were so close that the lantern light behind couldn't squeeze between them. Their hips arched forward, they danced, hands barely clapping now as eyes and feet flashed. Thrust, retreat. Thrust, retreat.

Breaths quickened on the sidelines—with one exception. Sir Lawrence set aside his half-full plate and rose.

The music crescendoed. Jeremy's legs disappeared in billowy white as the length of his body pressed against her. He was far closer than the dance required, but Jeremy had forgotten the spectators, or even that he danced.

In that last moment, they melded into one immutable force, moving together, hips weaving, faces so close that their noses brushed. With a final exuberant chord, the music stopped.

Jeremy should have retreated and bowed to his partner. He should have kissed her hand and fetched her a reviving glass of juice.

But Jeremy had never lived his life by etiquette. The thirst he saw in her eyes could not be quenched by liquid. He had put that need there, as surely as she had drawn the best of him.

With a harsh groan somewhere between a request and a demand, he pulled her into his arms. With a soft sigh of surrender, she went. Their lips met, but they only brushed before Sir Lawrence was upon them.

He pried Jeremy's arms away and pulled his daughter upright. "Mayhew! Lina! Our hosts will think us barbarians."

Two pairs of dazed eyes blinked, focusing on the ring of faces. Lina's heightened color deepened, then faded. She bit her lip and looked down.

Jeremy disguised his own flush with a rueful smile. "Sorry. The dance and the wine do rather go to one's head."

The excuse fooled no one, but, with Don Roberto's lead, they all retreated to the banquet.

Sir Lawrence hovered at Lina's elbow for the rest of the night. She toyed with the fragrant pork and tomato stew, responding to Baxter's overtures in monotones.

Jeremy let his eyes do the talking for him. Sir Lawrence glared, but he couldn't stop their silent communion. Lina's half-smile was headier than the maize spirit Jeremy consumed by the glassful. She'd forgotten everything during their dance, just as he had. Before them all, she'd proclaimed her response to him. He could afford to let Baxter monopolize her now.

She was his. Soon enough, she would admit it.

Late the next morning, a hasty breakfast of fruit and ham was interrupted by a workman. His clothes rumpled, his forehead bleeding, the man erupted onto the patio and broke into a spate of Spanish.

"What's the matter?" Sir Lawrence asked, breaking his silence toward Jeremy.

Jeremy listened. The relaxed expression he'd worn since he'd met them at dawn had changed to one of concern. "Some of the Maya of the area are rebelling again against Mexican rule. I was afraid of this. They resent Don Roberto as a representative of over 300 years of oppression. They sent warriors to try to burn his crop, but his men were better armed and they prevailed."

Cesar hurried after the worker. Don Roberto beckoned to Jeremy and led him to a quiet study. As soon as he closed the door, Don Roberto said, "Are you sure it's wise for you to go to Palenque? You'd all be safer here. I'm sorry, but I don't have enough weapons to lend you for your workers. I can only spare two for your friends."

Jeremy had already arranged with the boatmen to hire men from the villages in the area, yet now he wondered if that had been wise. Perhaps they should have restricted themselves to the workers Don Roberto could spare. But they'd made the entire journey without incident, so he'd hoped that the uprising he'd heard about had been exaggerated.

"My party will never agree to losing so much time moving back and forth. Besides, we pose no threat to the Maya. They know we'll only be here a short time."

"It's your neck, my friend. But the girl . . ." He sagged down into his chair. "I don't let my *niñas* off the plantation unless I send them with an escort. Of course, some of the young men could be in danger too . . ." His face grayed, and he rested his forehead on his palm as if he couldn't form the words.

"What?" Jeremy leaned his palms flat on the desk. "You don't have to mince words with me, Don Roberto."

"There are rumors that some of the Mayan priests are practicing human sacrifice again."

Jeremy jackknifed to his full height. "My God. Why didn't you tell me this earlier?"

"Because they were only rumors, and you were already here. Once I met the English, I knew they'd never agree to go back."

Jeremy sighed. "You're right about that. Least of all Lina. I'll just have to be vigilant. Besides, I can't really believe they've become that savage." Jeremy turned toward the door.

"I hope you're right, my friend," Don Roberto said as he joined Jeremy in the hallway. "I hope you're right."

Lina contained herself—barely—until, at last, they were all mounted on the sturdy horses Don Roberto leased them. Her embarrassment at her unseemly behavior last night slowly eased. The entire household had greeted her as an honored and respected guest.

Don Roberto, as usual, was spokesman. Responding to her warm thanks, he bowed and kissed her hand. "*De nada.* Come again. Soon."

Now, for the tenth time, she tried to peer through the trees at the waiting mountain. She told herself that her indiscretion was caused by sheer giddiness. After all, a twenty-year journey was about to end. Nothing, now, stood in her way but the last twenty miles. They should cover the distance by late afternoon, she calculated.

Finally, Jeremy quit speaking to Don Roberto, raised his hand in the air and led the party, single file, onto the jungle path. The leashed cub trotted along behind Lina. If he got tired, Lina intended to carry him in her arms, once her mount had grown accustomed to his scent.

Even after the week of captivity, he'd allow no one but Lina to touch him. Despite Jeremy's coaxing, she'd refused to leave him in Don Roberto's barn. She felt a curious responsibility toward the little cat.

Lina watched the easy sway of Jeremy's torso. He rode as well as he did everything else. Briefly, she wondered why he'd been so grim when he returned from Don Roberto's study. He'd waved away her father's query about the topic.

Lina's curiosity didn't last long, for, as the day wore on, her burning impatience grew. One plodding step after another seemed to stretch into eternity.

When they stopped for lunch, she wolfed down stew and *pozol,* a sugar-sweetened maize drink, and stood. The others were only half finished.

Wiping his mouth on the napkin he'd somehow managed to keep washed through every league of the trip, Sir Lawrence said, "Patience, child. We'll be there soon enough. Isn't the scenery spectacular?"

Lina barely restrained a snort. She'd seen enough exotic flora and fauna to last her a lifetime. The clear streams criss-crossing the landscape like crystalline ribbons were barriers now, slowing their pace. Even the flowers had grown tedious to Lina's overburdened senses. And the vast forest canopy that blocked the brutal sunlight had become a screen she longed to shove aside.

Jeremy stuffed the last of his tortilla into his mouth, chewed and swallowed. "We'd best hurry if we're to have time to set up camp tonight."

Lina smiled at him gratefully; he smiled back.

Grumbling, Baxter carried his food with him and mounted. Sir Lawrence did likewise. Lina had kneed her mount into a walk before they were firmly seated.

Several paces later, she said, "Jeremy, can't we trot?" She could carry the cub.

"Too dangerous. The going gets rough up ahead."

Indeed it did. Yet another ridge to scale. Lina dismounted long enough to fetch the cub, then held it before her on the saddle as her weary mare bunched her powerful hindquarters and began the climb.

Lina leaned forward, careful not to crush the jaguar, but he panted, seeming content to ride. She was so preoccupied in keeping her seat and not hurting the cub that the summit caught her unawares. Her hat slid over her nose. Her mare stopped. She clicked to it impatiently, but the horse didn't budge.

"Lina." Jeremy's voice shook with laughter as he backed his stallion next to her and pushed her hat back. "You're so busy covering the distance you haven't even looked around."

She looked up. "My God," she whispered.

Part Three

These cities . . . are not the works of people who
have passed away, but of the same great [race]
which . . . still clings about their ruins.
        —JOHN LLOYD STEPHENS,
                quoted in *The Adventure
                of Archaeology*.

Chapter 11

ACROSS YET ANOTHER tropical valley, Palenque beckoned to her. It was perched on a mountain shelf, yet looked down on its jungle domain. Peaks rose behind it, setting off the buildings that sparkled like diamonds in an emerald tiara. A stream wound a glistening ribbon down the hillside, ending in a waterfall that gave birth to lush growth that ultimately swallowed it.

Lina sighed in sheer delight. She'd seen many archaeological sites in her young lifetime, most of them disappointing, for little usually remained but ruins of the ancient kings who'd dwelled at Troy, Nineveh, and Knossos.

But here . . . these lordly buildings looked down on their domain, surely fitting abodes for the gods they'd served. The building mounds were strategically placed on the flat shelf in a design both natural and calculated. They seemed one with their surroundings, as innate as the sky above and the land below.

Lina knew all that modern science knew of these mysterious people, but this one look told her that if she returned annually for her lifetime, she would never exhaust the Mayan store of knowledge. Any people who could, with stone tools, wrest such beauty from the jungle, were civilized in a way beyond modern understanding—despite the evidence of torture and strange ritual in their carvings.

"If only," she sighed.

Her father had joined her on the slope. "If only what, child? Surely you're not disappointed. It reminds me of the Greek Acropolis, only it's better preserved."

"Yes. I was just wishing we had some way to decipher their writing, so we could really understand the history of the people who could build so well against such odds."

"That's why we're here, isn't it?" Without turning his head from the sight, Sir Lawrence said, "Well, Mayhew, what are we waiting for?"

Jeremy didn't answer for a long moment. Finally, Lina tore her gaze away and glanced at him. He frowned as he scanned the valley floor, then tracked each building, obviously expecting . . .

"Oh, dear Lord! Someone's beat us here." Lina urged her mount forward, but Jeremy caught the bridle.

"No! I'm going on ahead. You all follow twenty feet behind me." He pulled his pistol, spun the full cylinder, holstered it, then made his way down the ridge, leaning back in his saddle, throwing one arm out for balance.

Lina watched anxiously until he was safe at the foot, then followed. The descent was difficult, but her mare was agile.

"But Lina, I don't understand," her father protested behind her. "What's wrong?"

"Don't you see? The buildings. They're free of vegetation. Look at the jungle, Father. They should be buried under it, but someone's cleared it. Recently."

"Good Lord, you're right. Damn me, if Maudslay is already here—" Smashing his hat down on his head, Sir Lawrence kneed his mount to a faster pace once he quit the ridge.

The last quarter mile had to be traversed carefully, for the trail was choked by vegetation and blocked twice by woodland streams. Finally, hours later it seemed to Lina's impatient spirits, her mare climbed the steep hillside and burst onto the escarpment.

Lina found herself on the acropolis, but she was too busy searching for signs of human habitation to enjoy the lively architecture. She dismounted next to the sprawling palace, tied up her mare, and plunged inside. Most former explorers had bivouacked here, but she saw no signs of a camp.

The thick walls dripped with moisture, but the double galleries connecting to the inner courtyards allowed enough light for her to see where she was going. Reviewing in her mind the many drawings she'd seen, she traversed the harmonious, vaulted passageways until she reached the tower situated near one of the center courts. She climbed the crumbling interior stairway to the top, the third story.

This tower was the only one known in Mayan architecture. How many years had she dreamed of attaining its summit and looking down on the city it ruled, like the kings of so long ago? But again, she had little time to enjoy the fulfillment of a lifelong fantasy. When she stood in the tall, arched window, she dreamed not of bygone warriors but feared present interlopers.

From here, perspective made her appreciate what logic had already told her—someone had labored long and hard to clear the jungle away from the main buildings. But peer as she might, she distinguished no plume of smoke or beast of burden. The only inhabitants of Palenque were the monkeys screeching above her head and the snowy hawks circling over the palace.

She saw Jeremy exit one of the cleared temples. She cupped her hands about her mouth. "Find anything?"

He shook his head, then yelled back, "Get down from there. That thing doesn't look safe."

She smiled and shrugged, pretending she hadn't heard. As he approached the extended row of steps leading up to the terraced palace, she saw his black scowl. But she didn't move, for the journey had been too long, the dangers too harrowing.

She'd earned this moment.

She'd enjoy it.

Directly across, the smallest Temple of the Bas-Relief stood on its cleared mound.

To the southwest she spied the largest temple, the Temple of the Inscriptions. A steep-stepped pyramid led over one hundred feet up to the long, flat temple. Even from here, she could see the five doorways. She couldn't wait to explore the stucco reliefs facing it.

The Temple of the Cross towered atop still another pyramid, with a roof crest forty-two feet in height. Its stucco facade and wooden lintels had been carved with a grace and complexity the ages had marred, but Catherwood's meticulous drawings still proclaimed its former grandeur. It had a ten-foot long tablet on one wall.

It was toward the Temple of the Sun, southeast, that she looked the longest. It had the same distinctive sloped roof and elaborately carved comb. Inside stood an altar with carvings as familiar to her as the back of her own hand, for they were her favorite in all of Mayan architecture, as they had been to Catherwood.

She longed to see them in person, but the sun had lost its zenith, and Jeremy's steps rang as he climbed toward her. Sighing, she turned away and went to meet him.

"I couldn't see any sign of occupation from here. Did you find anything?"

"Nothing," he answered, offering his arm for her to descend. "But it bothers me. Who cleared the jungle? And why? It doesn't make sense, unless an expedition has come and gone. Yet I saw no trenches."

Frowning, Lina walked with him to the interior of the palace. "Surely we would have heard something. No, the only expedition other than our own that was being planned was one by the amateur Alfred Maudslay."

Baxter and her father were already setting up camp. Sir Lawrence glanced up at the name. He hurried over to them. "Anything?"

"No."

He wiped his brow. "Thank God. Come, my dear. It will be dark soon. You can listen as Hubert and I make our final decision about the first trench."

Lina gritted her teeth, but she sat cross-legged on the floor and listened as the two men ate a hasty meal of dried fruit and dried meat, conversing all the while. As darkness gathered, Jeremy set pine torches at intervals along the walls, but Lina knew he was listening.

"We've been through this before, Lawrence," Baxter said, swallowing a tough bite of meat. "The palace is the logical place to start. Surely any king would want his home to be his burial site."

"I'm not so certain, Hubert. I think one of the temples would be a more logical place. Religion seemed important to these people."

Lina had her own ideas, but since she'd not been asked . . . She started as a large warm hand covered hers. Jeremy had sat next to her and she hadn't even noticed. She swallowed, hard, as he smiled at her.

Somehow his silent support gave her courage to say, "Father is right. The temples are more logical. The palace must have been the center of activity. Surely a king would want a sacred, quiet burial place."

"No, no, no." Baxter flung his half-eaten meat into the fire. It sizzled, then curled into a brown husk.

The scent of burned flesh churned Lina's empty stomach. She looked around at the stucco portraits decorating the walls, blocking out Baxter's perorations.

In the bouncing shadows cast by the torches and the fire, the ancient priests seemed larger than life, looking down their patrician noses at a mere female. How fitting, she thought sardonically, that her father and Baxter should be obsessed with this culture. Women rarely figured in Mayan art. What would these learned priests have thought of a woman desecrating their tombs?

Lina shivered as cool, rain-swept air made the torches flicker. The feathered headdresses seemed to flutter, the strong limbs tense to step back into the world from the nether regions, eager for the blood of sacrifice. Lina thought of the many depictions she'd seen of torture in Mayan art: self-flagellation; thorns pulled through tongues, ears, and penises; priests drinking the blood of captives.

Yet Lina had always questioned that a people who could produce such powerful art and architecture were really so bloodthirsty. A debate raged in archaeological circles about the subject. Some said the mingling of the Aztec culture with the classic Maya had corrupted a gentle people who excelled in astronomy and math but who had never discovered the wheel.

Palenque, Lina had always believed, was the last flowering of a great civilization. The many archaeologists who'd come before her had compared it to Athens. The similarities were striking.

Yet, as she sat here in the flesh, surrounded by the art of men long dead, it was easier to give credence to the uglier theories of human sacrifice she'd scorned. Especially as, mysteriously, the torches guttered out, one by one. The hissing as rain swept through the lofty corridors was the logical explanation, but Lina's skin still crawled.

Once more, Jeremy showed how attuned he was to her. "We're safe enough in here. Snakes and jaguars will avoid the light. By the time the torches go out, we'll be in our hammocks."

"It's not animals I fear." Lina looked around at the portraits. "Funny. I couldn't wait to get here. Now that I am, in the darkness, this place gives me chills. At the moment, I'm remembering some of the more unpleasant renderings in Mayan art."

"Such as?"

"Have you ever heard of Diego de Landa?"

"No."

"He was one of the first Spanish priests to come to Yucatán. His work wasn't published until 1865." Lina's smile was both melancholy and reflective. "Seldom in history has one man had such an opportunity to influence it. He found books, manuscripts, some even mnemonically illustrated. They would have helped us immeasurably, no doubt, in analyzing the hieroglyphics. But he felt he had a holy responsibility to civilize these people. When he found that even the Christian Maya still practiced sacrifice of their own children, he gathered every book, idol, manuscript he could find of Mayan history and burned it. He even had his proselytes destroy some of the temples and use them to build churches."

"If his aim was to wipe the Mayan record from the globe, he succeeded pretty well. I doubt if we'll ever understand all of their culture without being able to decipher their writing."

"Yet even as he fanatically burned everything, Landa had Mayan scholars record the details of their daily life and tried to analyze their written language. Scholars today are still trying to piece together an alphabet from the record he left." Lina sighed. "My father has seen his manuscript, and he is not optimistic that it is sufficient help. It's probably the closest we'll ever get to a Mayan Rosetta Stone, however. If only Landa had actually translated the glyphs into Spanish, as the Rosetta Stone translated Egyptian glyphs into Greek and Demotic, we might have a chance to understand the Maya."

Jeremy, too, stared at the imposing portraits. "I'm not so sure we'd be doing either the ancient or modern-day Maya a service by publishing such a find."

Lina swung toward him. "Whyever not? The Indians who rowed us here have every right to be as proud of their lineage as I. I can trace my ancestry back to the Conqueror. Some of them may be descended from kings. Surely it would do them a world of good to know that."

"They've pride enough already. What good does it do them to have strangers pilfer their art and publish documents to feed the curiosity of the Western world? Both will ultimately draw more thrillseekers, perpetuating the cycle, until this heritage you describe so reverently is decimated piecemeal to decorate fine houses a world away. You must admit—you archaeologists do tend to take what you want, from the Elgin marbles to Schliemann's golden hoard."

"I didn't know you felt this way, Jeremy. If so, why did you bring us here?" She felt the intensity of his stare even in the growing dimness.

"You know why."

His whisper slipped about her like a cloak, both warming and constricting. She wanted to wrap him about her, but could not afford the luxury. When she moved slightly away, she found strength enough to retort, "I happen to agree with you, in part. Any finds we take away should be paid for in full to the proper authorities."

Jeremy snorted. "Indeed. The Maya hereabouts will be delighted to have you enrich the coffers of the goverment that oppresses them."

"Well, what would you have us do, then?" Lina moved farther away, but Jeremy sighed and caught her hand again.

"Nothing, angel. Dig where you want. Personally, I don't believe you'll find much, or do much damage." He pulled her under his arm and said into her hair, "Any more than you'll find gold."

Lina felt his smile. She was too tired to argue any longer, but she was disturbed at his opinions. Even if they worked out all their emotional differences, how could she form a relationship with a man so suspicious of the science she wanted to devote her life to?

The last torch spat, then died, abetting Lina's gloominess. Darkness gathered. What was that? Lina gasped as it flashed again. Eyes glowed at her from the darkness. She shrank against Jeremy. "Someone's watching us."

He chuckled. "Nothing to be afraid of, angel. It's fireflies. See how they bounce?"

Only then did Lina realize why the "eyes" had moved so erratically. She relaxed under Jeremy's arm.

The little insects seemed attuned to the environment, glowing brightly when the wind quietened, then fading as it whooshed through the stone corridors. Their bright cheerfulness was comforting. Somehow the shadows seemed less terrifying than before.

By firefly light, Lina settled the cub atop its mother's pelt, which she'd purchased from the Indians. It had stopped fighting the tether, but still paced the length of its captivity through most of the nights.

"You're not going to be able to keep him much longer. If you do, he'll be too tame to survive once you leave," Jeremy said at her side.

Lina leaned against him. "I know. Once he learns how to hunt, I'll let him go. Come on. Dawn will come early." Lina took her hammock from Jeremy. She'd long since become an expert at setting it up.

Only the fire and the insects offered light as, their plans made, Baxter and Sir Lawrence set up their hammocks.

"Good night, Lina." Sir Lawrence approached to kiss her cheek. "I've checked your drawing supplies. They've stayed dry, so you can start first thing in the morning on the palace walls. Hubert and I have compromised. We'll trench around the palace perimeter as soon as the workers arrive in the morning. If we don't find anything once we've gone all the way around, we'll move to the Temple of the Inscriptions." He moved away without noticing that Lina had not given her assent.

Her father swung into his hammock, unaware that Lina clenched her fingers so tightly that one of her mosquito-net strings broke. By the time she'd tied it together, she'd composed herself. Now was not the time to get into yet another argument. Only one thing would earn her father's respect for her ability.

Proof she knew what she was doing.

She had her own plans, as he would soon discover.

Lina was flipping back her netting to get in her hammock, boots and all, when Jeremy put a cup in her hand.

"Drink."

The fire was dying, so she couldn't see what the cup held, but she drank obediently. Watery tea with a bitter aftertaste. "Yuk," she said when she'd finished the brew. "What was it?"

"Never mind. Something to keep you strong. I take it myself, as you will, daily. I assure you I wouldn't poison you." Jeremy took the cup from her limp hand.

His concern touched her. The impulse was compelling to cup that strong cheek and kiss him, but she felt her father and Baxter watching. Jeremy smothered the fire and groped his way to his hammock.

Lina emulated him and expertly swung her weight into her own. The hammock swung gently, a soporific accompaniment to the nocturnal symphony of calling birds and whirring cicadas. Some sounds she didn't recognize, odd whistles and sonorous hoots. Once, she thought she heard a bark.

Baxter asked sleepily, "A dog? Do they roam wild?"

"No," Jeremy answered. "You're hearing a frog."

"Might have known. Everything is deuced strange here."

Strange, yes, Lina decided. But wonderful. And she fell asleep by the mystic light of fireflies, serenaded by the ancient rhythms of life.

Lina was up first the following morning. Alone, she made her way to the stream the Maya had tamed and coursed through their city. The sun was just peeking over the forest below, bathing every verdant blade and leaf in primeval light.

Hummingbirds darted among flowering vines, their delicate wings invisible. Dragonflies, purple and green wings beating with arrogant ease, chased gnats. A woodpecker hammered at a rotten tree nearby. She watched it admiringly for a moment before she recalled herself to her purpose and bent over the stream. Her fears had dissipated with the darkness. The disturbing conversation with Jeremy she refused to dwell on. She disagreed with him totally. The Maya stood to gain from the advancement of knowledge too.

This morning, Lina visualized breechclouted children gamboling in the water, watched over by women carrying infants on their backs. Perhaps, from a distance, their noble father regarded them fondly before he joined his peers for a morning ceremony that ensured the march of time.

Lina smiled at her fancifulness and bent to look at her image in the water.

She saw her own countenance, mysterious and lovely, framed by loose dark hair. Above it, she saw a dark, painted face topped by a quetzal headdress.

She leaped to her feet, whirling. The tall brush behind her quivered, but the only sounds disturbing the morning stillness were avian. No footsteps, no threat. Only the morning breeze and the quiet dawn.

Disturbed, Lina dried her face and hands on the towel she'd brought and hastened back to the palace. Was her imagination really too lively? The image had been so real. Exactly like one of the priests lining the palace walls.

In the end, the resemblance reassured her—it was *too* strong. She'd conjured up her picture of a priest because of the evocative atmosphere of Palenque.

Lina's unease didn't survive the morning, for the workers began trickling in from nearby villages as Sir Lawrence and Baxter tumbled sleepily from their hammocks. Lina took full advantage and pulled Jeremy into one of the secluded courtyards.

"Jeremy, I request your help. I want to start my own dig at the Temple of the Sun." Lina braced for a protest, but Jeremy didn't even look surprised.

"I suspected as much. I could tell even on the ship that you and your father differed not only on method, but site selection. I hired more workers than he requested so you could set up your own project."

Openmouthed, Lina stared at him. Then she squealed and threw her arms about his neck, showering his face with kisses. "You darling, I adore you!" She danced out of the tightening circle of his arms, and rushed away to meet the workers.

Jeremy stayed bolted in place, staring after her.

*   *   *

A mere fifteen minutes passed before Lina, by the use of sign language and pretty smiles, coaxed a baker's dozen of the strongest-looking Maya to help her load the mules and transport equipment to the temple several hundred yards away. She was mounting her mare when Jeremy came out of the palace, Sir Lawrence on his heels.

"What the devil do you mean she's already busy?" Sir Lawrence still held a straight razor in one hand. Half of his face was lathered. He made such a picture when his jaw dropped open as he saw the procession leaving the courtyard that Lina had to laugh.

"Good morning, Father." Lina was tempted to bolt after the Indians, but she quelled the instinct. He had to find out sometime.

"Lina, what in the name of the Queen are you doing? Where's your sketchpad?"

Lina braced her hands on the saddle pommel. "Catherwood made far better drawings of the palace murals than I can. We spent too much and came too far to duplicate previous efforts. Two concurrent digs will offer us a better chance of momentous discoveries."

"You have no idea how to lead a dig. I demand you get down at once and return to what you do best. It's why I brought you, as you well know." Sir Lawrence used the towel on his shoulder to wipe the foam away, obviously too distraught to remember he was only half shaved.

Lina closed her eyes, wondering vaguely why his attitude still hurt. She should be used to it by now. She opened her eyes and pinioned him with the blue stare so like his own. "You shall soon see 'what I do best.' " Reining her mare about, Lina cantered down the terrace toward the Temple of the Sun.

She heard her father chastise Jeremy. "Confound it, Mayhew, you've encouraged her in this folly!"

She didn't hear Jeremy's reply, but she knew she could count on him. The knowledge gave her strength as she began the greatest challenge of her life.

At the temple base, she paused and shaded her eyes. The latticed roof comb towered into the sky, blocking the morning sun. She longed to climb the crumbling steps and explore the magnificent altar Catherwood had drawn so well, but she contained herself. From the many digs she'd attended, Lina had learned that the most successful were accomplished systematically. Everything, no matter how unimportant it seemed, should be recorded *in situ*. Schliemann himself had regretted the destructive trench he'd dug at Troy and wished he'd logged the location of every find.

No matter how impatient she was to get started, Lina was determined not to make the same mistakes.

While the Indians unpacked the shovels, picks, buckets, and screens, Lina surveyed the temple by walking around it, looking for telltale mounds. She shoveled into several rises herself, but found nothing. When the Indians were free, she drew a mound in the air with her hands and showed them how to dig—carefully. Turning over each shovelful of dirt. She dug with them, side by side.

When Jeremy joined her several hours later, her gloved hands were stained, her skirt and shirt were mud- and grass-spattered, but she was humming.

He wiped a smear of mud from her cheek and pulled her hat lower over her face. "You'll burn to a crisp if you're not careful."

Smiling, Lina shook her head and arched her neck to look up at the temple. "I don't think so, if my hunch is right. We haven't found anything on the exterior. Finally, I get to go inside the temple." She nodded at the Indians. "Will you tell them to rest while I go inside and look around?"

Jeremy complied, then followed as she climbed the temple steps, walking behind her in case she should fall. "Your father is not at all happy with either of us. I've been passing his orders to his workers, but I don't seem to have appeased him much."

"Surprise, surprise." Lina didn't miss a step. At the top of the truncated pyramid, she paused to examine the four vertical panels fronting the temple. The two inner panels depicted life-size dignitaries, as lively and undistorted as any she had seen in Mayan art.

The end panels bore two scalloped, four-sided shapes containing more drawings she assumed were glyphs. Reverently she reached out to trace them with her finger, saw her dirty glove and snatched it off.

"Oh Jeremy. I'd give five years of my life if I could read these. Do you know what Stephens said when he came to Palenque? 'What we had before our eyes was grand, curious and remarkable. Here were the remains of a cultivated, polished and peculiar people, who had passed through all the stages incident to the rise and fall of nations; reached their golden age, then perished.' Aren't you as curious as I am, Jeremy? Don't you want to share this lost glory with the world, ultimately benefiting all humanity?" She continued to trace the lovely symbols, deep frustration on her face.

Jeremy cocked his head, obviously trying to get some of her perspective on the fading carvings. Finally, he shook his head. "No. They're long gone. They were a magnificent people, and as such, I think they should be allowed to keep their dignity. Can you imagine Palenque with children running around, throwing lolly sticks inside the altars, adolescents using pocket knives to carve hearts on the murals?"

When Lina shuddered, Jeremy smiled sadly. "Such is the inevitable result of greater knowledge, Lina. It's happened to Egypt. Look at the pyramids. They're wearing away because their outer stones have been stolen for other buildings. The sphinx is marred with hen-scratchings from Roman soldiers to modern children. Every time a new weighty tome is published by some glory-seeking archaeologist, more tourists come. Is that what you want to happen here?"

"But Palenque is more isolated. It's too hard to reach. That can never happen here."

"I hope you're right, Lina. Shall we?" Jeremy swept a hand before him toward the dark doorway. "You first. You've earned that right."

Still disturbed by the undeniable points he'd made, Lina plunged under the massive combed roof and entered the past.

The scent of the ages wafted into her nostrils. To many, the musty smell would have been unpleasant, but to Lina, it was heady. Long ago, upon these walls artisans had labored to incise the two huge glyphs. The mold growing on the walls, the cracked ceiling, the peeling stucco all marked the passage of time. Lina wasn't disappointed at the remnants of lost grandeur, for standing here in the dimness, it was easy for her to visualize this room freshly painted, filled with bedecked and befeathered priests.

The giant statues that had once stood in the niches had long since been stolen, but Stephens had seen them in one of the villages, and she imagined them there now. Her footsteps ringing on the floor, her heart pounding with excitement, Lina entered an even darker room.

Here, light barely penetrated, but unerringly Lina found her way to the altar. She pulled two candles out of her pocket, struck a match and lit them, handing one to Jeremy, keeping one herself.

They held them high.

"My God," Jeremy whispered. "It's magnificent."

Lina blinked away sudden tears. "It's all I hoped for. And more."

The altar was huge, this vaulted room obviously constructed to hold it. Two end panels contained life-size priests seeming real enough and strong enough to bear the weight of the slanted stone slab above their heads. Decorating the top edge of the slanted slab was a long figure that looked feathered, but the middle had faded, so Lina wasn't sure if it was a snake or a bird.

Beneath the slab, between the two feathered and fierce priests, was a recessed carving. Centered upon it was a gorgonlike face with a protruding tongue. More standing figures stood in reverent attendance on it, plus cross-legged mannequins.

Jeremy traced the face with his finger. "Astonishing. The artistry of the man who carved this is staggering. It's as fine as anything I've seen in Egypt. Do you think it's a sun symbol, perhaps?"

"That's what Stephens thought. Without interpreting these magnificent glyphs, I guess we'll never know for sure." Lina's regret was so acute that she barely felt the dart of pain in her hand. She looked down.

Wax had dripped, staining the back of her hand. She set the candle on the floor before the altar. Jeremy did likewise.

"You think there's something beneath the altar, don't you?"

Lina inhaled sharply. How could this man understand her so much better than her own father? "How did you know?"

Jeremy turned in a slow circle. "If I were a king, I'd want a resting place like this, guarded by a memorial like this."

In the flickering light, with his hair rumpled and his shirt half undone, Jeremy was the quintessential adventurer. Devil-may-care he might be, but uncaring he was not.

His smile was rakish. "And if my bones must be disturbed, I'd want a small, gorgeous brunette to do it." When she didn't smile back, he spanned the gap between them in one stride. "Lina, what are you thinking?" Cupping her face in his hands, he let her look her fill. As he looked his.

Despite the fact that she knew she was revealing too much, Lina couldn't turn away. This man had protected her over miles of dangerous terrain, anticipated her needs before she knew them herself, and stood with her now at the apogee of her life.

The revelation was blinding in that shadowy room.

She'd blocked the knowledge too long. Convenient or not, it was time she admitted it.

She loved him.

And though he'd never said it, somehow she knew he loved her too.

Flaws and all.

Her body had known almost from the beginning what her mind had rejected: This lonely, difficult man was meant for her. And she, prideful, reckless, but essentially kind, was meant for him.

Why else had she so uncharacteristically bartered her body and hoarded her soul?

Why else had he led her here against his instincts, investing so much money in a cause he didn't believe in?

But was caring enough to overcome their differences? He believed the past should be inviolate; she believed it should be explored. He hated the society she traveled in. And what kind of father would a wanderer make? Would he ever love her as much as the *Verdandi* and his freedom?

And most of all, how would he react when he found that she'd deceived him from the beginning? Somehow, she knew he'd prefer an honest wanton over a deceitful virgin.

Yet, if they both remained silent, no matter who won their wager, both of them would lose.

One of them had to bend, or they would break.

"Lina, darling, what is it?"

Tell him. Tell him you lied to get him here. Lina took a deep breath, but the words wouldn't come. It was too soon. She needed his support too badly. Words failed her, but actions— maybe this would be enough.

Making an incoherent sound of joy, she pulled his head down to her level and planted her mouth over his. She lavished tenderness upon him. She felt the stillness in his big body as he tried to understand.

Tentatively, he responded, his lips sliding back and forth upon her own. Not with arousal, but with a heartfelt warmth that grew with every shared breath. His arms clasped about her waist, and he held her gingerly, as if she would break.

Never had she felt stronger. With her mouth, she told him all her heart would speak could she give it leave. Jeremy absorbed the message with equal urgency.

For long moments, they stood linked among the past that had brought them together, uncaring of the future that could yet tear them apart. The present beckoned. Decay surrounded them, yet life unfurled within them. Lips melded, hands caressed as they communed, sharing the true meaning of life.

Without love, it was meaningless.

Between two people who loved one another, neither lost, for both won.

Neither took, for both gave.

Neither yearned, for they both were filled.

As that first exchanged glance eons ago had hinted, they both had hurts, but had found their healing in each other. Two solitary wanderers were linked now, and the stronger for it. Together, they could overcome all.

When they broke apart, each had to blink rapidly and clear clogged throats. Their panting breaths slowed. In the luminous candlelight, man and woman stared at one another, feeling the invisible, invincible bond neither could break. Raw, bare of subterfuge, they spoke simultaneously.

"Jeremy, you must know—"

"Lina, I l—"

Outside, two shots exploded in rapid succession.

Lina saw Jeremy's dilated pupils contract. She, too, had to blink before she could think clearly.

She whirled toward the doorway, but Jeremy was already two long strides in front of her. "Stay here!"

Shock slowed her for a second, but then she was bolting down the temple steps to begin the long, perilous descent. She spared one precious glance and almost paid dearly for it. She stumbled, her foot catching on a loose stone, but luckily fell backward and landed on her rump.

Breathing heavily, she stared at the edge of the jungle. Several Indians were hidden among the trees, firing arrows at someone she couldn't see. One fell as she heard another shot.

Lina hurried faster now, for she knew her father and Baxter must be the Indians' foes. Part of Lina realized the workers had disappeared, but it wasn't until too late that she'd wonder about the significance of that.

The rest of the lengthy descent was pure mental and physical torture, for she had to step carefully even as every nerve screamed haste.

She bolted off the last four steps and hit the ground running. Jeremy was meters ahead, loping toward the palace, his pistol at the ready. He disappeared inside the palace. Panting, sweat beading on her brow and under her arms, Lina finally plunged into the palace after him.

Her father and Baxter had taken cover at the rear opening, firing, reloading, firing, reloading with the old weapons they'd purchased from Don Roberto. Jeremy hunkered down beside them, pulling his pistol, but the Indians were already scrambling away.

"Dear heaven, look at that," Baxter whispered.

Through the writhing smoke, Lina saw a hazy figure bringing a gleaming ax down on the head of one of the Indians who'd fired at them. His bow slipped from his hands as his head flopped to the side. Blood gushed from the severed neck.

Lina whirled, gagging behind her clasped hands. Jeremy drew her face into his shirt. "He's gone, Lina."

Lina dared a look over her shoulder. She could barely

glimpse the body in the tall grass. "But . . . I don't understand. The man who used the ax—he looked like a Maya."

"I don't understand either. You'd think he'd be using that ax on us. But I'm going to examine the body. Maybe we'll find some clue on him. You stay here." Jeremy loped outside.

Lina trailed her father and Baxter back inside and fetched the bandages while her father helped Baxter off with his shirt.

"It's only a scratch," Baxter growled as Sir Lawrence cleaned his arm.

"Even a scratch can be dangerous in a tropical climate. Be still, man."

"What do you think, Lawrence? I swear the ax that priest fellow used looked exactly like a sketch of a ceremonial ax I've seen. Of course, they were some distance away, in the edge of the jungle, but a sight like that does rather leave an indelible impression. But deuce take it, why would one Indian shoot arrows at us and the other protect us? Doesn't make any sense."

Lina sat down on suddenly weak legs. "Priest? I didn't get a good look at him. Did he wear a headdress?"

Her father finished tightening Baxter's bandage, then glared at her. "What difference does it make?"

Lina persisted, "Was he wearing a headdress? Was his face painted?"

Baxter frowned. "Did you see him?"

Jeremy asked from the doorway, "Yes, Lina, did you see him?"

Lina swallowed. "This morning, early, when I went to the stream. I thought I saw a priest looking over my shoulder when I bent over the water, but when I turned, he was gone. I dismissed the incident as my imagination."

"Well, he carries a wallop for a figment. Almost took the other guy's head off," Jeremy said grimly.

Baxter looked torn between admiration and fear.

Jeremy's expression was not in the least ambiguous. "Why the hell didn't you tell me this earlier?" he said through gritted teeth.

"I told you, I—"

Voices called from outside, then two of the head workers

entered their gallery. They still looked shaken, but they said something to Jeremy. He responded in Yucatec Maya.

Baxter shrugged back into his shirt. "Well, at least we don't have to go after them now. Though I can't blame them for running off."

More Indians trickled in. Jeremy spoke briefly to Sir Lawrence, then jerked his head toward the trench. The Indians went obediently.

Lina stood and dusted off the limestone bits clinging to her skirt, but she saw the mud and grass stains and desisted. When she approached her father and Jeremy, they started apart. They'd been speaking too softly for her to hear. Grimly, she crossed her arms, having a fair idea of the subject.

Jeremy opened his mouth, but Lina said first, "No. I'm not going."

Jeremy's mouth snapped closed.

Her father tried next. "Lina, if I'd realized we'd be caught in the middle between two warring tribes, I'd never have brought you." He shuddered. Despite his wrinkled and stained garments, he still made the action look elegant. "You saw the way that blade took the man's head off. Probably obsidian, come to think of it. It was dark and shiny, and obsidian sharpens like—"

"Sir Lawrence!" Jeremy rapped.

Her father blinked, then glared sternly at his daughter. "The matter is not open to discussion. Jeremy will take you back to Don Roberto's. We'll visit you often."

"No. If I have to camp under a tree, I'm not going. I knew there were dangers entailed in coming here. If you and Hubert can risk them, so can I." Lina took two hesitant steps toward Jeremy. "Please, you of all people must understand."

That stony expression did not soften. "I was trying not to scare you, but since you're so foolish, it's time you heard some home truths. Sit."

Lina's mouth tightened, but she quelled the urge to go down on her haunches and bark. She folded her legs and sat down on a blanket.

Jeremy stood, legs spread wide, and glowered at all three of the Britons. "Several of the Mayan tribes in the area are not only warring with the Mexican government, but with each other. Perhaps as a result, they're trying to scare one another, but the end is . . ." Jeremy trailed off, then finished abruptly, "they're practicing human sacrifice again."

"By Jove!" Baxter exclaimed.

"Good God," whispered Sir Lawrence.

And Lina? Lina cocked her head. "You're just trying to scare me into leaving."

Jeremy reached out a long arm and hauled Lina to her feet. "Do you want me to show you what a decapitation looks like, Miss Scientist? Let's see how cool and curious you'll remain when you see a man's brains spilling out of his throat. If you're taken for sacrifice, you'll do well to die so easily. Sometimes men were drugged so they couldn't struggle as their hearts were torn out—"

Lina swallowed the urge to gag. "Not the classic Maya. I don't believe it."

"You're not among the classic Maya now. These Indians are an amalgam of three races and more heritages than you have in the whole of your British Isles. Who can say what they'll do? Or why?"

When Lina shivered, Jeremy made a rough sound and pulled her under his arm. "Please, Lina, be sensible. I'll stay here to guard your father. But think. Someone obviously resents our presence." Jeremy nodded toward Baxter's bandage. "And someone else wants to keep us here, but I doubt his motives are scientific. Why was the jungle cleared? We can't take the risk of something happening to you. You can come back when and if it's safe."

Lina squeezed Jeremy's arm with all ten of her fingers, praying he'd understand her feelings, as he had so often in the past. "Jeremy, if I were convinced I'd be secure at Don Roberto's, I'd consider going. But he hardly lives in a fortress, and he doesn't have many weapons to arm his workers with. If the Indians hate us so, his hacienda may be next. He told you himself he's worried, didn't he?"

Jeremy looked away.

"See? I'd not be that much safer. And I'd go out of my mind worrying about the rest of you. Here, I can do some good. The faster we dig, the quicker we can leave." When Jeremy didn't respond, Lina wriggled free.

Her eyes stung, but she refused to cry. It was ever thus. One moment she felt closer to him than any human being, the next, he was as cold and unreachable as the moon.

Thank God cowardice had kept her silent earlier. Love this man she might, but at the moment she wasn't happy about it. And neither, she had a feeling, would he be if she'd told him. She lifted her chin. "I'm going back to work."

"Lina, come back here!" her father yelled.

Jeremy didn't plead any more.

But she heard his vicious curse.

So much, she thought, tears unstoppable now, for the healing power of love.

It was an illusion.

To men, it was power. Bow to their invincibility, or be ostracized.

So be it.

Chapter 12

LATER THAT EVENING, Lina still worked, alone, long after the workers had departed. She'd sent them away early, for until she verified her theory, they had little to do. The lanterns and pine torches brilliantly lit the altar chamber, much to the dismay of the bats she'd displaced. Lina wrinkled her nose as, yet again, she stepped in a pile of guano.

Tomorrow she'd ask the workers to clear the droppings. Perhaps they obscured the cracks in the floor that might indicate a hidden stairwell. Certainly her searching fingers had found no evidence of an opening in the walls. She'd circled the room so many times her eyes were beginning to cross. Shadows lapped at the ring of brightness, and the wild night sounds echoed eerily through the mold-covered walls.

Resolutely, she quelled her fears. No feathered priests would rise to haunt her. If she *had* seen a priest, he'd been a very modern one dressed to frighten her. As for the tales of sacrifice, doubtless they were rumors calculated to scare the settlers in the area.

Lina rested her shoulders against the wall and blew her hair out of her eyes, staring at the altar. It seemed to dance before her bleary gaze, taunting her. She was right. She knew it. Somewhere under this room a king was buried. She stood in the Mayan equivalent of Westminster, reasoning that the Maya must have been a supremely logical people to have developed such complicated mathematics.

"Are you going to stay in here all night?" Jeremy asked irritably from the doorway.

Lina didn't even glance at him. "Maybe." One by one they'd

come to coax her away. She'd ignored her father and Baxter, continuing her search, until they left. She had a feeling Jeremy wouldn't be so easy to vanquish, but she deliberately kept her stride relaxed as she shoved away from the wall and approached the altar.

She'd never let him know how much he'd hurt her. She'd bared her feelings and her body to him, yet he still treated her like a child. Why couldn't he understand that her need for respect was greater than her fear?

What good was her physical safety if she hated herself?

Someday women would be revered archaeologists. Was it so wrong of her to want to be the first? Only in proving her competence could she crack the door of male dominance. She longed to tell Jeremy her feelings, but his words earlier today proved he had no more regard for her than her father did.

"Why did you have the workers remove the slab?" Jeremy nodded at the altar lid resting against the wall. The room was barely large enough to hold the altar, so it would be impossible to move it without dismantling part of the temple.

"To look inside, of course."

"Of course. What did you expect to find? A plan of the place with X marking the spot?"

Lina's teeth gritted together, but she didn't bother with a retort. Instead, she mounted the log ladder an Indian had brought her from his village and peered inside the altar yet again. "Jeremy, would you hand me a lantern?"

Jeremy sighed but complied. "This is an utter waste of time. It's almost ten. Come back with me so you can at least get a decent night's sleep—"

"Dreamless repose won't help me achieve my goal." She wouldn't be able to sleep anyway, but Jeremy didn't need to know that.

Lina held the lantern down inside the altar. She saw nothing but smooth-jointed walls. She hesitated, then thrust the lantern at Jeremy, grasped the side of the altar and levered herself over the edge, feet first.

"Lina, are you crazy?" Jeremy grabbed at her arm, but missed.

Her boots rang on the stone as she dropped, then her voice echoed, "Hand-d me-e the lantern-n, please-se."

Jeremy climbed the ladder until he thrust his arm down inside the well. Still, the altar was so tall that she had to stand on tiptoe to reach the handle.

"What are you trying to prove by this stunt? Dammit, if I'd known you'd be so unreasonable, I'd never have brought you here."

"So leave." Lina knelt, set the lantern down, and crawled along the sides of the altar, feeling with her fingers at the cracks.

"I ought to, and let you spend the night in the damn thing. Once the lanterns go out, we'll see how fascinating this place is." Jeremy's footsteps rang with aggravation, then faded.

Lina stood abruptly. "Jeremy?"

Only the wind answered, howling through the vaulted chamber. Lina's jaw tightened, then, moving with measured control, she knelt and resumed her search. Might as well take advantage of her position.

It took her ten minutes to find it. In the left end of the rectangle, squarely in the middle, lay a small, innocuous slit. At first she grazed over it, thinking the stone had been chipped upon installation. But, curious, she returned to the indentation. It was too well formed to be a chip.

Her heart lurched, then began to race. Minutely this time, she felt each centimeter of the mark that had been carefully carved.

To allow for leverage.

It wasn't exactly an X, but it was close enough.

When she heard stealthy movement, she called, "You can come out now, Jeremy."

Silence, then a male growl, "How did you know I was here?"

"I knew you wouldn't leave me alone all night. You only wanted to teach me a lesson."

"I can see you learned it very well." Jeremy's scowl thrust over the side of the altar.

"No sarcasm, please. You could stand a few lessons yourself." She held up her hand when his mouth opened. "I'm too happy to get into another argument with you. Look." She tilted the lantern until it illuminated the slot.

"Will a V do as well as an X?"

Jeremy stared down. "What do you think it's for?"

"To allow the bottom of the altar to be lifted out, of course. There must be a trap door underneath that leads to the center of the pyramid." Their eyes met by lantern light.

The admiration in Jeremy's warm gaze was balm to Lina's bruised self-esteem. "Your father will be proud of you, Lina."

Lina's elated smile dimmed. "I wish I could be so sure." Then, her expression settling into feminine lines of determination, she added, "Besides, let's not get hasty. If there is a tomb, it could well have been robbed in antiquity, like those in Egypt."

Jeremy stared down at the stone beneath her feet. "And getting to it will be no easy matter. My God, the bottom of this thing must weigh half a ton, at least."

"We brought enough rope to make a pulley." Lina looked up. "I just hope the ceiling is strong enough to support one. We'll start on it first thing in the morning."

She handed up the lantern. Jeremy took it, set it on the floor, then peeked over the edge again. He grinned when he saw her raised hand. "Ready to come out, are you?"

He offered a big hand to her, then snatched it back before she reached it. Lina wrinkled her nose at him.

The second time, she waited even when his hand came within reach. When he leaned forward, she snatched. Her fingertips brushed his, but still he pulled back too fast.

"Funny, Jeremy. If you want me to spend the night, fine. Just throw me a blanket and a bone."

Apparently Jeremy heard the weariness in her voice. He leaned over the side and offered both his hands, lifting her out. "Sorry, angel. I couldn't resist teasing you a bit."

When he pulled her onto his lap, Lina was too tired to resist. She cradled her head into his shoulder. For long moments they sat like that, on the rim of the altar, enjoying the contrast between their living warmth and the ghostly feel of this ancient resting place.

"I can almost see them, when I close my eyes," Lina said, doing so, "banging their fancy drums, shaking their rattles, chanting the ceremonies that marked the passing of the years. I think these buildings themselves were built mainly to help them celebrate their eternal calendar."

"Why do you say that?"

"Because, according to the books of Chilam Balam of colonial times, the Maya marked time in periods of twenty years called *katuns*, and 360-day years called *tuns*. Diego de Landa said they worshiped the passage of time, embodying the years themselves as gods. They sacrificed to it, built observatories to study it. If we ever decipher their glyphs, I think we may find that most of them are elaborate histories linked to the passage of time."

Jeremy stared around the vaulted room. "It's true. Time has a curious quality in these ruins. Both measured and incalculable."

Lina sat up, feeling that emotional bond with Jeremy again. This time, she fought it, for she was still hurt at his demand that she leave. She jumped down, the pads of her feet stinging at the impact.

Lithely Jeremy dropped beside her. "Lina, I must know— if we find a tomb, will you go on to the hacienda and allow your father and Baxter to excavate it?"

Lina pulled further inside herself. Oh God, what a fool she was to think any man, even this man she'd grown to love, could understand a woman's need to prove herself. Jeremy was wonderful at offering her a carrot, then beating her with a stick. And she was sick of being bruised.

Turning to the door, Lina mumbled, "Just leave me alone, will you?"

"Lina, I—"

"Not now, Jeremy. We have nothing to discuss until you understand that I shall not leave here until the rest of you do. I've told you before that my self-respect means more to me than my safety. If you cared you'd understand that."

She extinguished the pine torches and all but two of the lanterns. Lina hurried out of the temple, leaving him the other lantern.

The descent was treacherous in the best conditions. In the dark, the steps wet, she had to plant each foot carefully. Weariness made her falter a few times, but she'd almost reached the bottom before she lost her balance. She sprawled down the last three steps, landing on her hands and knees.

The lantern rolled, flared, and fizzled out.

Jeremy was there, running his hands over her. "Lina, are you all right?"

"Yes." She let him help her up, then hurried on ahead, memory guiding her steps as much as the weak glow from the palace. When they'd reached the foot of the steps, Lina blocked Jeremy's path.

"Please. Don't say anything to the others yet. We may find nothing tomorrow."

Jeremy frowned, searching her expression in the dimness. "Of course. If that's what you want."

"Thank you."

When she found her father and Baxter going over their notes by firelight, Lina pinned a bright smile on her face. "Good evening."

They both treated her to a glare, but her father sighed and replied, "Good evening."

Baxter nodded curtly.

"Did you have any luck today?" Lina asked.

"We found a few potsherds and beads, but no sign of a burial."

"Yet," Baxter inserted.

Sir Lawrence slammed his notebook closed. "I'll agree to surveying the palace until the end of the week, but then I want to move to the Temple of the Inscriptions."

"You're the boss." But, from the way he shoved his own notes inside his knapsack, the admission did not sit easily on Baxter.

"Yes, well, I just wish my daughter could see that."

From where she washed her face and hands, Lina pretended not to hear.

The next morning, Lina again sought her quiet time by the stream, but this time she was edgy. When a rustling sounded behind her, she whirled, holding her sturdy stick like a club. She relaxed when a tiny furry face peeked at her from the lower limb of a tree. Screeching her alarm, the monkey's mother swung down, snatched her baby under one arm, then scampered back up to safety.

Smiling, Lina bent over the stream again. She unbuttoned her blouse, wet her towel in the clear water, then bathed her throat and shoulders. Already the heat and humidity were stifling, and it was barely dawn. The mosquitoes had been unbearable last night. A few had even penetrated her net. She'd slept as restlessly as she'd predicted, so when the face swam over her shoulder again, she dashed the towel over her tired eyes.

She looked again.

The strong, painted face, topped by the distinctive blue-green of quetzal feathers, was no figment. Even wavering in water, the reflection was disturbingly real. Lina whirled, grabbing her club.

Dark eyes stared at her expressionlessly. They dipped to her open blouse. A familiar expression came into them.

Grabbing her blouse closed with her free hand, Lina backed off, opening her lips to scream.

As silently as he'd come, the priest left. She saw the bushes move, but she heard no footsteps. Then, even the bushes were still.

Lina's feet flew over the complex until she reached the palace. Only when she was safe inside their corridor did she drop the club. Just in time, she remembered to button her blouse. Then, composing herself, she approached the others.

"Jeremy, I saw him again."

Jeremy, his shirt still half unbuttoned, had obviously just swung out of his hammock. "I was coming to look for you. I've told you and told you not to wand . . ." He trailed off when she advanced far enough into the corridor for the sun shining from the courtyard to illuminate her face. "Saw who?"

"The priest."

All three men scrambled for their weapons.

"No, no," Lina said. "He's gone. He didn't do anything except watch me, anyway."

Jeremy propped his rifle back against the wall, but she saw the flexing in his jaw.

Apparently Sir Lawrence saw it too. "Why are you so worried about Lina in particular, Mayhew? Surely we're all in danger?"

Jeremy sat down cross-legged, and took a bite of tortilla.

Lina turned from ransacking their meager breakfast offerings, a mango in one hand, a tortilla in the other. She'd

assumed his male arrogance found her incapable of protecting herself, but something in his expression told her he was
evading a response.

She moved to stand over him. "Yes, Jeremy. Why me?"

Ravenously, Jeremy took a bigger bite.

Sir Lawrence had that vague expression that always indicated deep thought. Finally he nodded to himself. "I think
I know. You think she's in particular danger because of her
age, and ah, status. The Maya, according to conquest accounts,
found children and virgins to be of particular value to the gods
because of their innocence."

Jeremy choked on his tortilla. "Ah, sure, that's it."

Lina took her breakfast to the courtyard, unable to watch
Jeremy's discomfort anymore. She alone knew that wasn't his
reason. He didn't believe her virginal.

Why did the knowledge hurt her, when she'd fostered his
opinion? And if he didn't fear she made a particularly tempting
victim, then what was he so worried about?

As Lina hurried to the temple, Jeremy dogged her footsteps,
his rifle in his hand. She snapped at him yet again. "I'm fine.
Go do whatever great hunters do. Get us game, go see Don
Roberto, but just get out of my way."

"Don't you need me to interpret?"

"No. Sign language works well. Contrary to what my father
thinks, these men seem quite intelligent." Lina waved at the
workers already waiting at the temple base. She picked up a
stick, knelt over a clear patch of land and drew the design of
the pulley she wanted, pointing at the pile of ropes and metal
rings she'd lugged over earlier.

The men scratched brawny necks, talked among themselves,
then shrugged broad shoulders. The lead worker said something to Jeremy.

Jeremy laughed, but when Lina quirked an inquiring brow,
he, too, shrugged. She had a fair idea that they, as men, didn't
like to take orders from a woman.

In all her travels, she'd never met a worker who did.

Lina threw down the stick and rose. "All right, I'm sorry. I
do need you."

Jeremy's grin widened. "See, you didn't even choke on the

words." Jeremy tipped up her downcast chin. "Soon enough, angel, you'll be saying that to me in a more enjoyable context."

For a long moment, the heavy air shimmered with the tension between them. Lina couldn't look away despite their interested obervers.

Then Jeremy sighed and stepped back. "In a much more private place, I hope."

That old bold grin made Lina's skin tingle. Mosquito bites, she told herself. But, as Jeremy propped his rifle against the temple steps and picked up the ropes to begin tying them and stringing them through rings, Lina knew her itch could only be scratched by the man who'd incited it.

She had to force herself to concentrate as Jeremy expanded on her drawing. It was Jeremy who led the men into the temple, Lina who followed.

For the moment, she was content to let it be so.

Long, sweaty hours later, the slab shuddered, grinding against its resting place, then inched upward. Two of the strongest men held Jeremy's legs while he, upside down, inserted the tongue of the crowbar into the slot. Then he stuck the sturdy stick they'd hollowed over the handle to extend the crowbar. Two men on each side stood on ladders, grasped the long handle, counted in a strange tongue, and shoved in unison on the lever.

Lina saw their faces grimace with the strain, but finally she heard the telltale grinding of stone. Inside the altar, Jeremy was again held upside down, this time to loop rope over the slab as they lifted it. His voice rang out with a plea.

The men complied, pushing harder. Another man handed Jeremy a second rope and Lina knew he must have tied one end off.

Lina couldn't stand it. "Be careful, Jeremy." She paced, biting her knuckles. What if the lever broke with Jeremy's fingers underneath the stone?

Crrrkkk . . . Lina's head popped up. The stick? Was it about to break? She'd wondered if it would be able to stand the strain. She mounted the bottom rungs of one of the ladders until she could peek over the altar.

Jeremy's hands were busily tying the last rope under the opposite end of the slab.

The creaking came again, louder.

"Jeremy, move! The lever's about to break!"

"In a moment," he grunted. "Almost finished . . . Got it." He said something in Mayan to the men holding his legs. They began lifting him out.

Sighing their relief, the four burly Maya eased off on the lever. With a *thwak!* the stick broke.

The slab fell, crashing down with such force that the floor shook. Stucco fell from the ceiling and mold floated in the air, but Lina saw only Jeremy's triumphant face.

She hugged him. "Thank you. I couldn't have done it without you." He grabbed for her, but missed when she pulled quickly away and smiled at the workers. "Please tell them how grateful I am."

Jeremy did so.

After that, it was a simple matter to string the ropes through the pulley they'd attached to the ceiling and lift the slab. When it was clear of the altar rim, they lowered it until the men could grasp it, and cut the ropes loose. It took eight of them, but they managed to prop it against the wall next to the altar lid without dropping it.

Then they all wiped their sweaty brows and looked at Lina expectantly.

At last. The moment had arrived, but she was afraid to go on. She stared at the altar, her heart pounding against her ribs. "What if I'm wrong?" she whispered to Jeremy. "So much work for nothing."

"There's only one way to find out." He offered a big hand, palm up.

The moment she touched his hand, her nervousness eased. How right it felt for him to be here, so instrumental in the most momentous discovery of her life. He held her hands and eased her inside the altar, then turned up the lanterns they'd hung all about the stuffy chamber.

Between her feet, Lina saw only smooth, dusty stone. She bit her lip, then took the small brush from her belt and knelt, brushing carefully. Dust rose in a cloud in the hot, airless room, but she'd cleaned enough to see the pattern. She gasped and sat back on her heels.

The stones dovetailed neatly, and they were perforated in matching places, then plugged with filler. Lina pulled her pocketknife and scratched at the filler. It came out easily, leaving slotted holes obviously man-made.

Her voice trembling, Lina asked, "Jeremy, could you hand me the crowbar, please?"

"But why?"

"Just do it, please." He couldn't see what she was working over. When he handed her the crowbar, she stuck it into the hole and lifted.

The flagstone was heavy, but even by herself she could ease it free. She stacked it at one end, then continued until she had three quarters of the stones removed.

By now, Jeremy and the workers were hanging over the sides of the altar. "Lina, you were right! Why would the stones be removable if there's nothing there?"

The Indians, too, buzzed to one another in their strange tongue. Lina thought she heard the name "Pacal" bandied about several times, but she was too busy then to wonder at their excitement.

Lina was sure she stood over a burial. But could they get to it?

Glumly, she stared at the rubble blocking her. She brushed back the hair that had escaped her braid. "Well, whoever made this temple didn't want to give up their secret easily. If this stuff goes all the way to the center of the pyramid, we'll never reach it in one season. Maybe not in four."

"Don't lose heart. Here, let us help." With Jeremy's guidance, they started a line of diggers who filled buckets, then handed them up to others who took them outside and dumped them down the sides of the pyramid.

It was long, tedious work. The afternoon wore on, and finally they had to light pine torches to chase away the gathering gloom.

Five feet down, Lina's shovel struck solid stone. She inhaled, then coughed as dust entered her lungs. She dug more carefully, and soon had a long, smooth rectangle cleared. She rested her hands on her shovel.

"My God, Lina, it looks like a step!" Jeremy peered over her shoulder.

"It does, doesn't it?" Working in concert with Jeremy, she dug until another step was cleared.

When they came to the third step and still found only more rubble, Lina put her gloved hand in the small of her back and pressed. "This is not going to be a quick find, apparently. Tell the men to go home to their families. We'll start again early in the morning."

Jeremy was still digging. When his shovel struck more stone, he wiped his brow on his sleeve. "You're right, I guess. But it's maddening to leave it."

Lina smiled, wondering if her face was as dirty as his. His own frustration put hers into perspective. Of the many things she'd learned from her father, the most valuable was the criterion for any successful scientist: patience. "Whoever awaits us has been here for centuries. He won't mind resting a few more weeks." Lina looked at the full buckets handed up to the reaching hands above. "At least, I hope it's only a few weeks."

Yet, curiously, when Jeremy spoke to the men, they seemed reluctant to leave. The head worker even argued with Jeremy. Scowling, they collected their water casks and food pouches and melded with the night.

Puzzled, Lina followed them down. "How odd. I've never seen workers anywhere so willing—no, eager—to work."

"The Maya are not a lazy people. You've only to look about you to know that."

"True. Still . . ." Then, too tired to tease her brain further, Lina dismissed her unease. As they approached the palace, excitement again seized her.

"Jeremy, let me tell my father, please, in my own way."

"Of course. I wouldn't think of spoiling your surprise."

Pulling her sticky blouse away from her skin, Lina begged, "Then, may I bathe in the stream? It's dark. I'll take a gun."

Jeremy stopped abruptly. Lina turned and went back to him. Lit from below by the lantern he held, his face looked forbidding. "You don't know how to shoot."

Lina hesitated, then said softly, "No, but you do."

The flickering lantern flame seemed caught in his eyes. "Do you trust me to guard you? What if I decide to join you?"

"You have once before, and I was safe enough." Safe. What a dull word. How she longed to fling rectitude to the winds

and risk all on this man. Because she wanted it so badly,
Lina clenched her hands to keep herself from reaching out
to him.

Again, Jeremy showed a devastating bent for reading her
emotions. "Safe? You don't really want that, Lina. You're the
most daring woman I've ever known."

And he set the lantern down and drew her into his arms.

Warm lips tenderly caressed softer ones. Fireflies danced
ecstatically, reflections of the sparks arcing between the weary
adventurer and the lonely woman. The bond between them was
as ageless as the ruins they stood in—and as fragile.

It had been so long since he kissed her.

Lina's mouth trembled as she felt the deep emotion Jeremy
sometimes betrayed with a glance or a touch, but never with
a word. Lina's heart answered with a song that drowned out
all else. Who she was, why she'd come here, even who she
wanted to be, became secondary to the beauty of this man and
all he offered.

The stakes they'd wagered a world away had grown higher
with every shared smile and united thought. No matter if she
became the most famous archaeologist in the world, this was
the only supreme happiness she'd ever know.

No one, nothing, could ever replace Jeremy in her life.

Would her desperate gamble gain her a career and lose her
the only man she would ever love?

When they drew away to breathe, their hearts pounding,
Lina rested her cheek on his shoulder. Tell him, her conscience
urged. Tell him you lied to get him here. She took a deep
breath. "Jer—"

Jeremy tightened his arms about her. "Don't talk. Just let
me hold you a moment longer."

She subsided, needing this peace as desperately as he. Somewhere, the world marched on, but here in this aerie of the gods,
the embracing couple were born anew.

Finally, he sighed and released her. "Lina, do you understand now why I want you to go?"

"I know you're worried about me, but I still contend I'd not
be much safer at the hacienda."

Jeremy cupped her face in his hands. "Please. You've found
your tomb. Surely your father can conduct the dig as well?"

Hurt, Lina pulled away. "Perhaps. But this is my first, perhaps my only chance, to prove to him that I am truly as capable and dedicated as he is. How can you ask me to sacrifice all I've worked for all my life?"

Jeremy winced at the word "sacrifice" but responded passionately, "Because your life is very precious to me."

Lina kissed his cheek, her anger fading at his honesty. "I'm as safe as the rest of you. Now come along. I'm glad you'll be with me when I give my father the news. Will you then come with me to the stream?"

"If your father will allow it."

Her steps quickened. "He's not my keeper, though he likes to think he is."

When they arrived at camp, they found Baxter sketching the palace walls and Sir Lawrence brooding over the fire.

"About damned time," he snapped at his daughter. "I was just coming to look for you."

"Good. I was going to ask you to come see what we've found."

Baxter's pencil lead snapped. "Found? What could *you* have found?"

Lina flinched, but then her face lost all expression. "The morning is soon enough." Without another word, she went to her knapsack and pulled out fresh clothes.

Lina didn't see the glare Sir Lawrence shot at Baxter. "My dear, if you want to show us tonight, I'm willing. It's certain we've found nothing."

"Yet," Baxter insisted again.

"Nor are we likely to." Sir Lawrence watched his daughter bundle up fresh clothes. "What are you doing?"

"I can't stand this filth any longer. Jeremy is going to guard me while I bathe."

Baxter threw aside his sketchpad. "I'll do it."

Swiveling, Lina leveled an even blue gaze on him. "If you truly find me so helpless, sir, then I need a very, ah, experienced, strong man to guard me. You fail on both counts." Lina strode gracefully out of the palace, leaving Baxter with his mouth hanging open.

"What did I say?"

Jeremy shook his head. "Give it up, man. If you don't

even know how you've offended her, your suit is hopeless."
Jeremy followed Lina, but turned at the end of the gallery.
"By the way, the ineffectual little female may have just made
the archaeological find of the century."

Baxter surged to his feet, his fists clenched. "Don't patron-
ize me!"

But Jeremy was already gone.

Slamming a palm against the wall, Baxter snapped, "Are
you just going to let them go off like that alone?" He didn't
notice the stucco that flaked off.

Sir Lawrence did, for he watched the flakes float to the
ground before he glared at his erstwhile friend. He stalked off
to his hammock and flipped back his mosquito net. "How do
you propose I stop them? Besides, my daughter has obviously
made her choice. I can't say I'm thrilled with it, but she is
past her majority, after all. Mayhew's honorable enough, in
his own queer way."

Baxter spun on his heel. "Well, maybe you trust him. But I
don't." His steps echoed down the gallery.

Sir Lawrence jumped out of his hammock and sought a
lantern. As he turned up the wick and made his way to the
palace entrance, a small smile stretched his face. Lina would
have recognized it as his most manipulative one.

When they reached the stream, Lina and Jeremy paused to
enjoy the sight of the jungle moon riding the ripples. The
ever-present clouds had swept away, leaving the air pristine
and scented with greenery a-borning. The stream had broadened here as it prepared to tumble down the mountainside, as
perfect a bathhouse as nature could devise.

"I wonder how many ancient Maya bathed here before us?"
Lina asked dreamily. She sat down to remove her boots. "With
every day that passes, I see them more clearly."

Jeremy stood watching her a moment, but when she began
unbuttoning her blouse, he swallowed and turned away. His
voice sounded muffled when he said, "I just pray to God they
aren't seeing us as clearly."

Lina followed his gaze to the jungle lurking on all sides.
Her fingers paused, then she shrugged out of her shirt, stood
and unfastened her skirt. While Jeremy was still turned away,

she waded into the stream. She groaned in sheer luxury and sat down in the shallows, letting the current wash away her dirt and exhaustion.

"The water's heavenly." She dipped her head back and wet her hair, then splashed water over her torso. Vaguely she wondered why she felt no unease with him so near, watching her in so intimate an act. She only knew it felt right to have him here.

Jeremy tossed off his shirt and followed, sitting down opposite her. He watched her so intently that she quit splashing and peeked at him through a curtain of wet hair.

The moon was so bright that she could clearly read his expression. She caught her breath. The tenderness in his eyes was a prelude to the gentle caress that brushed the hair away from her face.

"Lina, is there anything you don't enjoy?"

The moment was mightier than pride. "Yes. Being away from you."

Groaning in need, Jeremy hauled her onto his lap and rained kisses upon her face, whispering between each one, "God, you make me feel ten feet tall. I haven't felt so alive in years."

Indeed, he surged with eagerness against her. She blushed. "I can tell."

"Be still." Jeremy raised his head and tried to frown, but the joy in Lina's heart was reflected in his eyes. "We came here to bathe, remember?"

"Did we? Just like you came here to guard me? Who's guarding *you*?"

Jeremy bit his lip and surveyed the jungle that crowded both sides of the stream. "Good point. You make me forget everything." He made to rise, but Lina locked her hands behind his neck and pulled.

She was finished with teasing. Only touching would satisfy her now. When his lips sought hers, she turned her head and tickled his ear with the tip of her tongue.

She felt the jolt run through him, then center in his groin. "Wench, are you toying with me?"

"No, Jeremy," she whispered in his ear, "I'm enjoying with you." She blew into the sensitized nerves.

His arms tightened until she could barely breathe. "But the bet. We don't know yet—"

Lina kissed his other ear. "Jeremy, I stopped caring about the bet a long time ago. How about you?"

The shiver that ran through him made his laugh shaky. "What bet?"

With a mere turning of their heads, their lips met. All the treasure they needed, or wanted, was here, in their arms.

The moon's sad face seemed to brighten as it beamed down on the two lovers. Rays lavished a golden blessing upon entwined arms and slanted heads.

But as treasures always do, they invited a marauder.

"You wanton," a harsh voice said from the stream's edge. "And you pretend to be a lady?"

Lina pulled slowly away. Damn Hubert. Jeremy had stiffened, but when he tried to set her aside, she wrapped an arm about his shoulders. There, on Jeremy's lap where she belonged, she faced Baxter. "It's about time you understood that, Hubert. I've never aspired to be a lady. It's more important to me to be a woman."

Hubert still watched Jeremy. "Well, that you are. I can vouch for that. She's every man's fantasy, what, Mayhew? She looks like an angel but acts like a whore."

Lina inhaled sharply. "This charade has gone on long enough. Jeremy, he's lying. I've never—"

But Jeremy wasn't listening. Rising, he carefully set her down and waded out of the stream. "That's enough, Baxter. Attack me all you please, but she's quite above your touch."

"She's obviously not above yours." Baxter met Jeremy halfway and took a wild swing.

Jeremy ducked and returned with a brutal punch to Baxter's chin. Baxter fell backward and cradled his head, shaking it.

His fists clenched, Jeremy stood over him. "Get up. I'm not finished with you yet."

"Yes you are." Sir Lawrence strode out of the bushes.

Lina wondered how long he'd been listening.

Baxter shook his head, then poked his forefingers in his ears.

Sir Lawrence glared at Baxter. "I hope your ears ring for a week. How dare you speak so to my daughter?"

Baxter only tilted his head and tapped his opposite ear. Sniffing his disgust, Sir Lawrence turned his attention to his daughter. "Lina, what am I going to do with you?"

Respect me, she longed to answer. Listen to me. She knew he loved her, but his condemnation of Baxter made her wonder if he was finally seeing her as a woman grown, not just as his daughter.

Lina strolled out of the water and drew her clean shirt over her chemise, putting Jeremy between her and Baxter. "We've accomplished something, at least, Father, if you'll quit pushing me toward Hubert."

"This trip has made me see how unsuitable he is for you," her father admitted quietly.

Hubert was still shaking his head and apparently didn't hear.

Lina hid a smile. Her father had deliberately sent Baxter on ahead to stop the inevitable, but she realized that, in his own way, he was trying to protect her. If he only knew. She wanted this American so badly that perhaps her father should be protecting Jeremy.

Their union had merely been delayed. When she was dressed, she shared a smile with him that said so. From the way his eyes darkened, she knew he understood.

"Hurry up," Sir Lawrence snapped when he caught the by-play. "I want to see this great discovery of yours."

"Fine. As long as you remember it is *my* discovery." Lina turned away from the stream.

A gentle hand caught her shoulder. Jeremy put his arm about her. "I can't wait to see his face, can you?"

Arm in arm, they strode to the temple. Jeremy climbed behind her, followed by Baxter and Sir Lawrence, who still carried a lantern. When they reached the doorway, Lina stopped. A dim glow emitted from the altar room.

"Jeremy, did you relight a torch after I left?"

"No. Why?" Jeremy stopped as he, too, saw the light. He fumbled for his pistol, then shoved her behind him. "Stay here."

Lina held a finger to her lips when her father and Baxter entered. She jerked her head toward the light. She tiptoed behind Jeremy.

Jeremy circled the altar, then looked inside. "Nothing." He

holstered his pistol. "I guess you didn't totally extinguish one of the torches. Still, it's odd it burned so long without being refueled."

Sir Lawrence spun in a slow circle. "What did you find? I don't see anything." Then his gaze lit on the paving stones they'd piled in a corner. He bent and fit two of them together. He ran his finger over the plugs they'd removed.

"My God." He rose abruptly. "Where is it?"

A smile playing about her lips, Lina let him wait.

"Dammit, girl, don't leave us hanging."

Baxter, too, bent over the paving stones, then surged to his feet and looked eagerly around.

Lina crooked a finger at them. "Follow me." She climbed one of the ladders, nodding for them to do the same, then dropped inside the altar. "Be sure you drop down at the end, where it's level."

When both men were standing beside her, Lina asked, "Jeremy, can you hand us the torch?"

Jeremy handed it down to Sir Lawrence. He gasped when he saw the steps. "How many have you uncovered?"

"Only four so far. If the burial is at ground level . . ."

The two pairs of blue eyes, so much alike, met. For once, father and daughter shared a common thought. Sir Lawrence said, "We'll never reach it before we have to leave."

Lina shook her head. "Maybe we'll get lucky."

Hubert was rubbing his chin. "We can start an assembly line. Maybe even rig up buckets on pulleys."

"That's a good idea," Sir Lawrence agreed.

"We've already done that," Lina snapped. "And it's me you should be talking to."

Sir Lawrence absently patted his daughter's shoulder. "Lina, I'm proud of you for finding this, but now you must let me do my job."

"Indeed. Go back to surveying the palace. You may still find something."

"This is more promising. Now, tomorrow we'll—"

"Tomorrow you'll leave me alone and let me do my job!" Deliberately Lina replicated his words.

Finally, that vague expression left his eyes. "My dear, surely you don't want to head this excavation?"

"I found it." Lina hesitated, then caught her father's arm. "Please, Father. Don't deny me this chance to prove that I, too, learned something in all those dusty camps. I love archaeology as much as you do."

"Ridiculous," Hubert broke in. "You don't even have the strength needed."

"I can shovel with the best of them." Lina held up her hands, palms out, and showed them the blisters that had rubbed through her gloves.

"Sir Lawrence, you must let her try," Jeremy said above them. "I'm not sure how the workers will feel if you take over. They're used to her now. She did find the steps, after all."

Sir Lawrence sighed. "Very well. I guess you're your father's daughter." He brushed her stubborn chin with a fist, but Lina saw the pride in his eyes.

Five years of turmoil quieted in that instant. Lina squealed and threw her arms about her father. "Oh, Father, I love you."

Sir Lawrence cleared his throat, glancing uneasily at Baxter, and pulled her away. "Yes, well, that's nice, but remember all you've learned. Never take anything for granted. Save everything, no matter how inconsequential, and record its position."

Lina hugged him again. "I will."

Awkwardly, he patted her back. "And promise me, mind, that the minute you find anything you'll come get me."

"I promise." Lina felt as if wings were attached to her feet, but Jeremy's strong hands might have had something to do with that. He lifted her over the altar, set her on the floor, then turned to help the two men out.

Lina heard a slight rustling. She was still so happy that she didn't heed it until she saw a blue flash behind the altar pieces they'd stacked against the wall. She looked at Jeremy, but he was headfirst inside the altar as he offered a hand to Sir Lawrence.

Lina hesitated, then she tiptoed toward the wall. Probably just a bird, caught in the room. When she was one step away, she knelt and peeked inside the gap.

Even in the shadows, she saw the flash of dark eyes. She barely had time to gasp before the man wriggled out of his hiding place and surged to his feet.

In the shadowy chamber, he seemed a carving come to life. His strong ankles and wrists were banded with jade. His quetzal headdress had several broken feathers, but was still imposing, even in the dim light. His breechclout was golden, with a long fringed sash in the middle hanging between his legs. His immense shoulders gleamed with sweat, rippling as he backed toward the door. Only then did she see the huge obsidian ax sheathed on his back. The ornately carved copper hilt gleamed as he moved.

Mesmerized, Lina couldn't look away from those compelling dark eyes. Like a supplicant, she knelt at his feet, too stunned to warn the others. He was so exactly as she'd pictured him. In fact, she'd seen him twice before. He'd been the one who watched her at the stream. Yet . . . her brow crinkled. He seemed even more familiar.

He smiled slightly, firming Lina's impression. He held a finger to his lips, still backing toward the door.

Baxter was just dropping to the floor. Jeremy had one foot on, one foot off the ladder when Sir Lawrence turned toward his daughter.

"Lina . . ." Sir Lawrence trailed off in shock.

Jeremy, too, turned his head. Both men stared in disbelief at the sight of Lina kneeling at the feet of the Mayan priest.

"Mayhew, your gun!"

Jeremy already had it out, but by the time he jumped down off the ladder, the priest had already covered the distance to the door in two great strides.

With a ripple of feathers and a slight rustling of cotton, he was gone. Jeremy ran after him, but Lina blocked his path.

Jeremy shoved her aside.

He came back a few minutes later. "He was too fast for me. He must have every crack in these steps memorized. Lina, why did you stop me?"

"Were you going to shoot him?"

"Probably. Didn't you see the ax about his shoulder?"

"Yes."

"That's no doubt the same ax that killed the Indian," Jeremy reminded her grimly.

"The same Indian who killed one of our workers, remember?"

"And could just as easily kill us," Baxter pointed out.

"Oh yes? Then why didn't he, when he had the chance?"

Jeremy frowned. "What do you mean?"

"You had your back turned for a good fifteen minutes while we were inside the altar. He could have easily come up behind you, Jeremy."

"That's true," Jeremy said slowly. "And if he didn't want to kill us, why didn't he leave while he had the chance?"

"Maybe he wanted to listen to our plans."

"You think he speaks English?" Sir Lawrence demanded.

"Why else would he stay? But I believe you're all asking the wrong questions."

"What do you mean?" Jeremy asked.

"Lina, be specific," her father admonished.

"Naturally, you know more than the rest of us," Baxter said, sotto voce.

Lina shot him a glare, then answered evenly, "You shouldn't be asking what his intentions are, but something even more basic—why did he come here?" She looked at the altar.

"Why has he been watching us since we arrived?" She approached the altar and rested a hand on it as if the contact would answer all her frustrating questions.

Then she swung to face the three men. "Most important—what does he want us to find?"

Chapter 13

Sir Lawrence exclaimed, "My word, you're right! Maybe he does expect us to find something." He strode up and down, muttering to his feet, "But how would he know? And if he knew there was something here, why didn't he just dig for it himself?"

Lina listened to her father ramble, knowing he'd not hear her if she interrupted. Eventually, he'd draw the same conclusions.

However, Jeremy was a different story. He'd said little, but judging by the way he fingered his pistol, he wasn't so sanguine about the priest's intentions. Lina knew that tense set to Jeremy's fine features. When he finally whirled on her as if he couldn't be still, she braced herself.

"Lina, I'll take no argument. It's too dangerous for you to remain here. Pack your clothes. You're going to Don Roberto's. Tonight."

"No."

Jeremy took an angry stride forward before he caught himself. "Lina, there's nothing you can do until we reach a tomb." His voice softened. "*If* we reach a tomb. I won't have you risk your life for nothing. If anything happened to you, I'd—" He bit his lip.

Anger fell in the face of his earnestness. Could she fault him for caring? "Jeremy, I'm in no danger. Why would the priest kill one of his own kind to protect us if he meant us ill? It doesn't make sense. No, somehow, his purpose allies with our own. I don't know how or why. But I mean to find out."

When his stony expression hardened to iron, Lina stepped

to him and put her hand on his arm. "Please, don't you see I'd go out of my mind worrying about you all? Jeremy, this is something I have to do. If you truly care about me, you'll understand that."

Jeremy's answer was wordless but definite. He flung off her arm and stomped out of the altar room.

Baxter's smug smile made Lina turn away so he wouldn't see her distress. God, why did it always come to this? No matter how capable she proved herself, even Jeremy reacted viscerally when she was in danger.

If she were a man, he'd not ask her to leave.

Despite his obvious concern, his request was an insult to all she was and wanted to be—in his arms. If the man she loved couldn't understand her need for self-determination, who could?

Lina dashed her tears off on her sleeve, whirled and sought peace alone in the jungle night.

Over the next month, peace proved even more elusive. Lina's only solace was the back-breaking, never-ending work. This time, the rift between her and Jeremy was too wide to bridge.

This time, she didn't even try.

Nor did he. From dawn to dusk, his weapons never left his side. Even as days faded into weeks, his vigilance was constant. Most of the time he stayed atop the tower or one of the pyramids, his rifle resting in the crook of his arm as he surveyed the jungle.

Lina seldom saw him for meals. The ache in her back accented rather than lessened the ache in her heart. Not once did she see a softening in those gray eyes that had once looked at her with such tenderness. In truth, sometimes she wondered if he hated her. The only time he touched her was when he gave her the daily dose of Maya medicine, diluted in her tea. Even then, he pulled his hand away quickly as his fingers brushed hers.

Then she'd lift her chin and turn away, denying, even to herself, the hurts he'd inflicted and the dreams he'd shattered. She could never be happy with a man who couldn't treat her as an equal. Jeremy had seemed so different. Now, increasingly, she wondered if her own loneliness hadn't invested in him the qualities she wanted to see.

Maybe her father was right. There, at least, she found some comfort. For the first time in years, he listened to her opinions. As the days passed and he saw how meticulous her methods were, from labeling and dating every find to sieving all the dirt they removed from the stairs, his grudging acceptance of her dig grew to excitement.

The two men had long since moved their excavation to the Temple of the Inscriptions. There, too, they'd found paving stones and hidden steps. There, too, they'd found rubble that had to be painstakingly removed.

The two digs had become a competition, but, for the first time in Lina's memory, it was a friendly one. At night, they'd each show off the trinkets they'd found.

"See here," Sir Lawrence said one evening, pulling a pottery fragment from his pocket with a flourish.

Lina turned the curved clay fragment over. "It looks like it came from a bowl."

"That's my guess. See the jaguar?"

"Yes." Lina shivered. Remnants of red paint still clung to the potsherd, delineating the setting behind the jaguar: a pile of human bones. Lina handed the fragment back. "Maybe a funerary bowl?"

"Maybe." Sir Lawrence gave the clay to Baxter, who dipped a pen in an inkwell and inscribed a neat number on it, then stuck it inside a crate lined with straw.

"And what did you find today, my dear? Anything of interest?"

Lina smiled and stuck her hand in her shirt pocket. "I'm glad you listened to my idea about the screens. Without them, we never would have found this."

"Best idea you ever had," Sir Lawrence agreed. "Well, let me see."

Of their own accord, Lina's eyes sought Jeremy. She ached to share her discovery with him, for it was the first evidence that she might be right. He sat against the wall, sharpening his knives. Not once did he look up, though she was certain he must feel her gaze.

Swallowing her hurt, Lina turned back to her father and handed him the tiny artifact.

"By Jove!" Sir Lawrence turned the smooth, cylindrical object over, holding it up to the lantern light to look through the hole drilled in its center. "Jade. Surely it's a bead from a necklace."

"That's what I thought."

Two pairs of blue eyes met. In that moment, the Colliers were not father and daughter, or even fellow Britons. They were archaeologists.

With an air of reverence, Sir Lawrence handed the bead back to his daughter. "Be sure you record where you found it."

"I've judged it as best I can, but we don't have room for the sieves in the altar room, so we've set the screens up at the bottom of the pyramid where we dump the dirt. I can't tell exactly what level it came from, but I can make a guess since we can only clear about three steps a day."

"Do your best, child." Sir Lawrence yawned and excused himself. When he stood, Lina noted that he limped.

She frowned. "What's wrong?"

"I don't know. My foot's been bothering me today. Help me get my boots off, will you?"

Lina complied. Sir Lawrence tugged off his sock.

Gasping, Lina held his foot up. It was swollen from the ankle down. "Have you fallen?"

"No. It's felt funny all day. Almost pulsating."

"Let me wrap it."

"That won't do any good."

Lina started and looked up at the tall shadow. Jeremy knelt next to her and turned Sir Lawrence's foot this way and that. Then he folded a clean towel under her father's ankle, stood, fetched the stiletto he'd sharpened and poured some carefully hoarded rum over it. Finally, he held the blade over the fire.

"What are you doing?" Sir Lawrence demanded, his gaze narrowing on Jeremy's knife. The tip was beginning to glow.

"Sir Lawrence, you'll get badly infected if the nest isn't drained."

Sir Lawrence paled. "Nest? What the devil do you mean?"

"Lina, give your father the rum." Jeremy pulled the knife

out of the flame. "I'd suggest he imbibe a healthy amount, because this won't be pleasant."

Lina crouched protectively before her father. "You're not going to hurt him."

Wounded gray eyes darkened, then went flat. "He has *niguas,* Miss Collier. They must come out, or he could get badly infected."

"What are *niguas*?" father and daughter asked in concert.

"Tiny blood-sucking insects. They enter the flesh under the toenails, eat their way inside and lay their eggs, which then multiply under the skin."

Lina gagged.

Sir Lawrence bolted to a seated position. "What?" He stared in horror at his own foot.

Baxter set down the artifact he'd been numbering and tore at his shoes and socks to feel his toes. He sighed his relief, then put them back on.

"I'm surprised you didn't have them before now. The medicinal herb I've been trying to get you to take protects against them and mosquitoes."

"Why the devil didn't you tell me that?"

"I did." Jeremy's lips stretched into that cynical smile that Lina hated. "But you doubted my warning, apparently." Jeremy squatted and lifted Sir Lawrence's foot on his thigh. "Take a few more healthy swigs."

For once, Sir Lawrence didn't argue. The bottle was half-empty when he finally lay down. "I'm ready. My dear, perhaps you'd better go outside for a moment."

Lina shook her head. "I'm staying." Strongly, she clasped his hand.

Jeremy's jaw flexed, and briefly, Lina saw her own torment reflected in his eyes. Then thick lashes shimmered in the firelight as Jeremy watched his patient's foot. He lifted the knife and made a swift, straight cut.

His back bowing, Sir Lawrence choked back a scream. The second cut was too much for him. His howl echoed through the ageless corridors.

Lina bit her lip until she drew blood, but then it was over. Jeremy squeezed Sir Lawrence's flesh. Pus and blood oozed out. Sir Lawrence winced, then sighed as the pressure eased.

Lina saw the tiny white dots swimming in the pus. Some of them even moved. She turned her head away.

Jeremy poured antiseptic over the cut. Sir Lawrence flinched and bit back a groan. Then Jeremy was winding clean bandages about the wound. "You'll need to stay off this for a few days. Do you want me to get some bearers to carry you to the hacienda?"

"No. I'll be fine."

Jeremy wiped up the mess with a rag, tossed the rag into the fire, then used the water bucket to wash his hands.

"Mayhew . . . thanks."

"Certainly. Would you like to start taking tea with Lina every morning?"

"Yes."

"Me too," Baxter added.

Jeremy nodded, then returned to sharpening his weapons.

Lina willed him to yell at her, shake her, somehow acknowledge her existence, but Jeremy could barely look at her, much less talk to her.

The knowledge ate at her like *niguas* throughout the night, into the next day, putrefying hope as the days marched into weeks. Lina knew only one antidote for the pain: work.

Ambition had lost her the only man she'd ever love, apparently. She might as well make the most of it.

From morning to night, she labored. They uncovered ten steps, then fifteen, then twenty. The deeper she was entombed in the darkness, the more determined Lina became. No matter how much gold they found—and they would find it, she assured herself, unable to contemplate losing the bet now— the expedition would be a failure unless they could answer the most pressing questions about Mayan history.

Who were these people? How had they lived? Why had they deserted their cities?

Compelling questions, all. To answer them they'd have to decipher these glyphs. Early one afternoon, tired from yet another sleepless night, Lina was tracing the glyphs with her finger for the umpteenth time, trying to see a connection, when she heard a commotion outside.

Lina stood, stumbling on her numb legs to the entrance. She shaded her eyes.

Horses stood before the palace, tails slashing at flies. Two of the animals wore sidesaddles. Lina hurried down the pyramid, her grim mood lightening.

Visitors were just what they needed. She hoped Cesar had come too. The charming Spaniard's admiration would be good for her bruised ego.

It wouldn't hurt Jeremy any either.

Lina's hurrying feet faltered as she reached the palace steps. She hated manipulative women—but dammit, Jeremy had manipulated her until she felt like a puppet. She had to know if he still cared for her.

Removing her gloves, Lina crammed loose tendrils back into her braid, took a deep breath, and practiced the happy smile that had once come to her with such ease. "Don Roberto! It's wonderful to see you."

Don Roberto gave her a courtly bow. "Señorita, the pleasure is mine, I assure you."

Jeremy turned from conversing with Carmen as Lina put her hand in Cesar's extended one. "We thought to relieve your drudgery with a party," Cesar explained. He kissed her hand, then cradled it in the crook of his arm.

From the corner of her eye, Lina saw Jeremy stiffen.

She smiled at Cesar. "You couldn't have come at a better time. What have you brought us?" Lina opened the huge hamper and peeked inside. "Scrumptious! Ham, cheese, wine, bread, and mangos."

"We thought you might be out of fresh food," Don Roberto explained.

"Long since," Sir Lawrence said, entering the courtyard, Baxter at his side. He shook Don Roberto's hand. "Capital of you, sir."

"Not at all. All I ask in return is to see some of your finds." Don Roberto grinned when both Englishmen couldn't seem to take their eyes off the basket. "After we dine, of course."

Carmen and Cesar spread blankets on one of the courtyards. Everyone tucked in with a will. Lina barely noticed when Cesar sat down beside her. Until this moment, she hadn't realized how tired she'd grown of beans and tortillas.

Cesar glanced from where Jeremy sat off to the side with

Carmen, to Lina. He quirked an eyebrow at his father. Don Roberto shrugged.

Slicing another piece of ham, Cesar inched closer to Lina and set the slice on her plate. "So, señorita, how do you manage to remain so beautiful even with dirt on your face?" Cesar wiped her cheek with his cloth napkin, the service more a caress than a chore. Then he cocked his head. "Perfect."

Lina flushed. "I don't. But it's kind of you to say so." She set her plate aside and scrubbed her face with her own napkin.

Cesar gently pulled her hands away. "Don't. You make me envious of a piece of cloth. Would you like some more wine?"

Mesmerized by the mellow warmth of those dark brown eyes, Lina nodded. Cesar topped up her glass, then clinked his glass against hers. "To ancient ties and new friendships."

The party grew merrier with every opened bottle of wine. Sir Lawrence and Baxter gestured as they conversed with Don Roberto about their mutual obsession. Carmen's sister sat next to Baxter, fluttering her eyelashes at the Englishman. Jeremy and Carmen shared another blanket, speaking in tones too low for Lina to overhear.

For the moment, she didn't care. She was enjoying herself so much that she almost forgot her ulterior motive until she threw back her head in laughter at one of Cesar's jokes and caught Jeremy's eye. He didn't seem to be enjoying himself, for he sat grimly watching her even when Carmen put her hand on his arm.

However, when Lina smiled at him hesitantly, he set his glass down, pulled Carmen up and escorted her toward the tower, carrying his rifle in his other hand.

Let him go, Lina's pride advised.

But she couldn't. Maybe she'd had too much to drink; maybe she was simply foolish. Whatever the reason, Lina's love was stronger than pride. She surged to her feet. "Jeremy, don't go. You need this respite more than anyone."

"Carmen is all the company I need," he said over his shoulder. Then he was inside the tower, unaware, and probably, Lina decided, uncaring of how he'd hurt her so publicly.

Lina muttered, "I want to check on my workers. Please

excuse me." She fled, barely making it out of the courtyard before the tears fell.

Footsteps pounded after her. "Señorita . . . Lina, please wait." Cesar caught her arm as she reached the foot of the palace steps. He cupped her cheek and turned her averted face up to him. He examined her closely. Regret flashed in his dark eyes, then he murmured, "He's jealous, you know. He wants to hurt you because you've hurt him."

Angrily Lina dashed her tears away. She hated herself for shedding them. "He'll not succeed."

"You are too honest to believe that." Cesar gently led her to the foot of the steps. "Tell me what happened. I thought maybe I had mistaken the way you both felt about one another, but obviously I was right the first time."

When they were seated, Cesar took her hand. His understanding clasp encouraged, but did not demand.

The words trickled, then rushed out in a torrent. When she was done, Lina felt much better.

Cesar shook his head. "You mustn't blame him for worrying about you. That is his right. I, too, would demand that you leave, if you were mine."

Lina tugged her hand away. "I might have known you'd take up for him. Why is it so hard for you males to understand that women, too, need to be independent and accepted on their own terms?"

Cesar's winsome smile grew roguish. "Ah, senorita, acceptance is such a very dull word for the excitement between men and women. If we truly understood each other, life would be boring."

Typical male arrogance. Mentally Lina threw up her hands, but before she could think of a rejoinder, Jeremy and Carmen exited the palace. Jeremy paused when he saw Cesar leaning intimately toward Lina, but then he tightened his grip on Carmen's hand and skirted them to descend the steps.

"Where are you going, my friend?" Cesar asked.

"Carmen wants to see the altar room." Jeremy didn't miss a step.

Lina was the one disturbed. The workers were still digging, and besides, the discovery was hers. It was her privilege to show off the altar room, and this was one triumph Jeremy would not spoil for her. She surged to her feet. "Now is not a good time—"

An arrow zinged into the steps where she'd been sitting. Lina froze, confused. Cesar stared dumbly at the broken shank of the arrow, which had bounced off the steps.

Only Jeremy's quick reactions saved them. Shouting "Get back inside!" he barreled up the steps, shoving Carmen ahead of him.

Lina and Cesar dived for the shadows as arrows showered down on them. Lina looked back over her shoulder as she ran, fearing for Jeremy's safety, but he'd crouched in the shadows and leveled his rifle to fire back.

"Give me your pistol!" Cesar shouted.

Jeremy slammed the butt of the weapon into Cesar's outstretched hand, then gestured angrily at Lina. "Take Carmen back to the interior hallway and get the others to bring their weapons."

For once, Lina obeyed without argument. She burst onto the courtyard, Carmen at her heels. "We're under attack! Jeremy and Cesar need help."

Sir Lawrence dropped his wine glass, not even noticing the spreading stain on the lovely quilt.

Don Roberto cursed and hurried to his saddlebag, flipping it open and removing an old but serviceable pistol. He rapped out orders to his daughters in Spanish. Obediently they trailed one another to the first tower floor. Don Roberto stationed himself at the entrance. "Señorita," he called to Lina, "Come. Here you will be safe."

Lina pretended not to hear and hurried back inside the palace to rummage through their supplies. She'd seen an extra pistol. Where was it? Her fingers brushed cold steel. She drew the pistol out of the crate, pointing it downward, and grabbed the box of bullets.

Maybe she couldn't shoot, but she could load.

Baxter snatched his own rifle, which he'd left next to his hammock. Lina passed him on her way back to the entrance. His eyes widened when he saw what she held, but his grab missed as she zagged sideways.

"Lina! Get the hell back here!" Sir Lawrence pounded after

her, his own pistol in his hand. "Go join the other women. At once!"

He spoke to air, for Lina had already made it to the entrance. Cesar was reloading, crouched behind one of the doorway pillars. Lina handed him the ready pistol and took his to finish loading it.

He scowled at her for her trouble. "Get back. You'll be hurt."

"So? Maybe you will be too."

Jeremy was sighting his rifle, but when he heard her voice, his arms sagged. Openmouthed, he stared at her.

The shock on his face slammed into Lina's gut, but she lifted her chin. "It's no more in my nature to sit and wait for deliverance than it is in yours." And she scooted on her elbows and belly toward him, Cesar's loaded pistol in one hand.

Since the men crouched on opposite sides of the entrance, she had to pass the doorway to reach Jeremy.

"Lina! No!" Jeremy instinctively inched forward to help her. A spear slammed into the pillar beside his head, smattering them with stucco dust. Then Lina was in his arms.

The pistol skidded out of Lina's hand across the paving. Sir Lawrence grabbed it.

Jeremy caught Lina in his arms and rolled with her back to safety. She felt the frantic pounding of his heart, and for one precious instant, she closed her eyes to revel in his concern.

Had she seen his face, she'd not have felt so safe.

Sir Lawrence nudged Jeremy in the shoulder. Automatically Jeremy released Lina and accepted the pistol. "I may kill you myself, angel, when I get the chance," he said through his teeth.

Her face white with stucco dust, Lina smiled up at him. "As long as you kiss me first."

Gilded lashes blinked rapidly, then Jeremy shoved her prone behind him. "Stay down!"

With Lina's help, the men were able to fire continually, so every time the Indians tried to approach, they were cut down. Their own position, looking down from the height of the palace, was also an advantage.

"What if they work their way behind us?" Cesar shouted over the reverberating fire.

"Unless they're already placed, they haven't had time," Jeremy called back. "But it wouldn't hurt for a couple of you to climb to the tower. Lina, you go with your father."

Her face stucco-white on one side, powder-black on the other, Lina scowled at him. "No. I'm staying with you." *Where I belong.* She longed to say the words, but now was not the time—if she ever mustered the courage to say them at all.

Danger had a queer way of putting things into perspective. Whether this moment was her last with Jeremy, or one of a lifetime with him, she would not leave his side.

Jeremy slammed more cartridges into his rifle. "Reason with her, Sir Lawrence."

But Sir Lawrence sighed as he saw the set of his daughter's mouth. "Be careful, child. We'll go check the other sides. Come on, Hubert."

Baxter and Sir Lawrence snaked backward on their stomachs. Their running steps rang as they reached the interior corridor.

The battle raged for ten more minutes, but the Indians' bows and spears were no match for their armament. In between loading, Lina glimpsed a strong brown body collapsing on the slope before the palace, blood oozing from a chest wound. She swallowed and hastily looked back at the gun in her hands.

Death was ugly, even when it came to an enemy. What else could they do but fight? When Lina heard gunfire echoing from the tower, she knew the end was near. Still, she continued to load steadily, hunkered down behind the pillar with Jeremy.

Cesar gave a wild howl. "They're on the run!"

Lina peeked. Bare-chested Maya ran down the hillside, some of them dragging their wounded along with them.

Even more telling, she glimpsed her own workers atop pyramids firing back. Some used muskets, but others had bows and arrows. She frowned, wondering why the men had brought weapons, but Jeremy shoved her back before she could see more.

His mouth worked as he slammed his rifle down, butt first, against the entrance. "I swear I'm going to beat you." He took a kerchief from his pocket and roughly swiped off her face.

"Look at you. You're driving me crazy! You don't listen, you don't care about anything but—"

Lina stopped his tirade by simple but effective means. She caught his head in her hands, drew it down to her level, and slanted her mouth over his. Jeremy latched onto her like a starving man, crushing her in his arms. Forgotten, the kerchief fluttered to the floor.

She could barely breathe, but what matter? Their mutual hunger had to be fed. For too many long weeks they'd fasted. Pride was a meager offering compared to this banquet of the senses.

The taste of him was divine. Sighing her pleasure, Lina opened her mouth to the thrust of his tongue. She twined hers about his, softening his aggression with response. His embrace gentled even as she felt his need growing against her abdomen. Lina ran her hands up and down his back, loving the virility tamed now for her pleasure.

At the moment.

A delicious thrill shivered through Lina, for she knew his strength was all the more powerful when it was restrained, all the more responsive when it was controlled. The right time, the right touch, and he would be a dynamo, she the switch.

Someone said, "Ah, Jeremy, señorita, we have visitors . . ." Cesar chuckled when he didn't get a response and said something in rapid Spanish.

Vaguely Lina sensed movement, then Jeremy's mesmerizing mouth was gone. Bereft, Lina reached for him again, but he set her firmly away and cleared his throat. "Ah, Lina, we have work to do."

Lina's haze cleared as she saw Don Roberto, her father, the girls, and Baxter staring at her. Self-consciously she patted at her hair. "Um, is all clear now?"

"Yes, it seems so." Don Roberto's solemn reponse belied the amusement in his eyes. "But now we must investigate the dead. I want to know which tribe hates us so. Will you come with me, Jeremy?"

His color heightened, Jeremy stood and led the way out. Lina made to follow, but Cesar caught her arm. "No. This time, be sensible. The sight is not a pretty one." He stared down at the lifeless heap on the slope before the palace.

Lina bit her lip and nodded. Sir Lawrence gave her a long-suffering look before he followed Cesar. Baxter skirted Lina, his mouth curled in distaste, and tromped down the steps.

Not for the first time, Lina thought Baxter should settle here, where his provincial attitudes were common.

"I'll help you pack your things," Lina offered as the girls continued to stare at her. All but Carmen smiled at Lina, obviously envying her boldness. Carmen sashayed back out to the courtyard.

Even from the interior, Lina heard the wine bottles clashing against each other. Sighing, Lina followed the girls.

Yet again, she was consigned to women's work, but she'd pushed the boundaries enough for one day. Besides, she wasn't sure she could stomach examining the dead. Enemies or no, the Maya had been human, with their own families, and beliefs.

Beliefs the expedition had challenged in coming here. Why did the Maya hate them so? And why did her workers fight against their own kind to save the foreigners?

Lina was to have her answers sooner than she expected.

The men buried the three dead Indians, marking their graves with simple stones so their tribe could find them if they wanted to recover the bodies. Then Don Roberto, Cesar, Baxter, her father, and Jeremy all hunkered down beside the fire, accepting the plates the daughters handed them. Don Roberto had decreed they'd all eat supper before returning. They knew the steep mountain trail so well they could traverse it even in the dark.

Lina accepted the inevitable and poured drinks for the men, tolerating their arrogance until the hasty meal was finished. But when the daughters retreated to a separate courtyard to wash, Lina balked.

She ignored her father's pointing finger and plopped down next to Jeremy. Their low-voiced conversation stopped, but she'd heard enough to realize they were discussing the warring tribes.

Sir Lawrence cleared his throat. "Ah, Lina, shouldn't you get ready for bed?"

"I have it on the best authority that I must wear my boots and clothes at all times. I'm as ready as I shall be. Don't mind me. I'll be as quiet as a little old mouse."

Jeremy sighed at her sarcasm. "Lina, we're not trying to exclude you, it's just that what we're discussing is not very pleasant."

"So? I saw men die today. I can't say I enjoyed watching that, but at least I want to understand why. I have every right to listen." More right, she thought, considering the sacrifices she'd made to get here. Her gaze slipped to Jeremy's mobile mouth.

And the ones yet to come. She smiled inwardly.

Sacrifice? Blessing, more like. The kiss she'd shared with Jeremy had gone a long way to blunting her anger and pain. He cared for her, despite their differences, as she cared for him. Somehow they'd work everything out.

But not if he persisted in his charming notions of "protection."

The kiss had, apparently, also appeased Jeremy, for he didn't flare up. He spread his hands wryly to the others, then drew Lina under his arm. His open, possessive touch warmed her more than the fire as he said, "We might as well let her stay. She'll worm everything out of us soon enough."

"Thank you, Jeremy," she whispered.

Don Roberto looked disapproving, but he gave a very Latin shrug that said "Women!" and continued. "I recognized one of the dead. His tribe is the one that started sacrificing again."

"Why do they want us to leave?" Baxter asked.

"And why do our own workers fight to keep us here?" Lina couldn't resist adding.

Don Roberto replied, "The first question is easy—they consider you interlopers desecrating their monuments. The second . . ." Don Roberto rubbed his chin. "I wish I knew. It's not uncommon for various Maya groups to fight one another, but I've never seen a tribe defend Westerners against their own people." Don Roberto warmed his hands before the fire, as if he'd suddenly grown chilled.

A log fell, shooting sparks into the air. Flames licked hungrily at the new fodder, casting eerie shadows against the muraled walls. Lina squirmed closer to Jeremy, for she couldn't shake the feeling that they were being watched. The only shadows wavering before her eyes were their own, she told herself.

But she started when a broad foot materialized. She squinted and saw the headman standing there, half in shadow, half in light. How did he move so silently?

Jeremy, too, jumped, but relaxed when he realized who it was. He said something to the man. The Maya answered, holding out his hand.

"What did he say? Why haven't they gone home?" Lina asked.

"He says one of his men was injured, but not seriously. They took him back to the village. The rest wanted to keep digging. He has something for you. Says they found it right before the shooting started."

"What?" Lina rose.

"I don't know. He insists on showing it to you."

Lina circled the fire. In his harlequin shades of bright and dark, the Indian looked mysterious, frightening. Lina's intuition had grown with time: These Maya worked because of a stronger motivation than money.

Today, her last doubt had dissolved. They'd literally risked their lives to keep them here.

Not because of greed.

Because of need.

They wanted something. But what?

Lina's heart leaped against her ribs when she saw what the man held. She gasped, caught his strong wrist and pulled him closer to the firelight. "Where did you find it?"

Jeremy translated her question. Sir Lawrence and the others rose, crowding around them.

The man answered.

"He said they hit a floor late this afternoon. They found the skeleton of a dog there and this statue. Both of them stood before a slab."

The clay figurine was chipped but intact. The vulture crouched in menace, wings folded, beak half open, ready to eat. Remnants of red paint remained about the mouth of the figure. Lina frowned as she drew it into the light. Something was wrong. This couldn't be from Palenque. The workmanship was crude compared to the grace of all the murals and the altar.

When she offered it to her father, Sir Lawrence gingerly picked it up. "By Jove, it's complete." He turned it over, examining it from all sides, then handed it to Baxter. "What do you think it was for, Hubert?"

"I've no idea." Baxter frowned. "But there's something odd about it."

"I thought that too. Lina, what do you . . ." Sir Lawrence's words trailed off when he saw no trace of his daughter, Jeremy, or the headman. "Where did they go?"

"The temple, I imagine." Don Roberto yawned. "Me, I've had enough excitement for one day. Tomorrow, you can tell me what you've found . . ." Don Roberto shrugged and went to round up his pride.

Baxter and Sir Lawrence had already run out of the palace.

The lanterns held by Jeremy and the headman illuminated the scene: Lina examined the front of what appeared to be a wooden-framed tomb. Frowning, she stood on tiptoe, feeling with her fingers.

Crudely jointed logs apparently supported the structure. "Why is this joist wood when the rest of Palenque is mainly stucco and stone?" Lina stepped over the dog skeleton and appraised the stone slab.

"Do we have enough workmen left to move this now?" Lina asked Jeremy. He translated.

The headman answered his query, set the lantern down, and ascended to the altar room to bellow something down to his men, who were gathered at the base of the pyramid.

Jeremy watched Lina walk in the limited space, craning her neck as she looked for an opening behind the slab. "Why aren't you thrilled, Lina? It looks as though you're right. There is a tomb."

Lina brushed off her dusty hands. "I hope I'm wrong, but it looks to me as if this tomb must have been put here long after Palenque was deserted. It just doesn't match. The workmanship of the statue was amateurish, and now we find a log tomb instead of the stone chamber we might have expected."

Jeremy frowned and said slowly, "I didn't think of that."

"Nor did I." Sir Lawrence slowly descended the steps to their level. "But I should have."

Before Lina could think of the ramifications of that admission, the workers came back into the altar room. Lina climbed out to allow the men more room.

With the Westerners' help, the Maya heaved the slab away from an opening. Lina was too busy watching to note that two of the workers in the altar room melted away.

As her father picked up a lantern, Lina held her breath.

Jeremy took a step toward him, but Lina caught his eye and shook her head.

Her father either accepted her of his own accord, or not at all.

Sir Lawrence moved closer to the opening, then he stopped. Pivoting, he called up to his daughter, "Well? Are you going to wait up there all night?"

A joyous smile drained the tiredness from Lina's face. She felt lighter than air as she tripped down the stairs. She flung her arms about her father's neck. "Thank you, Father."

He hugged her back. "You've earned this moment, daughter. Forgive me for not seeing it sooner."

His distinctive Collier eyes gleamed with pride as he watched his daughter pick up the lantern and step gingerly into the opening, illuminating the floor as she went. Sir Lawrence followed.

The remaining workers silently filed up the stairs.

Jeremy caught Baxter's arm when he would have entered the opening. "Leave them alone for a moment."

Baxter shrugged Jeremy off, but, a long-suffering expression on his face, he propped his shoulders against the wall near the opening.

Neither man noticed that the workers did not return.

As he waited, Jeremy tried to quiet the fast cadence of his heart. This was it. Would they find gold? Somehow, he didn't think so.

Jeremy clenched his hands, already feeling the silken touch of Lina's bare flesh beneath him. For months, he'd waited for her.

No, he corrected himself. For years. She was the woman he'd awaited his whole life long. They'd traveled across more than miles since they left Monte Carlo so long ago.

Their relationship had grown, and, he hoped, they along with it. The man he was now couldn't reduce their future to the baseness of a bet.

Through her, he again enjoyed the hummingbird's flight, the ancient majesty of these stone monuments, and the sleepy night sounds. His senses were alive again—now that he had something to live for.

A woman had never tasted so good to him as Lina had, flavored with powder and smoke, and sheer lust for life. Still, he could accept the fullness of her body only if she gave the fullness of her heart. Did she love him?

He yearned to believe so. Surely that had been love staring at him out of her powder-blackened face as she fought at his side. Yet . . . she'd been so remote these past few weeks. Of course, so had he. But he was half out of his mind with worry. If she loved him, how could she resent his concern for her?

The tortured uncertainty was interrupted when Sir Lawrence called, "Come along. See what we've found. What little there is."

Disappointment was rife in his voice.

Inside, they found Lina bending over a skeleton laid out on a straw pallet. Feathers about the head had crumbled to a blue-green dust. Bits of black hair still sprouted from the grinning skull. Armbands remained about the ulnas, but they were a curious green.

Jeremy bent over them. "Are they jade?"

Lina touched one gently with a gloved finger. Her glove came away stained green. "I think they're copper." She sat back on her heels. "So much for my instinct. So far as I'm aware, the ancient Maya didn't use copper."

Jeremy caught her shoulder. "Your instincts were good. You've found something obviously centuries old—"

"Not old enough. Look over there." Lina jerked her head toward the corner.

Taking a lantern with him, Jeremy stood. He whistled. "I'll be damned." In one corner of the room that was more a crude log hut, he found a full suit of armor, including the sword, musket, and ax.

Spanish armor. Rusty with the passing of the years. Yet, something bothered him . . .

Jeremy held the lantern high. "Look at the way the weapons are crossed, Lina."

Rising, Lina dusted off her skirt and joined him. She cocked her head. "They are situated strangely." The musket was propped across the front of the breastplate, the sword and ax crossed on the floor before it. "It's almost as if they're guarding something. I thought it was strange that this floor was dirt-packed when it's obviously solid beneath. Maybe they were trying to hide something. Father, will you sketch the placement of the weapons for me?"

Sir Lawrence sighed, but he took his ever-ready notebook from his pocket, flipped it open and began sketching. "This should be your job."

"Agreed. But I want to get something."

Lina disappeared outside, returning shortly after with a shovel. Sir Lawrence looked up, put a few finishing touches on his sketch, and nodded. "Go ahead. You think something's buried, don't you?" Sir Lawrence pocketed his notebook, then helped his daughter move the weapons aside.

"It's possible." Lina stuck the shovel in the dirt, then stomped down on it. "There's only one way to find out."

Jeremy had watched the byplay with amusement. Sir Lawrence had certainly changed his tune. But how could he fail to be proud of his daughter now? Jeremy knew better than to offer his assistance to Lina. This, too, was something she obviously wanted to do herself. She was digging carefully, for logs showed through in spots. The dirt was shallow.

The next time she stepped down on the shovel, she jumped off quickly and set the shovel aside. Kneeling, she dug through the soil with her gloved hands, removing a wrapped bundle.

The others gathered around her. The bundle was less than a foot square, covered in rough wool. The object was obviously protected by several layers.

Whatever it was, it had been precious to someone.

"Oh, please let this be what I think it is." Her fingers trembling with excitement, Lina pulled away a crumbling canvas cloth, revealing an oilskin. When she removed this, soft cotton was revealed.

All four of them were too intent on the find to hear the stealthy sounds in the stairwell. Even when the lanterns outside cast bouncing shadows on the walls, they didn't notice.

Lina peeled away the last layer. She caught her breath. "My

God. It . . . it . . ." She couldn't seem to finish. She turned the
object, which was about eight inches long by six inches wide,
over in her hands.

Jeremy was as stunned as the rest of them. "It looks like
a book." The material of the book was thicker than ordinary
paper. As Lina unfolded the first page, they realized it was
covered with delicate writing.

Sir Lawrence's voice shook as he exclaimed, "It looks like
the Dresden codex! Same screen-formed arrangement of pages.
This is an undiscovered Mayan text, Lina!"

"Are you sure, Father? This must be fairly recent. Isn't that
Spanish?"

Jeremy squinted. Was he seeing things?

Apparently not, for Sir Lawrence gently took the book
his daughter offered. "By Jove, you're right! The Spanish
is illustrated with hieroglyphics . . ." Sir Lawrence's excited
voice trailed off to a whisper.

Lina's eyes widened. Stunned, she looked up at Jeremy.

"Here's your Mayan Rosetta Stone, Lina." Regret amelio-
rated the happiness he felt for her, but he hoped Lina didn't
notice.

She'd made a wonderful discovery. What price would the
Maya pay for it?

Indeed, redemption lit Lina's eyes, but something deeper
and truer lurked behind the triumph. She took a step toward
him, leaving her father and Baxter conferring over the book,
and whispered for his ears alone, "I couldn't have found
it without you, Jeremy. It looks as though you were right,
after all."

The heartbeat thrumming in Jeremy's chest drowned out all
sounds from the stairwell. "About what?"

Lina stepped closer until her body brushed his. "Why, there's
no gold, Jeremy. Don't tell me you hadn't noticed."

"Oh, I noticed, all right. But Lina, we're not finished yet.
If there is another tomb dating earlier—"

She put her finger over his mouth. "I don't care any longer."

"Wha—" Jeremy cleared his husky voice. "What do you
mean?"

She burrowed into him. Jeremy clasped her carefully, for
she was so precious to him. Here were riches untold.

As she tilted her vibrant, lovely face back on his shoulder to answer, a new, unfamiliar voice spoke from the tomb entrance.

"*Gracias*, Miss Collier. I knew if anyone could find my ancestor's grave, you could."

Jeremy stiffened. Automatically he reached for his pistol.

His holster was empty. Only then did Jeremy remember he'd left in a hurry, intending to go back and clean the weapon which had seen such heavy, recent use. Jeremy tightened his arms about Lina, frantically searching the room.

Only the ancient weapons offered defense. They were so rusty they'd probably break if he touched them. The workers he'd grown to trust crowded into the stairwell behind the priest. Jeremy cursed them under his breath.

No wonder they'd been so helpful. They'd wanted to find this tomb and had used the Westerners as handy tools.

Lina, too, seemed to reach the same realization, for she lifted her head from his chest and glared at the priest standing in the doorway. The workers behind him held torches aloft.

The priest was lit in all his barbaric finery, from the quetzal headdress to his jade arm bands and fringed breechclout. His cultured Spanish was at odds with his appearance.

The priest came forward into the tomb and eased the book from Sir Lawrence's stunned hands.

A further shock awaited Jeremy.

Lina pushed away and stood on her own two feet. "How stupid I was not to recognize you earlier. You enjoyed terrorizing me, didn't you?"

The priest looked up. A smile tugged at his arrogant mouth. "Ah, so you know me at last. I'm gratified—*querida*."

Fear almost choked Jeremy then, for he realized two things.

Somehow, Lina had met this man before.

Obviously, this Maya admired more than Lina's scientific mind.

Jeremy began inching toward the ancient weapons.

Part Four

*What's old collapses, times change, and new love
blossoms in the ruins.*   -
—JOHANN CHRISTOPH
FRIEDRICH VON SCHILLER
"William Tell," act IV, sc. ii.

Chapter 14

THE PRIEST'S SMILE irresistibly reminded Lina of her Campeche gallant. She'd only seen him in his present guise a couple of times, but she still kicked herself for not recognizing him. "You used us."

That charming smile faded. "Those who are exploited eventually learn how to do the same."

"I've done nothing to your people—"

"You would steal our heritage and take it back to your cold isle."

"Why did you help us, then? Why did you defend us?"

"It was you!" Sir Lawrence interrupted. "You had your people clear the growth from the pyramids. You wanted us to find this tomb."

The priest gently folded the sheaves back into place. "This man was my ancestor from long ago. Through the ages my people have passed the old stories from son to son. For many years we let the legends rest as Westerners forced their customs and beliefs upon us. But we never forgot."

"Why now?" Baxter demanded, taking an aggressive step forward. He subsided when two of the workers leveled ancient but serviceable muskets upon him.

"Because more and more of you came. Eventually, this tomb would have been found. And once your people understood our ancient words, still more would come." Reverently the priest wrapped the book again in cotton. "The history of my people is for the children of Pacal alone. You whites have taken our lands, our culture, even our lives. Our history, at least, you will not steal while I have breath to fight."

"Pacal? Who was that?" Lina asked. A movement caught her attention. Jeremy inched toward the ancient weapons.

The priest, too, noticed. He took a musket and pointed it at Jeremy. "Señor, we do not intend to harm anyone—unless provoked."

Jeremy froze, his hand almost touching the old sword. Then he straightened and said evenly, "I won't fight you, as long as you take only what belongs to you." Again Jeremy drew Lina under his arm.

A dark gaze ran up and down Lina's dusty figure, landing on Jeremy's arm. "We are not so different, the two of us." Then, with a crook of his finger, the priest gestured for his men to leave. They filed out, but the priest paused at the doorway. "You have two days to pack your supplies. We've defended you against our enemies, but now we have the sacred book, you are of no more use to us. Remaining will gain you nothing, for your workers will not return. Leave while you can."

The priest left as quietly as he'd come, his precious bundle held protectively to his side.

Lina pulled away from Jeremy and slammed a fist into her palm. "Damn him, he'll not get away with this."

"It appears he already has." Sir Lawrence stared mournfully at the empty opening. "The secrets of the entire Mayan history could have been ours with that book. We've made one of the greatest archaeological finds of the century only to have it wrested from us by a savage."

"We?" Jeremy inserted. Lina smiled at him gratefully.

"Lina is my daughter, so I think the 'we' is justified," Sir Lawrence informed Jeremy.

"Why don't we get it back?" Baxter kicked at a protruding log as he hurried after the Indians.

The rotten wood splintered. Lina stared at what it revealed, but she hadn't time to investigate. She hurried up the tomb steps after Baxter. Sir Lawrence followed.

Jeremy ran after them. "Whoa there. We're outnumbered and outfoxed. Besides, you must consider something even more important: Who has more right to that book? The Western world, or the descendants of the people who wrote it?"

"Balderdash," Sir Lawrence tossed over his shoulder. He held the lantern high to illuminate the pyramid steps. Baxter hurried on down. Sir Lawrence descended more cautiously, continuing, "The Maya would benefit too. Just think of the way of life they'd soon enjoy—"

"Have you stopped to consider that they enjoy their present way of life? What's left of it, anyway." Jeremy paused on the steps to look down on the moonlit jungle. The last of the workers were straggling down the slope before Palenque to be lost in the night. "See? We're too late. They'll fight to the death to keep that book. Do you really blame them?"

Frustrated, Lina stared at the slope where the priest and his men had disappeared. Lina understood Jeremy's reservations, but understanding did not equal agreement. Somehow, she had to convince him to stay. "Father, will you go on? Tell Don Roberto we'll soon be there. I want to talk to Jeremy."

Her father hesitated, then he muttered, "If you're not back in thirty minutes, I'm coming after you." He picked his way down the steps.

Lina plopped herself on a pyramid step and drew Jeremy down beside her. "Can we blow the lantern out? We don't really need it. The moon is bright enough."

Jeremy complied. For long minutes, they sat in silence, drinking in the sight of Palenque marking off the phases of the moon, as it had for centuries. "Jeremy, look at it. The grandeur of this place belongs to all mankind. The modern Maya have no right to deny the rest of us. They can't own history."

"Lina, in an ideal world, you'd be right. But these circumstances are far from ideal. History will hardly be served if we all die here trying to preserve it."

That was one point she couldn't argue with. Wearily Lina rubbed the back of her neck. "But we've spent so much and have so little to show for it. Perhaps if we reason with them, they'll let us stay." Lina glanced over her shoulder at the temple. Silvered by moonlight, it was as handsome and elegant as an aged countess flirting in the dark. "I still believe an ancient tomb lies somewhere beneath this temple. Surely they want it found as much as we do."

Jeremy cupped her chin and tilted her face up.

Lina caught her breath at his expression. Scientific thoughts scattered on the winds of his raw emotion. Here was all the tender passion this man had hoarded, gifted to her as gladly as she would give her virginity to him. In this ancient monument to man's pride, Jeremy risked his own. Lina began to tremble.

"Lina, darling, for more years than I care to remember, I've wandered the world because I felt at home nowhere. Aside from my ship and my crew, I've had nothing and no one who cared if I lived or died. Even . . ."—He cleared his husky voice—"I regret to say, myself. Then you came into my life." Jeremy used his fingertip to trace the delicate curvature of her face.

"At first I wanted to spank you, then kiss you senseless. That day you got lost in Campeche, I knew then it was too late. No matter how much I told myself I didn't care, I died a thousand times for every one of the fifteen minutes you were out of my sight. That's why I tried to back out. To prevent what faces us now."

When her trembling increased, he groaned and hauled her into his arms. "Angel mine, don't you see? You're my first thought on waking, my last on sleeping. With you has come my enjoyment of life; without you, I'll be lost. Forever doomed to wander, like the Ancient Mariner, because I learned too late to love. Come back home with me. Be my guiding star."

Lina's eyes were so full of tears that his beloved face swam toward her through a haze. She blinked.

Briefly, the temple behind him filled her vision. But then Jeremy's face was in focus again, eclipsing all. If she found Coronado's gold but lost him, her emotional penury would turn her entire world to dross.

What good would it do her to be a famous, respected archaeologist if she died in the attempt? She was willing to risk her own life, but not his. With a last regretful glance at the temple she revered, she made her only choice. It was surprisingly easy, after all: Jeremy was more important to her than her own ambition.

The words came easily. "Love, we have too much to live for to risk it now." She covered his shout of joy with her hand. "Will you promise to bring me back, when the tribes have calmed?" She caught his smile with her hand. Her fingers curled around its warmth before she traced his cheek.

"I promise." His smile faded as he pulled her hand down

and drew it diagonally across both sides of his chest. Lina's pulse answered the racing plea of his own.

"Jeremy, don't you think we've waited long enough?" Was that really her voice? That husky siren's call?

The heart under her hand skipped a beat, then pounded harder. "What did you say?"

But yearning could not supply what boldness lacked. Lina burrowed her head into his chest. "You know what I mean." What would he do when he found her untouched? Again, she mustered courage to tell him; again, she failed.

Jeremy's hand trembled as he brushed the length of her braid. "Lina, I want you to know that I absolve you from obligation. I don't care any longer whether there's gold here or not. I couldn't win you on such terms and hold you. And—" His voice broke before he admitted softly, "I want very much to hold you. If you come to me it will be of your own accord." His face showing the strain, Jeremy set her firmly away.

Lina's mouth quivered as she appraised the short space between them. "So, you release me from the bet?"

"Yes."

"You would have me leave you now?"

"Yes."

"You're going to be generous and let me go back to my bed alone?"

"Yes."

"You're going to make love to me until my head spins?"

"Ye—" Jeremy stared.

Lina put all her heart into that smile.

It must have been a powerful one, for Jeremy bit off a curse and hauled her back into his arms. "You little wretch. Why won't you let me be generous?"

"If I wanted a gentleman, I'd be here with Baxter. You're something far more rare, as you've just proved . . ." Lina's beautiful eyes reflected twin moons that seemed to tug on Jeremy like the tides. As his head lowered slowly, inexorably toward hers, Lina finished on a husky rush, "You're a gentle man, with a bit of the rogue thrown in. I can't resist you, or what you make me feel, any longer. Make me yours."

"Dear God, I don't deserve you." Jeremy kissed her fragile

eyelids with ineffable gentleness, but his arms tightened as if, indeed, he would never let her go.

"Yes you do, Jeremy." *I only hope you feel the same when the night is done.* But Lina put aside all fears as she tipped her head up for his lips.

Palenque would wait. They could not.

Behind them, the stern, carved priests seemed to smile upon the couple who had crossed a world to find themselves in each other's arms. A night bird burst into song, his warbling, perhaps, a paean to the troth these old walls blessed anew for the first time in too many centuries. Love one another, Palenque itself whispered on the wind.

Time passes.

The world progresses.

Nations perish.

Bodies age.

Only love remains, passed from one generation to the next.

"Lina, come down now . . ." Her father's voice floated up to her from the bottom of the pyramid.

Jeremy's arms tightened, then he set her away. Even in the moonlight, she saw his uneven breathing, the flush at his cheekbones. "Meet me at the waterfall," he whispered. "When everyone's asleep."

"Gladly."

When they reached the bottom of the pyramid, her father's eyes narrowed on their linked hands, then settled on their flushed faces. "Well, what momentous decision have the two of you reached?"

"Father, Jeremy's right. We must leave. We can come back next year, when the tribes aren't so angry."

Sir Lawrence glared at Jeremy. "What nonsense have you filled her with?"

Jeremy sighed, but his voice was patient. "Why, good sense, sir. If we don't leave, we could all become part of this monument to human enterprise." Jeremy kissed Lina's hand. "And I, for one, have too much to live for."

"And if I refuse to leave?"

Jeremy's tone hardened. "Then you will stay here alone. Whatever happens, I'm taking Lina to safety. You have my word that I'll bring all of you back when it's quiet."

For the first time in Lina's memory, her father's indomitable posture wilted. "But our investors . . . our reputations . . ."

"We did find the one tomb. And we can describe the book, at least," Lina pointed out.

"That will make us look all the more ineffectual. We let savages steal the find of the century." He was still protesting when they reached the palace.

Baxter sat before the rekindled fire conversing with Don Roberto and Cesar. He leaped to his feet. "Well? What do we do next?"

"According to Mayhew, we leave."

Don Roberto nodded. "Most wise. You can come with us now." Don Roberto rose.

Baxter scowled. "I'll not cry craven."

"Then you can chortle alone," Jeremy retorted. "No doubt you'll still be crowing upon the sacrificial block."

"That's rubbish. These fellows have been Christianized."

Jeremy quirked an eyebrow. "Indeed. Decapitation is civilized compared to having one's beating heart slashed out." When Baxter would have argued more, Jeremy turned a cold shoulder and started packing a crate. "Lina and I are leaving and that's the end of it. You and Sir Lawrence can stay if you insist, but I do not advise it."

"Nor do I," Don Roberto inserted. "*Amigo*, you are an intelligent man . . ." Don Roberto pulled Baxter outside where their horses waited, and conversed with him in low tones. Baxter shook his head stubbornly. Resigned, Don Roberto mounted and made his good-byes. "You are all welcome whenever you decide to come." He waved, then led his pride down the path lit by a brilliant moon.

After they left, Lina went to the next gallery, where they kept the cub, and took him his evening meal. He yowled a warning at her. She stopped and tossed the dried meat to him. He'd grown in the past couple of months. His claws were formidable and she bore a couple of deep scratches from the last time she'd not jumped back quickly enough when she offered him a flopping fish. He'd become finicky unless they offered him fresh game, as his behavior this time again proved.

Sniffing, he stabbed the dried meat with his paw as if hoping the pile would show some life. He lapped at it, then he flopped down on his tummy in disgust, turning his head aside.

Lina laughed. "I'm sorry, your lordship, but I didn't have time to fish for you today." She cocked her head, but when she still heard arguing male voices from the next gallery, she sat down cross-legged, scooting near the cub gradually. No hurry to get back. She'd gladly leave the men to their arguments.

That proud little head lifted; green eyes glinted a warning. Lina snatched back her hand. "I only want to pet you. I saved your life, you know."

The cub's snarl revealed sharp fangs. Lina sighed and propped her elbows on her knees. "Very well. I can take a hint. Why should you be any more tolerant than your world?"

"Giving you trouble?" Jeremy asked from the opening.

"He won't let me pet him any more."

"Good. You'd be doing him no favors by taming him." Jeremy sat down beside her. "He's a handsome fellow, isn't he?"

"Yes." But Lina wasn't looking at the cub. Jeremy's eyes flickered with the banked fires she stirred so easily.

Then he was clearing his throat and helping her to her feet. "Baxter has finally agreed to leave. We intend to rise early in the morning to pack. Your father wants you to come to bed."

"He does, does he? And do you?"

Those fires didn't flicker as they swept up and down her slim figure; now they consumed. "Don't tease me, Lina. Unless you want me to sweep you up in my arms and steal you away, right here and now. I'm not sure I can wait another hour for you."

Indeed, the next hour passed at a tortoise pace, with Lina wishing the time a hare. Yet, as her hammock swayed gently in the breeze, Lina's tension grew. She had no doubts about her choice, but found that, despite her claims of equality, she was as nervous as any virginal bride.

With far more reason. Jeremy didn't know she was an innocent. And she still feared that when he discovered the truth, he'd be angry that she'd manipulated him. Nor had he made mention of marriage, but neither had she. Surely that was his intention, however. Had he not talked of wanting her by her side?

She'd sacrificed a lifetime's quest to chance happiness with him. The hour was at hand; she'd not fear it. Her tension eased as she remembered his loving declaration. He, too, was her guiding star. He would understand why she'd deceived him.

When Jeremy appeared soundlessly to offer his hand, she clasped it without a second thought. They tiptoed out, assured by the snoring issuing from various corners of the gallery. Jeremy tossed a clean quilt over his shoulder, then helped her grope in the dark along the galleries.

They paused on the steps to drink in the beauteous night. Fireflies vied with the stars for brightness. Trees sighed as they succumbed to the wind's embrace. Nesting birds cooed sleepily, reveling in the life Lina and Jeremy were about to celebrate.

At the foot of the steps, Jeremy faced her. "Lina, are you sure this is what you want? I won't object if you want to change your mind." Jeremy shifted uncomfortably. "It won't kill me—I don't think."

His self-deprecating humor reassured her further. She was doing the right thing for a simple reason: This man was right for her. No matter what came, she would never regret this night. Shyly she caught his hand. "I'm sure, Jeremy."

Joy lit his silver eyes. The laughter of lovers echoed off ageless stone as, holding hands, they ran down the slope to the waterfall. The moon smiled at them above the treetops, its reflection buoyant upon the water. A fawn and its mother lifted startled heads, then loped away into the brush. Flowers grew to the water's edge, bathing in the spray that refreshed Lina and Jeremy.

Lina lifted her face to it, glad when the mosquitoes buzzed away, defeated by the water's weight on their tiny wings. What better place to begin a lifetime of memories?

Jeremy seemed to feel the same, for he spread the quilt next to the stream, then exuberantly caught her up in his arms. "Luck smiled on me that day we met in Monte Carlo."

He spun with her, faster and faster, until she was dizzy and weak with laughter. "Stop, stop!"

He stopped. "I'll do anything you want. Laugh for me again, Lina."

Instead, her mirth died at the look in his eyes. "Oh, Jeremy," she whispered, cupping his cheek. His head ducked over hers, blocking the moonlight, blocking the world itself.

Homecoming. A world away from all she knew, Lina found all she'd ever wanted. The meeting of their lips was both an ending of her girlhood and the beginning of her full rite of womanhood. Vaguely Lina felt the ground beneath her as Jeremy set her down, following her with his long, loving body.

Hands dared where none had, but they were not intrusive. Lina arched to his touch when he unbuttoned her shirt. The chemise he'd purchased was gossamer in the spray, but restrictive to Lina's aching breasts. When he caressed her through the batiste, she felt his warmth. It was not enough; she needed the touch of flesh. She caught his wrists to voice the need, but then his mouth ringed the tip of her breast.

Speech was beyond her then. His gently sucking mouth drained her will, her very self, until she was an empty vessel waiting to be filled. The pride that had sustained her through many a battle was a hindrance now to the mating every woman longs for.

The strange thought flickered in the back of Lina's mind, but she welcomed it. Independence was a lonely luxury. Here, in the greatest intimacy a woman can know, she learned the value of belonging.

With the fullness of the heart he'd brought to vivid, pulsing life, Lina pushed him away. He made an inarticulate protest and tried to dip his head over her other breast, but he, too, was weak in his need.

She shoved him on his back, then pulled at his shirt. When his golden chest was revealed, she lavished the same care upon his male nipple. It hardened immediately in her mouth. Delighted, she stabbed her tongue at him.

His fingers flinched about her shoulders. "Witch."

Lina lifted her head to tease, "I thought I was an angel."

Slowly he pulled her down atop him, cradling her to his chest. "You are. Don't you know you've been my salvation?"

Tears misted Lina's eyes. Moved unbearably by the intensity of his stare, she buried her nose into his neck, inhaling the intoxicating scent of healthy, aroused male. She kissed the pulsing cord, then followed it to his ear. She circled the pleasing whorls there with her tongue. He inhaled sharply. The world spun about her.

Now it was he covering her like a living blanket, warming everywhere he touched. Lina had never felt so secure as in this moment when she risked all she was for what she could become. For a long moment they remained still, enjoying the sheer luxury of their closeness. Then, their feelings as syncopated as their pounding hearts, simultaneously they stirred to complete their union.

Strong hands faltered in their eagerness upon the buttons of her skirt. "Dammit, I was never so clumsy, even as a boy."

Lina laughed. "I'm glad, my charming rogue. Let me help." Lina soon found she was all thumbs too. The spray had made her heavy cotton skirt obdurate. Jeremy sat back on his heels in disgust.

"Your father planned this, didn't he? I've never seen a better chastity belt."

"You've probably never seen one at all. I suspect your previous problem is how fast women have removed their clothes for you."

"Except the only one who mattered."

Devotion was an odd expression to read in those quicksilver eyes that had, Lina knew, turned countless feminine heads. Some feminine reflex handed down to her through generations of loving women demanded her response. All thoughts of teasing flew out of her head.

Not giving herself time to think, she stood, took several steps back and with one sure movement loosed the heavy button at her waistband. With a supple sway of her hips, she let the skirt drop. She stepped out of it, then, her fingers trembling at her own boldness, she untied her chemise. The material gaped, showing a deep vee. Gradually, she parted it, revealing ivory arcs. The arcs grew into harmonious orbs capped by coral circles and ruby nipples. When the chemise fluttered to the grass, Lina reached for the last button protecting her chastity.

He was breathing so harshly she saw the rapid rise and fall of his chest, but he hadn't moved a muscle toward her. Lina touched the button at her split slip, her own heart sledging against her ribs. She saw how much her disrobing pleased

him, but it seemed her modesty was not as dead as she'd
hoped. She bit her lip and sent him a wordless plea.

He surged to his feet. "You darling. Come to me, Lina." He
held out his hand.

She crossed those two fateful steps to him, then her slip was
gone. Did he remove it, or did she? Ever after, Lina would not
know, for at that moment it didn't matter. She was bare, she
was ready, she belonged.

When his chest hair prickled her sensitive breasts, they
groaned. He pressed his hands into the small of her back and
rubbed against her, heightening the pleasure of flesh to flesh.
He ran his hands over all the valleys and peaks he'd crossed the
sea to conquer, murmuring husky praise at the beauty he found.

Lina sagged over his arm, her mouth open to his bold explo-
ration. New worlds opened before her closed eyes, worlds she
could find only in this man's arms. He wrapped one strong leg
about her, but still they weren't close enough.

She groaned against his consuming mouth, tugging weakly
at his breeches. "Off."

Laughter rumbled deep in his chest, a volcano stirring to
life. Passion shimmered between them like ash, warming all
it touched.

Jeremy released her, smiling when she swayed on her feet.
Slowly, his hand inched down to his own buttons. One pulled
loose. Two. Then three. The golden bush at his groin was
revealed, then he'd stepped out of his breeches.

Legs spread, hands propped upon his hips, he let her look
her fill. Lina admired the pleasing form that sloped from broad
shoulders, narrowing to trim waist and flat belly, down to . . .
Lina looked away.

The one glimpse was startling enough. His staff rose eager
and proud, proclaiming the power of his virility—and the feal-
ty it would demand. The silly fears she'd dismissed returned
with a vengeance. How could she possibly hold him all? She'd
never seen a naked man before, but even her inexperienced
eye knew he must be well endowed. The passion he'd stirred
within her began to ebb.

Jeremy crossed the gap between them in an athletic bound.
She backed away a step before she could stop herself. He
faltered, his bold smile fizzling. "What is it, darling?"

She shook her head, still staring at her feet. She flinched when his hands landed on her shoulders. They gentled, the conquerer vanquished by her delicacy. His hands praised her fragile collarbones, slipping down her sides to clasp her tiny waist.

When his hardness brushed her belly, she jerked away. Jeremy frowned upon her bent head. "Lina, what's wrong?"

Again, the impulse to tell him fought the fear of his reaction. If she told him, would he leave her be? Frightened as she was of the pain she knew would come, she was more terrified that he would pull away. No, she had to have him. No matter what the future held, she'd earned this night.

Renewed, she brought her hand down to all she feared and revered. The frightening power surged in her palm. She started away.

A harsh groan tore from him. His hands clenched upon her hips. "Again."

Stunned, Lina stared up at his pleasured expression. Fear dissolved at the astonishing realization: Her own power was as great as his. Here, in her hand, was the instrument God had made not just for the pleasure of man, but also for the pleasure of woman.

Lina cupped him again, this time savoring his own enjoyment. He rubbed himself into her hand. She was amazed at the paradoxical textures overflowing her palm. Hardness and softness, velvet-coated steel. Enthusiastic now at the purring she elicited with every stroke, she squeezed a bit too hard.

He caught her hand. "Gently, angel, or we'll end before we begin. My turn."

He bore her to the quilt. For a moment he knelt at her side, not touching, just looking. Molten silver started at her ankles, warming her slim legs and the spot between, pausing on her heaving breasts, then settling on her lips. His tongue licked the corner of his mouth, but still he didn't grab.

Thus Lina learned her second sensual lesson: Anticipation heightened the pleasure. Moisture oozed between her legs. Compulsively she reached out to him. "Jeremy, don't tease me."

Then she was bathing in molten silver as closer he came, closer, his eyes filling her with his essence even before he touched her. When he did, every sensitized nerve in her body reveled in his weight. For a moment he covered her, and she felt his hardness probing between her thighs. Instinctively she opened to him, but he bit off a curse and swiveled his hips away.

He buried his fingers in her hair, cupping her head. "Not yet. From this moment on, you'll know no man but me, remember no night before this." Now his lips and teeth completed the seduction his eyes had started, nibbling, sucking at the most peculiar places.

A third discovery hovered in the back of Lina's dazed mind: He knew the pleasure points of her body better than she did herself. How could he know that the hollow of her neck, the backs of her knees, the folds where groin met legs were so sensitive? Soon Lina was squirming, pulling at him.

He only laughed huskily and renewed his measured tracking of her body. Somehow he never touched her breasts, or her throbbing center. Lina began to pant and plead, but he held her wrists above her head and stabbed his tongue into her navel. Every nerve in her body was alive. Waiting.

"Please, Jeremy."

"Dear God yes, let me please you." His mouth drifted up her stomach to her breasts. They were so ready for him that when he finally drew her nipple into his mouth Lina bit back a groan. The shock traveled from her breast to her backbone, taking the last of her control with it. She became a wild thing beneath him, squirming to free herself.

All too briefly could he learn her taste and texture, for her pleasure had become an ache; finally Lina snapped. She pulled away from his lax grip and latched onto him.

Now it was his turn to groan. At a calmer moment he might have wondered at her awkwardness as she pulled him atop her and tried to position him. But months of wanting would no longer be denied.

Murmuring endearments, he helped her lead him to her moist, waiting well. The first tiny insertion popped sweat out on his forehead, but he drew a steadying breath and begged, "Lina, look at me." One thing yet remained before they joined.

Glazed blue eyes opened obediently.

"I love you, Lina." For only the second time in his life, he said the words. This time, his chosen mate was free and loved him in return. She hadn't said it yet, but he knew it was so. He saw the clarity return to her eyes.

"Oh Jeremy, I love you so. But wait—"

Ecstasy filled his heart; it bade him fill her body. "No more waiting, my darling. Just lie still . . ." He slipped deeper.

She caught her breath, but he mistook her pain for pleasure and pushed harder to fulfill them both. He was confused that he didn't slip right in, for he felt her slickness. Thinking his angle wrong, he pressed his hands beneath her buttocks and tipped up her hips.

Her eyes were closed and she was biting her lip, but Jeremy's eyes, too, were closed as he reveled in her warmth and welcoming softness. He paused only to bury his mouth over hers as, with one powerful thrust, he completed their union.

She cried out against his mouth, but Jeremy had already felt her chastity tear. He lifted his head to stare at her white face. Encased in her beautiful body, he tried to think. This could not be. She was experienced; she'd admitted it. He never would have . . . He groaned as her muscles tensed about him when she raised her head to take his lips.

"Never mind. I'm fine. As you love me, don't leave me now."

What man could resist such a plea? He couldn't think; she wouldn't let him. But in the back of his mind he felt her inexperience as her hips jerked upward in time with his downward slide. He went a bit deeper with every meeting. She held her breath, relaxed, then tipped herself upward again. He felt her discomfort ease.

She sheathed him well now, taking every engorged inch she'd swelled to bursting. Jeremy panted as the thrust, retreat, thrust, retreat, became as wild as the cadence of his heart. Lina, Lina, you lied, part of him said, but another part was primitively glad.

She'd had no other. The motherless little boy he'd overcome shouted his joy over the man's suspicions. No leftovers now. This exquisite, intelligent woman had saved herself for him alone.

Later, the man could ask her why.

Not now. She harbored him in all the mystery that was woman, but only with Lina did he feel he'd come home. He reached, and reached . . . almost there. Her cries rang out over the pounding of the waterfall. He felt her spasms grip him and pull him deeper. A final time he withdrew, his full length throbbing with passion, coated with her dew, before he buried himself and erupted.

Her breasts rose against him as she gasped, and even at the acme of his pleasure he was sensitive enough to understand that she was shocked at the moisture streaming into the most intimate part of her body. He was helpless to stop it. Pleasure such as he'd never known geysered from him, to her, the pulsing jets so powerful he shook with the force. She opened to his spray like a flower, unfurling again and again to share the gift of life.

The trickles died slowly, and even then he felt the aftershocks that tremored through her. His own legs quivered, and he knew if he tried to stand he'd fall. Only when he could catch his breath did he find energy to move. But when he tried to slip aside, she clenched her arms about his waist.

"I'm too heavy."

"Hmmm." She sighed. "If I'd known it was like this I would have come to you weeks ago."

He was touched at the words. Still, they forced him to face the unpleasant truths their pleasure—what an inadequate word that was for the cataclysm that still made them shake—had delayed. Lina was all the woman he could ever dream of, but before he could feel she was truly his he had to know why she'd chosen him. Even more important, he had to know why she'd lied.

Still nestled inside her, Jeremy turned until Lina was atop him. "Don't you have something to tell me?" He tried to make his voice stern, but knew he failed miserably.

Her eyes fluttered open. Even in the moonlight he saw the flush start in her cheeks, then wash over her neck to her chest. "It's a little late for that, I think. You know the truth now."

Jeremy twitched his hips aside and set her on the quilt. She held her arms out, but he sat up and clasped his own about his knees. "A hell of a way for me to find out. I've done many things in my life, but I've never yet despoiled a virgin."

"Is . . ." She steadied her voice. "Is that the way you'd describe what happened between us?"

Jeremy tightened his arms to keep from grabbing her and saying that it didn't matter. Nothing mattered except holding her, loving her. But he'd allowed his urges free rein long enough. Their bodies communicated well enough. What of their minds? "Lina, this night has been the best of my life, but how could it have been the same for you? I wouldn't have been so . . . eager had I known you were untouched."

Her tense shoulders relaxed. "Is that all? If you recall, sir, it was I who . . ." She blushed.

"Pulled me in? But I wasn't sole possessor of your, ah, most cherished possession at that point."

"Had you known ahead of time, would you have stopped?"

Jeremy opened his mouth, but then he ruefully shook his head. "Not as long as I had your consent. I didn't intend a quick roll in the hay, Lina. I intended this night to be the first of many."

The last of the shadows were dashed from her glowing smile. "Then there's no problem, is there?" Kneeling, she threw her arms about his neck.

Helplessly Jeremy opened his arms to her. She was his, only his, part of him exulted, but the remnant of the rejected little boy resented her lies. He felt torn in two, his mental torment all the worse now that his body was so satiated.

The feel of her soft, unfettered breasts heightened the wrong instinct. The other instinct that had kept him safe in many a brawl and protected him from many a slur howled louder. Firmly Jeremy set her from him. She wasn't like the others. He knew it. She was probably just too embarrassed to tell him. But he had to have the reassurance from her own lips.

"Lina, why didn't you tell me the truth in Monte Carlo? Surely you know that I never would have made the bet with you."

"Are you here with me because of the bet?"

"No, of course not. I already told you the evidence is not conclusive. Someday, gold may be found here."

"Then what does it matter?" Lina caught his hands.

Jeremy tugged away, his heart beginning to pound at her evasion. "Why didn't you tell me?"

Lina sighed, then she lifted her chin. "Because I knew you wouldn't guide us if you knew."

Pain sliced through Jeremy. Oh God, not her too. He would have staked his life on her honesty. He wished, of a sudden, for his clothes. He looked around for them, but Lina shoved him down on his back and planted herself atop him.

"Dammit, maybe I was wrong, but *you* tell *me*—would you have led us here if you'd known?"

"Yes. No. I don't know."

Lina's tremulous smile pressed against the barriers his instinct was trying to erect. She brushed his damp hair away from his brow. Not since he was very young had a woman shown him such tenderness. The barriers slipped a bit.

"Jeremy, so many times I've tried to tell you. Do you know why I didn't?"

He shook his head, his throat clogged with emotion.

"Because I loved you and I didn't want to lose you," she said simply.

The craven instinct whimpered and slunk away to the shadowy corners of his mind. "Angel, I guess it doesn't matter. We were meant to be together, and if you hadn't lied, we might never have learned that."

He believed the words as he said them, but part of him was still hurt. However, he loved her too much—and wanted her too much—to let his old fears alienate him from the one person he needed most. He'd gambled once and won; he'd do so again. He pulled her down for a kiss that spoke of his yearning and his need.

Joyfully she responded, then she rose and tugged on his hand. "Get up, lazybones. I want to bathe." They waded into the shallows and soon were splashing like children. Happy laughter rang above the roaring falls.

Some distance away, Sir Lawrence buttoned his breeches and lifted his head. What the devil was that?

He traced the sound to the stream. Parting the lush bushes, he lifted a foot to step onto the bank. His foot froze in midair. A gasp escaped him.

Lina stood bare as a naiad, waist-deep in the stream, splashing the man who faced her within comfortable touching reach.

That pale gold hair and powerful back could belong only to one man. Sir Lawrence stamped down and took one step toward them, furious protests trembling on his lips.

How could they commit their indecency under his very nose? He hadn't even realized they were gone. Where was the innocent, moral young girl he'd raised?

Sir Lawrence strode toward them. Then Lina tipped her face up to Jeremy for his kiss. Even from where he stood, Sir Lawrence heard Jeremy's hoarse groan. Sir Lawrence's furious rush lost impetus. Again, he froze.

He didn't stop because of Jeremy's obviously emotional reaction to the beautiful temptress who lifted her arms about his neck. He stopped because of his daughter's expression.

In that moment, he saw his own dear Elaine, the only woman he'd ever loved. How many times had she looked at him so, as if he were the only man in the world for her? She'd worn that exact expression on the night Lina was conceived. Sir Lawrence winced and lifted a shaking hand to his eyes.

He prayed Lina would not conceive. He was obviously too late to insure that. Then he forced his hand back to his side to look again at the daughter he adored.

They were still kissing, with all the unbridled passion of lovers. Yet it was not Lina's youth he saw in that moment; it was her womanliness. She'd become a woman without him knowing it.

Obviously she loved Mayhew. He couldn't say he was thrilled with her choice, yet he'd come to realize Mayhew, in his own way, was one of the most moral men he'd ever met. He was apparently wealthy. Yet how could her father countenance his daughter's marriage to a man who had no home but a ship, no matter how fine it might be?

Sir Lawrence sighed. After a last worried look, he swiveled and went back the way he'd come. And somehow, there in the evocative ruins that still whispered of times past, he seemed to hear his wife say over his shoulder, "You did the right thing, my love. Let her be happy."

"You'd better treat her well, Mayhew," Sir Lawrence said through gritted teeth. His hammock was lumpy as he waited a very long time, it seemed, for their return.

*   *   *

Back at the stream, Jeremy lifted Lina into his arms and carried her to the bank to lay her on a bed of flowers. She laughed as she shifted her shoulders. "It tickles."

"It does? How does this feel?" Jeremy tore a handful of the scented blossoms, crushed them in his hands, then rubbed her torso with exquisite care. "Does it still tickle?"

Lina arched herself to his touch in reply. Her eyes drifted closed as his hands lowered to her legs to learn their pleasing curvature. His teasing smile died. His lips parted with quickening breaths.

His mouth hovered over her torso. The very tip of his tongue came out to flick her nipple with a dart of fire. Lina tried to pull his head closer, but he resisted, blowing on the flesh that hardened in quick response. He leaned back to savor her wanton beauty.

She was a study in nature's glory. Her black hair was night personified, blanketing the flowers in velvet luxury. Her body was white and plush as the clouds he'd longed to ride as a boy. Unable to stop himself, he cupped his hand about the vee between her legs. Here was his seat to the heavens. But he'd not take it until she was ready to go there with him . . .

For long, patient minutes, he courted her. And he found that Lina loved as she did everything else: enthusiastically. Again, he wanted to throw his head back and yell his pride to the elements. She was his! By her own choice.

Instead, he showed it to someone more important—Lina. The first time had been his. This time was hers. Leisurely minutes later, she writhed beneath him, her face flushed, her eyes alight with starfire and womanfire. When he resisted her pulling hands, the sensual haze cleared in a Lina-like glare.

"Damn you, you've explored enough!"

A smiling mouth lifted from her dimpled knee. "A man surely has the right to revel in virgin territory before he settles there." And his head dipped again.

"My bold adventurer"—Lina caught her breath at a particularly wicked slash of his tongue—"plunder."

"The treasure is mine?"

"Such as it is."

"Lina, don't you know how beautiful you are?" Jeremy sat

up to admire her from end to end. "A man could search the world over and never find a woman so irreplaceable." Jeremy traced under her eyes. "Twin Stars of India." He cupped her breasts. "Solomon's pearls." One hand winnowed down her belly to the cleft still wet with him. "And here"—his breath caught before he steadied it—"the fountain of youth."

Lina took full advantage of his rapt study. She cupped the twin spheres that based his towering manhood. "And these. The golden apples of Hercules, perhaps?" She stroked them gently.

They hardened in her hand. Then his mouth was buried in hers, his tongue and manhood demanding entrance. And Lina found that the second time was better, for it lasted longer.

Indeed, they rode to the moon together. For several pulsing instants they became elemental, bits of stardust and moonbeams that drifted slowly back to earth. When they opened their eyes, each knew their world had been forever altered.

They would never be alone, or lonely, again.

Lina saw her own tears misting Jeremy's eyes. He cleared his throat, then helped her on with her wrinkled clothes before he dressed.

In hushed silence they climbed back to the palace, both afraid to break this precious unity. Much remained between them to be resolved, but neither wanted to speak of it now.

Where would they live? How could Lina pursue her work if she sailed with Jeremy? Did he fully trust her?

Though she felt rested, the tiny worry that had never stopped whispering at the back of her mind grew to a clamor.

Why did he make no mention of marriage?

Chapter 15

LIGHTS BLAZED FROM the corridor. Lina and Jeremy paused, blinking back to reality.

"What's wrong? Why is everyone up?" Lina wondered aloud.

Jeremy hurried into the gallery. It was empty. "What the hell?" Instinctively he grabbed all his weapons.

Lina was already rushing back outside. "I think I know where they are."

As she suspected, she saw a dim glow from the top of her pyramid. As she climbed to the top, she sighed wistfully. "Her" pyramid. If only.

But she'd promised Jeremy. The temple would wait until she could return next season. She clasped his hand tighter, reflecting on the night past. Her blush warmed the regret away. The pleasure they granted one another overshadowed every experience of her life—even finding the tomb.

However, her father and Baxter seemed to feel differently. Lina wasn't surprised to see them pulling furiously at the rotting log floor to reveal paving stones similar to the ones they'd found in the altar.

She lifted the lantern set against the wall and cast its light over the patch they'd cleared. "I knew it! I knew there had to be a reason for them to put a log structure inside stone walls. They didn't just make a crude burial; they made a shield."

Setting the lantern down, Lina went to help her father pull at a stubborn piece of log.

"Dash it, if you knew, why didn't you say something?" Baxter demanded, straightening. "We only came back because

Sir Lawrence couldn't sleep and wanted to take a last look about."

"If you recall . . ." Lina grunted and stumbled backward as the log ripped free. She toed the dirt away with her boot to reveal yet another stone. "We had to leave in rather a hurry. But I thought I glimpsed a smooth patch of stone."

"So you knew . . ." Jeremy cleared his hoarse voice, "another tomb was here? Before tonight?"

If she hadn't been so tired and so excited, Lina would have heard the strain in his voice. "I suspected. Where's the crowbar?" Lina spied it against the wall and grabbed it.

Her father took her hand, his own scratched and bleeding. "Child, are you all right?" Again, he glared at Jeremy.

Lina saw only the paving stone beneath her feet. "Of course. But I'll be better when we finally find Pacal." Pulling away, Lina winnowed the end of the crowbar into the plug and, with a heave, lifted the stone free.

The scientific curiosity she'd learned in her cradle gripped her so strongly that she was unaware of the present undercurrents filling the stuffy tomb.

The past tugged at her now. Smells wafted out of the gaping hole: death, decay, and mold. These plugs had been here for ages on end, any amateur nose could have concluded. Lina's itched with her need to explore further. Dammit, two days wouldn't be enough. Could she, maybe, coax Jeremy into giving her a week?

She didn't see Jeremy's grim suspicion, her father's anger and worry, or Baxter's curiosity. With every paving stone she pulled away, the smell grew stronger.

"Lina, what are you doing?" Jeremy demanded. "There's no time to—"

Sir Lawrence propped a fist on his hip. "Of course this changes things. We can't go now. Right, Lina?"

"Hmmm," she answered, unaware of what he'd said. A two-foot hole gaped now—enough to hold a lantern down.

"And naturally, after tonight, Mayhew will make no objection."

Jeremy stiffened.

Sir Lawrence strode to face the man he obviously feared trifled with his daughter's affections. For Jeremy's ears alone, he whispered, "You owe her, Mayhew. She's waited all her life for this day. Do what you need to do, hire opposing Indians to protect us if you must, but help us stay."

"You saw? At the stream?" Jeremy asked quietly.

Sir Lawrence's fists clenched. "Yes. I wanted to blow your brains out. But my daughter obviously wanted something else." Sir Lawrence took another step and stabbed his forefinger into the taller man's chest. "I may yet kill you if you make my daughter unhappy. And forcing her to leave the find of her life will do exactly that."

Jeremy slapped Sir Lawrence's hand away. "That's rich. You lecturing me about respect for your daughter. I respect her as a woman *and* as a scientist. But even if I didn't . . . care for her, it would be my duty as your guide to see that we all get away safely."

On her way back to the hole with the lantern, Lina's steps slowed as, finally, she noticed the tension. She inclined her head, trying to hear the heated whispers, but both men were speaking too softly. She frowned. "What's wrong?"

Sir Lawrence stood back. "Nothing. We understand one another perfectly. Here, dear, let me help you."

Lina let him take the lantern, but made no move toward the hole. "Jeremy, why are you looking at me like that?" That precious devotion in his eyes had warmed her so briefly, but now those quicksilver eyes stared at her with . . . suspicion?

"Lina, I would speak with you. Alone." Jeremy turned on his heel and stalked out.

Lina passed her father on her way out. His hand caught her arm.

"Darling, remember you're descended from the Conquerer himself. Don't let him talk you into leaving. Not now, when we're on the verge of a momentous discovery." Sir Lawrence picked up the lantern again. "Help me, Hubert."

Alarm grew as Lina followed Jeremy. What had happened between the two men she most loved? She found Jeremy sitting on the top pyramid step. She sat down next to him. Even in the dim light the hazy clouds allowed, she could see the tension in his face. "What did he say to you, Jeremy?"

Jeremy's jaw flexed. "He saw us tonight."

A flush began at Lina's hairline and spread down her throat

to her toes. "Oh no." Sometime she'd intended to confess—
but not this fast. "Did he insult you?"

"No more than usual. Actually, he was quite restrained
under the circumstances. Said he'd like to blow my brains out
but could see you wanted something quite different." Jeremy
slowly turned his head. "The question is—what is that?"

"I don't understand. Surely I made it quite obvious what I
wanted. As you did." It still bothered her that he'd made no
mention of marriage, but she felt his ambivalence and knew
now was not the time to broach his own reticence. Nevertheless, her alarm began the slow rise to anger.

What terrible deed did he suspect her of? "Quit dallying and
get to the point."

Jeremy's smile flickered briefly, then extinguished. "Lina,
why did you choose tonight to come to me?"

"Because I didn't want to wait any longer."

"And it had nothing to do with seeing the paving stone?"

"No. Why would you—" She gasped. "My God, you think
I was manipulating you? That I . . . lay with you so you'd feel
obligated to let me stay?"

The look on his face was all the answer she needed. Lina
surged to her feet, wondering vaguely that she could still stand.
Later, she'd have the luxury of misery. Her father had been
right all along. For now, she had work to do.

"In for a penny, in for a pound." Gracefully she pivoted on
her heel and ducked back inside the temple.

"Lina, wait!" *Argue with me, tell me I'm wrong,* Jeremy
cried inwardly. But she was already gone.

For good?

Jeremy clenched his fingers about his knees so hard that
his knuckles went white. He didn't even feel the self-inflicted
pain. The old wounds that had scabbed over but never healed
now throbbed as years of loneliness, suspicion, and anger
swelled to bursting.

Precious memories battled with the facts as he knew them:
She'd lied about being experienced to get him here; she'd
bedded him this night knowing another tomb lay beneath
the priest.

Was she a product of the high society he detested? Or was
she in truth the vibrant, moral woman he loved more than

life itself? Jeremy cupped his fingers about his bursting head, feeling torn in twain.

The pressure built until he was almost screaming, then, as they always did, his seaman instincts took over. Down went his hands; up went his chin. Enough of this maudlin self-pity. It gained him naught. Lina, like the sea, was elemental, both beautiful and dangerous. No matter her composition, he'd be drawn to her for the rest of his life. And, like the sea, she was generous only to those who respected her.

He'd give her the benefit of the doubt, as she had done for him. He would not make the mistake that he had with Aimee and his mother. This time, he'd see not what he wanted to see, but what was . . .

Decisively he rose and strode toward the temple doorway.

"Lina, look at this," Sir Lawrence said, by all appearances headless as he peered down into the hole. Baxter held his feet. The words had a hollow sound as if they echoed off vast space.

Lina gritted her teeth and by sheer force of will mastered the waves of pain. How could Jeremy . . . but no. No time for that. She'd give him his two days, damn him, and then leave like a good little girl. And when he came crawling to her she'd pretend all the indifference she would from this moment cultivate. No man who could believe her so shallow could care an iota for her.

Especially after . . . those thoughts, too, she blocked, along with the smidgen of guilt. She had lied to get him here, after all, even knowing how it would hurt him.

Her steps were as firm as ever as she approached her father. She knelt and tried to peer around him, but his shoulders blocked the hole. She tested the strength of the stones by rapping them with her knuckles. "Is it safe?"

Sir Lawrence tapped Baxter with his free hand. Baxter pulled him backward. Sir Lawrence sat up. "From the little I could make out, the paving blocks seem bolstered by supports. The construction holding up this floor would have to be strong just to support the altar. But the lantern is too weak to illuminate whatever lies below."

Baxter was already reaching for rope.

Lina forestalled him. "I'm going." Baxter dropped the rope as if scalded.

Sir Lawrence opened his mouth, but Jeremy said from the doorway, "We'll both go."

Jeremy might have been a Mayan ghost for all the credence Lina gave him. "This is my find, Father. And you know I'm experienced in climbing. I'll be fine." Lina picked up the rope and began tying a makeshift sling.

"What of snakes? Or bats?" Jeremy tried to take the rope from her.

Lina jerked it out of his hands. "I'm not afraid of snakes. Eden was spoiled by one, don't you know?" For the first time since he'd entered she looked at him.

Jeremy winced, then his face lost all expression. He swiveled and exited.

Telling herself she was glad, Lina hastily finished her sling and slipped it about her hips. "I'm ready."

"Lawrence, you're not actually going to let her—"

"Hush, Hubert. Daughter, this is not wise."

"It's eminently sensible, Father, considering we have one day left to work." Lina jerked her head toward the entrance.

Sir Lawrence and Baxter turned automatically to meet the dawn that was beginning to peek curiously into the chamber above. Disgruntled, Sir Lawrence caught the other end of the rope and looped it several times around a sturdy protruding log.

"You win, daughter, but for God's sake be careful."

"I will."

When she was suspended over the hole, Lina took the lantern Baxter handed her. Jeremy hurried back in, a rope wrapped about his shoulder, just as the other two men began lowering her. Her last sight of him showed him frantically knotting his own rope about a log.

Then wonder eclipsed all, even her pain and resentment. "My word," she whispered, casting the lantern light this way and that.

Around her was a fairy world of glittering stone. Wetness dripped everywhere in this corbeled vault, forming stalactites that stabbed down from the ceiling and stalagmites that lunged from the floor. All fear dissolved as, slowly, they lowered her further. She gasped and held her arm out to its full extension.

A bold eye seemed to blink against the light. Her heart skipped a beat until she realized marching figures were carved in exquisite bas-relief against the stone walls. Their postures were explicit of both protection and respect.

For the dead?

Lina looked down. This time her gasp didn't supply enough of the dank air. Her head swam until she coughed. Her eyes cleared as she saw the complicated carving about to brush her feet.

Lina pushed off against the wall, slipped her hips out of the sling, and dropped to the floor.

The men above must have seen the rope slacken as her weight dropped free, for her father called down, "Lina! Are you all right?"

"Fine," she yelled back up, her voice echoing. Her feet skidded against the slick, moss-covered floor, and something slithered across her boot, but she didn't even notice. Lina reached out to touch the slab, her senses alive to the man she knew must be buried here. This stone monument almost filled the long, narrow room. She judged it must be at least twelve feet long and seven feet wide.

An altar? Or a sarcophagus? She lifted her lantern to get a better look at the smooth limestone top. She heard an exclamation above her and tilted her head back.

Jeremy descended on a separate rope. "My God, it's magnificent."

Lina brushed at the layer of mold and dirt with her glove, revealing stone carving so finely detailed that she was stunned. Tears started to her eyes as again she rested her hand on the artistry men of her own world could scarcely match with all their modern tools.

Everything had been worth it. All the bites, the sleepless nights, the bickering, the dangers. To stand here in the resting place of the man who must have watched Palenque rise—with Jeremy. Despite her anger, she was glad he was here to share it with her.

Standing beside her, he caught his breath and reached out to cup her cheek. "Angel, forgive me. I know—"

"What do you see, L—" Her father's words stopped abruptly, but Jeremy and Lina saw and heard only each other.

Sighing, Lina pulled away. "I'm not sure yet," she yelled up, circling the slab.

Her knee knocked against a masonry box. Something rattled.

She pushed at the lid. With Jeremy's help, she slipped the cover off enough to illuminate the contents. Lina stumbled backward until the rough stone wall pressed into her back.

Skeletons littered the box. Jeremy held the lantern high and counted. "I see six skulls. Six sacrifices. This must be the burial of a very important man."

"Pacal," Lina whispered, staring again at the slab.

"Pacal?"

"Don't you remember? The priest called his people the children of Pacal."

"Of course!" Jeremy abruptly went silent and looked up. "Your father hasn't said much in some moments."

Lina didn't even hear him, for she was investigating the room that she was increasingly certain must be a burial chamber. "Jeremy, can you wipe away as much of the mold as you can so I can see the top slab?"

Jeremy complied, using the rags he'd slipped into his pockets.

At one end, Lina found an urn. She tipped it over. Hard objects pinged against the floor and went rolling. Lina held one up to the light. It was a tiny jade carving, as finely made as anything she'd seen from any other culture. She set it down gently and picked up a pearl. It was slightly tinged with pink, the size of a penny. More jade shone with a dull luster in the light, but she didn't take time to examine it now. Instead, she scooped all back into the urn. In a recess, she found more pieces of pottery.

"It's as clear as I can get it without soap, Lina. Come look."

Lina stood and hurried to Jeremy's side. In silence, they looked upon the reclining figure of the man they both knew must be Pacal. Even with his eyes closed, being swallowed by the great fleshless jaws of some underworld monster, he was a striking figure, strong of nose and muscles, wearing jade adornments at arms, ankles, ears, and neck. Behind him rose a carving she couldn't make out.

"It looks like a ceiba tree," Jeremy said from his greater height. "Curious. The source of life and death all in one striking depiction. I wish we knew what these glyphs say."

Glyphs ringed every edge of the slab. Traces of red paint still decorated some of the glyphs on the sides. Lina gently touched one of the more evocative ones. "We could read these someday if we still had the book."

Frustration rang in her voice, then she picked up the urn and stepped back into her harness. "We need to get the photographic equipment down here to take pictures. Getting this slab loose will be no easy task—especially in one day."

Before she could tug on the rope, Jeremy took a great stride forward and caught her arm "Do you mean you still intend to leave on schedule?"

"I never intended otherwise." She slipped neatly out of his closing arms, honesty compelling her to add, "At least, not unless you agreed. I was considering asking for a few more days—but only for a few days. Not any longer. And I hope my *obedience*"—she emphasized the word bitterly—"satisfies you, for *I* shan't any longer. After all, I've paid my debt to you. Apparently there's no gold. But we said nothing about a lasting relationship."

"Lina, I didn't mean to hurt you. I came back to help. Despite everything, I still believed in your honesty."

Lina searched his eyes, but she no longer trusted the feelings in those gray depths—or her own. Resolutely turning away from his pleading expression, she tugged on the rope, cradling the urn in one arm.

"I'm ready to come up," she yelled. She wondered at the speed with which she was pulled out. She'd not realized her father and Baxter were so strong.

Jeremy hastily gripped his own rope and began pulling himself out, using his feet against the sloping walls. The climb was tiring, for he slipped often. His feet slowed as he neared the top and heard the voices.

Lina was grabbed the second her feet cleared the opening. She blinked against the torches blazing around her, momentarily blinded. But when her feet touched ground, a tall figure wearing a headdress came closer to her, closer, forcing her back into the wall.

Lina held the urn protectively to her breast.

Gently the priest removed the fine pottery. "Thank you."

"You promised us two days," Lina managed over her frightened heartbeat.

"Two days to pack, not loot," he chided her gently. "And where is your other admirer?" He looked around.

Lina shrugged. "Hunting, I suppose." A glance assured her that her father and Baxter were safe. They'd been herded up the steps like cattle and huddled on the top, but aside from a cut on Baxter's lip they looked unharmed.

Lina pretended to call to them. "Our fine priest keeps promises no better than the Spaniards he hates, wouldn't you agree, Father?"

Warning received, loud and clear, she hoped.

Indeed, Jeremy halted his climb. He hung precariously fifteen feet above the stone floor, a dark void lapping at his boots, indecision twisting his face. He tilted his head to listen.

"Obviously," Sir Lawrence said, impervious to the scowl the priest leveled on him.

"If your motives are so pure, señorita," the priest said, swinging back to Lina again, "then you will gladly help us complete the discovery you have begun, no?"

"No." Lina's blood chilled as those almond-shaped dark eyes slitted, but she continued easily, "At least, not as long as you hold us prisoner. Let my father and Baxter go and I'll gladly lead your excavation. The slab below is too heavy for us to lift without your help, anyway."

"Lina, I won't leave you," her father exclaimed.

"Nor I," agreed Baxter.

Lina continued as if they hadn't spoken. "And further, you must agree to let us take part of the finds back to England. We spent thousands of pounds getting here. You'd never have found the book, or the tomb, without us. Surely we deserve some compensation. You have my word that the finds will be treated with reverence and will go into public museums for all the people of the world to learn the greatness of your culture." Lina held her breath.

Below, Jeremy did the same. She couldn't, she wouldn't

endanger herself that way—she would. He heard the smile in the priest's voice.

"You drive a hard bargain for a woman. A lovely woman, at that. But I knew the first time I saw you that you were both intelligent and spirited. Agreed, señorita." He commanded something in his language.

The men standing over Sir Lawrence and Baxter moved back. The two Britons hesitated.

Lina was touched at the anguish in her father's face. She took a step toward him. "Go to where the lion sleeps, Father. I'll be fine. They won't hurt me because they need me."

Hope flickered in Sir Lawrence's strong face. Tugging on Baxter's arm, he turned.

"And if you bring Don Roberto back with guns, you will be met in kind," the priest warned. "I would hate for your lovely daughter to be caught between us. ¿Comprende?"

"Yes," Sir Lawrence said dully. His ringing footsteps retreated.

As the priest took two steps toward her, Lina lifted her chin and pretended not to be afraid. This time, she didn't back off, even when his strong, bare chest filled her vision.

"Are all the women of your country so brave?" A brown finger traced Lina's high cheekbone.

"Oh yes. But not all of them are so tolerant." Lina turned her head aside from his touch.

The priest smiled, then stepped back briskly. "So, show me what you have found."

Lina's spine wilted, only partly at her command. She'd not slept a wink and was exhausted. Even more important, she had to get these men away so Jeremy could climb out.

"Please, let me take a nap first. I worked through the night, and I need to be rested before we start cataloguing the tomb."

"Cataloguing? What is this?"

"To make a written record, so if anything is lost—"

A strong hand waved her to silence. "We need no such record."

Lina tucked her hair back into her braid. When she could speak evenly, she said, "I won't help you unless you let me make a record. Especially considering the fact that I'll only be taking part of the finds back with me."

That dark scowl settled on her again, but Lina's lovely face was set just as stubbornly.

His dawning smile reminded her of Cesar at his most Latin, and for the first time she realized that this man was a product of two warring cultures. Her curiosity was piqued, but all scientific consideration fled at his next words.

"*Ay, Dios mio,* you are stubborn. You will have fine children."

Lina cleared her throat when his dark gaze wandered over her. "Ah, may I go now?"

He waved her before him, pausing to leave two of his men on guard.

He escorted her to the palace, himself crossing his arms to station himself at the opening to the corridor. Lina climbed into the hammock, wondering if she'd awaken to find everything a dream. Surely her imagination could never devise something so fantastic . . . She yawned, her hammock swinging as the morning rain began.

When she was almost asleep, her deepest feelings held sway. "Jeremy," she whispered. Somehow she knew he would come. She was safe enough. She slept.

Hovering between two unenviable options, Jeremy was anything but safe. He didn't dare light the lantern they'd left below, yet he heard voices from above. He had no idea how many men remained. His arms and legs were tired, but terror for Lina troubled him far more than his aching muscles. Her bold gamble had apparently succeeded. He'd calmed somewhat until the priest made his comment about Lina's potential as a mother.

How many times had he thought the same? Dammit, she was his, by her own choice. No one had the right to speak to her so, or lust for her. Every primitive impulse he'd long thought himself immune to blanketed him as surely as the darkness. He didn't stop to recall his doubts about her; he didn't stop to fear for the future that would require diligent compromise.

Sheer instinct drove him upward. Only ten minutes had passed, he judged, since the priest took Lina away, but he'd have to risk it. At least this time he had his weapons. When he reached the opening, Jeremy braced himself with his feet,

took out his stiletto and stuck it in his teeth. He'd rather no
use his pistol, if he could avoid it.

Inch by inch, he lifted his head until he could see above the
hole. To his relief, the log tomb was empty, though he saw
two stalwart bare backs guarding the entrance.

His face beaded with perspiration, Jeremy kept pulling unti
his feet, blessedly, cleared the hole. He couldn't avoid making
some noise as his boots landed on stone, but the two men were
conversing quietly in their own tongue, a slightly differen
dialect to the Yucatec Maya Jeremy knew.

Behind them, Jeremy rubbed his scraped, bloody hands or
his breeches and grasped the knife. Then he hesitated. If he
killed them, the priest would be angry. Angry enough to hur
Lina? Jeremy didn't think so, but he couldn't take the chance
If he could escape to the jungle, he didn't think they'd pursue
him long. They'd assume he, too, would go to Don Roberto.

Not hardly.

Sheathing his knife, he picked up the ancient musket. It was
rusty, but the wood was still intact. The butt should make
a good club. Jeremy walked soundlessly on the balls of his
feet, closer, closer. When he stood directly behind one man,
he lifted the musket high and crashed it down on that dark
head. The Maya dropped in a heap.

Before Jeremy could bring the weapon up again, the other
man whirled; he received his blow on the chin.

"Hellfire and damnation!" Jeremy propped the gun agains
the tomb wall. He'd hoped to catch them both unawares, but
now one of them had seen him. Jeremy dragged them into the
tomb and trussed them, then stuck rags in their mouths. At
least this should give him some time to get away.

He stole their water casks and *pozol* supplies and hurried
outside to survey the compound. It was empty of all but a few
men who snoozed in the shade of a temple. Sir Lawrence and
Baxter had apparently left, for their horses were gone. Surely
Don Roberto and his men would be here soon. Jeremy loped
down the steps. He could keep to the brush and wend around
to the palace. He might have a chance of snatching Lina . . .

Lina awoke with a start. What was that? She glanced
through the haze of netting and saw the priest sitting in

the doorway. However, his head was slumped on his broad shoulders. Was he asleep? If he hadn't spoken, what had awakened her?

"Angel," the soft call came again. Lina shoved the netting away and bolted out of the hammock. Only two men called her angel and her father was gone.

"Where are you?" she called back, a wary eye on her guard.

"The interior courtyard. Come."

Lina tiptoed around the priest, who was indeed slumped in sleep. A few more steps, and she was in Jeremy's arms. The frantic pounding of his heart told her all she'd doubted about his feelings.

She tipped her head back to his descending mouth, but the kiss was, of necessity, hard and brief. "God, I can feel gray hairs growing as we stand here," he said harshly against her mouth. He tugged on her hand. "Guards surround all the entrances."

"How did you get in?"

His bold grin sent a shiver through Lina, as did his words. "You do like to climb, don't you?"

She saw then that he was leading her to the tower. "And you call me reckless?" But she went willingly—at first.

However, her feet slowed along with her excitement. As Jeremy wrapped the rope he'd used to climb the tower about her, she covered his hands. "Jeremy, if I leave now I'll never know what lies under that slab. Nor will the world, for the priest will secrete it all away, as he took the book."

"Lina, I know that's frustrating, but we don't have a choice."

"We always have a choice." Their eyes met.

His hands slowed, then dropped. "And I made mine. No matter how you got me here, you've given me the greatest happiness of my life. If you insist on staying, you endanger not only your own life, but mine. For without you, I'll go back to being a wanderer with Polaris ever leading nowhere."

Lina's hands clenched with the need to reach out to him and erase that desperate look from his face. But he didn't know what he asked of her—for little reason. "Jeremy, if I truly believed myself in danger, I'd come, no matter what. But the priest won't hurt me."

"And what of your promise to leave? The same promise you reaffirmed just hours ago in your precious tomb?"

"I fully intended to honor it, even after we found the remains, but that was before the Maya came." Lina shoved the loose rope down to the ground, stepped out of it, and put a pleading hand on Jeremy's arm. "If I leave now, I'll betray every ideal I've fought so hard for. How can I prove myself as capable as a man if I let such a magnificent discovery be lost? I came here knowing this journey could be dangerous— as you yourself warned me."

"If I'd known the Maya were interested in Palenque before we came, I never would have brought you." Jeremy covered her hand with his own and squeezed with unknowing strength.

Lina schooled herself not to wince. She met his eyes square-ly, but fear twined about her insides like ivy. Instinctively she knew her future was far more at risk in this moment than when the priest captured them. She'd leave the Yucatán safely—but would she do it without Jeremy?

He, too, seemed to realize the stakes, for his grip relaxed, then he took a tiny step back.

The significance of his action was not lost on Lina. He might as well have drawn a line in the sand.

"Lina, perhaps I could sympathize with the sacrifices . . ."— he closed his eyes briefly at his choice of words, then opened them and rushed on—"you're willing to make if I believed in your cause. But I think you know I don't and that I never have. Leave these people, dead and living, their dignity. How would you feel if some future archaeologist robbed your family mausoleum and put their funerary finery on display?"

Lina couldn't suppress a moue of distaste. "But it's not the same. My people don't supply the answer to the riddle of a great civilization. If they did, I wouldn't begrudge the world the right to gawk at their remains."

Jeremy's hands clenched at the conviction in her eyes. Very quietly he said, "And what of our happiness? Should that not come first?"

Tears started to Lina's eyes. "If it rests on so flimsy a base, then it's not worth sacrificing my integrity for. I'd not ask you to dump irreplaceable cargo over the side even if it would save us from pirate attack."

"But I would. Without hesitation if it would keep you safe." The words hovered in the air between them like a shimmering but indestructible curtain. They couldn't go through it, but they could sweep it aside.

Neither moved to do so.

"And there lies our basic difference. Some things are worth dying for, Jeremy, such as honor and integrity."

"Agreed, Lina. But those aren't at stake here. No one will blame you for letting the finds go under the circumstances. Why do you care what society thinks?"

"I don't. I would blame myself. I could never stomach being an archaeologist again. Don't you see that?" Lina held a pleading hand out to him.

He didn't take it. "I see much. Much you helped me learn. One lesson above all: Some compromises are worth living with. Come with me, Lina. We've earned a chance at happiness together."

Still, no mention of marriage. She had to know. "And how would we live? Roam the seas together?"

Jeremy frowned. "I don't know. I suppose so. I can't imagine being landlocked. To be honest, I haven't given the specifics much thought. Once we're away we can make plans."

Lina rubbed her elbows, feeling chilled despite the oppressive humidity. "And how am I to conduct my work at sea?"

Silence.

Darkness danced before Lina's eyes as she swayed with the surging pain. Dear God, to come so far, love him so much, and learn that, in the end, he was like the rest. It was the woman's place to follow her man. Cherish came before obey in the marriage vows, but seldom in practice.

Even Jeremy put obedience first.

Had he, in that moment, cherished her first and demanded her obedience second, she could have climbed down with him and deserted her past for the future she longed for. Had he asked her to marry him or even bended enough to say he'd occasionally accompany her on a dig, she'd have flown into his arms where she belonged.

He did none of those things—he only stared at her with that quiet control she hated. He would always keep part of himself inviolate, yet he would not allow her the same luxury. The truths were bitter, but Lina accepted them as she must: If he loved her, he'd not force her to such a choice. Besides, it was too late. Even if she went with him and turned her back on all she'd strived for, they'd never be happy now.

A mere step stood between them, but in the end, it was a chasm.

Lina dropped her hands and straightened to her full height. "Jeremy, I . . ." She couldn't say the words, but found she didn't have to.

Those gray eyes were the clearest she'd ever seen them. No smoke or mirrors now. She saw anguish, she saw yearning, and finally, she saw angry acceptance.

He swiveled and ducked to pick up the rope, his movements jerky. "Go then. I'll do what I can to watch out for you. I owe you that as the man who led you here. But that's all."

"That's all," Lina agreed huskily. Her nails dug into her palms so hard they drew blood as he lowered himself out the window, braced his feet, and gave her one last look.

Then he was gone. Even the sounds of his passing were soon muffled by the screech and rustle of wildlife.

The memory of his eyes haunted Lina as she stumbled back to the palace. Beneath the wounded male pride lay the little boy she'd sometimes glimpsed. He'd won his shiny red wagon, touched it, ridden in it, only to have it dump him on the ground and leave him in the dust. Far lonelier now that he'd so briefly won his heart's delight.

As was she.

Through the days and nights that followed, not even the intellectual challenge of the tomb consoled Lina. Jeremy was never far from her thoughts. With every exquisite piece of jade they found, every pearl and stunning figurine, her anguish grew. How had they been so close, only to end as living proof of their deepest fears? To Jeremy, she was the worst example of a society woman interested more in ambition and appearance than in loving support.

To Lina, Jeremy was the worst example of a man who wanted her unquestioning respect, then condemned her for asking for the same. How could they ever overcome differences so basic?

They couldn't, whispered the winds skipping through the palace.

They couldn't, shrieked the birds.

They couldn't, laughed the monkeys.

"Señorita, why have you been so grim?"

As Cantul sat down beside her, Lina started. In the past two days, she'd lost all fear of the priest and now called him by his Mayan name. How could she fear a man who behaved like a teasing older brother? Their mutual respect had grown with every find they shared. Tomorrow, they hoped to finish lifting the enormous top slab to see inside the sarcophagus. She should be excited, happy.

She was neither, for she had another worry now besides regret. She set aside the piece of jade she'd been sketching and wrapped her arms about her knees to stare moodily into the fire. "I'm worried about my father. I don't understand why he hasn't come back."

"Perhaps Don Roberto could not come yet."

Lina smiled at him wryly. "You knew they'd gone to get him?"

"Of course. My people, too, often call him a lion. And where is your friend Jeremy?"

Lina's smile faded. "I don't know."

Truthfully, she didn't. If he was watching, he was doing so very stealthily. Sometimes, she thought she'd glimpsed him lurking in the tree across from the temple, but then the leaves would rustle and she'd see a monkey poking its head out of the branches.

"He is watching." Cantul picked up a stick and threw it into the fire.

"How do you know?"

"Because if you were mine, I would watch." Those dark eyes slanted in her direction, then quickly away.

"I'm not his." Lina swallowed and grasped her knees tighter.

"No? My wife, she used to say that, too, before I took her to my mat. She never said it again after that."

"You're married?"

"I was. She was Spanish, a good Catholic girl who came to help the nuns at the mission."

"Was?"

His strong jaw flexed. "She died having my son. He lived only an hour."

Lina gasped. "I'm . . . so sorry." That explained so much. The odd blending of cultures she'd seen in him, his command of English. He had gone to Campeche to trade quetzal feathers, which had explained his long, bulky, sack. Only now did she understand why a Mayan priest had been inside a Catholic church. He'd obviously gone inside to light a candle in honor of his dead wife.

He went on dully. "The town doctor, he would not come because she had betrayed her people by marrying me. They never let her in their fine house after that. The midwife did what she could, but the birth was breech."

The rendition was all the more powerful for its simplicity. It also explained why he was determined to keep his heritage alive. Under the same circumstances, she, too, would hate the whites who tried to incorporate everything different into their cruel society. "That's why you fight."

"Yes. And because it is right. We should be proud of her ancestors, not ashamed as they have tried to make us."

"And the other tribe? It seems to hate you too."

"They want to rule all our people, force us back to the jungle into the old ways of sacrifice and war. I believe the old ways should be remembered, but they are not always best. I could never sacrifice one of my own children to Chac."

"Chac?"

"The rain god."

Lina shivered.

Cantul stood. "Come, enough sad stories. Tomorrow, we feast after we look upon the face of Pacal. Tonight, we will make our own offering to the gods."

"We will?" Lina took the hand he extended.

"You promised to let the cub go. If you do so now, perhaps it will be a good omen."

Lina's steps slowed. "Oh, please, not tonight."

"Tonight."

Only once had he grown angry with her—when he'd found her feeding the cub. "Do you want to anger the gods? *El tigre* is not meant to be a pet." He'd crossed his arms over his formidable chest and glared at her.

"But he would have died if we hadn't taken him."

"Better an honorable death than to be led about by a halter."

His bold Mayan nose had quivered in disgust as he eyed the tether tying the cub to a pillar. He'd made her promise then to let the cub go.

Now, as they stood and stared at the jaguar, Lina wondered if she could keep her promise. The contrary little beast had become far more dear to her than any of the dogs she'd had as a child. Perhaps he represented the wild beauty of the jungle itself, or perhaps he symbolized her love for the people who had obviously revered him.

For whatever reason, when Cantul gave her a little shove, she balked. Then, sighing, she went to the pillar, untied the tether, and approached the cub.

Slitted green eyes watched her warily until she tossed him the piece of fresh goat meat Cantul had given her. The cub descended on it, growling his contentment. While he was distracted, Lina quickly loosened his rope collar and slipped it over his head.

He slapped at her, spitting, when she interfered with his meal by moving his head, but she dodged. His tail twitched, then he lowered to his feast again.

Despite the danger of injury, Lina brushed the soft fur at his nape, unable to resist touching him a last time. His head lifted.

Wild green eyes met hers. His jaws were bloody, but his whiskers twitched as he sniffed her familiar scent. He bent his head again, suffering her touch as he finished his meal. When he was content, Lina stood and stepped back, watching as he paced to the limit of his tether—and beyond.

The look of shock on his face was comical. With that distinctive raspy howl of his breed, he bolted. At the doorway he stopped. Lina would have sworn the yowl he gave was a feline goodbye, then he'd padded silently away.

And she knew she'd done the right thing. He was meant to rule the night.

Cantul lifted her chin and wiped the tears away from her eyes. "You did right, *querida mia*. Your God, and mine, will be smiling on us tomorrow."

His words proved prophetic, for the next day went smoothly. The pulley they'd rigged held as they heaved up the immense slab and maneuvered it aside.

Beneath they found a fish-shaped cover stone and two stucco heads. Lina exclaimed and held one to the light. The long nose, narrow chin, and slanted eyes were distinctively Mayan. The detail, from the curves of mouth and jaw to the lines serrating the headdress, was astounding.

"Their artistry never ceases to amaze me," Lina said. "Do your people still know how to do things like this, Cantul?"

Bitterness twisted his dark face. "No. The priests have tried for many years to make us forget the old ways. They have almost succeeded." He gently picked up the second head. "But not totally."

They handed the heads to two of the tribesmen, then worked on the plugs in the fish-shaped cover until the men could pry it loose. With a shifting of dirt and the stale whiff of ages past, the cover groaned and revealed its secret.

Lina gasped.

Cantul crossed himself.

His men stared in disbelief.

Pacal lay before them in a splendor that was still impressive despite his skeletal state. He was a tall man; for his time, he must have been a giant.

His sepulcher was painted red. It made an imposing background for the king's ransom in jade he'd taken with him into death. Jade disks from a collapsed diadem rested on his head, as did fragments of a polished jade mosaic mask.

Earrings engraved with hieroglyphics lay where his ears had been and a hefty necklace of tubular beads still decorated his chest cavity. Other necklaces littered the sarcophagus, some finely carved depictions of fruit, others exquisitely modeled flowers. Rings enhanced all the bony fingers. A jade statuette lay at his feet.

For long minutes, Lina looked her fill. She could see him in all his splendor, lording over his subjects from his throne, garbed in jaguar skins and weighted with jade. What had that time been like? Somehow, she believed people then had been much the same as people now. They wanted sustenance, and shelter, and children.

And love.

Tears misted Lina's eyes. She whirled and set up the tripod. When the photographic equipment was ready, she had the men hold the torches high to illuminate the cavity. She used all the plates that had survived the moisture and humidity, hoping it would be enough of a record.

Again, she mourned that she couldn't take all the finds back with her—until she looked around her at the wonder and pride in the dark faces lined with toil. This man was their ancestor; they had more right to his legacy than anyone.

In this, at least, Jeremy was right.

But that didn't ease her frustration. Late into the night they worked, Lina sketching and cataloguing, the others helping her where they could. After a brief rest, the next morning they crated the finds in straw and carried them out.

Then most of the workers gave her a grave smile as, for the first time in days, they departed to their village. Cantul remained with Lina, along with several of his men.

He gave her a white dress one of his men had brought. "You deserve to be dressed as a princess for the feast."

Lina ran the fine cotton through her fingers. Exquisite Mayan designs clustered at hem and puffed sleeves. She looked down at her filthy clothes. "I'll dirty this lovely gown if I don't bathe."

"Go then. I will guard you."

When they reached the stream, Lina kept her undergarments on, peeking over her shoulder all the while, but that proud dark head never turned. After she was clean and dressed, she approached him. "You can look now."

He inhaled sharply when he saw her, but then sadness blanketed the desire in his eyes. "Come. We have more work to do," he said abruptly, turning on his heel.

Lina followed, alert to the slightest movement in the jungle. Her head was turned the wrong way when a strong hand clenched about a tree branch so hard that the branch split. Jeremy climbed down from his perch and tailed them as they returned to the palace.

Lina sat down, her heart in her throat, and watched Cantul sort through the crates. She let him give her what he wished, expecting him to keep the best of the finds, but to her amazement, he was scrupulously fair. Whenever there was a duplicate, he gave her one object. Those that were unique, he kept—with one notable exception.

Gingerly he picked up a piece of the jade mosaic mask and turned it this way and that. He tried to mate it with another one, then another, and finally set it down. "This can never be repaired."

Lina choked back a laugh at his disgust. "Yes it can. You'd be surprised what patience can do."

"Can you put this back together?"

"Eventually. If I have all the pieces."

He sorted through the crates until he found what seemed to be all the loose bits of jade mask and put them in one small box. He offered the box to her with a grave bow. "Take them. I want your people to look upon the face of Pacal and know what a great man he was."

Lina's hands trembled as she accepted the box. "Thank you. You honor me with your trust. I promise not to break it." Two different pairs of eyes met, reflecting two different cultures that could, when liking was allowed, work in harmony.

Neither of them saw the long shadow reflected on the corridor adjacent. It stayed still. Waiting.

Soon Lina had a pile of four large crates and the box containing the mask. She bit her lip, wondering if she should take the gamble. But what did she have to lose?

Cantul cleaned his hands in the bucket, then dried them on a rag. "Now, señorita, will you honor us with your presence at our feast? Then I myself will escort you to Don Roberto."

Lina nodded. "I will be delighted. But first . . ." Cradling the small box holding the mask to her bosom, Lina rose. "The tomb was magnificent, Cantul, but its significance pales in comparison to the book. I'll gladly return to you all the pearls and jade if you'll let me take this one mask and the book back to England." Her heart sank, for Cantul was shaking his head before she'd even finished.

"The book is not mine to give. It belongs to my people, and their sons and their grandsons. It is as sacred to us as your Bible." He sighed at the disappointment in her face, went to the pack he'd brought with him and pulled something out.

Lina's eyes widened. All this time, he'd had it with him! Why hadn't she thought to look? If only she hadn't used all the plates, she could at least take a picture.

Peeling the wrapping away, he set it before her. "You can

see it again, if you wish." He pulled apart the first leaf.

They were both bent over it, absorbed in the harmonious inscriptions, when that long shadow slipped closer, then stood directly behind them. Cantul slumped sideways, knocking Lina off balance.

She screamed—but a smile broke across her face when she looked up. "Jeremy!" She scrambled free and tried to embrace him, but he caught her wrist and tugged her after him to the door.

"Hurry. They're coming."

"Who's coming?"

His only answer was to drag her after him faster.

"But what if you hurt him? You hit him hard." She jerked her arm free. "Wait a minute. We can't leave the book just lying about like that . . ."

"Shut up, Lina." He pulled her behind him again. "Sometimes I wonder if you have good sense. Why do you think he's dressed you up like a lamb to slaughter?"

"Because he wanted me to look nice for the feast. His people are coming back." Lina stared up at the tree he pushed her toward. "I'm not dressed to climb this. Besides, it's totally unnecessary."

His hands shoving at her shoulder blades showed his disagreement. "I told you they're practicing sacrifice again."

"That's not his tribe." But Lina climbed, the leather sandals Cantul had given her perfect for the task. When they were safe, he'd listen.

They'd barely made it onto the platform Jeremy had built into the trees before angry painted Indians burst onto the escarpment. Their weapons were primitive, but it was the hatred in their faces that chilled Lina's blood. They ringed the palace and brandished their spears and bows, shouting insults.

Her blood slowly congealed in her veins as she saw proof of their fury.

Bringing up the rear, several men shoved bound and bleeding prisoners before them.

Even from this distance, Lina recognized that blond head, that graying leonine head, and that proud dark head.

No wonder her father and Baxter hadn't come . . .

Chapter 16

"DO YOU STILL think there's no danger, Lina?" Jeremy asked grimly in her ear.

"We've got to help them!" She tried to reach the edge of the platform, but Jeremy hauled her back by the waist.

"Are you insane? We can't help your father if we're prisoners too. We have to bide our time. Your priest's friends will hear the news at their own village and hurry back—with weapons. Then maybe we can do some good."

Cantul, a rag held to the back of his head, came to the doorway. The leader of the rebels, his face ugly with a savagery accented by the paint, climbed two palace steps and jerked a thumb over his shoulder toward the prisoners, shouting something.

"Do you understand what he's saying?" Lina asked.

"Only bits and pieces. His dialect is different. Something about how the invaders are not so powerful when met with force. That your priest was wrong to submit to their arrogance." Jeremy inched closer to the edge of the platform, but the exchange was hard to hear from this distance. He shook his head. "This is getting nasty." Jeremy kept watching the escarpment that connected Palenque to the jungle. "Come, on, dammit, hurry up."

Lina, too, yearned for the workers to reappear, but their village was some distance away. Even if they heard about the attack the minute they arrived, they'd barely had time to make it back yet. "Jeremy, we can't wait. Isn't there something we can do? Cantul is my friend."

The words were scarcely out of her mouth before the angry

Maya chief arched his arm back to throw his spear. Lina bit back an alarmed cry, but Cantul apparently was expecting it, for he bolted into the palace before the spear was away.

The chief dropped his arm and yelled something over his shoulder. His men surged up the steps after him.

Cursing in languages Lina didn't recognize, Jeremy checked to be sure his pistol and rifle were loaded, then he swung his legs over the edge of the platform. "Do not, and I repeat, *do not* leave this tree. Understand?"

Lina was too busy watching the prisoners to respond. They were held next to the edge of the jungle, propped against trees. Two men stood guard over them. The rest of Palenque was deserted, but battle cries echoed from the palace along with the muffled retort of musket fire. Could Cantul and his three men possibly hold off the entire tribe with single-shot muskets? Still, she couldn't help him. But the prisoners . . .

Jeremy followed her gaze and exploded, "Dammit to hell, don't you know that dressed that way you're a perfect celebratory sacrifice if the wrong side wins?"

"So? That's certainly the case if I remain here. They'll find me eventually if you're all killed. I promise to remain outside, hidden as best I can. But it's my duty to try to release my father."

"You're the stubbornest woman I've ever met." He blew a breath through his teeth. "Very well, we'll do it my way. For once." Jeremy helped her down the tree, then shoved Lina behind him. "Stay down. Do what I do."

In a zigzagging crouch, he kept to the buildings and undergrowth, working his way to the edge of the jungle where the prisoners were held. The stealth was unnecessary. The guards were obviously not happy at their role and were attentive only to the sounds coming from the palace complex. When the bushes beside them rustled, they didn't even turn their heads.

Lina used Jeremy's stiletto to free all three prisoners. Baxter said, "Thank God," before he could stop himself.

He bit his lip as he met Lina's eyes.

The guards turned—five seconds too late. One guard met Jeremy's skinning knife in the throat; the other fell backward, a jagged red hole rimmed with powder burns in his chest. Lina glanced at them, then quickly away, swallowing. Jeremy had no choice but to kill them, but the ease with which he'd done so troubled her.

Her father embraced her roughly. "Thank God. I've been so worried about you."

Lina ran her hands over him. "Are you all right?"

"Fine. They slapped us around a bit. Come on, we've got to get out of here."

Lina pulled her wrist away. "Wait." Hesitantly she asked Don Roberto, "Where is the rest of your family?"

"I sent Cesar into the jungle with my daughters. He took them to a hiding place upriver. Thank God I can go to them now."

The musketfire wasn't coming as frequently now. Lina held her hands out to him pleadingly. "Please, help Cantul and his men. They had nothing to do with this."

Don Roberto's aristocratic nostrils flared. "Why should I risk my life for an Indian who despises me?"

"Because he's risked his life for you."

Don Roberto frowned. "I don't understand."

"The other Maya hate him because he won't follow their savage ways and counsels peace with the settlers."

Lina found little sympathy in the four masculine faces. Indeed, her own father said, "I can't pity a man who kidnapped my daughter and stole our find."

Lina grabbed the rifle from Jeremy's lax grip. "Do as you must. But Cantul is my friend." She ran toward the palace.

"Lina, dammit, come back!" Sir Lawrence bellowed.

Her running steps scarcely touched the ground.

Jeremy bolted after her.

Baxter followed.

Don Roberto and Sir Lawrence exchanged a grim look, then picked up the obsidian axes their guards would no longer need and ran after the others.

Their assault totally surprised the warring Maya. Jeremy picked off three with his pistol before they realized their rear was under attack. Baxter grabbed the rifle from Lina and emptied it rapidly, hitting flesh with every shot. Lina accepted the pistol Jeremy tossed her and rapidly reloaded it.

Meanwhile, the warriors regrouped, brandished spears and axes, and charged. The Westerners retreated to the palace steps and made a stand at the doorways, where they could face their exiting opponents one by one. Sir Lawrence and Don Roberto learned how to use their axes very quickly when their lives were at stake.

Baxter's empty rifle made a good club. Jeremy emptied his pistol, then drew his knife. Lina grabbed the pistol, but this time she never had a chance to load it. More warriors pushed at the ones in the doorways, slipping through. Jeremy faced two Indians, kicking at one, slashing at the other.

Lina was too busy then fighting for her own life to worry about helping Jeremy.

A brutal grip forced the stiletto from her numb wrist. A painted, grinning face filled her vision as the smelly warrior forced her down the steps, an obsidian knife held to her throat. When she reached level ground, Lina's instincts took over. Leaning back away from the sharp blade, she slammed her knee into his groin.

The Indian grunted and bent over, but he still didn't release her wrist. Lina kicked again, but her slippers didn't do much damage. The warrior forced himself erect, panting.

Black menace was personified in that face. He raised the knife. Lina closed her eyes, awaiting the slash of the blade, thinking vaguely that she'd never thought to die this way. She felt his shadow blocking the sunlight.

A hoarse scream surprised her. His rough hands let go. Astounded, she stared at the Indian. He was doing a peculiar jig in place, awkwardly jabbing in the area of his own back. When he danced sideways, Lina understood why.

A speckled piece of living jungle was attached to him, all four claws digging into his bare back. The cub gave an angry yowl when the knife nicked his paw and sheathed his claws. He dropped lightly to the ground, leaving four deep, bleeding furrows in the broad back.

The Indian turned on him. The cub stood his ground, tail slashing, spitting his own brand of fury. He was accustomed now to the scent of man. He had no reason to fear it.

"Run," Lina screamed, rushing forward, waving her hands. The Indian drew back to throw.

His arm stayed extended as, slowly, he toppled backward. An arrow protruded from his chest.

Lina glanced at the slope leading to the acropolis. Cantul's men swarmed up it, armed with spears, bows, and firearms they were using to good purpose. Lina's weak legs gave out, but she cupped her hands about her mouth and yelled toward the palace, "They're coming!"

Just in time. A Maya warrior had taken the ax from Sir Lawrence. Sir Lawrence held his wrist with both hands, but still that bloody edge came closer, closer until it nicked the Englishman's Adam's apple. When the man glanced up at Lina's shout, Sir Lawrence stamped down, hard, on his bare foot.

Howling, the Maya let go to hop about like a one-legged jackrabbit, cradling his abused foot in his hands.

Sir Lawrence kicked his muscled buttocks. The Maya sprawled down the steps, then leaped to his feet at a dead run.

Baxter's assailants released him and fled. Baxter gave a deep-throated war cry and shook his fist. "Bloody wise decision," he yelled after them.

Jeremy's knife was coated with sticky red that ran down onto his fingers. The man who faced him looked at the blood streaking his opponent's hands and chest, then chose the better part of valor.

He fled to fight another day. His leader lay dead inside the palace, killed when Cantul came down from the tower to pursue his distracted enemies. One by one, the other surviving Maya seemed to reach the same conclusion. Cantul, the wound pouring blood at his shoulder apparently not slowing him, ran down the steps in hot pursuit. His men followed.

Soon both tribes had disappeared into the jungle.

Don Roberto sat where he stood. He held his hands out before him, appraising the red spatters. "I'm too old for this."

Sir Lawrence sat next to him. "Me, too, but I'd say we acquitted ourselves favorably. Are you happy now, Lina?"

Lina didn't answer. Sir Lawrence surged to his feet. "Lina!" The cub crouched at the foot of the steps washing his face, but Lina had disappeared.

Tiredly Jeremy nodded toward the interior of the palace.

"Inside. Checking her precious finds, no doubt."

Energized, Sir Lawrence ran into the palace. Baxter and Don Roberto followed.

Jeremy stared grimly about at the dead and wounded littering the clearing before the palace. He wiped his knife off on his pants leg, then sheathed it with angry efficiency.

They were lucky to be alive, and all she cared about were her damn artifacts. The battle wasn't her fault, for the Indians would have revolted and threatened Don Roberto and Cantul even if they'd never come. But the outcome certainly would have been different if she hadn't insisted on intervening. Cantul would be dead. Why the hell did she risk her very life for an Indian she barely knew, but she wouldn't set aside her own ambition for the man she claimed to love?

Angrily he climbed the palace steps three at a time. This time he'd not let her send him away without an explanation.

Inside, he found Sir Lawrence and Baxter exclaiming over one crate, Don Roberto over another. Lina was searching a pack against the wall, her movements frantic. Jeremy knew what she was looking for.

"It's not here!" She scrambled to her feet and looked wildly about. She searched her own pack, throwing her clothes helter-skelter about. "My notebook's gone too! It has all my drawings in it."

Jeremy went to help her, but a long search of every container revealed neither her notebook nor the book. He sat back on his heels. "It's gone, Lina. One of the warriors must have taken it."

"Nooo!" Lina rose again, but then she stopped dead. Her nostrils quivered. "What's that smell?"

Jeremy sniffed. "Something's burning." Their eyes met. With one motion, they swung toward the courtyard.

A small pile of ash was all that remained of the fire. The breeze had picked up again, which explained why they hadn't smelled the fire until it was too late. Lina fell to her knees and used a stick to stir up the ashes. Her face went white. The stick fell from her hand.

Jeremy squatted to see the small piece of oilskin and another that looked like canvas. He pulled her into his arms, wondering why the angry chief had burned the book but left the rest of the artifacts alone. "It's probably just as well, Lina. The destruction of this book may have saved a culture."

She stiffened, then pulled away. "How can you say that? It's a tragedy. Not just for knowledge, but for Cantul and his people. Don't you understand me any better than that?"

Spiky lashes adorned eyes that were huge, resentful. Where had all the love gone? The undying devotion they'd pledged by the stream must have been a dream called up by this evocative place. His own anger hardened. "Apparently not. No better than you understand me."

"I haven't asked you to give up the sea." She rose, her fists buried in the folds of her skirt.

Jeremy stood also, but his towering height didn't seem to intimidate her. It never had. "No, you haven't. It wouldn't do you any good, anyway."

Without another word, she pivoted and stalked away. Jeremy watched her go, his eyes burning, the heart she'd coaxed open closing with a rusty bang. He took a deep breath and schooled his expression to indifference before he followed.

Inside, he cried.

How would he survive the long trip back? With her so near, yet so very far away?

"My notebook's gone, Father. All I have are the photographs now, assuming they survive the trip home." Lina was surprised her voice was so steady. Even the danger they'd suffered together couldn't heal her rift with Jeremy now. For him to so lightly dismiss the loss of the key to the Mayan civilization, then rub her nose in the dirt by emphasizing the fact that he'd never leave the sea . . . well, he couldn't have made his feelings more plain.

Time for more of those unpleasant truths her life seemed to be governed by.

Sir Lawrence shook his head mournfully. "Dammit, if we hadn't been captured—"

"What is the matter?" Cantul entered, his shoulder bandaged with a piece of his fringed sash.

"The others?" Don Roberto interrupted, looking warily behind Cantul at the palace steps.

"Fled. With news of our united victory against them, they should not trouble us again for some time." Cantul's elation faded as again he took in Lina's troubled expression. "What is it?"

"The book has been burned, Cantul." Lina was astonished when he shrugged without concern.

"I hadn't time to save them all. I regret that I couldn't find your own book, Sir Lawrence," Cantul said.

"What do you mean?" Lina demanded.

Cantul disappeared and came back shortly—carrying Lina's notebook. "As soon as I awoke, I realized we were under attack and hid this above a lintel."

Lina wasn't about to tell him that Jeremy had hit him. She grabbed the notebook and flipped it open. She sighed her relief. "It's all here. Thank you, Cantul." She bit her lip, then added, "And the manuscript?"

Jeremy entered on the words. All present fixated on Cantul's bruised and battered face.

He glanced from Lina's hopeful expression to the others, then back at Lina. He shook his head.

Lina's shoulders slumped.

Jeremy met Cantul's eyes over her head. Cantul arched an eyebrow—but his stare was not as direct as usual.

Jeremy turned away. "I'll see if I can round up the mules so we can head out." He disappeared outside.

Cantul hesitated, then he approached Don Roberto and held out his hand. "Thank you, señor. My people will be grateful for your help. Should you need us for anything, send someone to my village and we will come."

Don Roberto shook the dark, bloodied hand. "*Gracias, amigo.*" He hurried outside, obviously yearning to get back to his hacienda and check on his children.

Sir Lawrence and Baxter closed the four crates Lina indicated, and hauled them outside.

Cantul and Lina were left alone. She appraised his strong face and cradled her notebook close, wishing she'd taken time to sketch Cantul. Somehow she didn't think she'd ever forget him anyway. "Thank you for everything, Cantul. Your ancestors would be proud of you."

Cantul cupped her cheek. "No. They would call me a fool for letting you go."

Lina smiled gravely. "I give you my solemn vow that their treasures will be displayed with honor, and I will write of you and your people as fitting heirs of their greatness."

"Thank you, Miss Collier." Cantul stepped back.

Understanding his need for the distance, Lina nodded. "Good-bye. I hope to see you again one day. Be happy."

"You too. But happiness is like the mango—you have to reach for it to enjoy it." Wise black eyes stared into hers, then he pivoted and left, his bare feet silent on the floor. He paused in the next corridor, and when he departed the palace, he carried a rag-wrapped bundle.

When they arrived at the hacienda, girls burst out of the door, chattering in excited Spanish. Don Roberto hugged them, one by one, then clapped Cesar on the shoulder. "Thank God you are all safe. But why did you return?" Don Roberto appraised his outbuildings. Some had been set afire, but the heavy rains had kept them from burning totally. They wouldn't be difficult to rebuild.

"One of the servants came to say it was safe, that the Indians were gone and had been defeated." Cesar held his hands up to Lina and lifted her lightly to the ground. "You are looking well for one who has survived a fierce battle. But what is this sadness I see?" Cesar's finger traced her turned-down mouth.

Inexorably Lina's gaze sought Jeremy. The barriers were firmly in place again. She could read no more in those mirrorlike eyes than the first time she'd seen him. Less. She gave Cesar a wide smile. "I'm just tired. I'll be fine after I eat."

"Come, then. We've managed to find enough for a meal. Tell me what you carry in those crates."

The gentle weight of his arm about her shoulders was her only comfort throughout that interminable meal. Jeremy, too, played with his food. Finally he tossed his fork down and interrupted Carmen's chatter.

"Cesar, isn't it about time for you to go to Campeche again?"

"*Sí*. Especially now so many of our supplies have been stolen."

Jeremy cleared his throat. "Ah, would you be amenable to guiding Sir Lawrence and his party back to Campeche?"

The buzz of conversation at the table halted.

Lina's teeth clamped down so hard on her tortilla that she bit her lip. Slowly she drew the flat disc out of her mouth and forced herself to chew the mouthful. It felt like straw, but in truth she didn't taste it.

Cesar's arm dropped from Lina's shoulders. Lina felt his appraisal, but she kept her eyes down so no one would see her devastation. Jeremy couldn't even say her name. Dear God, she'd given this man her virginity, her love, only to hear him foist her off on another man as part of the Lawrence party. Vaguely Cesar's response impinged on her consciousness.

"If Lina wishes it."

Everyone looked at her, but Lina showed inordinate interest in her plate.

Sir Lawrence said gruffly, "It's foolish for two parties to make the journey."

Jeremy said, "I . . . need to get back to my ship and can travel faster alone. It should be safe enough now the uprising has been defeated."

Lina's chair scraped back. "Ah, I've had enough. I'm very tired. If you'll excuse me . . ."

"You sleep in Carmen's room again," Don Roberto called after her.

Lina nodded as she hurried out of the *sala*.

Conversation resumed, but it had a forced tenor. Jeremy Mayhew listened, a polite expression on his face. Under the table, he was slowly ripping his napkin to shreds.

Hours later, when the house was quiet, Lina finally gave up trying to sleep. They'd be leaving with the dawn anyway, for they'd packed and hired boatmen that very night. She shoved back the sheet and padded out to the veranda, wearing only the sheer night rail Carmen had lent her. The tears were past now. They had provided little comfort.

She felt dead inside. What a good analogy, she thought wearily. All that Jeremy Mayhew had brought to vivid, pulsing life was gone. Hope for the future, enjoyment of her own femininity, physical delight. If she gave in, followed him blindly to the sea and set aside the dreams he'd helped her fulfill, she could still have those things.

But Lina knew herself well. She was not a make-do person. As an archaeologist, she could not be content as an assistant; she had to lead. As a woman, she could not follow blindly; she had to stride side by side.

Jeremy wanted blind obedience, and that she could not offer, even to him.

A movement outside caught her attention. She stiffened, wondering if she should fetch Don Roberto, until she caught the gleam of pale blond hair.

Jeremy, too, couldn't sleep. He was striding about the clearing before the hacienda, as if he could not be still. Even his pace was jerky, without its usual swift grace.

Tears started to Lina's eyes again. Her feet obeyed her heart, even though her mind screamed a protest.

This would be the last time she saw him. A future they might not have—but one night was left of their present to store up memories of the past. Lina could think of no sweeter good-bye.

She drifted down the steps toward him, her toes curling to the lush grass beneath her feet, her legs tingling as soft cotton wrapped about them in the breeze.

When she was ten feet away, Jeremy lifted his head. He went stone-still until she was within touching distance. Then he, too, seemed to forget all but the moment.

He grabbed her about the waist and hauled her against his chest. "Lina, I—"

A slim finger pressed the words back into his mouth. "Don't talk. Tonight, we only feel." She slipped her hands behind his neck and drew his mouth to hers.

Fireflies danced about them, glowing and fading in their mating ritual. The plump moon played hide-and-seek with svelte clouds. Trees soughed in background harmony to the cooing night birds.

Lina heard nothing, felt nothing, but the beating of her own heart, the potency of male flesh pressing into her from neck to toes. Their lips slanted hungrily, tongues battling for dominance, but in this field of valor there were no losers.

Only winners.

She wrapped her calf about his legs, but still she couldn't get close enough. Then her world tilted crazily as he swung her up into his arms and carried her away from the hacienda. She lay quietly, her own heartbeat keeping frantic time with his.

Straw prickled her neck as he laid her down inside the unburned barn on a sweet-smelling, fresh bed of nature's design. Lina's curious mare nosed over its pen at the intruder, whickering.

Lina didn't hear her, for strong hands were lifting the night rail, baring ankles, calves, knees, and thighs. Then he stopped.

The barn was dim, so Lina couldn't read his face, but she heard the strain in his voice. "Lina, are you certain this is what you want?"

In wordless reply, she reached for the buttons of his shirt. He tugged the gown the rest of the way up her body and cupped her breasts.

He groaned. "I never thought to know this joy again. Why do you deny us both?"

"Don't. No talk." And she dipped her head to tease his nipples with her tongue.

Talk was indeed superfluous. The touch of flesh to flesh was the ultimate narcotic. They forgot all, forgave all to steal this pleasure from an unkind fate.

Jeremy buried his hands in her hair, then tipped her head back. But he didn't take her yearning mouth. He nipped and lapped, sucked and nibbled. Beginning at the pulsing cord in her neck, he charted her desire for him like the great tracker he was. He abandoned her arched, shivering neck to mine the treasures above her heart, traveling on to the secret valley between her legs only he had known.

And when he touched her there, his path was lush and inviting. He took it instinctively, kicking his breeches away and settling his hips where he belonged.

She gasped at the swift merging, but not in pain. This, this she was meant for. No matter that this moment was a soporific to her future pain. It was meant to be. She was his, and would remain his when half a world separated them.

She wanted him to know that, take it with him into his lonely nights. This moment would be a link between them always.

Tears gathered in her eyes as she felt the exquisite tenderness he, too, gave in full measure of a devotion that was not meant to be. He did not take with measured, greedy thrusts; he slid softly, gently upon her, each stroke reaching high to coax more dew from her pearl.

Shudders racked her, but vaguely she knew that he, too, trembled. Their straw bed became a cloud as they strove harder, reaching, reaching for all they could be. They found, as lovers had in ages past and would in ages yet to come, that only in giving could they attain that summit.

For one eternal, blissful moment, they found it. One last time their bodies arched in graceful union, casting them high above the earthly vale. Linked, they looked down on the baseness of pride, and ambition, and past hurts. Lina was full with him; he was merged in her. Neither had room in heart or body for anything else.

But, as the exquisite pulsing died, they were cast down from Olympus to a simple bed of hay. Again, they were two people with hearts too big to compromise. Jeremy cradled her to him, stretched on his side, still nestled within her. Lina sighed and buried her nose in his clean male scent, trying not to think of the dawn only a few hours away.

"Lina—"

"No, Jeremy. Talking always gets us in trouble. Just hold me and keep the dawn away." She rose above him to scatter kisses everywhere gold dusted him.

He sighed and let her have her way. Again, they dared fate. And once more, just before dawn, they linked, this joining the most poignant of all. Lina couldn't restrain her tears after that, but, to her relief, exhaustion had finally claimed Jeremy.

She sat up, drew her gown over her head, and contemplated her only hope of happiness. Was she doing the right thing? Surely she would never love another this way again.

She traced the strong lines of his mouth. If they were not so iron-willed, one of them could compromise, maybe even both. But too much had gone before. He would not abandon the sea, she could not leave her dreams of being the first famous woman archaeologist. They had sustained her for too many years.

But sweet heaven, he was so beautiful in unguarded sleep. If God willed, maybe she carried now the seeds of his strength within her. She had to acknowledge to herself that the secret wish had partially been responsible for her recklessness.

But only partially. Now he would know, when he awoke to find her gone, that she had truly loved him. Her eyes burned, but no tears came out. She bent her head and kissed his earlobe to whisper into it, "I love you, Jeremy. Remember me, as I will remember you."

Then she rose and left without another backward glance. She didn't dare.

Jeremy awoke with a start when a worker came into the barn. The man stared at him in astonishment, then retreated modestly. Blushing, Jeremy scrambled into his clothes.

Lina! He had to catch her before she left. She loved him, after all. Now that he knew that, he could conquer anything that held them apart—even if it meant he had to give up the sea. Carrying his boots and socks, he rushed into the hacienda and burst into Don Roberto's study. "Where is she?"

Don Roberto studied him from top to toe, then shook his head in genuine regret. "Gone. This hour past."

Jeremy sank into the chair before the desk. The boots dropped from his numb hand. By the time he hired his own boatman, they'd be leagues ahead.

"I wondered why you didn't come to tell them good-bye. I can see you, ah, had a busy night. Sir Lawrence left this note for you." Don Roberto handed him a folded sheet of paper.

"Mayhew, we haven't always seen eye to eye, but I am very grateful for your help and forbearance. We would not have survived this trip without you. Once the finds are sold, we will divide the profits as you were promised. You can pick up your share at the Hotel de Paris in Monte Carlo six months from today. Forgive my own intemperance, but my daughter is very important to me. I want her to be happy. With gratitude, Sir Lawrence Collier."

Jeremy folded the note and stuck it into his pocket, his mouth wry. Only a gentleman of Sir Lawrence's standing could put him in his place so politely. Yet, there was something odd about the tone of the note. And why didn't the man just mail him the cheque to the Marseilles address? Jeremy's heart skipped a beat, then he shrugged.

He didn't give a tinker's damn what Sir Lawrence thought. The man would just have to live with him as a son-in-law. If things worked out as he hoped, Sir Lawrence would have no reason to be ashamed of him. Jeremy rose decisively.

"Well, my friend, what will you do now?" Don Roberto asked sympathetically.

"I'll do what I should have done years ago." At the doorway, Jeremy swung about, his cheeks creased in that bold adventurer's smile Lina loved. "I'm going home. It's time I saw my mother."

Part Five

See golden days, fruitful of golden deeds, with joy and love triumphing.
——MILTON, *Paradise Lost*, Part III

Chapter 17

SIX MONTHS LATER, Evangeline Collier brushed at the bugle beads on her gray gown. Why had her father insisted she wear it? With the weight she'd lost over the past months, it hung loosely on her. She stared in the mirror. She looked like a woman now rather than a girl. She cupped her flat stomach, sighed, and turned away.

She'd been devastated when her monthlies started as they reached Campeche. Her last link to Jeremy was gone, save for the memories. For six months, they'd been her only solace, especially the residual warmth from that last sweet night. So many times she'd longed to write to him.

But what would she say? That she was lonely? That she missed him? That the adulation she'd received since her lectures at the British Museum were small compensation for what she really wanted?

The museum had paid handsomely for the finds. Her father had believed they could receive more from private collectors, but Lina had insisted on honoring her promise to Cantul. Pacal's treasures resided in magnificent display cases for all to admire. The museum had been so impressed with the artifacts and her copious, organized notes and sketches that they'd raised the funds for her to conduct a dig at Knossos. She was supposed to start as soon as this brief vacation in Monte Carlo ended.

She still didn't understand why her father had insisted they come here. He'd hemmed and hawed about the proximity to Crete, but she knew him too well. He was scheming again.

At least he hadn't flung suitors at her feet lately as he had so often in the past.

Come to think of it, why? And what would he say when she told him that being here had revived too many painful memories? That she'd finally broken her self-imposed vow of silence and sent a letter to her only address for Jeremy, the one in Marseilles. It would probably take months for him to get it if he was sailing, but at least she'd taken the first step.

Even if marriage was unthinkable between them, surely they could still see one another. She was already a fallen woman, so she might as well make the most of it. Achieving her lifelong dream had brought her contentment and self-respect. But not happiness.

Only Jeremy could supply that.

The knowledge had crept upon her slowly as she cleaned, finished cataloguing and photographing her finds. Often she wondered about Cantul, hoping that he had found some lucky woman to share his life. Finally, when all else was complete, she turned her attention to the mask.

It had taken her two months of assiduous work to reassemble it. And when she looked upon the face of Pacal, instead of triumph, she knew regret. Those black jade eyes so like Cantul's looked at her sternly, chiding her for obeying her mind instead of her heart . . .

"Are you ready, daughter?"

Lina started. She hadn't even heard the door open. She turned and smiled at her father, grateful again that the pain of the last year had brought her something, at least.

She had now the relationship with her father she'd always wanted. He consulted her and actually listened to her suggestions, for she'd proved herself. When they arrived back in England, he'd insisted that the reporters who wanted to talk with him speak instead to his daughter, who had been head archaeologist on the tomb excavation.

"Aren't you eager to play some roulette?" he asked, shutting the door behind him. "You used to love it."

Lina took his arm. "I've lost my taste for gambling, I think. We can't afford to lose now. My salary is not very much, as you know."

He patted her hand. "I hope it hasn't been too hard on you, losing your home."

"No. I was glad to get the debts paid off. I'm doing the work I've always wanted anyway. The estate was a wonderful place to grow up, but since it looks as if I won't be having children of my own . . ." She cleared her husky throat, missing Sir Lawrence's secretive smile. "But at least I know we did the right thing. The investors seemed pleased enough at the quality of the finds even though they didn't make much above the dig expenses."

"Pity we didn't find gold." Sir Lawrence opened the door. "Still, I'd not trade what we did find for all the gold of the Aztecs."

Lina watched her feet descend the plush red-carpeted stairs. Funny how the hotel still looked exactly the same. Somehow, it should have changed, the way she had. "How did Jeremy react to his cheque?"

"He hasn't collected it yet. Or so I've heard."

Lina sighed. He apparently wasn't pining for her. She wondered how many ports he'd landed in, and if he'd seen Aimee.

When they reached the casino, she tilted her chin and emptied her spangled reticule. The pile of chips was small, but it should be enough to while the hours away. She grabbed a glass of champagne from a passing waiter and carried it with her to the roulette table. Her father stood beside her, but he kept shifting restlessly, watching the door.

Finally, when she'd lost her first three bets, she glanced at him irritably. "Go on, then. You don't need to stand guard over me." She assumed he wanted to talk to some of his cronies, who were also going to Knossos with them to dig on a different part of the palace.

Sir Lawrence stiffened, looking toward the door. Then he smiled his handsome smile at his aggravated daughter. "I'll see you later. Don't be out too late, mind."

What on earth did he mean by that? She'd be back to her room before midnight. Lina decided she'd had enough "fun" and put her last two chips all on one number. After her gamble with Jeremy, no game of chance could ever compete.

A big browned hand matched her bid. Lina traced the hand to the wrist cuffed in a white shirt, up to a tailored black tuxedo arm, past a muscular shoulder to that achingly familiar mouth.

"Jeremy," she whispered.

The roulette wheel spun as fast as her brain. Why had he come? Was he as glad to see her as she was to see him? She could read nothing, as usual, in those smoky eyes—until he smiled.

Lina didn't hear the ball click as it landed. Or see that it lodged on her number. Silver eyes glimmered with promised delight, a lode waiting for her that only she could mine. Jeremy caught her arm when she swayed. "We won, Lina."

"We did?" The croupier deposited a huge pile of chips in front of each of them, inclining his head with interest as he tried to listen.

Lina didn't even see the payoff, for she knew Jeremy wasn't talking about roulette. His voice said so, his eyes said so, his touch said so. When he scooped their winnings into one bag and tucked her arm in his, she followed.

Blindly, as she had always sworn not to. When he'd changed their chips, he dumped them all into her reticule.

"No," she protested, but a brown finger touched her lips.

"No talk. Save it for when it matters."

He led her to the door. As they exited, Lina saw her father watching them. She held her breath, but he smiled broadly and waved her out. Her mouth dropped open. "He planned this."

Jeremy nodded at Sir Lawrence and received a cheery wave in return before Sir Lawrence returned to talking with his friend. "He summoned me here."

Lina's heart fell until Jeremy added, "But I would have tracked you down no matter where you were."

"You would?" The words burst out of their own accord. "Then why did you wait so long?"

He laughed, drawing her outside onto a bench secluded in a gazebo. "Did it feel as long to you as it did to me?"

Lina nodded, her eyes burning with the residue of the eternal, lonely nights.

His mirth faded. "I missed you, angel."

"Oh Jeremy, if you only knew how many times I've regretted not giving up my work—"

"Shhh. I was wrong to demand it. My only excuse was that I was so tired, so worried about your safety, that my old instincts took over. You were the most important thing in the world to me and I wanted you to feel the same. But the choice I gave you wasn't fair. I realized how wrong I was that night you came to me."

Lina's voice wobbled. "I hoped you'd feel how much I loved you."

He tugged her to his heart. "I could scarcely avoid it. And did you feel the same?"

"Yes. But I still didn't think you'd give up the sea for me. I never wanted that, anyway. I only wanted each of us to sometimes accompany the other. As long as we could come home together, I felt we could work anything out. But you never offered me that compromise."

"I do now." He drew back to look at her.

Lina's breath caught as love filled those indomitable eyes. "What do you mean?"

"I mean, angel mine, that I've docked the *Verdandi* in London. My stepbrother has been wanting to open an import-export office in London. He asked me years ago to head it, but it wasn't right for me at the time. Now it is."

"Are you sure, Jeremy? I don't mind spending six months at sea with you if you'll go with me on some of my digs."

"I don't intend to give up the sea entirely. I hope you'll voyage with me when your schedule allows."

She'd sail to the ends of the earth with him now, but she could only manage a choked, "You won't be able to keep me away."

They shared a kiss that banished the shadows of pain and offered a shimmering glimpse of the happiness compromise had granted them. When it became too passionate, Jeremy groaned and drew away. "Not again. I've promised myself that the next time we bed we'll be wedded. I owe your father that much."

Lina's heart sang with happiness, but she had to know. "Jeremy, did you go back to New York?"

"Yes. I'd run from my past long enough. You made me see that too." He traced the shadows under her eyes. "My mother was delighted to see me. And I find that I am much like her in many ways. I want you to meet her soon." His voice lowered as he added, "I saw Aimee again. She's a lovely woman, but her eyes are not as blue, nor is her laugh as loud. I still care for her, but as a sister. No one can ever compete with you in my heart."

Lina hiccuped and threw her arms about his neck. "Oh Jeremy, marry me soon. Don't make me wait."

His mouth brushed hers, then moved quickly away. "Temptress. I have the special license in my pocket as we speak. Come, let's go find your father."

He surged to his feet, pulling Lina up with him.

Laughing, Lina tugged her hand away and ran down the gazebo steps. Walking backward, she called to him, "But first, I have a wager to make."

He stalked her steadily. "Oh yes?"

"Yes. Would you care to bet on whether we'll find gold at Knossos?"

"What are the stakes?"

"The same as before."

Jeremy arched an interested eyebrow. "Sounds to me as though I win, either way." He pounced.

As she settled into his arms, Lina sighed. "That's the beauty of it. We both win."

And there, in the brilliantly lit garden in front of the casino, they scandalized the patrons. Kissing passionately, they pledged to their golden future.

If you enjoyed this book, take advantage of this special offer. Subscribe now and get a

FREE
Historical
Romance

No Obligation (a $4.50 value)

Each month the editors of True Value select the four *very best* novels from America's leading publishers of romantic fiction. Preview them in your home *Free* for 10 days. With the first four books you receive, we'll send you a FREE book as our introductory gift. No Obligation!

If for any reason you decide not to keep them, just return them and owe nothing. If you like them as much as we think you will, you'll pay just $4.00 each and save at *least* $.50 each off the cover price. (Your savings are *guaranteed* to be at least $2.00 each month.) There is NO postage and handling – or other hidden charges. There are no minimum number of books to buy and you may cancel at any time.

Send in the Coupon Below

To get your FREE historical romance fill out the coupon below and mail it today. As soon as we receive it we'll send you your FREE Book along with your first month's selections.